He knew that if he took Jasmine to bed now and made love to her, she would respond with a passionate eagerness and warmth, satisfying him in a way he had never found with any other woman.

Yet, always, he was aware there was some essential part of the woman in his arms that eluded him, no matter how closely he held her. And that, afterward, her beautiful face, wiped clean of passion, would once again be coolly remote, her eyes, like now, staring at him, unfathomable, holding their own secrets.

For the first time in his life, Morgan faced a disturbing truth. He wanted more than the body of this woman, seductive as that body was. He wasn't even sure what more he did want.

After all, he thought, bewildered, what more could a man want from a woman?

JASMINE

Marcella Thum

FAWCETT GOLD MEDAL • NEW YORK

A Fawcett Gold Medal Book
Published by Ballantine Books

Library of Congress Catalog Card Number: 84-90879

ISBN 0-449-12672-2

Manufactured in the United States of America

First Ballantine Books Edition: July 1984

For Clara and Sam

Chapter 1

"Well, I say it's sinful, the way the girl flaunts herself before every man aboard the ship. Why, even last Sunday at evening services, she ogled Brother Micah all the while he was preaching."

The speaker was a bony-faced woman with sallow skin and a long, thin nose. The nose fairly twitched with irritation as she glared across the deck at a young, slender woman in a dark green bombazine dress, standing beside the rail. The bark, *Jeremiah*, four months out of Boston, was scudding westward before the trades. As the ship pitched slightly in the choppy sea, the girl placed one hand on the rail to keep her balance and the other on the sleeve of the black-frocked man standing beside her.

"Look at her now!" the woman continued, her voice a low hiss of outrage, "hanging all over Brother Micah." She gave her gray-haired companion a severe glance. "It's your Christian duty, Sister Emily, to warn the girl of the error of her ways before she strays completely from the paths of righteousness. After all, didn't you say you knew Miss Babcock's family in Honolulu?"

For all that her face was covered with a web of wrinkles, Emily Palmer's blue eyes were as bright and alert as a young girl. At the moment, she kept her eyes fastened on the petticoat she was mending. If there was one thing Emily had learned since she had sailed to the Hawaiian Islands in 1824 as a very new missionary's wife, it was to curb her tongue. Twenty-five years ago, she thought wryly, she would no doubt have taken pleasure in pointing out to Sister Cora that when one attended divine services, it was to listen to the word of God, and not to judge the behavior of the other worshippers.

Now she put that thought charitably aside and said instead, her voice placid, "I knew Jasmine Babcock's mother, and only briefly. Caroline Babcock and her daughter accompanied her husband on his whaling ship. When she learned she was expecting another child, she stayed in Honolulu with her daughter while her husband continued with the cruise to the coast of California. Captain Babcock hoped to return to Hawaii before the baby was due, but he was delayed. The mission doctor delivered the child. It was a difficult birth, and Mrs. Babcock and her baby died. Before her death, Mrs. Babcock asked me to look after Jasmine until her husband returned."

It had been two months before the captain returned to Honolulu, Emily recalled. By that time she and Samuel had become deeply attached to the five-year-old Jasmine, a warm, loving child with traces of the beauty she was to become already visible in her delicately featured face. She had even hoped that Amos Babcock might be persuaded to allow Samuel and her to raise the child with their own two daughters. The captain went on a wild, drunken spree upon learning of his wife's death, and it was two weeks before he showed up at the Palmer home, his clothes rumpled as if he had slept in them, his eyes bloodshot.

Each day of those two weeks, Jasmine had gone into the small front parlor of the Palmer home with her packed suitcase in hand and waited, her eyes fastened on the door, for her father's return. When he finally came striding into the room, a radiant smile lit up the child's face. Without a word, she had gone to her father and slipped her hand into his.

The captain had nodded stiffly to the Palmers. "I thank you for caring for Jasmine."

At a nudging glance from his wife, Samuel Palmer had said, "We've enjoyed her company. As a matter of fact, my wife and I would be most pleased if you would consider allowing us to continue the care of the child. We would raise her with the same love and devotion we give our own."

Amos Babcock's face had reddened. "What sort of savage do you take me for?" he asked gruffly. "To give up my own flesh and blood? I'll raise my daughter myself, thank you."

"How can you?" Emily had blurted. "Your whaling voyages take you away from home for months; sometimes, years at a time. And you can hardly bring up a young girl on a whaling ship."

Amos Babcock's mouth set in a tight, obstinate line as he reached down and lifted Jasmine into his arms. "I'll leave the sea, then. James Cavendish has his store up for sale. I've always had a hankering to be a merchant." His eyes glinted with shrewd amusement beneath thick, grizzled brows. "There's money to be made in these islands since you missionaries have taught the natives the sin of slothfulness and put the fear of God into them."

Samuel Palmer winced. It was his secret sorrow that it was the harsh, inflexible tenets of their stern, Calvinist faith that the brethren seemed intent on passing along to the native Hawaiians. And the natives who came to the mission church, remembering their own cruel, pagan gods, accepted such harshness without question. "It's love, not fear, of God we are trying to teach the Hawaiian people," Samuel said quietly.

Emily, a sudden, painful twisting in her heart as she looked at Jasmine, made one last attempt. "What do you, a man alone, know of raising a daughter, Captain? She'll need proper schooling and a chance to meet suitable Christian men when it's time for marriage."

"She's a mite young to be thinking of such things now." The captain chuckled as he strode to the door, his daughter's arms looped contentedly around his neck. "I thank you for your kindness, but Jasmine and me, we'll manage quite well by ourselves from now on."

"I heard Miss Babcock mention that she had several sisters and a brother in Honolulu," Sister Cora said, her sharp, curious voice cutting through Emily's reverie. "I assume that Captain Babcock remarried?"

Again Emily took her time answering. "Jasmine has a half sister Lani," she said slowly. "And a stepbrother and stepsister, Kale and Lilikoi."

Sister Cora's mouth dropped open. "Those are Hawaiian names! Are you saying that Captain Babcock married a native woman?"

Emily sighed to herself, thinking how much her companion, who was traveling to the Sandwich Islands to visit her missionary brother, had to learn about the life of the foreign residents in the islands, particularly the relationships of the males with the native women. But then, she remembered, she had been dismayed herself when she had first arrived in the islands, almost twenty-five years ago, and discovered the numerous casual liaisons between the *haole* men and the Hawaiian women. At least, Amos Babcock had married his Hawaiian mistress, plump, good-natured Malia, who had brought a young son and daughter with her into the Babcock home, and then had borne Lani an indecorous six months after her marriage to Captain Babcock. Emily suspected that the captain would not have bothered to legalize his relationship with his mistress except, of course, he could not bring his mistress and raise an illegitimate child in the same house with Jasmine.

When Emily didn't answer at once, her companion continued sternly. "The church doesn't condone such marriages, surely? Why, only last year I read in the mission-board news that one of the brethren was expelled from the church for marrying a native girl."

Emily knew the case in question. She also knew that Samuel had spoken out against the expulsion of the young minister, to no avail.

Sister Cora inched forward in her chair, her voice

dropping to a scandalized whisper. "Is it true what I've heard about the native women, Sister Emily? They walk around stark naked and brazenly bestow their favors upon any man who strikes their fancy. Certainly no decent man would marry such godforsaken creatures."

"No creature is ever godforsaken, Sister Cora," Emily said in quiet reproach. "It is true that when the mission families first came to the Sandwich Islands, the Hawaiian women were not . . . accustomed to wearing gowns, except for their native *pa'u*. That's why the mission wives devised a long, loose gown to cover their nakedness. But that was many years ago. Today, many of the Hawaiian women, especially those in the royal family, dress in the height of fashion. As for the present Mrs. Babcock, I have never seen her other than properly clothed. Malia's a fine, Christian woman and a devoted mother to all the Babcock children."

Sister Cora's sharp glance darted once again across the deck to where Jasmine Babcock was now promenading slowly back and forth, her hand resting lightly on the arm of Brother Micah. A gust of wind tugged the demure, green-silk poke bonnet back from the girl's face, and the black, silken curls released at the temples danced across delicately arched brows. The face was finely featured, only the mouth had a sensual, full lower lip, and the slightly tilted brown eyes set in a frame of thick black lashes had a disturbing boldness about them as the girl smiled teasingly up at her companion. Emily Palmer felt her breath catch in her throat. She had forgotten how lovely the girl was.

"Miss Babcock is hardly a child," Sister Cora said tartly.

At that moment, the wind snatched at the green bombazine gown, outlining the taut, full breasts, a tiny waist, and the graceful swell of hips that were not at all childlike. It was also immediately apparent to the two women that the bodice of Miss Babcock's gown fit much too snugly, and that somehow the top three buttons of the high, ruched neck of the gown had become unbuttoned, exposing an immodest view of a creamy throat.

Oh, dear, Emily thought, dismayed. She had hoped that the years at Miss Ander's Academy for Young Ladies had molded Jasmine into a properly demure young lady. For even at age twelve, when Jasmine had been a student at Emily's mission school for girls, she had been a problem. Not that the girl wasn't intelligent, more so than her sisters, the indolent Lilikoi and soft-spoken, shy Lani, but it was always Jasmine who got into trouble. She wore forbidden flower wreaths to school, sneaked off to swim with the native children, and raided the mission sugar barrel. However, it was when Emily noticed the eyes of the young Hawaiian chiefs from the nearby Royal School gleam with appreciation as Jasmine walked by with an innocently provocative swing to her hips that Emily had had her conversation with Captain Babcock at his mercantile establishment on Fort Street.

"But to send the lass all the way to Connecticut to school," the captain protested unhappily.

"It's for Jasmine's own good," Emily insisted. "You want your daughter to make a suitable marriage with a man from a proper background, don't you? What sort of husband can she find here in the islands but drunken seamen and dissolute *haoles*, many running away from shameful secrets in their past." She paused tactfully. "And there's Jasmine herself. Not that she isn't a sweet, loving child, but there's an unfortunate wildness, a headstrong side to her nature that must be controlled if she is to find the path to God—and a good marriage," she added practically.

"Aye," the captain agreed gloomily. "She's a handful, all right, always has been. Stubborn as a mule, with a temper to match. Can't imagine where she gets it. . . ."

Emily repressed a smile. Captain Babcock's own obstinacy and quick temper were well known in the islands, and the years had only increased his acerbic reputation.

"A man couldn't ask for a better wife than Malia, but

she has the Hawaiian way of spoiling children," the captain continued, then shrugged ruefully. "Not that I'm much better. Oh, I take a strap to them when they need it, except Lani, of course. You only have to frown at that child and she bursts into tears. But it does no good. Lilikoi and Kale are pure Hawaiian. Nothing will change their natures. As for Jasmine, she's like quicksilver in my hand. When I try to hold her, make her behave, she slips away from me."

"Miss Ander's Academy is highly recommended. It's where Samuel and I sent our own two daughters."

The captain spoke softly, as if in mourning. "The lass is still a babe. To send her away for so long—it's like tearing out my heart."

Emily remembered her own sorrow when she had watched her two young daughters leave the islands for school in America, watching their tiny figures on shipboard slip from sight, not knowing whether she might ever see them again.

Still, she thought now, forcing the pain back into a corner of her heart, she should thank the Lord for His blessings. She had been able to go back to America for her oldest daughter's wedding and saw that her youngest daughter was happily set up as a schoolteacher in Boston.

When she had boarded the *Jeremiah* for her return voyage to the Sandwich Islands after her visit with her daughters, she had had been surprised to find Jasmine Babcock as a passenger aboard the ship. A week out from Boston she met the girl alone on deck and said curiously, "I saw your father just before I left Honolulu, and he said nothing about your returning home."

"Oh, he doesn't know," Jasmine said blithely. "I was bored to death at school and I decided it was foolish to waste Father's money by staying any longer." She shivered. "And those New England winters! They seemed to last forever. Even in the summer I never felt warm."

Emily couldn't help glancing at the girl's left hand and murmuring, "I would have thought . . ." Her voice drifted off tactfully.

"You mean marriage?" Jasmine shrugged indifferently. "Oh, I had my share of proposals." A look of distaste stiffened the young, lovely face, her dark eyes puzzled. "I can't imagine why any girl wants to get married and put up with those wet kisses and groping hands." She giggled suddenly. "Though it was fun outwitting the chaperones at the school. That's the trouble," she said rebelliously. "After a man's married, he can still have all the fun he wants, but the wife is stuck at home with a houseful of children." At her companion's shocked glance, she added hastily, "Oh, I suppose someday I'll have to marry. What else is there to do? But I'm in no hurry."

Emily felt it her duty to protest such a lighthearted approach to matrimony. "My dear child, it's a woman's duty and great joy to marry and bear children. There is no greater happiness."

Then she fell silent, sensing that her words were sliding off the girl like water off a stone.

A peal of female laughter drifted across the deck, interrupting her thoughts, as the ship suddenly dipped into a trough. Emily's mouth tightened disapprovingly as she watched Jasmine clutch at the arm of her companion. She wondered, annoyed, what Brother Micah could be thinking of, encouraging the girl that way with his poor wife hardly able to stir from her cabin, ill from the terrible storm the ship had encountered rounding the Cape. Emily sighed and picked up her sewing. Still, it would take a man with a heart of ice to resist Jasmine's seductive beauty. Poor Captain Babcock. If he thought his daughter had been like quicksilver when she left the islands, Emily sensed that Jasmine was now like a volcano waiting to erupt.

Jasmine, smiling through fluttering eyelashes up at Micah Beale, was well aware of the two sets of disapproving eyes watching her from across the deck. How silly of them to think that she had any interest in a dried-up stick of a man like Micah Beale, she thought, amused. If there were any other presentable males as passengers, she wouldn't have given the man a second glance. But after four months at sea, she was bored with her own company and she had to amuse herself with someone, didn't she?

Now she let her hand press lightly on the man's arm as she murmured, "I did so enjoy your sermon last Sunday, Mr. Beale, although I must admit I found it a little frightening." She shivered delicately. "All those poor lost souls in hell."

Enjoyment wasn't exactly what she had felt, Jasmine reflected. There had been something decidedly unpleasant about the wild sheen in Micah Beale's eyes as he described in graphic details the terrible agonies that would be endured, after death, by those souls who had not found salvation.

"I preach only the truth, as the Bible tells us," he said, his long face somber. "The unrepentant damned will burn forever in hell's fire. It is for this reason that I joined the ministry. If I can pull only one burning brand from the fire, redeem one sinner before it is too late . . ."

The pale gray eyes resting full on Jasmine's face had a slick, oily sheen that was not, Jasmine realized uncomfortably, the silly, infatuated look she was accustomed to seeing in men's eyes. There was, in fact, something almost menacing in Micah Beale's gaze. Abruptly she pulled her hand from the man's arm, laughing a little nervously. "I prefer the Hawaiian gods. They're sometimes cruel, too, but much more forgiving."

"I've read of the primitive idols and pagan gods the natives in Hawaii worshipped," Micah said, frowning. "We can thank God that our missionaries put an end to such heathen rituals."

"Oh, no," Jasmine protested. "It wasn't the missionaries that destroyed the Hawaiian gods. It was after the death of the great Kamehameha that the people themselves rose against the *kahunas*, before the first missionaries arrived." She smiled, her eyes sparkling mischievously. "My father always said that if the first Kamehameha had been alive when the missionaries

arrived, he would have sent them and their religion
marching into the sea if they had tried to convert him!"

At the mocking laughter in the girl's face, Micah
Beale felt a terrible spurt of anger, making his hands
tremble and his mouth grow dry. It was an anger that
his teachers at the seminary had warned him he must
learn to control. But surely his was a righteous anger at
this young woman who laughed so disrespectfully at a
minister of God. Of course, he should not have expected
any more, he thought, gazing coldly at the girl. At his
first glimpse of Jasmine Babcock, he had known the
young woman for what she was, no better than a harlot,
despite her fine manners and expensive gowns.

It was his duty, he knew, to try to save her soul, but
despite all the time he had spent with her, she continued stubbornly to resist him. And what was worse, he
felt sure she was trying to seduce him. He had to
remind himself constantly, when he was with her, of the
Bible's admonition: "To resist the woman whose heart is
snares and nets, to lust not after her beauty in your
heart, neither let her take you with her eyelids."

It was difficult, though, he was discovering, to resist
his companion's corrupting beauty. His eyes, unwillingly,
returned to the swell of the girl's breasts so clearly
outlined beneath the green bombazine, the creamy flesh
temptingly visible through the unbuttoned neck of the
gown. Unbidden, words from the Song of Solomon
leaped into his mind. "Thy neck is as like a tower of
ivory, thy two breasts like two young roes that are
twins which feed among the lilies."

No matter how he tried to free his mind from fleshly
lusts, a painful tightness swelled in his loins whenever
he was with Jasmine Babcock. He was furious at his
own weakness, knowing that such desires of the flesh
were an abomination. And he was even angrier with the
girl for deliberately arousing such sinful lusts within
him, with her smiling lips that he could almost taste
beneath his, "sweet as honey and smoother than oil."

He glared at the mocking laughter in the girl's dark,

lustrous eyes. Such a carnal spirit cried aloud to be broken, to be made submissive to God's wrath, before she was lost forever to eternal damnation.

"Brother Micah."

For a moment, the minister stared blindly at the woman who had come up beside him, then realized she had been speaking to him and he hadn't heard. He saw the bowl held in Sister Emily's hands and caught just the hint of disapproval in her voice as she murmured, "The cook made some chicken broth for your wife. I thought perhaps you'd like to bring it to Sister Mary."

"Yes, of course," he mumbled, his face flushing as if Sister Emily could see into his mind and know what he had been thinking. "I'll take it to my wife at once."

He almost tripped over a coil of rope on the deck in his haste to get away, and he could have sworn he heard the girl giggle at his clumsiness. When he entered the tiny cabin that he and his wife shared, despite his anger and humiliation he could still feel the pressure building up inside him, a need that would not be denied no matter how he prayed for the strength to overcome his frailty, this sinful desire for a woman's flesh beneath his hands, the softness of her body between his legs.

His wife was half asleep, her face against the pillow an unattractive gray. She had been thin when she married him, just a month before they had sailed, but whatever softness her body had possessed her constant seasickness had worn away, until her breasts hung pendulously and her shoulders were bony knobs. Micah had felt no great fondness for her when he married her, but a minister needed a wife, and no other woman had shown any interest in him. There was, too, to be practical, the handsome estate Mary had inherited from her wealthy banker father.

"Micah," she murmured, trying to smile, to stir herself to greet him, knowing how her illness aggravated him. Then, to her dismay, she saw that her husband was removing his trousers and she hastily turned her eyes away. It embarrassed her to see a man's nakedness, even after five months of marriage. No one had warned her what marriage would be like, the shocking thing that happened between a man and a woman in bed.

Moaning, distraught, knowing what was about to happen, she tried to jerk her body toward the bulkhead away from her husband, but the berth was too narrow. Abruptly he pushed her cotton nightgown up toward her breasts and flung his body down on top of hers. In a few minutes it was over, and Micah's face gleaming with sweat, his body now relaxed and drained, rolled away from his wife.

But her smell was still in his nostrils, that disagreeable odor that always seemed to hang around his wife since she'd become ill. Unbidden, the scent of that Jezebel he had stood with on deck, only a few moments before, swept back over him, a light flowery scent, teasing, delicious.

A frustrated anger pulled at him when he thought of Jasmine Babcock. Was her presence aboard this ship the Lord's way of tempting him, as Bathsheba had tempted David? But then all women were the same, arousing a man's lustful nature with the devil's own wiles, even Mary, staring at him, her soft eyes wide and cowlike in their devotion and pain.

Hurriedly he pulled his wife out of the bed, forced her to kneel on the floor beside him and join him in a guilt-ridden prayer of repentance. "Oh, Lord, forgive us for our many sins. . . ."

Chapter 2

It was daybreak, one month later, when Jasmine heard the cry of "Land ho!" and, dressing quickly, she climbed up on deck. At once, she recognized a special softness in the air, a land scent in her nostrils.

The eastern horizon was streaked with pale gold, but overhead the billowing sails were a ghostly white against a still-dark sky. It was toward the west that Jasmine gazed, though. Her hands tightened on the rail with excitement as she saw what looked like a white cloud floating in the distance above the black water. Then gradually, as the sky brightened, she could see other clouds gathered, but one cloud remained unchanging, majestic, towering above the others, and she recognized the glittering, snow-capped peak of Mauna Kea.

As the bark sailed closer, she could see the dramatic shoreline, sheer rock walls slashed with waterfalls that plunged into the ocean below, and, beyond the black cliffs, lush green fields and forests.

"Is that the island of Oahu?"

Micah Beale had joined her at the rail, and she pushed back a feeling of resentment at his presence. She had wanted to enjoy these first moments alone, after all her lonely years away from the islands. Then she saw that not just Mr. Beale had gathered on the deck but the rest of the passengers as well, even poor Mrs. Beale, who looked as if she had dragged herself from her death bed and was clutching her husband's arm as if she would collapse if she let go.

"We won't sight Diamond Head until tomorrow," Jasmine said. "That's the island of Hawaii and the volcano Mauna Kea you're seeing." She couldn't resist adding, "The Hawaiians believe the goddess Pele lives in the volcano. When she's angry, she causes the volcano to erupt."

Mrs. Beale shuddered. "You don't mean there are active volcanoes in Hawaii?"

Mrs. Palmer had joined them, and she gave Jasmine an annoyed glance then said soothingly, "There are no active volcanoes on Oahu, where we're going, Sister Mary." Taking Mrs. Beale's arm, she said gently, "Come and sit down. You shouldn't have left your bed."

Micah did not follow his wife. Instead, he turned to Jasmine and said, "We've missed you at our evening prayer meetings, Miss Babcock. And these last weeks, I have the feeling that you've been avoiding me. Have I perhaps in some way offended you?"

The obsequious note in the man's voice, the way his pale gray eyes shone when they rested on the bodice of her gown and then looked away, repulsed Jasmine.

"You're mistaken, Mr. Beale," she said coldly, deliberately turning her back on him and strolling toward the bow of the ship. To her annoyance, he trotted after her.

"I had hoped, Miss Babcock, that we could pray together for the salvation of your soul. It grieves me to think of a young woman like you facing eternal damnation. I would feel as if I had shirked my duty if I didn't make one last attempt to help you find God's grace. Perhaps I could stop by your cabin this evening."

If his face had not been so long and solemn, his eyes burning with such an odd, feverish intensity, Jasmine might have laughed aloud. Instead, she said firmly, "I'll be busy packing this evening." And then to change the subject, she gestured toward a passing ship. "I wonder where she's off to?"

Like the *Jeremiah*, the vessel was three-masted and

square-rigged but with a blunt nose and square stern. Despite its cumbersome look, the ship seemed to leap buoyantly over the white-crested waves.

Reluctantly Micah pulled his gaze away from the girl. "She's a whaler," he said, his thin mouth pursing with disapproval as he observed the figurehead on the bow of the ship, a beautifully carved nude torso of a young woman with long hair flying, as if she were gleefully breasting the waves with her voluptuous bosom. "Scandalous! But then, even at the seminary, we heard that the whaling man hangs his conscience on Cape Horn before he reaches the Sandwich Islands. And it's common knowledge, the vile manner in which whalers comport themselves in the ports of Honolulu and Lahaina, gaming and drinking and exhibiting licentious behavior with the native women."

Anger flashed suddenly like golden sparks in Jasmine's eyes as she faced the minister, her voice scathing. "My father was a whaling captain, Mr. Beale, and there's no finer man anywhere."

Embarrassment flushed Mr. Beale's face as he stammered apologetically, "I—I assure you, Miss Babcock, I meant no disrespect."

Almost, Jasmine felt sorry for him, he looked so miserable. And she wasn't so naive that she didn't know he was partly right. She had seen the seamen from whaling ships swaggering through the streets of Honolulu or staggering from one grogshop to another. And she had heard the stories of the native women who swam out to the whaling ships to service the seamen. When the early missionaries had tried to put a stop to such wanton behavior, the whaling men had stormed ashore and attacked the missionaries with clubs and stones.

Nevertheless, Jasmine gazed wistfully at the passing vessel, so close now that she could glimpse the huge try-pots on the deck of the ship, the smoke-blackened sails. Even though she had been only a child, she remembered vividly her days aboard her father's whaling ship, the freedom with which she had roamed the decks, the burly seamen shaping toys for her out of whalebone and telling her tall tales of their adventures chasing the elusive sperm whales. As she watched, the tiny figure of a man climbed the rigging of the whaler, swinging with a daredevil insouciance to reach the masthead hoops. How wonderful it would be to have such freedom, she thought longingly, not to be tied down to schoolwork and housekeeping and wearing the proper clothes, saying the proper things, before being carted off by some man into marriage, tied down to a home and children for the rest of your life.

So engrossed was she in watching the whaler that Jasmine didn't notice that Mr. Beale was once again importuning her, until she felt his hands on her arms, tugging at them, trying to pull her down to her knees.

"We can pray here, Miss Babcock," he urged exultantly. "On deck in full sight of God, we can beg His forgiveness, for I am as much a sinner as you."

Jasmine was at first too startled to resist the wiry strength of the young minister's arms. She cast a quick glance across the deck, not sure whether she was relieved or dismayed to discover that the other passengers' attention was focused on the island of Hawaii.

"Mr. Beale, please!" she hissed, furious now as his hands dug into her arms, his face so close she could see the traces of old smallpox scars and catch the unpleasant, sour smell of the man's breath.

On the quarterdeck of the whaling ship, the *Louisa*, Captain Morgan Tucker was nursing a cup of coffee and a headache. How much had he had to drink last night? he wondered gloomily, trying to ignore the painful, mallet-like pounding at his temples. And there had been a *wahine* in his cabin, hadn't there? Or had there been more than one? At least one, he vaguely recalled, slim and dark-skinned, heavy-breasted, with tiny, white teeth that had left painful marks on his shoulder and earlobe. What was her name? Lili . . . Lilikau—something like that. All he could remember for sure was the way she had never seemed to tire in his arms and had little tricks to tease him, which drove him to possess her time and time again, her body squirming happily beneath his, her long, lovely legs scissoring around his hips, pulling him more tightly against her.

Finally, exhausted—last night in port or not—he had carried her, giggling, in his arms up on deck, her dark hair streaming down her back, and dropped her unceremoniously over the stern of the ship. He had watched her surface, still laughing, her white teeth flashing in the moonlight, her body silver as she swam effortlessly toward the shore. For a moment now, he felt a second's guilt at the way he had gotten rid of the girl, then he shrugged mentally. Undoubtedly he had paid her well, and all Hawaiians were half fish anyway.

"Ship off the port beam, Skipper," the helmsman called.

Morgan had already seen the bark. He picked up his glass and surveyed her deck. She was carrying a heavy cargo, riding low in the water, and passengers, too, he noted. Two in particular in the bow near the bowsprit caught his eye, a man and a woman who strangely seemed to be engaged in some sort of wrestling match. Regretfully he could not see the woman's face, hidden as it was beneath a bonnet, but she had trim lines, Morgan thought, smiling at the glimpse of a curved, slender leg beneath a flurry of petticoats as the young woman struck violently out with her foot. Thrown off balance, her companion staggered. Before he could recover, the woman struck him full in the face with her hand then stalked away, leaving the black-frocked man slumped, almost as if in prayer, on the deck.

Morgan grinned. Now there was a hellion worth taming, if you could get past her claws. What had set her off? he wondered. A lover's spat? Somehow he was sure the lanky man wasn't her husband.

Well, it wasn't any of his concern. He lowered the glass and picked up his coffee. He had work to do with the charts in his cabin if he was to set a course for the coast of California. Ordinarily, this time of year, the

Louisa would have been heading toward the whaling grounds off Japan, but an instinct within him that Morgan had long ago accepted without question had made him decide to head to the grounds off California instead. It was this instinct of Morgan's that had made the *Louisa* one of the luckiest whaling ships afloat. Greasy luck, other whalers said enviously. After almost two years at sea, the holds of the *Louisa* held over eighteen hundred barrels of sperm oil.

As Morgan left the quarterdeck, he cast a quick but all-encompassing glance up at the rigging, making sure the sails were properly set, the rigging in perfect order. Not that there was likely to be any slackness aboard the *Louisa*. Although the clouted rope was not used by the officers of the *Louisa* as it was so liberally used aboard other whaling ships, the men were well aware of the skipper's short-fused temper.

By the time he reached his cabin, Morgan had already forgotten the amusing incident he had witnessed between the young woman and her male companion. As he pulled out his charts and studied the whirling lines that were the flow of currents, his deeply tanned face was set in a thoughtful frown; the hazel eyes under dark, straight brows turned a deep brown with concentration. The Pacific Ocean was his trackless jungle and, once more, he was the merciless hunter, his whole being centered passionately on only one thing—his prey, the great sperm whale.

The *Jeremiah* lay to in the narrows leading into Honolulu harbor the next morning waiting for daylight to go through the passage. The customhouse officer came on board shortly after the ship anchored, but it was several hours before the passengers were able to debark, carried by boats to the waterfront. A stone fort with high, thick coral walls, begun by the Russians before King Kamehameha had driven them from his kingdom, still stood guard over the harbor. The fort's ancient cannon rusted peacefully in the hot June sun.

Although most of the whaling fleet had left, not to return till fall, the outer harbor was crowded with foreign merchant ships, just as the waterfront itself was crowded with grogshops, pool halls, saloons, chandlers' shops, and the thatched stalls of open-air markets, all jostling for space in the narrow, winding dirt streets.

The smells from a nearby meat market, the odor of rancid oil and decaying vegetables, made Jasmine's nose wrinkle fastidiously. She lifted her skirt to keep the hem from the dusty street while trying to avoid the mass of humanity pushing and shoving around her. There was a Chinaman with a long pigtail flopping down his back; seamen in patched jackets and trousers, babbling in a dozen different tongues; dark-skinned Hawaiian men with only *malos* wrapped around their waists, balancing *mamaki* poles with calabashes at either end; and, of course, there were the urchins, wearing nothing at all, begging on the street corners.

As Jasmine had expected, her father was waiting for her. No doubt, the customhouse officer had gone straight to the Babcock store to inform the captain of his daughter's presence aboard the *Jeremiah*. Although he was only a few inches taller than his daughter and had a broad chest and short bandy legs, to Jasmine her father had always seemed a giant. Forgetting all decorum, she flung herself into his waiting arms, pressing her soft cheek against his stiffly bearded face. "Oh, Papa," she cried happily. "How good it is to see you!"

For a moment, her father held her tightly, then thrust her away as he grumbled, "None of that now, missy. Who gave you permission to take French leave of your school and book passage on the *Jeremiah*?" He frowned, searching Jasmine's face. "You're not in any trouble?"

He felt a wrenching ache as he studied the delicate oval of his daughter's face. How much she was like her mother, Caroline. Except Caroline's eyes had always held a serenity, which was like a soothing, cool hand on a man's aching brow, while there was none of that cool tranquillity in his daughter's luminous eyes. They shone with a disturbing willfulness, a challenging lust for life that Amos Babcock uneasily suspected could tempt a man beyond endurance.

"Of course not, Papa." Jasmine laughed, tucking her arm into his as they walked to the waiting carriage. "I was just so homesick for you and the family and the islands that I couldn't bear it a moment longer." Her hand tightened on her father's arm. "Everyone's all right at home, aren't they?"

"Everyone's fine," her father assured her, helping her into the carriage then climbing in beside her and taking the reins. "I sent a boy home from the store to tell the family that you'd arrived. No doubt Malia already has the servants in an uproar, preparing a grand feast for you. As for the others, Lani's still helping out at the mission school. Your brother shipped out on a whaler but came back a few months ago. Now he's thick with a group of ne'er-do-wells who blame the *haoles* for everything that goes wrong in the kingdom. Still, I guess we should be glad he didn't run off to the California gold-fields like so many of the young *kanakas.*"

"And Lilikoi?" Jasmine asked. "How is she?"

"God only knows what that one's up to," the captain said, exasperated. "Malia tries to keep an eye on her, but she's too big now to take a switch to, not that it ever did any good."

As they talked, Jasmine was squirming around, trying to see everything at once. They had left the waterfront and lower Nuuanu Street and were driving up into Nuuanu Valley, the Koolau Mountains, which stretched like a verdant backbone across the island, rising before them. Swirls of dust rose beneath the carriage wheels as they rode by grass-roofed huts with red and pink hibiscus spilling out of adobe-walled courtyards. Occasionally the carriage had to swerve to avoid hitting a swine rooting happily in the middle of the road or a primitive two-wheeled cart drawn by a muscular Hawaiian man. The carts and grass huts, and the *malos* the men wore, were much the same as when Captain Cook had discovered the islands, in 1778.

Yet Jasmine couldn't help noticing the modern wooden-and-stone two-story homes intermingled with the grass huts, and the number of handsome carriages on the street being driven by men in modish frock coats and accompanied by women in fashionable western gowns, holding dainty parasols over their heads. Even the native women strolling along the street, although they might be wearing flower wreaths in their hair, more often than not wore the loose, missionary-inspired *holokus*, or western dresses, rather than traditional *pa'us*.

"The town has grown so," Jasmine said, surprised. "I don't remember houses being built out this far before I left."

"Aye, Honolulu's a boom town these days." Her father nodded. "There's so many ships in the harbor, you can walk from one to another without touching water. And last year the king moved his court here from Lahaina, got himself a new palace on King Street. There'd be lots more new buildings, too, if the price of wood hadn't skyrocketed with all the lumber being shipped off to the California goldfields. Of course, I've made a nice profit myself in the gold trade," he said, giving his daughter a smug glance. "I stripped the store and shipped everything I could to California: blankets, picks, knives, at ten, fifty times their usual price. But even the high prices don't stop the *haoles* from streaming into the islands. Wouldn't surprise me someday to see more white than dark faces on the streets of Honolulu."

"Surely that's not possible!"

"It's true enough. When the white men first came to the islands, they say there were about a quarter of a million natives here. Now there's little more than seventy or eighty thousand left, and more and more dying off each year. The missionaries say it's God's curse upon the land for its wicked ways. Your brother claims it's the fault of the foreigners for destroying the Hawaiian gods and bringing in their white man's diseases."

"What do you think, Father?" Jasmine asked.

The captain shrugged. "I'm a businessman, child, not a philosopher. All I know is that each man has to fight to hold on to what's his. It's the way of the world, always has been. Probably always will be." He gave his daughter a teasing, warning glance. "Remember what I say, missy. Always fight like the devil for what's yours, no matter what the odds." His deep blue eyes sparkled with relish. "Even if you don't win, you'll still have had the fun of a good scrap."

Jasmine laughed, her glance resting affectionately on her father's grizzled face, feeling once again the deep, unquestioning love that she and her father had always shared. How much she had missed him these last years, she thought, squeezing his hand.

The carriage was passing a pedestrian, a small, fussily dressed man with a russet mustache and a brown plaid vest. The captain stopped and, leaning out, called, "Can we drive you somewhere, Mr. Wyllie?"

The man doffed his hat and smiled at Jasmine when the captain made introductions, then, speaking with a slight Scottish burr, said, "No, thank you, Captain Babcock. It's just a little way I'm going." He pulled a wry face. "Another meeting with the French consul. More new demands on the king, no doubt."

The captain frowned. "I heard talk at the store. What are the Frenchies wanting now?"

The diminutive man spread his hands. "The demands are always the same. Separate Catholic schools, reduction of the import duty on French brandy, requiring the French language to be spoken in all dealings with Frenchmen. They even want an official apology from the students at Lahainaluna School for dabbling their hands in the holy water."

Jasmine glanced back curiously at the debonair little man as he walked away. "Who is Mr. Wyllie, Papa?"

The captain urged the horses forward again. "The stories are that he's a minor Scottish laird of considerable fortune, though I'd not be knowing the truth of that.

When he stopped off in the islands several years ago, Dr. Judd brought the man into the government as the Minister of Foreign Affairs. Of course, it's really Judd who runs Wyllie's office."

"The newspapers back in Connecticut call Dr. Judd 'King Judd,' " Jasmine said.

"There's not much humbleness about the man," her father agreed, chuckling. "And he's made a lot of enemies since he left being a missionary and joined the Hawaiian government. Even Mr. Wyllie has split with him over the high-handed way Judd runs the kingdom." The captain added thoughtfully, "Still, you have to give the man credit for putting the country on a sound financial footing."

"What of King Kauikeaouli? Why doesn't he do something about Dr. Judd?"

The captain shook his head. "The king's clever enough to know he hasn't the skill or training to run the country properly alone." He smiled dourly. "Anyway, Kauikeaouli has other . . . pursuits to keep him busy away from the palace."

"You mean he's found a new mistress?" Jasmine asked matter-of-factly.

Her father turned and stared at her, his face growing beet red as he bawled, "And what do you know of such things, Jasmine Caroline Babcock? Is that what they taught you at that fancy school?"

"Oh, Papa, of course not," Jasmine said, lowering her eyelids demurely. "But, after all, I'm not a child any longer." And it certainly was no secret in the islands, even before she left, that King Kamehameha III preferred drinking and sailing and relaxing with his friends, usually young, pretty *wahines*, to ruling his kingdom.

"It's enough *pilikia* your sister Lilikoi causes," the captain muttered, giving his daughter a scowl. "I'll not be having you bring disgrace on the family, too."

They had crossed Nuuanu Stream now and were climbing into the valley, the road a streak of red earth winding between rows of kau trees, the branches arching between the carriage and the soft blue sky. The air felt softer, cooler, with the sweet fragrance of a maile vine that grew near the road. The Koolaus still loomed in the distance, and as Jasmine watched, a filmy gray mist that had been shrouding the mountaintop parted, and she could see jagged green peaks glistening in the sunlight. Then the carriage left the road and turned into a private driveway. Crushed coral rock flew up beneath the wheels as the carriage came to a stop before a low, rambling coral-stone house with a wide veranda surrounding it.

Almost before the carriage stopped, Jasmine had caught her skirt up in her hands and leaped to the ground, running toward the enormous woman who had stepped out onto the veranda. The woman's black hair was piled up high around a tortoiseshell comb, her light brown face was wreathed in a smile, and, for all her bulk, she moved toward Jasmine with a gliding, youthful grace. Malia enfolded her stepdaughter in her arms, kissing the girl in the Hawaiian fashion, by putting her nose against Jasmine's cheek and giving a sniff as if inhaling the fragrance of flowers.

"Aloha, Malia," Jasmine whispered, snuggling happily into the woman's arms, remembering how, even as a child, being embraced against her stepmother's soft, deep breasts, was like being enfolded in fragrant pillows, making all hurts disappear.

Then her stepmother was holding her away, studying Jasmine's slender figure, appalled. "You are nothing but skin and bones, child. Didn't they feed you at that school?"

"Oh, Mother," a low, musical voice drawled from the doorway. "You should know by now that all *haole* women are skinny with long necks. Why else do they torture themselves with whalebone corsets and high, tight collars? Unless they keep themselves all covered up for fear they might possibly attract a man." The voice lifted mockingly. "Perhaps my sister is afraid, too. Perhaps that's why she's come home without a *kane*."

Jasmine smiled at the young woman lounging in the doorway, her voice amused. "When have you ever known me to be afraid, Lilikoi?"

The two young women exchanged glances. Lilikoi's brown black eyes with the glossy sheen of the kukui nut fell away first. Perhaps she was remembering when they were children and Jasmine had bloodied her nose in a fight. She shrugged and laughed. "Welcome home, little sister. It's been dull around here without you."

Unlike her mother, Lilikoi's supple body was not encased in a voluminous Mother Hubbard gown. She wore a panel of red and gold silk knotted over her breasts and falling loosely to her knees, and as she glided with a sinuous grace toward Jasmine, it was obvious she wore nothing at all beneath the *pa'u*.

At eighteen, Lilikoi's body still had the precocious ripeness of a girl of the tropics, with firm, deep breasts and dark skin with a burnished glow. The curve of the hips, though, was already tending toward plumpness and, in a few years, would be padded with layers of fat. A scarlet hibiscus was tucked into shining, dark hair that fell in a long swatch over her shoulder and smelled faintly of coconut oil as she embraced Jasmine.

"I've missed you, too, sister." The new voice was soft, the smile sweetly beguiling, as a second young woman moved hesitantly out of the shadow of the doorway and onto the veranda.

Jasmine turned and stared, delighted. "Lani! Is it really you? I can't believe it. You were just a *keiki* when I left. Now you're all grown up and beautiful."

Her half sister, Lani, had enough *haole* blood in her from the captain so that her skin was like dark, aged ivory. Her features, though, were her mother's, from the full, molded lips to eyes the color of ebony, and her hair was as dark as a blue black mynah's wing. She wore a full gown with full gigot sleeves, that covered her modestly from the neck to her ankles. But even the billowy gown couldn't completely conceal the young, blossoming figure beneath, the firm young body and tiny, budding breasts.

Lani's face was flushed with happiness as she flung herself into Jasmine's arms; her dark eyes, holding a mixture of naiveté and solemnity, sparkled with tears. "Oh, it's been lonesome without you," she cried childishly. "Promise me you'll never go away again."

Jasmine held her close. Sweet, sweet Lani, she thought, and felt tears sting her own eyes. "I promise, sweetheart."

Behind her, her father cleared his throat loudly. Open displays of emotion always embarrassed him. "Well, now, how long must a man stand on his own porch?" he blustered. "First we'll have a good meal and then afterwards, we'll all go for a drive. I'll show Jasmine that nice piece of land I bought up in the valley. It'll make a fine sugar plantation one of these days, you mark my word, daughter."

"Land that you *bought?*" The voice was as furiously contemptuous as the face of the young man who had come silently around the side of the veranda. "Don't you mean land that you stole, Captain?"

Chapter 3

Jasmine studied the bronzed young man walking, with an almost studied arrogance, toward the group on the veranda and thought, well, at least her brother had not changed greatly. Kale had been a handsome young boy when she had left Hawaii, tall and strong for his age, with surprisingly classical Grecian features in a broad

Hawaiian face. Charcoal black brows arched over dark brown eyes that could be suddenly, unexpectedly, softly luminous but were often fierce or sullen. Now, at age twenty, he stood more than six feet tall, with massive shoulders and muscles pulled taut as cords across a broad chest. He wore a bright red *malo* tied around his slender hips and a shark's tooth on a necklace of braided human hair around his neck.

Behind her, Jasmine heard Malia draw in her breath, then she spoke so swiftly in Hawaiian to her son that Jasmine, who hadn't spoken Hawaiian since she had left the islands, was at first unable to follow the words.

Kale came to stand before Jasmine, inclining his head toward her in a beautifully perfect, if mocking, bow. "My mother scolds me for not dressing properly in my sister's presence. I apologize if my native garb offends you, but, of course, I did not know of your arrival, little Pikake," he said casually, calling her by the Hawaiian name for jasmine, as he always had.

He was baiting her, Jasmine knew, the way he had teased her when they had been children, but always at the point when he had plagued her beyond endurance he would flash that mischievous, charming smile at her and her anger would melt helplessly away.

Well, she wasn't a child any longer, she thought. She smiled coolly at her brother and murmured, "You don't offend me at all. I think you look very handsome." Laughter danced in her dark eyes. "But then I'm sure you know that."

When she stepped forward to receive his brotherly embrace, instead, his mouth, warm and caressing, moved suddenly to cover hers. The kiss lasted only a second, but when Jasmine stepped back, her face was flushed.

The luminous, teasing brown eyes shone down at her, a smile hidden in their depths, as he said softly, so softly that only she could hear, "You've grown into quite a tempting morsel, Pikake. It's good to have you home."

Clutching at something to say to break the awkward

silence almost palpable in the air between them, Jasmine blurted, "What did you mean? You know Father would never steal land from anyone."

The smile disappeared as her brother's eyes hardened, opaque with anger. "What would you call it when their own land is taken from the Hawaiian people and given to foreigners?"

"That's not true, Kale." Lani's voice was softly reproachful, but her eyes held a tender warmth as she gazed at her brother. "In the old days, only the kings and the chiefs had the right to own the land, and the common people owned nothing, not even a taro patch. Under Kauka Judd's new law, all Hawaiians have the right to buy and own a plot of land, even foreigners, if they first become Hawaiian citizens."

Her brother's bow-shaped lips twisted in a sneer, his voice contemptuous. "And how quickly *haoles* like the captain and other merchants have leaped to become Hawaiian citizens! Even your missionary friends, little sister. Isn't it amazing how many of them have suddenly left their churchly callings to become landowners, farmers, and planters?"

Lani's childishly curved chin quivered unhappily beneath her brother's fierce glare, but she persisted. "The king himself granted land to the missionary families for the great good they have done for the Hawaiian people."

"What good?" her brother demanded. "They brought their foreign god and laws to our land. They burden us with taxes to support a government that is theirs, not ours. Your Dr. Judd struts around, fancying himself the Cromwell of the Pacific, yet to other nations of the world we are a laughingstock, a plum ripe to be picked."

"That's enough, Kale. This is your sister's homecoming. I'll not have it spoiled with your wild, foolish talk." Captain Babcock glowered at his stepson. "And you know very well that I paid more than a fair price for the land I bought from John Kahuli."

Before Kale could protest further, his mother said firmly, "Come along. The food will be growing cold."

She gave her husband a quick, silencing glance.
I'm sure, husband, that Jasmine is too tired from her long voyage to spend the afternoon driving around in a hot carriage."

Captain Babcock might be a force to be feared in the business and trade houses of Honolulu, but at home it was his wife who ruled. Without another word, he followed her into the spacious Babcock home, where carved teakwood chairs from China sat on thick *lauhala* mats, and on the English rosewood dining table a polished calabash was neighbor to a fine-cut crystal bowl. All the high-ceilinged rooms opened onto a veranda so that every room had a cooling breeze as well as a view of the lush green gardens that surrounded the house.

Kale excused himself and when he returned to the dining room he was wearing trousers and a white linen shirt, but the shark's tooth still hung around his neck. Jasmine remembered that in the old days only chiefs and members of the royal family were entitled to wear the shark's tooth, an emblem of power. She saw her father glance irritably at Kale's decoration and wondered whether Kale wore the necklace as a reminder that Malia was the daughter of a chief who had fought beside the great Kamehameha or simply to annoy the captain.

Then the food was being served: buttered fish, steaming sweet potatoes sweetened with coconut syrup, taro cakes, fresh mangoes and bananas, spicy *lomilomi*, and, of course, the inevitable *poi*.

For a while, Jasmine forgot everything else as she happily stuffed herself in a most unladylike fashion. No matter how much she ate, though, Malia kept insisting that she eat more, until finally, laughing, Jasmine pushed her plate away. "I can't eat another spoonful, Malia, or I'll burst."

After he finished his meal, Captain Babcock decided to return to the store, and Malia, as was her custom, returned to her bedroom for a nap. Jasmine's trunks had been brought to the Babcock house from the

...ped the servant with the unpacking.
...ster bed and all the chairs in the bed-
...ered with a flurry of lace and ruffles and
...s. Lani and Lilikoi, watching and giggling
...oolgirls, admired this gown and that bonnet,
...ed on trying on the lisle stockings and white kid
gloves. Snatching up a pale yellow shot-silk gown with
bouffant lace sleeves, Lilikoi held the dress up before
her, studying herself, pleased, in the dressing-table
mirror.

"I think I'll wear this one at the next reception at the
palace," she announced, her eyes sparkling. "Even Prince
Lot will forget his broken heart over Princess Pauahi
when he sees me."

"I thought you wrote me that the prince and Bernice
Pauahi were betrothed," Jasmine said.

"Prince Lot thought so, too," Lilikoi said, shrugging
her bare, rounded shoulders. "It turns out that the princess had other plans. She wants to marry Charles Bishop,
an American she met when she was attending the Royal
School. Prince Lot is desolate, and Bernice's parents are
furious. They believe the missionaries encouraged the
marriage so that Bernice's fortune will fall into the hands
of a *haole*."

"They have no right to think that," Lani protested.
"Why, you only have to look at the princess and Mr.
Bishop together to know how much in love they are."

Lilikoi turned maliciously upon her sister. "And what
do you know of love, little sister? You wouldn't know
what to do if a man so much as touched you."

"While you know only too well, don't you?" Kale
drawled from the open doorway. "You should. You've
bedded half the *kanes* in Honolulu."

Lilikoi eyed herself complacently in the mirror, running her hands over the generous curve of her hips.
"I've had no complaints," she said, a small, catlike smile
on her full lips.

Lani's face stained a deep pink beneath the ivory, her
dark eyes filled with unhappiness as she stared at her

sister. "It's a sin," she blurted, "to sleep mischievously. God will turn his face away from you."

Kale's face stiffened, his muscular body moving with a lithe grace across the room to stand before Lani, staring fiercely down at her. "It's a *kapu* of the missionaries' *haole* god that a man and a woman are forbidden to find pleasure in each other's bodies," he said harshly. "Our Hawaiian gods make no such *kapu*."

Lani did not shrink from the fury in Kale's face, only her voice trembled a little. "There is only one God, my brother."

Watching the two of them, Jasmine had a sudden feeling of unease, sensing that Kale's anger and Lani's stubborn resistance were only a cover for a deeper, more profoundly disturbing emotion. It was not a thought, however, she cared to pursue, and she stepped forward quickly. "Did you come to see my new gowns, too, Kale?" she asked, smiling teasingly.

The anger faded from her brother's face as he tweaked at a curl of Jasmine's hair that had escaped confinement at the nape of her neck. "It's a warm day, Pikake. I came to ask if you want to go swimming."

When Jasmine hesitated, Kale taunted her, "Or perhaps you've forgotten how to swim. You always did splash around like a beached *kohola*."

Lilikoi let the silk dress drop carelessly to the floor and said at once, "I'd love a swim. I'll have the servants fetch the horses."

"I can still beat you in a race to the reef," Jasmine replied indignantly. "Just give a minute to change into my riding habit."

Then she saw that Lani was standing in the middle of the bedroom, looking forlorn. "Come along, Lani," she said. "We'll show Kale who are the best swimmers in the family."

The girl hung back. "I—I don't think I should."

Jasmine remembered then that the missionaries had always frowned upon Hawaiians spending their time frivolously on water sports instead of their daily labor and were particularly forbidding of young native women swimming openly with men.

"Please come, Lani," she pleaded. "It'll be like old times, the four of us together, having a picnic at the beach."

Kale took his half sister's hand and said very solemnly, although his dark eyes gleamed with laughter, "I have read your Bible from cover to cover, and there is no *kapu* against swimming." He pulled at her hand, smiling. "You don't have to go into the water. You can watch from the beach."

Lani felt a familiar weakness creeping over her. With her gentle, submissive nature it was difficult for her to refuse anyone, especially Kale, who, even when they were children, had been able to make her laugh or cry with his smile or frown.

A few hours at the beach shouldn't be a great sin, she thought, and it was Jasmine's first day home. "All right," she said softly, "just this once."

It was an hour's horseback ride from the Babcock home to Waikiki. Years before, the captain had had a small thatched hut built upon a raised platform of stone where the girls could change their clothes and Kale could store his surfboard and outrigger canoe. A coconut grove sheltered the house from the sun and a lanai stretched out in front of the hut with a view of the sea.

"Nothing's changed," Jasmine said, looking around her happily. Perhaps the thatch was torn in places, the wicker chairs on the lanai a little worn, but the ocean itself, stained a dozen shades of blue, the white foam breaking over the coral reef, and the dark, brooding Diamond Head at the far end of the beach were the same. So was the pungent scent of seaweed and the sounds of the surf lapping at the sand and the rustle of tattered palm fronds, exactly as she remembered when she used to lie awake at night in her bedroom at the academy, too homesick to sleep.

Lilikoi lent her a flowered-print *pa'u*, and she hastily removed her riding habit and wrapped the cloth around her body, tying it tightly over her breasts before she joined Kale and Lilikoi. Together they splashed out through the shallows and then plunged headfirst into the softly breaking waves.

"What about that race?" Kale asked, suddenly surfacing beside Jasmine and gesturing toward the breakers, tumbling over the distant reef. It was, Jasmine discovered quickly and ruefully, no contest. Although she was a good swimmer, she hadn't been swimming in years, and her body was no match for Kale's, with muscular strength in his arms and legs as he cut through the water, always ahead of her.

But Jasmine didn't care that she had lost the race. It was much too enjoyable, floating on her back in the ultramarine sea, taking a sensuous pleasure in the water, warm and silken soft, caressing her breasts and limbs. Like the hands of a lover? she wondered, remembering suddenly the greedy, smug smile of pleasure on Lilikoi's face when she spoke of the enjoyment she found in a man's arms. Someday she would find a lover who would make her feel that way, Jasmine thought dreamily. She could already imagine what he would look like: tall and slender, with blue eyes and blond hair like a golden god. The sun beat down on her closed eyelids. Her thoughts slipped away drowsily.

On the beach, Lilikoi, too lazy to stay in the water for long, had returned to the beach hut. She curled up like a puppy on the springy-soft *lauhala* mats and instantly fell asleep. Lani took off her shoes and strolled down the beach. The incoming tide, washing over her bare feet, felt deliciously cool, and she looked longingly out at the blue green ocean. She was not as strong a swimmer as Lilikoi or Jasmine, but she remembered what fun it had been as a child, dashing into the waves, letting them tumble her over and over.

She glanced around. There was no one in sight. Impulsively she pulled off her warm, voluminous gown and folded it neatly before placing it on the sand. She wore a long, white muslin shift under the gown, and when she stepped into the ocean, at first cautiously, then swimming with reckless abandon into the deeper water, the material clung to the lissome, almost boyish curves.

The ocean buoyed her up gently as she swam out to the line of larger waves curling and rushing toward the shore. She braced herself as the waves swept over her, tumbling and pulling her under into a dazzling, brilliant world, then sent her, gasping, to the surface again and into the sparkling, sun-warmed air. She felt as if she were a child again, happy and carefree.

How could her pleasure in the water be sinful, she wondered, bewildered, remembering how one of the mission teachers had reviled swimming and water sports as "heathen revels."

But then, although she tried hard, Lani had never completely understood why it was evil to wear flower garlands to church, or why idleness was a sin and labor beloved of the Lord God, Jehovah. Still, Lani thought, suddenly fearful and guilt-stricken, one didn't question the wisdom of the *haole* God, especially when eternal damnation was the lot of those who defied his commands. It had been wicked of her to come to the beach and, worse, to take pleasure in her wickedness.

She half turned to start back to the beach when a wave, larger than the others, bore down upon her. The crest of the wave swept over her, tossing her head over heels before she could take a breath, then pulled her swiftly down in its undertow. The salty taste of seawater was in her mouth as Lani tried to kick her way back to the surface, but the long white shift wrapped wetly around her lgs like tentacles of seaweed, trapping her so that she couldn't propel herself upward. The water that had seemed beautifully blue and crystal clear was now a black, deadly wall falling on her, crushing her.

She was flailing, panic-stricken, with her arms when she felt an arm around her waist and she was being jerked to the surface. For several seconds, she was too busy gasping and choking, pulling air into her tortured lungs, to realize that it was Kale's arms around her, carrying her to the beach and placing her gently on her feet. His hands, circling her tiny waist, supported her as she clung, exhausted, to him.

His dark eyes studied her face anxiously. "Are you all right, little sister? For a moment, when I saw you weren't coming up, when I wasn't sure I could reach you in time . . ." His voice broke and she realized that the hands on her waist were trembling.

"I'm—I'm fine . . . I feel so foolish."

"You should feel foolish," he said, anger fighting with the concern in his face. "That's a *pupule* costume to wear swimming. You could have drowned."

But she was aware that it was more than anger and concern in his eyes as his glance ran over her soaked shift. The wet sheer muslin material clung so closely to her breasts and legs that she might as well not be wearing anything at all, she thought, feeling all at once uneasy yet breathless as she saw a luminous warmth replacing the anger in Kale's eyes. His eyes seemed to burn with a flame from within as they lingered on her small, pertly upthrust breasts. It was a flame that seemed to burn her, too, as his hands pushed aside the shoulder straps of her shift, slipped beneath the material, seeking the blossoming softness beneath.

Then, alarmed, she tried to pull away. "No, Kale, you mustn't!"

"I want you, little sister," he whispered huskily. "I have ever since I watched you turn into a woman. And you want me, too. I can see it in your eyes."

For a moment, appalled, she stopped struggling. Could it possibly be true? she wondered, dismayed. Was there a deep-seated evil, some sinful perversion inside of her, that responded to Kale's touch? She could not deny that she felt a breathless sense of excitement when she was in the same room with Kale. And when he smiled at her, there was a rush of warmth through her body, like a fever, so that when the feeling left her, she felt chill.

"I want to marry you, *makamae* Lani," he whispered. "I want to be with you."

Now, with a strength she didn't know she possessed in her slender arms, she managed to push him away. "No!" she gasped, horrified. "It is forbidden."

"Not by our Hawaiian gods," Kale said, his face black with anger. "Have you forgotten that we are the grandchildren of a great chief? *Niau Pio*, a brother marrying a sister, has never been *kapu* between members of the *alii*. How else have we kept our bloodlines pure? Our own king married his sister, Nahienaena, and still mourns her death." His voice was warm as a caress reaching out to her, coaxing her. "Please, my sweet Lani, let me make you happy. Listen to the singing in your blood, to the voice of your ancestors, not some alien god that lives far away in a foreign land."

"You mustn't . . . we mustn't talk of such things. It is a great sin!"

Trembling, Lani snatched up her gown and slipped it over her wet shift. Tears of unhappiness spilled down her cheeks as she turned and, half running, half falling in the soft sand, fled back down the beach toward the beach house.

Jasmine, swimming toward shore, had seen Kale carrying Lani through the surf toward the beach, but Kale's broad shoulders had hidden the rest of the scene from her view.

Now she scrambled out of the water to Lani's side, frightened by the tears streaming down her sister's face and the wide, frightened look in the childishly soft dark eyes. "What is it, Lani? Are you hurt?"

Her sister took a deep, shuddering breath. "I—I went out too far. . . . A wave pulled me under."

Yawning, Lilikoi strolled down the beach, gazing curiously at her brother, who stood behind Lani, his face as dark as a thundercloud. "What's all the *kulikuli*?"

Jasmine slipped a comforting arm around her younger sister, shocked at the violent shudders shaking the small body. "Lani almost drowned. Thank God, Kale was close enough to pull her out. We'd better get her home."

Lilikoi shrewdly studied Lani's flushed face and the

look of frustration in Kale's dark, furious gaze. She had long suspected her brother's desire for Lani and had once even teased him about it. After all, wasn't she much more available and twice as desirable as bland little Lani, but Kale had never so much as touched her. An icy warning in her brother's glance, though, told her that this was not the time for further teasing. She turned spitefully instead to Jasmine. "You'd better get out of the sun, too, sister, or you'll be brown as a *hapa-haole*. And what *haole kane* would want you without your pale white skin?"

Jasmine was beginning to feel a prickling sensation on her face and shoulders. She had forgotten how merciless the Hawaiian sun could be, but she smiled sweetly at Lilikoi. "Oh, I've never had any trouble getting boyfriends, Lili. Or were you afraid I'd take away one of yours?"

Lilikoi's eyes glittered. She took a threatening step toward Jasmine. "You so much as look at one of my sweethearts, and I'll scratch your eyes out."

Kale stepped hastily between the two young women. "Nothing has changed," he said irritably. "Even as *keikis*, you and Lili always fought like two cats in a bag."

He gave Jasmine a gentle shove toward the beach hut. "Run along and change your clothes, Pikake. You're right. We should get Lani home."

Chapter 4

Over the next weeks, though, as one golden summer's day followed another, Jasmine realized that a great deal had changed. Always before when she and Lili had quarreled as children, they had made up just as quickly. But she sensed there was only a wary truce between them now. Kale was gone a great deal of the time with a group of friends who called themselves the Sons of Kamehameha and regarded all foreigners in the islands with dark suspicion. Lani spent more and more of her time working at the school or with her nose buried in a Bible, and ever since the day at the beach, her soft brown eyes held a haunted look. As for the captain, he was no longer the simple shopkeeper he had been when Jasmine had left the islands. Now her father seemed to have a finger in a great many pies—land and banks and shipping—so that he, too, was seldom home.

At first, Jasmine was resentful of the changes in the family, of their new interests in which she had no part. Then she told herself firmly that she was being childish. Had she really expected everything to stay exactly the same, just waiting for her return? Only Malia, thank goodness, was unchanged and unchanging, placid, warm, and loving.

Then, as word rapidly spread of the new beauty who had arrived in Honolulu, invitations began to pour into the Babcock home, and Jasmine soon forgot her misgivings. Quickly she was swept up in the gay social whirl of the royal court, as well as the small, cliquish social world of the foreign community, people who made their home in Honolulu. She was invited to parties at private homes, teas at foreign consulates, and receptions aboard the naval vessels from a dozen different countries that sailed into Honolulu harbor, as well as soirées and balls at Iolani Palace.

Daily trips to the beach had darkened Jasmine's skin, but the smitten young men who gathered around Captain Babcock's daughter didn't seem to find the tawny golden shade of her face and arms displeasing. Jasmine wondered, amused, what they would think if they knew that her whole body was the same gleaming tawny shade. When she went to the beach alone, she would often remove her *pa'u* after a swim, stretch out in the seclusion of the beach hut's lanai, allowing the sun free access to her entire body.

Certainly Jeremy Smyth-Wright, assigned to the British legation in Honolulu and Jasmine's eager escort to a reception at the palace one evening in August, couldn't seem to keep his admiring gaze away from his companion. There was, Jeremy decided, something peculiarly alluring about the contrast of the raven black hair and thick-lashed dark eyes against the pale gold face. It was, in a way, like having on his arm one of the exotic native beauties who paraded along Fort Street and, it was whispered, danced at night naked in certain selected saloons along the waterfront. Not that Jeremy made a habit of visiting such establishments. However, it was pleasantly disturbing to know that his companion was as beautiful as any of those shameless creatures; while at the same time, of course, it was gratifying to know that only pure white blood ran in Jasmine Babcock's veins, a well-bred young lady who could grace the finest drawing rooms in London.

Jasmine was aware of her companion's flattering gaze. She gave him a devastating smile, as if she were equally entranced, even as she glanced absently around the throne room, where the reception was being held. King

Kauikeaouli and Queen Kalama sat upon a dais covered with crimson velvet. The king, Jasmine thought, looked particularly imposing with a broad sash of crimson and gold worn across a blue Windsor uniform, which was embroidered with gold taro leaves on the collar and cuffs.

The queen was a plump, pretty woman who looked slightly uncomfortable in western clothes. Court attendants stood on either side holding the royal *kahilis*, and the two young princes, Alexander and Lot, sat in smaller chairs next to the dais. Both boys—like the king, their uncle—were over six feet tall, but while Alexander, heir to the throne, was slender, with fair skin, Lot's skin was dark, his large head sitting low upon broad shoulders, and his expression taciturn. Near the throne stood Dr. Gerrit Judd, a small man with crowns sewn onto his coat lapels and a firm, purposeful stare on his face that made him seem larger than he was.

Jasmine and her escort had already been through the reception line, Jasmine making a low, graceful curtsy to the king and queen that brought a proud smile to Jeremy's lips. He decided that no other woman in the room could match Jasmine Babcock's beauty and regal bearing, as if, he thought, pleased, she had been born to the purple.

Later, as they were served refreshments, Jeremy noted, "I see that Wyllie isn't here this evening. I suppose he's concerned about the two French warships that arrived this morning. I wonder if the French consul isn't deliberately trying to provoke a confrontation between France and the Hawaiian kingdom, probably hoping to take over the islands, the way the French have done in Tahiti and the Marquesas."

Jasmine waved her fan indifferently. "Oh, the French have threatened to attack the islands before, and it was all a bluff." She gave her companion an amused, sidelong glance. "After all, it's no more than the British did in forty-three, when Lord George Paulet sailed into Honolulu harbor and forced the king to cede the islands to England."

Jeremy's face turned a bright pink as he replied stiffly, "That was entirely different. Paulet acted outside the scope of his instructions. As soon as Admiral Sir Richard Thomas heard of it, he, of course, restored the independence of the Sandwich Islands immediately."

"Of course," Jasmine said demurely, hiding a smile. It really wasn't much fun teasing Jeremy, she decided. He was so serious and pompous. Still, he was tall, blond, and blue-eyed, with beautiful manners. And her father had pointed out to her that Smyth-Wright's father was a lord. Although Jeremy, being a younger son, had little chance of inheriting the title, he did have a large private income. If only, Jasmine sighed, Jeremy had the slightest sense of humor.

Nevertheless, she felt sufficiently contrite at having baited him that on the carriage ride home, she allowed her companion to slip an arm around her waist. Emboldened, Jeremy turned her mouth toward him and pressed his lips against hers. Jasmine's petal-soft lips did not part beneath the pressure of his mouth, but, of course, since Jasmine was a carefully brought-up young lady, he would have been shocked if she had known how to kiss properly.

"My precious girl," he murmured, finally releasing her but still breathing the faint jasmine scent that clung to her hair and skin. "How lovely you are."

Jasmine's dark-fringed eyes, which could be velvet brown in the sunlight but were now almost black in the moonlight, were cast modestly downward. There was a faint flush beneath the golden skin, which Jeremy attributed to maidenly excitement stirred by his kiss.

The truth was Jasmine was feeling only irritated and bored. Jeremy's kiss, though not unpleasant, had caused no answering response in her blood, and she was regretting the fact that he had undoubtedly crushed the nosegay of white pikake she wore at her waist.

"How I'd love to take you to London and introduce you at court," Jeremy said eagerly. He laughed, nodding back toward the palace. "Of course, it would be a real court, not a slapdash affair like the one at Iolani Palace."

"Oh, you find the Hawaiian court amusing?" Jasmine asked, an annoyed note in her voice that Jeremy missed completely.

"The king's a good enough chap when he's not in his cups," Jeremy said indifferently. "And when Dr. Judd and the mission people aren't trying to turn him against England. Still, it wasn't more than thirty years ago that the king's father was practicing his savage *kapus* and these islands were completely uncivilized."

"Are white men so much more civilized?" Jasmine asked, her chin lifting angrily. "The French are threatening to turn their guns upon the fort. If they do, all of Honolulu could go up in flames."

"Oh, I doubt if the French would go that far," Jeremy said heartily, then, realizing that the topic of warfare was hardly conducive to wooing a maiden in the moonlight, he once again tried to slip an arm around Jasmine's waist.

His companion drew quickly away. "It's late," Jasmine said, her voice chilly. "I think you had better take me home."

Escorting Jasmine to the veranda of her home, Jeremy asked hopefully, "Would you care to go horseback riding with me tomorrow? We could ride up into Manoa Valley, bring along a picnic lunch."

"We'll see tomorrow," Jasmine said, not sure whether her anger was directed at Jeremy's disparaging remarks about the royal family or at his having given up so easily making love to her.

The next day, however, there was no possibility of going horseback riding. Early the next morning the citizens of Honolulu were warned that the French planned to attack the city. Foreign residents scurried around town, hiding their valuables or moving them to places of safety. Captain Babcock, swearing loudly and sweating in the August heat, supervised the removal of the goods from his store near the waterfront where the French frigates were anchored, ready to turn broadside and open fire upon the town if the French demands on the Hawaiian government were not met.

Before leaving to keep an eye on his store, Captain Babcock gave strict orders to his family that none of them were to leave the house "until this damn French matter is settled one way or the other." When a mutinous darkness settled over Kale's face, he added curtly, "I'll expect you to stay home, Kale, and watch over your sisters. Thank God, your mother's safe on Kauai. Not that I expect the Frenchies will get this far up into the valley, but tempers are running high."

By afternoon, bored and restless, the young Babcocks gathered on the veranda, looking down toward the harbor, where an ominous silence prevailed.

Lilikoi prowled the veranda, her mouth drooping sulkily. "If we only knew what was going on," she complained.

"At least we haven't heard any cannon fire," Jasmine said, fanning herself with a fragrant sandalwood fan. The day was hot without a breeze stirring, even on the shaded veranda. She was wearing her coolest gown and had removed as many petticoats as she modestly could, but she was still uncomfortably warm. "If the French ships were firing on the town, we'd hear."

"It's so foolish," Lilikoi said, frowning. "Why doesn't the king just agree to the French demands?"

Lani had been sitting quietly, curled up in a wicker chair. Now she looked at her sister, shocked. "That would mean allowing more and more Catholic priests to come to Hawaii, snaring the souls of the people with the delusions and superstitions of Rome."

Kale turned from staring broodingly down at the harbor and gave Lani a sharp glance. "Is the *mana* of your *haole* god so weak then, little sister, that he fears all other gods? Is that why your mission church allowed the persecution and imprisonment of Catholics and tried to expel all priests from the islands?"

"The missionaries never approved the persecution of

those poor misguided souls," Lani said, her face troubled. "Anyway, that was ten years ago."

"For myself," Lilikoi said, smiling smugly, "I like the Frenchmen. There was one French sailor I remember." She frowned absently. "Or was it a Yankee whaling captain? We went for a midnight swim together and while we swam together, he took off my *pa'u* and . . ."

Jasmine saw Lani's ivory face turn a painful, embarrassed scarlet and she snapped, "Oh, be quiet, Lili. No one wants to hear about your rutting with every man in sight."

"It couldn't be that you're jealous?" Lili purred. "Poor Jasmine. How dull it must be, being courted by that Englishman. Everyone knows the English have ice water in their veins." Her eyes narrowed spitefully. "Or is it that you don't know how to arouse desire in a real man?"

Jasmine's fan snapped shut. "Jeremy happens to be a gentleman," she said. "But then you've probably never met one among your acquaintances on the waterfront."

"Shut up, both of you," Kale ordered wearily. "Isn't it enough we have the French attacking us without you two battling?"

"I wish Father would come home," Lani wailed softly. "Suppose the French have killed him!"

Kale pressed her shoulder gently, tenderness flooding his impassive features as he looked down at the girl. "No one's harmed the captain. You'll see. He'll be home soon."

A gloomy, uneasy silence settled over the veranda as the afternoon dragged by and there was still no word of what was happening in town. It was early evening when the captain returned, his face weary as he greeted his family, still assembled on the veranda.

When he didn't speak at once, instead sinking, exhausted, into a chair, Kale demanded impatiently, "Well, what happened? Did the French attack?"

"They came storming ashore, boatloads of French sailors, early this afternoon," the captain replied. "The only damage they did, though, was to wreck the fort, spiking the cannon and destroying the muskets and bayonets, letting the gunpowder pour into the harbor. They also ransacked the governor's house and destroyed everything they could lay their hands on, as well as stealing the king's yacht."

"And no one tried to fight them off?" Kale demanded, outraged.

"With what?" the captain asked wryly. "The kingdom has no army or navy."

"Kamehameha would never have allowed such desecration," Kale said bitterly. "His army would have attacked the French with only clubs and their bare hands." His dark eyes shone savagely. "Tonight when the French sailors are asleep, my friends and I will creep among them and . . ."

"You'll do nothing of the kind," Captain Babcock growled, jerking to his feet. "This whole affair will blow over in a few days. But what do you think the French will do if any of their men are killed? It's just the excuse they want, some incident to give them a reason to take over the government completely."

Afraid that Kale and her father might actually come to blows, Jasmine stepped forward swiftly, but Lani was there before her. She stepped between the two men and placed her hands on Kale's chest, whispering, "Please, Kale. I could not bear it if you took a man's life or if you lost your own. You are too dear to me. . . ." Her voice stumbled, her face becoming pale, as she stammered, "To—to all of us. Promise me you won't go near the Frenchmen."

Jasmine could see the warring of conflicting emotions in her brother's proud, handsome face as he gazed down at Lani. Then he nodded, thrusting Lani away from him, and stalked off the veranda into the darkness in the garden.

For several days, the French sailors and their commanders marched importantly around town, their drums beating, but as Captain Babcock had predicted, within a week the French frigates sailed from Honolulu bound for France.

Life once more for Jasmine became a round of parties and receptions and teas. She tried to forget what Lilikoi had said about Jeremy and her. Surely she knew better than to pay any attention to Lilikoi's malicious teasing. Yet she found herself flirting with Jeremy in a much less ladylike way than she had before, using her fan provocatively to draw attention to the tempting fullness of her breasts above bodices cut daringly low and letting her hand linger on Jeremy's arm, leaning close to him to whisper in his ear.

Then one afternoon when they were taking a horse-back ride together across the plain to the beach at Waikiki, she pretended to catch her foot in the stirrup as Jeremy helped her dismount and almost fell into his arms. To Jeremy's startled but delighted surprise, Jasmine did not immediately pull away from him but leaned more closely against him. Her face was lifted to his, her mouth half-parted in a tantalizing smile.

When she did not resist his searching mouth on hers, he became bolder. His hands fumbled at the buttons of her trimly tailored English riding habit, desire whipsawing through him so that he wasn't aware of how very still Jasmine was in his arms.

Damn the clothes that women wore anyway, Jeremy thought, perspiration breaking out on his forehead as he struggled with the buttons on the jacket. Then there was the silk blouse beneath, and the ruffled linen chemise beneath that, finally revealing the shadowy hollow at the base of Jasmine's throat, the silken swell of breasts the same tawny color as Jasmine's face. But before his hands could reap their reward and caress that desirable softness, Jasmine murmured a sharp "No, please. You mustn't! Let me go."

Her hands, knotted into fists, pushed hard against Jeremy's chest, catching him off balance. The perspiration on Jeremy's forehead felt suddenly cold as he realized what had almost happened. In another moment, he would have taken Captain Babcock's daughter there on the beach, as if she were some common prostitute from Fid Street. He watched uneasily as Jasmine walked quickly away from him toward a grove of coconut trees half slanting toward the water.

Yet . . . Jeremy frowned. Surely he hadn't imagined the invitation in Jasmine's eyes. Was it possible she wanted him, too, but was too shy to say so? However, once he told her his news, he thought confidently, all that would change.

He crossed to the girl's side and said firmly, "You needn't be concerned, my dear. After the letter I received yesterday, I had planned to speak to your father anyway."

Jasmine had managed to rebutton her jacket and adjust her riding hat with its yellow plume, tilting it at a rakish angle over her smooth black hair. "What letter?" she asked.

Jeremy put on a properly grave mien. "I received word from my family that my father is very ill. I've already handed in my resignation at the consulate. I'll be sailing for England within the week."

"But you'll come back?"

"I doubt that. I'll be needed at home to help run the family estate." He frowned thoughtfully. "It'll mean a hasty wedding here in Hawaii, I'm afraid, unless you prefer to wait and be married in England."

Jasmine concealed her annoyance at the offhand way that Jeremy seemed to assume that she would, of course, accept his offer of marriage, and asked cautiously, "You mean we would live in England?"

Jeremy stared at her, surprised. "Of course. We could hardly live here in Hawaii like outcasts, now, could we?" He added jovially, "Why, even Dr. Judd is willing to sell these islands to the highest bidder."

"What do you mean?" Jasmine stared at her companion, bewildered. "Dr. Judd is accompanying the young princes on a world tour."

"It was supposed to be a secret," Jeremy admitted.

47

"Only Mr. Wyllie informed my consulate that Judd has carte blanche during his trip to transfer or sell the sovereignty of Hawaii."

"The king would never permit it," Jasmine protested, outraged. "It would be like selling his own people."

"I'm sure it will make very little difference to the natives," Jeremy said, impatiently reaching for Jasmine's hand. "You'll love London, my dear. If you'd like, we can honeymoon in Paris or Venice. There's so much of the world I want to show you."

Leave Hawaii, Jasmine thought, dismayed, staring into Jeremy's flushed face. How could she do that? She remembered the desolation she had felt those years she had spent away at school, as if some essential part of herself had been left behind here in the islands.

Taking her silence for consent, Jeremy once again drew her into the circle of his arms. Earlier, when Jasmine had allowed him to kiss and caress her, she had only wanted to prove that Lilikoi was wrong, that she was quite as capable as Lili of arousing desire in a male. Instead of feeling pleasure, though, when Jeremy's tongue had thrust into her open mouth, when she had felt the damp warmth of his hands on her body, she had only felt repulsed and a little guilty.

This time, however, when his mouth sought hers, she turned her face away and was furious when Jeremy's eager, questing tongue, frustrated, found instead her ear and nibbled at her earlobe. "Don't!" she said, incensed.

Jeremy's arms tightened around her. "It's all right, my dear," he whispered hoarsely, struggling to hold her twisting body. "We're going to be married. It's different now. You'll like it, you'll see."

"I said no!"

Jeremy, startled, stared into the face of an icy virago, a Jasmine he had never seen before, her eyes like ebony and just as hard.

"And we're not going to be married," she snapped. "Not now, or ever."

Then she turned and ran, stumbling across the sand

to her horse. Grabbing the reins, she mounted quickly, kicking the horses' flanks savagely as she raced back toward Honolulu, leaving a disconsolate Jeremy on the beach, staring after her, bewildered.

Chapter 5

"Hurry up, Jasmine."

In the darkness of the garden, Lilikoi's voice was disembodied, held to an impatient whisper so as not to awaken the sleeping household.

Jasmine hesitated halfway down the veranda steps. Like her sister, she was dressed in a flowered silk *pa'u*. Lilikoi's *pa'u* was a scarlet print, matching the hibiscus in her hair; Jasmine's, a pale yellow, was worn with a wreath of fragrant pikake blossoms in her dark hair and around her neck.

Earlier in the evening when Lilikoi had stopped by Jasmine's room and asked, "Do you still remember how to *hula*, sister?" her words had not been so much a question as a challenge.

Malia respected the *kapus* of the missionaries, but she also respected certain traditions of her ancestors and had taught all her daughters the *hula*, although none of them could dance as gracefully or skillfully as Malia herself.

Jasmine looked up from her packing. The Babcock family was leaving the next morning to visit Malia's family on Kauai. "I haven't danced the *hula* in years," she said and then added curiously, "Isn't it still forbidden?"

"Oh, yes," Lilikoi answered carelessly. "But the police can't be everywhere. Some friends of mine are giving a *luau* this evening, and there's sure to be dancing. You can come along, if you want."

Jasmine hesitated. "I still have packing to do."

"You can finish that in the morning." A jeering note crept into Lilikoi's voice. "Unless, of course, you're afraid . . ."

No, Jasmine thought, annoyed, she wasn't afraid. What she was was jumpy and restless, her nerves on edge, the way she felt before a thunderstorm broke over the Pali and swept down into the valley. Except there were no thunderclouds overhead. It was a clear, moon-bright night, with just a faint breeze wafting into her bedroom, carrying the scent of ginger and maile and night-blooming jasmine from the garden, filling her with vague yearnings, for what she didn't know.

Jeremy had left for England almost a month ago now, and the suitors that had taken his place aroused only tedium and indifference in her. She was even beginning to wonder if she had made a mistake turning down Jeremy's proposal of marriage. Perhaps, in time, she would have grown accustomed to Jeremy's beautifully tended hands roaming over her body as if he had a perfect right to do so, trading her sunny, fragrant islands for one that she heard was more often than not fog-covered, cold, and rainy.

No! Not yet. Rebellion surged in Jasmine. It was too soon to settle for a life of matrimonial dullness, one monotonous day merging into another, growing old and never knowing. . . . Her thoughts stumbled uncertainly, for she wasn't really sure what it was she didn't know. Was it the look on Lilikoi's face when she described the exploits of her lovers, that languorous, self-satisfied gleam in her heavy-lidded eyes, a look that Jasmine had never seen on her own face?

At the moment, though, Lilikoi's eyes held only irritation as she said petulantly, "Well, are you coming or not?"

Impulsively, Jasmine reached for her shawl. Why not? There couldn't be any harm in just attending the *luau* and watching the dancing. No one need ever know.

"You'll have to wear a *pa'u*," Lilikoi said. "Otherwise, everyone there will think you're a *malihini*."

Jasmine had often worn the *pa'u* when she was alone at the beach but never out in public. But she supposed Lili was right. She would be too conspicuous at a native feast wearing her western-style gown and poke bonnet.

Quickly she slipped out of her gown and wrapped herself in the silk *pa'u*. Then catching sight of herself in the mirror, the shocking expanse of gleaming flesh above her tightly bound breasts, she nimbly arranged sprays of pikake into garlands around her neck and another smaller wreath for her hair. As she finished, she was aware that Lilikoi was watching her, a look of secret amusement in her dark eyes that made Jasmine suddenly feel uneasy.

The uneasiness returned as she left the house, making her pause uncertainly on the steps.

Lilikoi appeared before her in the darkness, her hand pulling impatiently at Jasmine's arm. "Come along. We'll have to hurry or all the *kalua* pork will be gone."

Jasmine's uncertainty disappeared, banished by a sudden attack of down-to-earth hunger pangs. She could almost taste the delicious morsels of pig that had been slowly baking all day for the *luau*, wrapped in leaves and buried in an earthen pit lined with kiawe wood and hot lava rocks, cooked so long and slowly that the tender meat fell apart in your mouth.

This time, when Lilikoi tugged at her arm, she did not hesitate but followed her sister through the darkness of the garden to the back gate, where several *kanaka* friends of Lilikoi's were waiting. There were whispers and giggles, and Jasmine felt herself being lifted on horseback by strong male arms. Her mount followed the other horses obediently as the party traveled along narrow moonlit back roads between taro patches and mullet ponds, through softly rustling banana groves, and past small, dark thatched huts, where an occasional dog rushed out to bark at them as they rode by. After a few turnings, Jasmine was lost, although when she caught the distant pungent scent of seaweed, she knew they were traveling *makai*.

After about an hour's travel, she could see tiny flames of bonfires and the golden flickering light of kukui torches, hear the soft soughing sound of the surf rolling over a beach. By the time they arrived at the *luau*, the feasting had already begun. Crisp, succulent pig, baked yams and breadfruits, and fresh mangoes and bananas were being served on woven mats with ti leaves as platters. Gourds of a potent bitter-tasting liquor, which Jasmine suspected was kava, were being passed around.

Jasmine was still eating happily when the music began: the pounding of the *pahu* drums, the beating of gourds against the ground, the eerie high-pitched nose flute. Several seated men started chanting in a monotone in time to the music, and here and there a woman rose to her feet and began to dance.

Jasmine watched, fascinated. She had forgotten how beautiful the *hula* was: the flowing movement of the arms, the hands like birds in flight, the sinuously swaying hips of the women moving as one to the sharp beat of the drum, the cries of the chanting men. The tempo of the music quickened, the drums grew louder, the dance faster and faster, until it reached a sudden, crashing climax.

Then a young man wearing only a *malo* and dog-teeth anklets leaped to his feet and began to dance solo. All his movements were obviously those of a man attempting awkwardly to make love to a woman, first prissy and stiff, while his audience roared with laughter. Belatedly Jasmine understood that the dancer was mocking how missionaries made love; then, as his gestures and the movements of his hips and arms became more adroit and virile, the Hawaiian *kane* made love. Jasmine found herself laughing, too, especially when the young man pretended to mount a horse, lifted an umbrella over his head, missionary-style, and rode off stage.

Once again the young women picked up the dancing, and Jasmine found herself swaying to the rhythm of the *pahu* drum, caught up in the infectious gaiety of the *hula*. Lilikoi had joined the dancers, and like the other women, she now wore her *pa'u* tied around her waist in the traditional style. A red lehua *lei* and her black hair streaming down over her shoulders were all that covered her full, brown-tipped breasts, which gleamed like polished walnut in the light of the kukui torches. The music picked up tempo, and Lilikoi's supple body swayed faster to the left and right, to the enthusiastic commands of the chanting men.

Then a tall, handsome young man left the onlookers and moved purposefully toward Lilikoi. The other dancers drifted away. The young man's hips rotated slowly as he advanced toward Lilikoi, his hands making short, quick movements while his eyes never left the girl's gleaming breasts. She slowed her dancing to the rhythm of his as she allowed him to approach her, so closely that her breasts brushed his chest as her hips moved in perfect unison with his.

Around her, Jasmine felt the crowd grow quiet, her own throat tightening as she watched. Then suddenly, smiling wickedly, Lilikoi danced swiftly away, followed closely by the man who pranced behind her, to one side then the other, leaping spread-legged in front of her, but always she managed to elude him. Discouraged, he moved away. Immediately she began to pursue him with swaying hips and breasts, her pink tongue playing over her moist mouth, her hands and body encouraging then taunting, repulsing him.

It was an erotic courting dance as old as the islands themselves, the playful invitation to lovemaking, the teasing rejection, until the desire for culmination when the movements of the dancers rose to a frenzy and, at last, the dancers sank exhausted to the ground.

Delirious with excitement, the onlookers cried, "*Hana-hou! Hana-hou!* More! More!"

Lilikoi regained her feet gracefully. In one swift movement, she crossed to Jasmine's side and pulled the girl to her feet. Startled, Jasmine tried to pull away.

Lilikoi's hand tightened on her arm. Beneath her breath, she whispered, "You said you could *hula*, sister, or was that all big talk, too? Are you afraid that they clap for me and will laugh at you?"

As if sensing the tension between the two women, the crowd began to urge Jasmine on, beating time upon their crossed legs. The musicians began to play again, the beat of the *pahu* drums throbbing through the night. Jasmine gave her sister a furious glance. It was, after all, hardly a fair contest. She hadn't danced the *hula* in years. But as Lilikoi pulled her forward into the circle of flickering light, she knew she had no choice. She must at least attempt the dance or give Lilikoi the satisfaction of knowing she had bested her.

Hesitantly she took the stance of the dancer: feet flat on the ground, knees flexed, arms gracefully extended. At first, her hips moved slowly, uncertainly; then gradually as the chanting of the men and the rhythmic beat of the drum and gourd and flute crept into her blood, her hips began to sway faster. Almost of their own volition, her slim arms and hands with tapering fingers formed words and phrases, telling an ancient love story of a young Hawaiian girl who had had the misfortune of falling in love with a god.

As her hips rotated more swiftly, the chanting and music became faster, more staccato, the pins fell from her hair and it cascaded to her shoulders, floating like a black cloud around her face. Flickering light from the kukui flames caressed the lissome body that caught the firelight like tawny gold. The tightly wound silk *pa'u* outlined even as it concealed the proud, upthrust breasts the tiny circle of a waist, and the seductive swell of hips and was somehow more disturbing to the watching men than Lilikoi's uncovered breasts and deliberate, blatant sexuality.

"*Auwe*," a man whispered to a friend. "This one was made to tempt the god Ka himself."

Their eyes fastened hungrily on Jasmine's body, swaying with a languorous grace like a willow touched by a breeze, each sinuous movement filled with an artless innocence. Her softly shining eyes were those of a woman slowly being aroused to love, her mouth curved in a dreamy half smile, as her hands flew to her lips then, open-palmed, to her audience in the traditional gesture of the *hula* dancer offering herself to her lover.

Jasmine was no longer aware of the onlookers. She was caught up in the abandonment of the dance, her heart pounding in time with the *pahu* drum and the surf crashing on the shore, her breath mingling with the soft, fragrant night air. All the fires of passion banked inside of her for so many years, all the inexplicable yearnings of her vibrant young body, were suddenly released, concentrated in the movements and gestures of the dance.

In the darkness of the grove of trees surrounding the cleared *luau* area, a dozen sailors from the recently arrived whaling fleet had joined the festivities. After months at sea, they greedily eyed the golden girl swaying in the moonlight, imagining how it would feel to hold that supple body in their arms, feel those hips rotate beneath them for their own private enjoyment.

Two men standing off by themselves watched the dancers silently until the one man, shorter and stockier than the other, whispered hoarsely, "I've never seen that *wahine* before, have you, Captain?"

Morgan Tucker shook his head, his gaze appreciatively following the inviting movements of the girl's hips. Finally he lifted his gaze to the oval, finely featured face, the delicately arched brows above dark, lustrous eyes, the mouth with a full sensual underlip that curved upward at the corners with an almost childlike smile of innocent delight.

No, he decided, he didn't know the girl. Not that Morgan's memory was all that good when it came to women. There had been too many since he'd gone to sea as a lad of twelve. In the dark, who could tell them apart? he had always thought cynically. Still, there was something about this particular *wahine*. If he had held her in his arms, he was sure he would remember.

Jasmine was only half-consciously aware of the tall, dark man in the blue jacket with gilt buttons. Then, as she swayed closer, the flame from a torch bent in the night breeze so that for a moment the man's face was illuminated in the firelight. She saw clearly features that were much too craggy to be handsome in a broad, bony face, a square-cut, jutting chin without the customary beard, a long, firm mouth and dark hair cut unfashionably short. The face was deeply tanned with white lines splaying around the narrowed eyes so that Jasmine would have known at once that he was a seaman, even if it hadn't been for the jacket he wore.

It was the man's narrowed gaze, though, that caught and held her, as if he had physically reached out his hands and arrogantly seized and held her. The hazel eyes traveled slowly over her body with an appraising look, as if, Jasmine thought furiously, now fully aware of the man, she were a prize sperm whale and he was sizing up how many barrels of oil she'd make.

Deliberately she danced nearer, her hands flying teasingly toward her breasts then out to the man, her palms gracefully cupped upward as if coaxing a lover into her arms, her swaying hips never missing a beat. As she danced closer to the man, she could see a slight scar like a dimple in the square-cut chin, that one slanting brow was higher than the other. She caught the scent of tobacco and whiskey and whale oil that she remembered from her father's clothes.

When the man instinctively stepped toward her, his arms stretched out to seize her, she laughed softly, tauntingly, into his face and danced away swiftly, turning her back deliberately on the man, yet still moving her hips provocatively, her back and shoulders like shimmering golden silk beneath the fall of black hair. The contemptuous gesture of her swaying backside brought a roar of laughter from the crowd and a dull flush to Morgan's face as his hands fell to his side.

His third mate, Harry Otis, quickly hid a smile at the girl's impudence and asked the captain, "Do you suppose she's the girl Lilikoi was telling me about?"

Morgan's face was still flushed with anger, but his voice was deceptively quiet as he growled, "Whether she is or not, she's the one I want."

The tempo of the dance was moving to a crescendo now. When the chanting and drums crashed to a sudden halt, Jasmine fell back swiftly and gratefully, blending into the darkness. She was limp with sudden exhaustion, her legs trembling.

"More . . . more!" the onlookers cried, but Jasmine retreated still more deeply into the darkness of the palm grove, shock racing through her trembling body now that she was released from the spell of the chanting and drums. How could she have danced like that, like some common girl from Fid Street?

Lilikoi appeared beside her and said grudgingly, "That wasn't bad dancing, for a *haole*."

"We have to leave," Jasmine wailed. "I should never have come here in the first place."

Lilikoi shrugged. "If you want, but my friends won't want to go this early. The dancing's just beginning. We'll have to ride back by ourselves."

"Do you know the way?"

"Of course. Come with me. Our horses are down this path."

As soon as she and Lilikoi left the lighted *luau* area, darkness descended like a black cape around Jasmine. She had to strain her eyes to make sure that Lilikoi was still ahead of her as she hurried down the narrow, winding path, moonlight blotted out by the overhanging palm and koa branches. When they had followed the path for about five minutes, and still had not come to where the horses had been tied, Jasmine protested, "Are you sure we're going the right way, Lili? It . . ."

Her words were abruptly cut off as an even deeper darkness descended, a thick, black weight flung over her head. She heard a scuffling sound of footsteps, muffled by the blanket over her head, imprisoning her within its suffocating folds.

When she cried out, the blanket was pulled tighter around her, the roughly woven material pressing against her mouth and nose, scratching her skin. She felt herself being lifted bodily onto the back of a horse, someone else mounting behind her. A man's arm encircled her waist like a vise.

As she struggled furiously against that arm, she heard a low, chuckling voice. "She's a real *kolohe*, ain't she?" Then she heard the sound of a man's laughter, and for a moment, startled, she thought she heard Lilikoi's rippling laughter, too.

As the man reached for the reins, his grip loosened a little, and Jasmine swiftly dug back with her elbow into his ribs hearing, pleased, a swift, painful expulsion of breath from her captor followed by an angry oath. Then the arm around her waist tightened slowly, cruelly, like pincers, squeezing the breath out of her. With the blanket cutting off the air from her mouth and nose and the arm crushing her waist, her only struggle now was to breathe, each tortured breath a jagged thrust of pain into her lungs. Then the darkness outside of her seemed to explode within her mind into a dozen pinwheels of scarlet and gold, and there was no more pain, only a dark oblivion.

Chapter 6

When Jasmine recovered consciousness, the blanket was still flung over her but held loosely so that she was able to breathe. She became aware that she was no longer on horseback and that she was being carried, as unceremoniously as a sack of flour, flung over a man's shoulder. There was something else different, too. From the way the man walked, she could tell they were no longer on land, and even through the blanket, she caught the faint smell of gurry, a mixture of brackish seawater, decayed whale meat, and rancid whale oil. It was an odor that she immediately associated with her childhood on her father's whaling ship.

Then she was being carried down a narrow, steep staircase, and, the blanket still wrapped around her, she was dumped onto something soft and yielding. By the time she had untangled herself from the folds of the blanket, she heard the sounds of retreating footsteps and of a key being turned in a lock. She tossed the blanket to one side and sat up, too confused and shocked to do more than stare blankly around her.

The room in which she found herself couldn't have been more than six by four feet, with a dimly lit whale-oil lamp hanging from the timber over the bed. The room's sole piece of furniture was the three-quarters bed on which she was sitting. Beyond the partition of the stateroom was another, slightly larger cabin. Even before she stepped cautiously inside of it, she knew what it would contain: a horsehair sofa, a chair, and a compass hanging over a desk. Both cabins were almost identical to her father's quarters aboard his ship, except the bed in this room was of carved mahogany and set on gimbals so that the sleeper would remain upright even in a heavy, rolling sea.

The familiarity of her surroundings brought back memories of a happy childhood spent in just such rooms as these and made her forget for a moment the circumstances of her being here. Her own small bed, she remembered, had been built above a similar horsehair sofa, with a railing to keep her from falling out. Instead of a child's berth in this cabin, there was a shelf built above the sofa and the shelf was filled with books. Aside from the books and some charts spread out on the desktop, the rooms had a spartan air about them with nothing to reveal the character of their owner.

She moved quickly to the door, which she was sure led out into the saloon where the ship's captain and officers ate their meals, but, as she expected, it was locked. The only other exits from the quarters were a grilled skylight above her and a small stern port in the sleeping cabin, neither of which was large enough to allow her escape. As she prowled back and forth between the two tiny cabins, a raw, burning anger began to take the place of her fear.

How dare she be treated in such a high-handed fashion? Just wait till her father found out how she had been manhandled, no doubt by drunken whalers. He'd have the whole town turned upside down looking for the men involved.

Furiously she began to pound at the locked door, even though she doubted that any officers would be in the saloon at this time of night with the ship undoubtedly in port. Probably the captain was ashore, too, or the man who kidnapped her wouldn't have dared to use his quarters. Still, it made her feel better just to beat at something with her bare fists.

When the door did suddenly open, she stepped back,

startled, her hand still half raised. A man stepped across the threshold, the bulk of his body filling the doorway, his dark head almost brushing the top of the door. It was the seaman from the *luau*. He was looking at her now in the same measuring way he had then, his eyes narrowed, his glance speculative as he closed the door behind him and tossed his jacket onto the chair. He said briskly, "Sorry to keep you waiting . . . Jasmine, isn't it?" He began unbuttoning his shirt. "Don't worry. We'll soon make up for lost time."

She stared at him, too outraged at his calm self-assurance to speak; then, as the shirt casually followed the coat to the chair, revealing a broad, muscular chest with a mat of short, springy, curling hair, she began to sputter, "What do you think you're doing? How dare you . . ." She broke off, startled. "How do you know my name?"

"From your sister. At least, she says she's your sister." The appraising look lingered on the slim, oval face with the delicately drawn features. "Not that I see much family resemblance."

"Where is Lilikoi?" Jasmine asked, belatedly remembering that she had not been the only one to be set upon and carried off. Her voice tightened with fear. "If you've harmed her . . ."

A dark eyebrow slanted upward in amused bewilderment. "Now why should she be harmed? Your sister's in very good hands and no doubt enjoying herself thoroughly." A half smile quirked the corners of the long, sensual mouth. "Though I'll admit the arrangement of partners may not be exactly as your sister planned."

What did he mean? Jasmine wondered, bewildered. What plan? And why was he behaving as if it were perfectly natural, her being here? She was too wrapped up in her own confused thoughts to notice the look of impatience that had slipped into the man's eyes, mingling with the warmth of his gaze as he studied the slim, graceful figure standing before him.

The girl was even more beautiful than he remembered,

Morgan decided. Close up, the tawny skin was flawless, with the shimmering texture of the finest, peach gold Chinese silk; and although the dark hair hung tangled and disheveled about her shoulders, he was relieved to see that she didn't coat it with coconut oil as so many of the local beauties did. The garlands of pikakes she wore around her neck were now brown and wilted, but they still managed to half conceal from his gaze the tempting curve of her breasts. With one swift motion, he reached out and disposed of the *leis*. Then, just as swiftly, before she realized what was happening, his hand reached out again. This time the pale yellow silk *pa'u* followed the pikake *leis* to the floor at her feet.

She gave a shocked gasp and bent quickly to snatch up the garment, her hands trembling with fear now as well as anger as she attempted to rewrap the silken folds around her body. Watching her, Morgan frowned irritably. What was wrong with the girl? With a familiar pressure growing stronger by the minute in his loins, he hadn't the inclination for a leisurely seduction.

It had been almost six months since he had held a woman in his arms, months of back-breaking, dangerous work chasing the giant sperm whale with a tiny cockleshell of a whaleboat, never knowing when the maddened, harpooned giant would turn and crush the boat with one flip of its tail or bite the boat in two with its monstrous teeth. Then after killing and dragging the whale back to the ship, there was the stinking aftermath of cutting up and trying out, boiling the whale oil out of the blubber.

Not to mention the gale that the *Louisa* had run into along the line that had snapped her mizzenmast and brought the ship limping back to the port of Honolulu for recruiting and repairs. He had been looking forward to his first night in Honolulu and having a *wahine*, as willing and eager as he was, in his arms. And remembering the provocative way the girl had danced at the *luau*, the tantalizing swaying hips, and the half-dreamy look in her eyes, he was sure she was as ready as he was for lovemaking.

Now he growled angrily, "Take off that damn thing!"

When she didn't move, standing as if frozen in shock, his hand whipped out and once more removed the offending garment before pulling her hard against him. One arm circled her waist, lifting her from the floor, the other hand pressing her softly rounded backside so that her body could fit more pleasurably against him. His mouth covered hers easily now, without the inconvenience of cricking his neck bending over her.

The soft warmth of her body against his hardness, the shape and feel of her mouth under his searching tongue, sent shock waves of pleasurable sensations through Morgan so that at first he didn't notice that the girl was passive, an unresponsive weight in his arms, her mouth still and cold beneath his. When he released her as suddenly as he had gathered her into his arms, she half staggered, then retreated quickly away from him. The wide, dark eyes lifted to him were not filled with passion, he saw, surprised, but with something much closer to open hostility.

"You'll have to kiss better than that or you'll prove to be a great waste of time," Morgan growled, stung in spite of himself by the loathing in the girl's gaze.

Jasmine felt her face grow icy cold, then flushed red-hot with fury. Waste of time! The insufferable, unfeeling brute! Is that all it meant to him, abducting her, forcing himself upon her, just so he could wile away a few hours' time? Terror was forgotten in the anger consuming her, choking her. Her hands reached up to fly at that face, to claw that expression of possessive arrogance away.

Her one hand connected with his cheek, feeling a savage satisfaction as her nails raked his flesh, but then, with a pantherlike swiftness, he caught her other hand and whirled her around, twisting her wrist behind her so that tears of pain sprang to her eyes. She had retreated, without realizing it, from the cabin into the small stateroom and now, when he pushed her away from him, she sprawled across the bed.

His face was dark with anger as he said grimly, "You might get away with behaving like a bad-tempered bitch in your Cape Horn crib, maybe your customers on Fid Street enjoy it, but when I entertain a woman aboard my ship, I expect a different sort of behavior."

As he was talking, he was removing his trousers. Having spent her early years in the relaxed sexual climate of the islands, where native children frolicked naked on the beach and their parents' casual attitude toward clothing often left little to the imagination, it was not the first time Jasmine had glimpsed a man's nakedness. It was, however, the first time she had seen a male with his manhood engorged. Shocked at the sight, she hastily turned her eyes and, panic-stricken, tried to scramble away.

The narrow bed, however, left her very little room to maneuver, and before she could do more than utter a brief scream that was more like a frightened squeal of dismay, he was in the bed beside her. His leg was flung across her body, pinning her to the mattress, and his mouth covered hers, effectively cutting off any more protests.

She had not struggled against him when he had first kissed her because she had sensed it would not only be a mistake but futile as well. Now, however, with his mouth bruising her lips, forcing them apart so that his tongue could seek the softness within, and his hand lightly, familiarly caressing the length of her body, the only instinct she had left was terror at what she sensed was about to happen. Even though she knew it was hopeless, that her slim strength was no match for the man's, that in fact her struggles apparently only served to arouse him further, she was no longer thinking clearly. Sheer panic had taken hold of her, turning her into a wild, squirming creature. She clawed at any available flesh she could find while her writhing body twisted and turned with the slipperiness of an eel, trying to find any escape from the relentless weight of the body flung over hers.

Yet the more she fought against him, the more brutally searching and demanding his mouth became on hers, as if he were drawing the very breath from her body. Her lungs felt as if they would explode; the blood pounded in her temples. Her fists beating at his chest, trying to push him away, became weaker. Did he mean to kill her? she thought, dazed, when suddenly he withdrew his mouth from hers. The relief she felt was short-lived. As she gasped for breath, she felt his lips, burning against the coolness of her flesh, trail down the column of her throat, pausing a moment to explore with his tongue the dark hollow at the base of her throat before moving downward to catch and hold with his lips one rose-tipped breast.

"No!" She thought she screamed, but it was only a whispered moan of dismay pushed past the rawness of her throat.

Once more, feebly, she reached out to push him away, but this time he caught her hands roughly in one of his and pulled them impatiently above her head. While his tongue lazily caressed the velvet-soft peak, his other hand moved downward over the cool, satin-soft flesh of the faintly rounded stomach, only to discover, surprised, that the girl's thighs were pressed tightly together, as if to deny him entrance. What sort of game was she playing? Morgan thought, anger mixing with the painful pressure building up inside of him, demanding release. Was it money she was after? He remembered he hadn't discussed payment with her, but then he seldom did with native girls. Most island *wahines* were eager to share a man's bed, with or without a gold coin in payment.

Then suddenly, triumphantly, he felt the rose-petal-soft peak of her breast grow taut beneath his tongue, heard the girl give a sharp, surprised gasp, her eyes widening, charged with wonder, as if caught unawares by pleasure. He felt her thighs parting almost involuntarily for just a moment, but it was only a moment he needed to position himself above her and thrust fiercely inward. The slight resistance he met with surprised him but did not stop him from taking swift, urgent possession of her body. When she cried out, he thought it was a cry of rapture to match his own moan of pleasure. Then he looked down into her face and saw, vaguely startled, that her eyes were bright with tears, the lashes shiny black points against her cheeks, her face glazed with shock and pain. But by then it was too late for him to stop even if he had wanted to, as helpless before his own driving passion as if he were a brig being torn apart by a sou'wester rounding the Cape.

Afterwards, in the stillness following the storm, he could hear her crying softly. She had pulled as far away from him on the bed as possible as soon as he had released her. She lay curled in a ball with her back to him, her black hair splaying down over her shoulders, hiding her face from view.

Morgan scowled at the girl's back. How the hell could he have known the girl was untouched? he thought, remembering the provocative way the girl had danced at the *luau*, the frankly sexual appeal in her swaying hip movements, the teasing come-hither smile. No prim and proper young lady would ever attend a *luau* or dance a *hula* in the first place. Not to mention the fact that Lilikoi had made it very clear that her sister was as eager as she was to board the *Louisa*. Nevertheless, looking at that quivering, somehow vulnerable-looking back and listening to the low, childish sobs, Morgan felt an unexpected stab of guilt, an unfamiliar emotion for him, and a deucedly uncomfortable one, he was discovering.

Still scowling, he went into the adjoining cabin, found his decanter of whiskey and poured himself a stiff drink. Although in the years since he had shipped out on his first whaler he had encountered a wide variety of women, he had always avoided virgins like the plague. To his mind, virginity was a vastly overrated quality and one to be avoided at all costs. What was the sense in choosing ignorance over experience in a woman, any more than it made good sense for a captain to pick greenies for the forecastle instead of seasoned hands? Of course, someday in the distant future when he married and settled down back in New Bedford, naturally, Morgan would choose a virgin for a bride. But that was different. And at the moment marriage was the furthest thing from Morgan's mind. His immediate problem was the girl and what to do about her.

Pouring a second glass of whiskey, he carried it back into the stateroom. The girl had stopped crying and was sitting up in bed staring bleakly into space, the coverlet half-pulled around her.

"Here, drink this," he said. She started at the sound of his voice, her hands clenching at the coverlet. "I'm sorry," he said gruffly. "I didn't mean to gally you."

She turned and gave him a blade-sharp scathing look that cut into him like a flensing spade slicing into whale blubber. "No, thank you." Her small rounded chin lifted haughtily. "And I'm not a whale to be gallied!"

With one part of his mind, Morgan found himself wondering how the girl happened to be acquainted with whaling lingo even as he saw, concerned, that her lips were a bluish white and her hands trembled as they clutched at the coverlet. Impatiently, he thrust the glass at her, his voice a brusque command. "Drink it!"

For a moment, her dark eyes met and clashed furiously with his, but there were few, even hardened, mutinous seamen, who could stand up to Captain Tucker's quelling gaze. Reluctantly Jasmine took the glass and swallowed the liquor. At first it felt as if she had swallowed a lightning bolt, then the whiskey spread a heartening warmth through her body. The trembling like butterfly wings inside of her slowly stilled, and her nerve ends, which had become numb with shock, once more returned to life.

Beneath lowered eyelids, she covertly studied the man who stood beside the bed and whose overwhelming physical presence seemed to fill the tiny stateroom. For all the man's height and bulk, there was not an inch of fat on his body. The wide, square set of his shoulders, the flat, muscular chest narrowing down to lean hips, which she saw thankfully were now wrapped in a towel, reminded her somewhat of Kale. Except there was no wiry mat of black hair on Kale's chest, and her brother's flesh had a look of warmth and softness about it. This man's body seemed carved from the same rich brown mahogany as the bed and was just as unyielding to the touch, while his rough-cut face reminded her of a description she'd often heard about New Bedford whaling men: "Hard as nails afloat." Remembering his bruising mouth on hers, the steellike muscles in those thighs that had held her imprisoned, she could attest to that hardness. She winced mentally at the memory and turned her gaze away.

Then suddenly it occurred to her that, incredibly, she didn't even know the man's name. And the way he had found the whiskey, his proprietary air toward the cabin, made her gaze return to him, startled. "These are your quarters?"

He nodded, then a half smile replaced the grim line of his mouth. "We didn't get around to introductions, did we?" He gave her a slight, mocking bow from the waist. "Morgan Tucker, captain of the *Louisa*, out of New Bedford. And you're Jasmine . . ." He waited, lifting a slanted eyebrow.

Jasmine hesitated. For the first time since she had been brought to the cabin, she felt a faint stirring of hope. If he didn't know who she was, then it was possible she might still save her reputation, even if she had lost something infinitely more precious. Yet if he knew Lilikoi, why wouldn't he know her last name? Unless . . . She gave him a scornful glance. "I gather then you didn't bother to discover Lilikoi's name either, before you raped her."

If she had expected to disconcert him, she was disappointed. He gave her a surprised glance, then threw back his head and laughed, a low, rumbling sound that seemed to come from deep in his chest and bounce off the timbered walls of the stateroom. "Rape Lilikoi?" he gasped, the laughter dying down to an amused chuckle. "Now that's what I call an impossibility. More than likely it would be the other way 'round."

Color surged into Jasmine's face. How dare he? First, abducting and humiliating her, using her body in a way she had never dreamed possible, and now laughing at her. Fury such as she had never felt before, hadn't even known she was capable of feeling, jolted through her. She sprang at her tormenter with a low cry of fury.

Just before her fingernails could tear at his face again, his hands caught and held her wrists, holding her struggling body away from him as easily as if she were a child having a temper tantrum. "At least, you and Lilikoi have one thing in common," he commented, watching her violent struggle with a mixture of irritation and bewilderment. "You're both cats that like to claw."

"Let me go!"

"Gladly, but not until you promise not to try and scratch my eyes out," he said dryly.

Eyes blazing, she tried to lunge at him again, and his hands tightened their grasp on the slender wrists. He saw the flicker of pain cross her face, but she did not cry out. She had courage, anyway, he thought grudgingly. And then feeling the fragility of those wrists in his hands, he felt suddenly ashamed and released her abruptly. She sank down onto the bed, biting at her lower lip to keep the tears from her eyes at the pain throbbing in her wrists. She wouldn't give him the satisfaction of seeing her cry again, she thought savagely.

"How long do you plan to keep me a prisoner here?" she asked bitterly.

Once again she saw a look of surprise touch briefly the man's gold-flecked, hazel eyes before he gave her that sardonic half smile she was beginning to hate. "How can you be a prisoner when you came here of your own free will?" he asked.

Her own free will! Once more Jasmine felt the anger leap inside her, but this time she held it fiercely in check, having learned that physically attacking the man was as futile as beating with her fists at the locked door. She said icily, "Do you call having a blanket thrown over my head and being carried aboard this ship half-unconscious my own free will?"

Morgan studied the girl's face. Was she telling him the truth? When he had come aboard earlier, he had met Otis in the companionway. The man had smiled and, winking broadly, jerked his chin toward Morgan's cabin. He hadn't said anything about overpowering the girl and dragging her aboard.

Probably the girl was lying, and yet . . . Morgan frowned uneasily. There was something different about the girl. With her delicate features and tawny coloring, she obviously had a lot of *haole* blood in her veins, and from the way she spoke, she must have had more education than the usual native girl. However, Morgan had entertained *hapa-haole* girls on the *Louisa* before, half-native, half-white *wahines* who had attended the mission schools and received a patina of western education. He even agreed, amused, with the missionary who had complained that educating the native girls only made them more sought-after as mistresses for the white men in the islands.

No, it was something else about the girl, he decided. Even with her tear-stained face and disheveled hair she still had a natural beauty that stirred him in a way he had never felt for any other woman. She had snatched up the coverlet again, but he could still glimpse the soft slope of shoulder, the gentle curve of hip, the almost luminous quality of her tawny skin. He remembered only too well the texture of that skin beneath his hands, the scent of jasmine from her hair in his nostrils, the silken softness of that hair twining around his fingers.

He sat down on the bed beside her, feeling the overpowering need to touch her again, to feel that cool flesh grow warm beneath his hands. He reached out a hand and lightly stroked the arm that clutched at the coverlet, smiling coaxingly. "Are you so eager, then, to leave? I'm sorry we got off to such a bad start, but I couldn't have known, could I, that you were untouched? I can promise you it will be much more pleasant the next time."

She jerked away from his touch as if it were a red-hot poker. It was the first time Morgan had experienced rejection from a woman, and he was both intrigued and challenged. And Captain Morgan Tucker, who had a reputation among whaling men for chasing down the most wily whale and riding out the stormiest sea, was not a man to turn down a challenge. Besides, he was sure that he hadn't imagined that swift, sweet gasp of pleasure that had come from her throat when his lips had found her breast.

"Pleasant!" she protested, outraged. "As pleasant as a Nantucket sleigh ride!"

His curiosity was once again piqued by her knowledge of whaling activities, but it was a curiosity that faded as he pulled her gently toward him, tugging the coverlet from her grasp and cupping her breast in his hand. His narrowed eyes never left her face as he teased the soft peak with his thumb.

"You'll see," he murmured as his mouth lowered over hers, his lips caressing the corners of her mouth, slowly, insistently. Jasmine knew now what to expect and that to struggle against the man's strength would only cause her more pain. What she did not expect was that even as her mind braced itself against the onslaught, her body would suddenly, incredibly, betray her to the enemy. As his hands roamed freely over her body with long, gentle, searching strokes from breasts to thighs, she all at once felt as she did when she sunned herself on the beach-hut lanai without a stitch of clothing on. The warmth of his hands on her body was like the heat of the sun, making her feel as relaxed as if she were a flower, its petals slowly, deliciously opening to the sun, her lips and thighs parting so that the delicious warmth could reach every part of her body.

This time, when Morgan took her, he knew he did not imagine the cry of joy that came from her half-parted lips. Nor the brilliance like sea fire gilding her wide, dark eyes for a moment before she closed them, the lashes sooty black against her cheeks.

Afterwards, spent and content, he lay with his arm flung across her, and murmured, pleased, "You're a witch, my sweet Jasmine, a sea witch. I've half a mind to take you with me when we sail."

At his words, he felt her body stiffen, and even before she pulled free of his arm, he guessed what she was about to do. He was at the door to the outer cabin only a second after she reached the door and was frantically tugging at the latch. He whirled her around to face him. Towering over her, his hands pinned her shoulders to the door, his voice a low, furious growl. "Where the hell do you think you're going?"

"I'm going home. You can't make me stay." Her eyes met his defiantly, but her voice was a childish wail of terror.

He could feel her shoulders trembling beneath his hands. Was his touch so repulsive to her then, he thought, not sure whether it was anger or wounded pride that made him shove her to one side and pull open the door. "Go on, then! No one's stopping you." His glance flicked over her, golden glints of amusement in his eyes. "Only how far do you think you'll get at this time of night, dressed like that?"

She had edged by him nervously and picked up her *pa'u*, and she wrapped it hastily around her while he watched grimly. When she started again for the door, he grabbed her arm. "Don't be an idiot. The streets of Honolulu are crawling with seamen just looking for a willing, or unwilling, *wahine*. You'd be raped or worse before you reached Fid Street."

She glared up at him, the color running from her face down to the generous swell of her breasts. "And if I stay here, I'll be safe?" she demanded hotly.

Morgan said a few choice words beneath his breath then bellowed, "Daniel!"

After a few seconds, a young man who couldn't have been more than twelve or thirteen came hurrying into the mess room. His blond hair was tousled as if he had just awakened. He cast a quick glance at Jasmine as he tucked his shirt into his trousers, and his blue eyes registered no shock at finding a half-naked woman in the captain's quarters. No doubt it wasn't that uncommon an occurrence, Jasmine thought bitterly.

"Fetch one of your shirts and a pair of trousers," Morgan ordered. "And be quick about it."

Now a look of surprise did dart across the boy's face, but he rushed away immediately and returned with a reasonably clean blue shirt and much-patched trousers.

Jasmine pulled on the pants and shirt quickly, rolling up the sleeves and trouser legs so that they fit better. The captain was waiting for her in the saloon and, giving her only a fleeting glance, turned to the cabin boy. He handed the boy a small pistol. "I'll expect you to see this *wahine* safely to where she wants to go. If there's any trouble, use this. Do you understand?"

The cabin boy swallowed hard. The captain's eyes boring into his made it perfectly clear what the unhappy results would be if he disobeyed Morgan's orders.

He shoved the gun into his belt. "Yes, sir."

Without another word, Morgan turned and strode back into his cabin, slamming the door behind him. Jasmine stared at the closed door, relief warring with indignation on her face. So that was all there was to it as far as Captain Tucker was concerned, was it? Kidnap a woman, rape her, then send her on her way without even a backward glance, as if he'd already forgotten about her.

A coldness like a frost settled over Jasmine's features. Well, she wouldn't forget, she vowed. Captain Tucker would regret the day he had taken, with callous cruelty and indifference, what should have been her most precious possession, to be given freely and with love to her future husband. Somehow, some way, Jasmine promised herself, her dark eyes glittering with rage, she'd make Morgan Tucker pay.

Chapter 7

Sitting in the Babcock pew in the Kawaiahao Church in Honolulu, listening to a sermon that seemed to go on forever, Jasmine fought off waves of drowsiness. Not a breath of air stirred in the church, where natives wearing bits and pieces of western clothes rubbed shoulders with nattily dressed officers from naval ships in the harbor and merchants in sober black broadcloth sat beside their bonneted wives, whose hands were primly folded in their laps.

"Look not upon the wine when it is red. At the last, it biteth like a serpent and stingeth like an adder!" thundered from the pulpit. The Reverend Samuel Palmer had already spent almost an hour preaching on the evils of alcohol and adultery, casting stern glances at the royal pew as he spoke. All of Honolulu was aware that the king was drinking more heavily than usual these days and had a new favorite royal mistress.

A sudden queasiness in her stomach pulled Jasmine's attention away from the sermon. She reached hastily for a small vial of smelling salts in her reticule and saw Malia watching her with an anxious look on her face.

"You've been moping around the house ever since we returned from Kauai," Malia had scolded that morning when Jasmine had said she was too tired to attend Sunday church services with the family. "And you hardly touched your breakfast this morning. I think you should pay a visit to Dr. Cary."

"I'm perfectly all right," Jasmine had protested. "But perhaps some fresh air would help."

Later, though, as she had followed the family into the pillared, coral-stone church, she swallowed a yawn and only hoped she could manage to stay awake during what she knew would be a long, dull sermon. At least, she thought, glancing surreptitiously around her, as she did almost instinctively wherever she went, she didn't have to worry about running into Captain Tucker. She certainly couldn't imagine the man attending church services.

As always when she thought of Morgan Tucker, she could feel a trembling start deep inside of her as she helplessly relived the pain and humiliation of those moments aboard the *Louisa*. It wasn't only the shock of the encounter that had remained with her, though; it was a new, frightening sense of vulnerability. She had been terrified, when the family returned to Honolulu, to discover that the *Louisa* was still in port. Honolulu wasn't that large a town. How could she be sure not to meet Captain Tucker on the street or at someone's home? The thought of that appraising, ruthless gaze passing with an amused, familiar knowledge over her body made Jasmine turn hot and cold by turns.

Or suppose, somehow, he had discovered that the woman he had bedded so casually was Jasmine Babcock? How long before the scandalous gossip would spread like wildfire through Honolulu so that she'd never be able to hold her head up in polite society again. She'd heard how men liked to brag about their female conquests, especially when they'd been drinking.

Oh, damn Morgan Tucker, Jasmine thought. And damn Lilikoi, too. She would never forgive her sister, never! She remembered the guarded look on Lilikoi's face when she had accosted her sister the next morning. "Why are you making such a fuss?" Lilikoi had shrugged indifferently. "How was I to know those men would drag us off to the whaler?" Her eyes widened with injured innocence. "You surely can't think it was my idea."

"You know Captain Tucker," Jasmine had said indignantly. "You knew he'd be at the *luau*."

"No one forced you to go with me," Lilikoi had pointed out. Her voice suddenly became venomous. "And I was the one that the captain wanted, not some silly *haole wahine* who doesn't know the first thing about pleasing a man in bed. It was all a stupid mistake."

Why, she's jealous, Jasmine had thought, stunned. Whether or not Lilikoi had helped in planning last night's abduction as a cruel trick on her sister, it was clear that Lilikoi had expected to be the captain's partner and that she was furious because Jasmine had taken her place.

She had stared at Lilikoi, feeling sick all at once, the same way she had felt when she had awakened that morning and the memory of what had happened to her the evening before had flooded back in a scalding wave.

Something in her sister's stricken face had made Lilikoi feel suddenly, uncomfortably guilty, and she had looked away. Why did *haoles* make it so important, she wondered irritably, what happened between a man and woman in bed? Until the missionaries had come to the islands with their laws and *kapus*, Hawaiians had accepted the simple, innocent pleasure that a man and woman found in each other's bodies without question, the same way they found delight in eating and drinking and gliding shoreward on a skimming surfboard. To be sure there were always those men who were more virile than their friends, more skilled at bringing pleasure to a woman, men who never tired even after a night of lovemaking. Morgan Tucker was such a man, Lilikoi thought, her face softening in memory of the night she had spent aboard the *Louisa* with the captain the last time he had been in port. Usually Lilikoi forgot her lovers quickly once they were gone from her bed, but somehow she had never been able to forget Captain Tucker, as if he had planted a seed of desire in her that had taken root and would not be removed.

She had glanced at Jasmine, her eyelids lowered to hide the anger and jealousy that clawed at her at the thought that the captain had chosen Jasmine over her last night.

"Are you going to tell Father what happened?" she had asked. And she thought vindictively, it would serve Morgan right, conveniently forgetting her own part in last night's abduction.

"No!" Jasmine had said sharply. "You mustn't say anything either. Promise me, Lilikoi. Father would kill the captain."

Her sister had nodded grudging agreement, then had said mockingly, "So you don't hate the captain so much that you want to see him dead?"

Jasmine's hands clutched at her reticule, anger churning inside of her as she remembered that she hadn't dignified Lilikoi's ridiculous insinuation with an answer. Of course she hated Morgan Tucker. But she would chose her own time and place to get even. What good would it do her to have the man destroyed if her own reputation was destroyed as well? She could only hope that Captain Tucker would have enough sense to keep his mouth shut if he learned it was Captain Babcock's daughter he had raped and not some island girl.

Jasmine was so consumed by her own worries that she didn't notice that Lani, sitting beside her, didn't look too happy either. Her sister's soft brown eyes, almost hidden beneath the gray bonnet she wore, were terrified as she listened to the minister's sermon. Reverend Palmer seemed to be looking directly at her, Lani thought, as he warned darkly, "Be not deceived, God is not mocked. . . . You cannot hide your wickedness deep enough within you that your sins will not be found out. Renounce the devil and all his works, the sinful desires of the flesh, or you will know eternal fire and damnation. . . ."

Was her wickedness so plain, then, Lani wondered miserably, that it could be seen on her face? This terrible longing like a fever in her blood to be with Kale every minute; the heat that raced through her body when he smiled at her, the weakness that left her limp when he touched her. Last night in the garden he had pulled her into the dark shadows of a kau tree, and when his hands had found the softness of her breasts, his mouth warm and searching on hers, she had had the odd feeling that she had split apart, one part aghast at what was happening, the other wickedly, sinfully never wanting Kale to stop, as if she would die if he took his hands away from her. Then a servant had come down the path, singing tipsily from too much rum, and she had been brought back to reality. She had fled from Kale's arms to the safety of the house. Help me, O Lord, she prayed numbly, help me to turn away from temptation. . . .

When the services finally ended, Lani hurried to the Babcock carriage while her parents stopped to talk to friends clustered around the entrance way to the church. Feeling the need to stretch her limbs, Jasmine wandered around to the back of the church to the small cemetery filled with the graves of missionary families. Some of the wives, Jasmine noticed from the tombstones, had lived only a few years after reaching the islands, often dying in childbirth. Many of the women, she knew, had known their husbands only a few weeks before marrying them, men who were virtually strangers, and embarking for the Sandwich Islands. How had such brides felt on their wedding nights? she wondered. As shocked and terrified as she had been aboard the *Louisa*?

But thinking about that night made the queasiness she had felt earlier in the church sweep over her again. She was reaching for her handkerchief when a voice spoke behind her. "I thought I saw you at the services, Miss Babcock. What a pleasant surprise that we should meet again."

She turned, startled, to find Micah Beale standing, watching her, hat in hand.

Remembering their last encounter aboard the *Jeremiah*, Jasmine had to force herself to smile politely at the man. "Good morning, Mr. Beale," she murmured. She gestured with her hand toward the plain tombstones with their mute stories of lives ended tragically young. "I was thinking how sad they seem."

"They died doing God's work," Micah said and then added almost absently, "Mary's grave is there in the corner."

"I didn't know," Jasmine said, startled. "I'm sorry. When did she die?"

"Only a few weeks after we reached the islands. Her heart was never very strong. The doctors advised her against making the trip, but, naturally, she felt her place was beside me when I received the call to these islands."

He didn't, Jasmine thought uncharitably, sound particularly saddened at his wife's death, only a little aggrieved that she should have had the effrontery to die on him.

She started to turn away toward the carriage, where she could see Lani waiting, but Mr. Beale put out a hand restraining her. "I hoped we might talk for a moment, Miss Babcock." There was an urgency in his voice that made Jasmine pause. Micah's face was flushed except for the pox scars, which remained a dead white. "I'm leaving the ministry," he blurted. "I've given up my church."

He did not think it necessary to add that he had been quietly asked by the mission-governing board to submit his resignation. There had been stories of the Reverend Micah Beale's unseemly behavior among his parishioners. Vicious lies, all of them, Micah thought bitterly now. He had done his best to place the fear of God in the lust-filled hearts of savages who knew no shame. Even those natives he thought he had brought to God's grace turned out to be backsliders. There was the woman and man from his church who were planning to be married. He had gone on horseback to the woman's hut unannounced and found her embraced with her sweetheart. He had watched their obscene copulation for several minutes before they realized he was there. He hadn't even realized he still had the horsewhip in his hand until he began applying it vigorously to the woman after the man had scrambled quickly out of the hut. Then the man had returned with his friends, and Micah had been dragged away to the police. Of course, the police had done nothing, because the woman refused to testify against Micah and it was against the law, in any case, for a man and woman to sleep together outside marriage.

"Will you be returning to Boston?" Jasmine asked, although she wasn't really interested. The warmth of the sun was making her feel dizzy, so that in the distance, the extinct volcano Punchbowl seemed to recede before her eyes.

"No, my dear Mary left a sizable estate. I've bought land near Nanakuli and plan to try my hand at raising sugar. I was brought up on a farm, you know."

"I wish you luck," Jasmine said. "Now, if you'll excuse me . . ."

But once again, his hand tightened on her arm, clammy cold for all that it was a hot day. "I've—I've thought of you often since our days aboard the *Jeremiah*, Miss Babcock. I hoped I might see you again, come to your home. I've taken the liberty of speaking to your father. He's given me his permission to call upon you."

He looked down into the girl's face framed by the lavender silk of her bonnet. She was thinner than he remembered, but she still possessed a radiant beauty, which for all that it was wicked and corrupt, still had the power to stir disturbing feelings inside of him. He would save her from herself, he thought exultantly. From the first moment he had met Jasmine Babcock, he had realized it was his God-given mission in life to bring this young woman to a state of grace. And the nights he had suffered the torments of the damned, twisting and turning on his narrow cot, thinking of the girl, fighting off the fires consuming him, were only part of the price he knew he must pay for doing the Lord's will.

Even now here in the sunlight, he had to struggle against feelings of lust within him, the desire to touch that pale peach gold flesh, his gaze dropping to the breasts outlined boldly by the tightly fitted, shirred bodice, a shameless invitation to all eyes.

"I know you have not found God's grace," he whispered hoarsely. "But it will be my duty as your husband to help you find salvation."

Jasmine stared at the man, too dumbfounded to reply. Was he really proposing to her, here, in a cemetery? Poor Mr. Beale, she thought, a bubble of hysterical laughter rising in her throat. He didn't know how far from grace she had fallen. She tactfully swallowed the laughter, murmuring, "You do me a great honor, Mr. Beale, but it would be a waste of time for you to pursue any further friendship between us."

Unlike Jeremy, though, Micah Beale was not put off so easily. He smiled unctuously at the girl. "I understand, Miss Babcock. A young lady wants to be courted properly. I've been too precipitous. Your father warned me that you might reject my attention at first, but I've discovered that a woman seldom knows her own mind. She must be shown the way."

Jasmine jerked her arm from Micah's grasp, the furious words on her lips forgotten as she felt the taste of nausea rising in her throat. "Excuse me. . . . I'm not feeling well."

When she hastened to the carriage and climbed inside, she had to grip the handle to keep the world from spinning around her.

"What is it, Jasmine? Did Mr. Beale say something to upset you?" Lani glanced back toward the cemetery, toward the tall, black-frocked figure casting a dark shadow in the sunlight. She shivered. "The Reverend Beale preached at the mission school once. When his eyes looked at you, it was like looking into the face of judgment."

Malia had come up to the carriage with her husband. She took one look at Jasmine's face, which was coated with a fine gleam of perspiration, gathered the girl into her ample arms, and said briskly to the captain, "*Wiki-wiki*, we must get this child home."

Once the carriage pulled into the Babcock driveway, Jasmine made a dash for her bedroom, where, for a few helpless moments, she was violently sick. Afterwards, Malia gently washed her face and helped her into bed.

Captain Babcock, who had been pacing up and down in the hall, stuck his head in the door, his voice gruff with anger. "How is the lass? Shall I fetch the doctor?"

Lilikoi joined the captain in the hallway. "What's wrong?" she asked sleepily.

"Jasmine took sick after church services," Lani said.

"No." Jasmine shook her head. "I didn't feel well this morning when I awoke, or yesterday morning, either. I suppose I must be coming down with a fever."

Lilikoi laughed, her eyes roving over Jasmine, her face bright with malicious amusement. "What you have, sister, I wager it will take nine months to get over."

"Nine months?" Jasmine echoed blankly then felt the breath leave her lungs, as if someone had jabbed her in the ribs. No, she thought, no, it couldn't be. She counted back quickly, frantically. She had missed her last period. But then her periods weren't always regular, she reminded herself. And the morning sickness could be . . . Oh, God, she couldn't be carrying a child, not that man's child!

Malia sat down on the bed beside her and asked quietly, "Is it possible, *keiki*? Could you be *hapai*?"

Jasmine stared mutely at her stepmother then nodded, unable to force the words from her lips.

The captain thrust his way into the room. "What are you saying?" His eyes beneath the bristling brows blazed at his daughter. "It was that blasted limey, wasn't it? I'll drag him back here by the scruff of his neck."

"No, Papa," Jasmine said wearily. "It wasn't Jeremy."

"Then who? Who was the bastard?"

Jasmine did not answer, as if suddenly, inexplicably, she was unwilling to expose Morgan Tucker to her father's murderous wrath.

"Well, are you going to tell or shall I?" Lilikoi asked.

Captain Babcock whirled upon his stepdaughter. "Aye,"

he growled. "I've no doubt we'll find you're involved in your sister's shame."

Lilikoi backed away from the anger in the captain's face. She said sulkily, "It wasn't Jasmine's fault. We attended a *luau* together. Afterwards, on our way home, we were set upon by drunken whalers and dragged aboard the *Louisa*. Jasmine was taken to the captain's quarters."

"The *Louisa*?" the captain said disbelievingly. "That's Captain Tucker's ship. Why, I know the man, and his father before him. Morgan's a hard man, but I can't believe he'd . . ." He shook his head and turned back to Jasmine, his voice stern. "I want the truth now, lass. Was the man Morgan Tucker?"

She nodded helplessly then burst into tears. "I'm sorry, Papa," she gasped through her sobs. "It all happened so quickly. He thought I was a native girl, and afterwards . . . I thought as long as he didn't know who I was . . . it was better to not say anything."

A terrible anger turned Captain Babcock's eyes into slivers of ice, but none of the rage he was feeling showed in his voice as he patted Jasmine's head awkwardly. "There, there, lass," he said. "It'll be all right, you'll see. I'll take care of Captain Tucker."

"Papa, please, you mustn't!" she wailed. She remembered the strength in Morgan Tucker's hard, muscular body, and he was half her father's age. "Please, Papa, wait. . . ."

But the door had already closed behind the captain. Jasmine sank again into Malia's arms, her body shaking with violent sobs. Malia brought her a glass of some bitter-tasting liquid, then held the girl's hand until at last, drugged, she drifted off to sleep.

When Jasmine awoke again, she could hear the patter of light rain against the leaves and shrubs in the garden. Still half asleep, she stretched. She must have overslept, she thought.

A soft knock came at the door at the same time memory returned in a rush, and tears stung her eyes.

What good would crying do, she thought bitterly, wiping them away with the back of her hand. Tears wouldn't ger rid of the baby that was growing inside of her, or turn back the clock so that she could once again be the Jasmine Babcock whose only worry was what dress she should wear to a party or what she should have for breakfast.

The knock came again at the door. Pulling a robe over her shoulders, she opened the door to find Lani standing in the hall with a tray in her hands.

"I thought you might want some breakfast," she said shyly.

Breakfast? Jasmine thought, startled. She had practically slept a whole day away. Then, frightened, she asked, "Father? Is he all right?"

"He's fine. He wants to see you in the parlor after you've eaten." Lani's face pinkened. "I'm so sorry, Jasmine, about the baby. I mean, not the baby itself. You know how I love babies. And, of course, it's not the baby's fault, is it?" She broke off, shaking her head sadly. "Oh, dear, I'm not making any sense, am I?" Her gentle voice rose indignantly. "That Captain Tucker should be horsewhipped. And Lilikoi, too. She told Kale what happened. She knew those men were waiting to take you two to the whaling ship. I've never seen Kale so angry. I think he would have killed Lilikoi if I hadn't stopped him. And then he was going down to the harbor to find Captain Tucker, but I told him not to be foolish. That he'd only cause more scandal and that you were in enough trouble . . ."

Jasmine winced, and Lani gasped. "Oh, I didn't mean . . ."

Jasmine gave her a quick hug. "I know you didn't. Now, run along and tell Father I'll be down in just a minute."

Her appetite having suddenly left her, she pushed the tray away and, dressing quickly, hurried down to the parlor. Malia was sitting quietly on the sofa, but her father was pacing up and down the room. He searched his daughter's face anxiously when she entered the room. "You're feeling better, lass?"

"Yes." And then she said in a forlorn rush, "Oh, Papa, I'm so sorry for all the trouble. . . ."

He interrupted her quickly. "Hush, lass, what's done is done. And it could be worse. The babe will have a name. I've spoken to Captain Tucker, and he's agreed to marry you."

Chapter 8

At first, Jasmine couldn't believe she had heard correctly. Marry that arrogant, scowling brute who had her dragged aboard his ship and then forced himself upon her, not once but twice? Her father couldn't be serious.

Before she could do more than sputter indignantly, however, her father held up his hand, silencing her. "Let me finish, lass. Morgan Tucker has accepted full responsibility for the child. And he agrees that a marriage is necessary, not only to protect your reputation but to give the child a name. Naturally he had no idea that you were my daughter or he would never have . . ." Captain Babcock cleared his throat uncomfortably, searching for the proper words.

"Raped me," Jasmine said bitterly. "That's what he did, isn't it? And I suppose his offer of marriage makes everything perfectly all right."

"No, of course it doesn't," her father said irritably. Not that he blamed the girl for feeling as she did. He had been ready to blow Morgan Tucker out of the water himself when he'd stamped aboard the *Louisa* yesterday and headed for Morgan on the quarterdeck. Some of the men on watch, seeing the lust for blood in the old man's eyes, had reached quietly for marlinspikes, but Captain Tucker had stood, legs braced, watching the man approach. His face was a guarded mask as he gestured the men away with just the slightest motion of his chin then nodded to his visitor, his voice quiet. "We'll talk in my cabin, Captain Babcock."

The guarded expression had stayed on his granite-hard face, but Captain Babcock had not missed the momentary shock that had slipped for a moment into the narrowed eyes as the captain had explained the reason for his visit. Morgan Tucker had neither explained nor apologized, nor had Amos expected him to. Instead, when the captain had finished, Morgan had said gruffly, "It seems, Captain, we have a bit of gammoning to do."

Now Amos stared into his daughter's furious eyes, torn between his love for his firstborn and a reluctant sympathy for Morgan Tucker. But then how could a woman possibly understand how it was for a man at sea for months at a time aboard a stinking whaler with no creature comforts? Naturally he sought what a man needed when he reached port. And if the women were eager and more than willing, as the native women on the islands spread across the Pacific generally were, what was the harm in it? Captain Babcock could remember only too clearly those years when he had been a virile young man aboard a whaling ship, with a young man's natural yearnings. If a beautiful, apparently willing *wahine* had hove into view, he wouldn't have bothered asking too many questions either, he thought ruefully.

"I'll never marry that man," Jasmine said coldly.

Malia saw the anger gathering in her husband's face and, leaning toward Jasmine, spoke quickly, "The *Louisa* is leaving Honolulu for the Japan grounds in two days. So the wedding must be tomorrow, if at all. Captain Tucker could be gone for as long as a year. By the time he returns, the child will have been born, and whatever talk there might be about your hasty marriage will have been forgotten."

She sighed at the obdurate look on the girl's face, so like the stubbornness she so often saw in her husband's face. "You must be practical, child. Think of the baby." No Hawaiian, she knew, would ever think the worse of an illegitimate child, but Malia was only too well aware of how the *haoles* in Honolulu would treat such a child. "There are even laws against those who bear such children," she pointed out. "Just last summer, if your father hadn't used his influence, our gardener's son could have been put in prison when his wife had a child too quickly after their marriage."

Jasmine listened, her hands clasped tightly before her, her whole body rigid. "I'll go to prison rather than marry a man I despise," she said proudly.

"No one's going to prison," her father exploded. "But I'll not have a bastard for a grandchild. Marriage is the only answer. If you don't want Morgan Tucker, though, mind you, I think you could do far worse, then there must be some man you'll have." He thrust out his lower lip thoughtfully. "There's that preacher, Micah Beale, who came around to see me the other day wanting my permission to court you. He'd make a good husband. I understand he inherited a large estate from his dead wife and plans to go into the sugar business."

Jasmine winced, remembering the clammy feel of Micah's hand upon her arm, the oily sheen in the gray eyes when they looked at her. At least for Morgan Tucker she felt a healthy hatred. For Micah, she felt an uneasy, shivering distaste. Unfortunately, she knew that Malia was right. If she were ever to be accepted in society again, she must have a husband to give the baby a name.

Sensing that the girl was weakening, Malia added, "If after the captain returns, you still want to be free of him, there's always divorce." A divorce, Malia knew, would cause gossip, too, but not as much scandal as Jasmine's being an unwed mother.

It was raining harder now, one of those torrential showers that suddenly swept down over the Pali. Jasmine went to stand at the window, listening to the rain beating against the veranda steps and watching the sheets of silver water streaming down the windowpanes. The garden was almost hidden by the mist of spray that rose from the beaten ground.

It isn't fair, she thought, her mouth tightening rebelliously, trying to shake off the unnerving sensation of walls closing inexorably in upon her; not just the gray opaque wall of rain or the walls of the spacious parlor but her very skin itself felt like a silken trap enclosing her and the baby within her body. Why should she be punished and the man who had caused all her problems get off scot-free?

Except, the thought suddenly occurred to her, that Morgan Tucker wouldn't be exactly free. He'd be saddled with a wife and, she suspected, the captain didn't want a wife any more than she wanted a husband. In a way, the captain would be trapped in the same way she was.

Perhaps even more so. A thoughtful smile relaxed the tightness at the corners of Jasmine's lips. She remembered the whaling wives she had met at parties, women left behind in Honolulu while their husbands were away on whaling cruises. They didn't seem to lack for masculine companionship or a gay social life. And if their husbands, returning after months at sea, might wonder how their wives had occupied themselves when they were away, that was their problem, wasn't it? If a wife were properly discreet, who would know; and if she were not discreet enough, well, it was the husband who wore the cuckold's horns, wasn't it? And how the arrogant Captain Tucker would hate that, Jasmine sensed, a delicious excitement stirring within her at thought of the man's being humbled. She savored the sweet taste of revenge. And once she had her revenge, as Malia had said, there was always divorce.

Jasmine turned slowly to face her father and stepmother, her dark eyes luminous in the half-shadows of the room, a small smile playing across her mouth as she said, "I'll marry Captain Tucker."

Her father gave a gusty sigh of relief. "Good! That's my sensible girl." He turned triumphantly to his wife. "I told you, Malia, didn't I, that Jasmine would come around when we explained matters properly to her?"

"Yes," Malia said, but her glance rested uneasily on Jasmine's face, on the brightness of the girl's eyes, and that odd little smile on her face, reminding Malia of how Jasmine had always looked as a child just before she embarked on a particularly outrageous piece of devilment.

The wedding of Jasmine Caroline Babcock to Morgan Tucker took place at four o'clock the next afternoon in the Babcock parlor. By necessity, there were only a few guests: a dozen or so close friends, Emily Palmer, whose husband was performing the ceremony, and members of the immediate family. The parlor was decorated with fragrant plumeria, jasmine, ginger, and maile leaves; the cascading bouquets arranged by Lani filled the room with an explosion of color.

The bride wore a simple peachblow silk gown and a wreath of pikake blossoms on her head. The sun, pouring into the parlor, limned the figure of the bride with a pale, golden glow. The dark hair, pulled back smoothly from the oval face, showed to perfection the delicate features and the long, graceful column of a throat that was bare of any jewels.

The groom was waiting by the improvised altar, his black frock coat and trousers, dark hair and sun-browned skin a stark contrast to the rainbow of flowers and glistening sunlight.

Jasmine gave her husband-to-be a quick sideways glance as she joined him at the altar, noticing, surprised, the expensive tailoring of the jacket fitting snugly over broad shoulders, the handsomely embroidered waistcoat, and the snowy-white shirt of the finest handkerchief linen. He could pass for a gentleman, she thought grudgingly. Some women, she supposed, might even call Captain Tucker handsome, although personally she didn't care for dark men.

Then she saw that the hazel eyes with the circle of gold around the iris were observing her as closely as she was studying him, and she stiffened as she felt that scowling, appraising gaze travel over her body. His eyes lingered on the pikake wreath in her hair.

She wondered if he was remembering the pikake garland she had worn around her neck the night they had met, which he had dispatched of so summarily along with her silk *pa'u*, leaving her as vulnerable as she suddenly felt now beneath that embarrassingly familiar gaze. She averted her own eyes quickly. She couldn't go through with it, she thought, suddenly panic-stricken.

As if from a great distance, she heard the minister asking the couple standing before him to join hands. She stood paralyzed, unable to move, while every instinct within her was warning her to turn and run. Then she felt a large warm hand close over hers, imprisoning her tiny hand firmly in its grasp so that she could not have fled even if she had been able to. Once again she was unwillingly reminded of the relentless strength of the man standing beside her, of how easily he had overpowered her in his quarters on the *Louisa*.

She could remember nothing of the rest of the ceremony. She must have given the right responses, because finally it was over. Relieved, she had half turned away when she felt Morgan's arm around her waist, turning her around to face him, that sardonic half smile on his face. "You've forgotten to kiss the groom," he murmured.

She forced herself to stand perfectly still and closed her eyes amd mouth tightly and primly tilted her face, waiting. She expected his mouth to assault hers bruisingly, the way he had aboard the *Louisa*. Instead, his lips barely brushed hers fleetingly, and when her eyes flew open and stared at him in surprise, he said softly, his hazel eyes gleaming and amused, "One of these days you really must learn how to kiss properly."

Her face flushed, but before she could reply, the guests were gathering around to congratulate the bride and groom. Malia's eyes were damp as she hugged Jasmine close. Lani's face was wet, too, as she clung to Jasmine, casting a fearful glance at her sister's new husband. Captain Tucker looked so fierce, she thought, almost like a pirate, with his dark, scowling features. How frightening it would be, she thought with a shiver, being married to him.

She flung her arms around Jasmine and whispered, "Nothing's changed? You won't leave me?"

"Nothing's changed," Jasmine assured her. "Why should I leave you?"

Then Mrs. Palmer was pressing her cheek against Jasmine's face, smiling happily and saying, "May God grant you every happiness in your marriage, my child." Her bright blue, wise eyes searched the girl's face. For a moment, she thought the bride, standing at the altar, had looked scared to death. And the rush to get the girl married, this hasty wedding. Quickly Mrs. Palmer set aside such thoughts. The important thing was that Jasmine was married and would settle down, God willing, in time! It was too bad, of course, that Captain Tucker wasn't a church-going man, but he had a good reputation as a whaling captain, a hard man but fair. And, no doubt, Jasmine Babcock needed a strong man for a husband or she would walk right over him, Mrs. Palmer thought wryly.

Remote from the other guests at one side of the room, Kale and Lilikoi watched the festivities, a similar brooding expression on both their faces so that they looked very much like brother and sister.

At last Kale said tauntingly, "It seems, sister, that your trick has turned out badly for you. Your sister has your captain now, and you have nothing."

An emotion that might have been pain, and certainly

was anger, touched Lilikoi's black eyes as she gazed at the groom. "What do a few words spoken before a *haole* preacher matter?" she said, shrugging her shoulders. She glanced at Lani, who was talking to a guest, a young man gazing admiringly down into her lovely face. "You haven't managed so well yourself, brother. If you're not careful, little sister will find herself a *haole* lover."

Anger flared in Kale's eyes, but before he could retaliate, Lilikoi had already moved away, threading gracefully through the guests to reach Morgan's side.

She smiled mockingly up at the captain, her voice teasing. "Should I offer congratulations or condolences, brother-in-law?" Then her dark arms reached up to encircle his neck and pulled his mouth down to hers, her own lips moist and open, moving hungrily against his, her hands tightening in his hair while her body molded pliantly against his.

Jasmine heard Lani give a soft little gasp and, turning, discovered Lilikoi in a passionate embrace with her new husband. The embrace lasted only a few seconds before Morgan managed to pull himself free of those soft, entwining arms, like ropes of silk, holding him fast. Jasmine could not see Morgan's face, but Lilikoi looked directly across the room at her, a smugly triumphant smile on her lips.

Malia moved forward quickly, gesturing toward the dining room. "Come . . . eat. . . ."

Then Malia was beside Jasmine, slipping an arm around her waist and pulling her firmly toward the dining room. "Come along, child. You must be starved. You haven't eaten a bite all day."

Reluctantly Jasmine followed her stepmother into the dining room and even more reluctantly swallowed a few pieces of the baked chicken and pineapple. She must be laced too tightly, she thought as she felt her stomach quivering in protest against the food. Or perhaps it was nerves. Her hands felt cold as ice and yet the rest of her body felt uncomfortably warm, the floor unsteady beneath her feet.

She took a few sips of the fruit punch. Because of the presence of the missionary guests, the Babcocks had refrained from serving wine or liquor, although Jasmine suspected that her father was making an exception for certain nonmissionary guests in his study. She almost wished she could have something stronger than punch to help her get through the rest of the afternoon. Her mouth ached from smiling; her backbone was stretched like a taut wire as she forced herself to stand proudly erect and to ignore the occasional speculative looks she saw in the eyes of some of the guests as they glanced her way.

"The wedding was so romantic," one woman murmured, her eyes sliding down to the bride's tiny waist and lifting again swiftly to Jasmine's face. "Captain Tucker must have swept you off your feet. You surely couldn't have known him very long?"

Long! Jasmine fought a sudden hysterical desire to laugh; she was afraid that once she started, she wouldn't be able to stop. She glanced across the room at the stranger who was now her husband, standing, for the moment, alone. His feet were braced and his arms held behind him as if he were on the quarterdeck of his ship. If he was aware of the ripples, the undercurrent of curiosity about his hasty marriage, he gave no indication as he gazed, unperturbed, over the heads of the guests. For all of his stillness, though, he seemed to dominate the room with his presence; the same autocratic way, she was sure, he ruled the *Louisa* and her crew, not by height and bulk but by that indefinable air of command that every good whaling captain possessed.

As if feeling her eyes on him, Morgan turned. Gazing at his new bride, the expression on his face did not alter in the slightest. But, the next moment, he was standing beside her and the woman was being effectively shunted aside as he leaned over Jasmine and said quietly while his eyes studied her pale face and the lips drained of all color, "I think it's time we took our farewell of our guests, don't you agree, madam?"

It was not a question, she realized, but an order. Anger temporarily pushed aside her bone-deep weariness. Did he think she was one of his crew to jump at his slightest command? Well, he would learn differently. "I don't care to leave yet," she said, annoyed that her voice sounded petulant rather than firm. "I'm enjoying myself."

"I can see that," he said dryly, but he moved away from her.

Jasmine gazed after him, suddenly apprehensive. Surely her father had explained to Captain Tucker that he would not be spending his wedding night with his bride. Her mouth felt dry suddenly, and she swallowed more of the fruit punch. The fluttering like butterfly wings was in her stomach again, and her head was beginning to pound. She gazed with distaste at the guests still milling around the food table. Would they never go home?

Then she saw, relieved, that a few people were leaving and Malia was tactfully but firmly shepherding the rest of the guests toward the front door.

Lani came over to Jasmine, her face concerned. "You look tired, Jasmine. Why don't you sit down?"

"Yes." Jasmine heard her own voice, sounding oddly faint and far away. Lani's face swam before her and the room spun dizzily around her.

She heard Lani call out, frightened, "Papa, come quick!"

Then arms were around her, lifting her; her head was resting against a hard-muscled chest and she was being carried up the broad staircase to her bedroom. Her father? she wondered, remembering how he would carry her, half-asleep, upstairs to her bed when she was a child.

Then she was in her bed and hands were deftly removing her fawn-colored kid slippers and loosening the high-buttoned lace collar from around her neck. Except the hands weren't papa's, she realized, all at once alarmed. Papa's hands had never been so skillful and by now, exasperated, he would be yelling for Malia.

She thrust the hands away and, pushing herself to an upright position, demanded indignantly, "What are you doing here?"

Morgan's dark brows slanted together so that they almost met above his nose. "I'm your husband, remember? You were feeling indisposed, and I carried you upstairs." He was removing his coat as he talked, tossing it casually onto a beruffled chair beside the bed.

As his fingers moved toward unbuttoning his waistcoat, she said coldly, "I'm feeling better now, so you can leave." Then, feeling at a disadvantage lying on the bed, she swung her feet to the floor and stood, facing the man, her chin tilting with an unconscious arrogance that matched his own.

"Leave a bride on her wedding night?" One black eyebrow slanted upward. "How ungallant."

"Gallant!" she snapped. "The word should choke in your throat. Or is it your idea of gallantry to drag a woman aboard your ship and force yourself upon her?"

Morgan's face darkened and his eyes glittered with anger as he walked toward her. She did not retreat, although her hands balled into fists at her side at his approach. Her voice was icily contemptuous. "We're not aboard the *Louisa* now, Captain. Come one step closer and, I warn you, I'll scream the house down!"

Morgan stopped. For a long moment he studied the girl's rigid body, the wide, dark eyes, shimmering bright and hard as diamonds, and he knew she meant exactly what she said. So that was the way the wind blew, he thought, feeling almost the same sense of shock and dismay he had felt when Captain Babcock had exploded his bombshell in his quarters. Not that he had doubted the captain's story. He cursed his own stupidity for not having guessed at once that the beautiful creature in his cabin that night was not some simple native girl. Except, he admitted ruefully to himself, even if he had known, he doubted that it would have made any difference.

But marriage, which the captain had strongly suggested was the only honorable step for Morgan to take, was another matter entirely. And it hadn't been only a suggestion. Morgan had been well aware that Captain Babcock was a power in Honolulu, a friend of the royal family and of the autocratic Dr. Judd. If Babcock passed the word, he could make life difficult for a whaling captain. Provisions would be delivered slowly, if at all, and repairs would be done in a slovenly fashion.

Not that Morgan hadn't always planned to marry someday. He had more than enough money to support a family with the fortune he had made from his whaling voyages. It was the idea of being forced into marriage that galled him. Still, he had pondered as he had poured a drink for his guest, he would go far to find a more beautiful wife than Jasmine Babcock. And it wasn't only her beauty that intrigued him; it was the hard core of courage the girl possessed, along with a deeply passionate nature that he sensed lay beneath the cool, touch-me-not exterior.

Intrigued him enough so that the next morning he had questioned Daniel closely about the address to which he had delivered the girl the night before. It turned out that Jasmine had left Daniel in the vicinity of lower Nuuanu Street and not returned to some waterfront grogshop on Fid Street. Questioning the men in the forecastle about the supposed sister, Lilikoi, had brought no better results. The men had all spoken highly of Lilikoi's sexual prowess, but none of them had thought to ask her last name. Over the next weeks, deliberately taking his time seeing to the repairing of the *Louisa*, Morgan had surprised himself at how often his thoughts had turned to wondering about the girl: who she was, where she had come from, and where she had gone.

As for the third mate, Otis, who had brought Jasmine to the ship, when summoned to the captain's quarters the next morning and questioned, he had insisted that the girl had come quite willingly along with Lilikoi to the ship. Morgan, however, had known at once that the man was lying through his teeth. He hadn't said a word, only stared for a long moment at the man standing before him. A flush had spread over Harry Otis's face; an eyelid began to twitch nervously under that ruthless, probing stare. Finally, desperately, he had confessed that, yes, he had brought the girl aboard the ship against her will. "But you said yourself you wanted the girl, Captain," he had said, his gaze shifting evasively away from Morgan's face. "Lilikoi said the girl was shy, just needed a little coaxing." And then, in a blustering attempt to regain his courage, he had protested, "Hell, Skipper, what difference does it make? I never met one of these native girls yet that wouldn't jump into bed with a white man for a piece of gold, or less."

For several seconds, Morgan had toyed with the tempting idea of disrating the man and sending him to the forecastle. But Otis was one of his best harpooners, seldom missing placing the deadly iron into a whale. And there was a grain of truth in the man's defense. Morgan remembered that he had told Otis that he wanted Jasmine and no other.

Nevertheless, he had taken a vicious delight in dressing the man down, reaming him up one side and down the other with his tongue, until, finally, he allowed the shaken and perspiration-soaked mate to leave the cabin.

Now, as Morgan studied the girl standing stiffly before him, her eyes watching him warily, he felt an unaccountable pang of guilt. He remembered how slight that slender body had felt in his arms, how easily his strength had overcome her soft woman's body despite her struggles against him, and he wondered suddenly how he would have felt if the situation had been reversed.

Irritably he thrust that uncomfortable thought aside. After all, he had done the right thing, hadn't he? He could have denied all responsibility for the girl's predicament. Instead he had accepted his responsibility and married her. What more did the woman want?

With an effort, he kept the anger from his voice as he said slowly, "I understood from your father that you had agreed to the marriage."

"I agreed to a marriage ceremony, nothing more."

"You're carrying my child," he pointed out brusquely.

She flinched, a flush running in feather strokes across her face. How dare he mention the child, as if, somehow, it gave him certain proprietary rights over her. Impulsively, wanting to hurt him as he had hurt her, she blurted, "Your child? How can you be so sure it's your child?"

Almost immediately, she regretted what she had said and was even more dismayed when she saw the black anger she saw clouding her new husband's face. She backed instinctively away from him.

Had it all been a lie, then? Morgan wondered furiously. Could he have been mistaken about the girl? He would have sworn that he was the first. Was it possible that she could have been putting on an act for his benefit?

For the first time, it occurred to Morgan that the unvarnished truth was that he knew very little about women. Oh, he'd taken more than his share of females to bed, but beyond enjoying their very enticing bodies and the pleasures those bodies gave him, he had spent very little time trying to fathom a woman's mind or even conversing with his bedmates. Not that the women he had made love to were all that interested in conversation, anyway. As for the so-called nice women, he'd only met a few, briefly, while in New Bedford on his infrequent trips home. They had either bored him, with their silly chatter, or annoyed him, with their prim airs.

The only woman that Morgan knew well was his mother, a shrewd, hard-headed New Englander, and even though he admired and respected her, mother and son had never been particularly close.

Morgan wondered wryly what his mother would think if she learned of the circumstances surrounding her son's marriage. Never one to mince words, she would have undoubtedly called him a dozen kinds of a fool for allowing himself to be tricked into such a marriage in the first place. Captain Babcock and his daughter had set their iron just deep enough into his hide, Morgan thought, scowling, then played the line cleverly so that he hadn't a chance of escaping.

Still scowling, he turned and, picking up his jacket, slipped it on. When he turned back to Jasmine, he saw the quick relief flooding her face, could almost sense the tension leaving the slim, rigid body. He felt a swift, searing rage at her eagerness to be rid of him and an even more explosive anger at how easily she had duped him.

Uneasily Jasmine saw the muscles in Morgan's face pull taut, the hazel eyes looking almost golden with the blazing fury in their depths.

Too late, she opened her mouth to scream. Morgan had already covered the distance between them, moving with amazing swiftness for such a large man. His mouth covered Jasmine's completely, choking off the scream, while his arms tightened around her in a bearlike grip. Then slowly, relentlessly, his arms forced her body ever closer so that her soft thighs fit snugly against his and her full breasts were crushed against his hard, unyielding chest. Just as pitilessly his mouth assaulted hers, forcing her lips to part helplessly beneath his.

Jasmine could feel her heart pounding in great, wrenching strokes against her rib cage as she fought, in vain, for breath. Remembering the savage fury she had seen in Morgan's face, an icy terror gripped her. For the first time in her young life, she realized, incredibly, that she could die here and now, her life snuffed out as easily as the man now crushing her in his arms could snap a man's neck with his powerful hands. A whimper of fear started deep in her throat, a soundless cry.

Then darkness invaded her mind, and the next thing she knew she was lying on the bed, gasping for breath. Her breasts ached and her body felt bruised from the pressure of those arms against her soft flesh.

Morgan stood beside the bed, looking down at her. For a split second, she saw reflected in his shocked eyes the same terrible fear she had known: that he might have killed her, without even meaning to, in a blind, insensate rage.

Then all expression was wiped from his face, leaving his eyes an opaque brown as they roved over her slim body. Her gown was tumbled up around her slender legs, her breasts rising and falling in agitation beneath the silken gown. She could feel her flesh shrinking from that gaze, not from the passion but from the icy scorn she saw there, and she began to shiver.

Mistaking the shiver for fear, Morgan scowled down at her, his voice a low, rasping growl, "I don't like being threatened or gulled, madam. You'll do well to remember that in the future."

Then he was gone, the door closing quietly behind him.

On the bed, Jasmine began to cry, without quite knowing why, and could not seem to stop.

Chapter 9

Daniel hesitated outside Captain Tucker's quarters, a cup of hot coffee in his hands and an uncertain expression on his young face. Ordinarily he wouldn't have thought twice about disturbing the captain, but on this last cruise of the *Louisa*, Captain Tucker had been an entirely different person from the man for whom the cabin boy had conceived a shy, almost painful hero-worship. Ever since the ship had left Honolulu for the Japan grounds, late last fall, the captain had been short-tempered and moody, either staring gloomily out to sea or bellowing at the men for the slightest shirking of their duties. And for the first time since the *Louisa* had left New Bedford, three years before, the ship's "greasy luck" had run out. Only a dozen or so whales had been spotted, and they had managed to elude the *Louisa*'s whaleboats, one even using her flukes to toss a boat over so that it was a miracle the men aboard had survived.

The crew had begun to squabble among themselves: a fist fight had broken out in the forecastle between two of the Portuguese and several of the men in the forecastle were even whispering of jumping ship when it returned to Honolulu.

Not that every man aboard the *Louisa* didn't know what was ailing the captain. Any man would have a foul disposition after marrying a reported beauty like Captain Babcock's daughter and then having to leave his bride after only one night of wedded bliss. Daniel had hoped that as the *Louisa* drew closer to the Sandwich Islands the captain would become more cheerful at the prospect of seeing his wife again. Instead, if it were possible, the captain had become more irascible, and when they had anchored last evening in Honolulu harbor, he had announced that there would be no shore leave for the men until the *Louisa* was scoured with sand and soap from stem to stern.

Sighing heavily to himself, Daniel lifted his hand, knocked gingerly, then pushed open the door. To his surprise, the captain was already in his shore clothes, although he hadn't yet been to breakfast. He whirled around when Daniel entered and snapped, "Is the carriage waiting for me at the dock?"

Daniel blinked. "You—you didn't say anything about wanting a carriage, Captain," he stammered.

Morgan scowled. "Damn it, do I have to think of everything myself? Do you expect me to walk into Honolulu? Tell Mr. Otis to arrange for a carriage right away." As Daniel turned hastily to obey the captain's bidding, the coffee cup hit the edge of the desk, spilling coffee onto the charts on the desktop.

The captain gave the boy a scathing glance. "I'd expected that after three years at sea you could manage to handle a cup of coffee without spilling it."

"Yes, sir." The boy nervously mopped at the coffee with his shirtsleeve, only making the stain worse.

Morgan saw the hurt in Daniel's eyes, the slight trembling of the still boyishly formed mouth, and felt a twinge of remorse for taking out his own irritation and frustration on the lad.

"Never mind," he said gruffly. "There's no great harm done."

As the boy scurried from the room, Morgan's mouth clenched in a tight, angry line as he realized that he was just as jumpy and nervous as his cabin boy. It was ridiculous, he thought, annoyed, that a man who could handle a crew of rough seamen should worry about dealing with a slip of a girl.

Always before when he was at sea, he had easily put out of his mind any memories of the women he had met in port. A whaling captain shouldered too many responsibilities, had to make too many dangerous, split-second decisions, to waste time lollygagging over a female like a besotted schoolboy. Yet during the last nine months, memories of Jasmine had somehow managed to intrude into his thoughts time and time again. Memories of the way her black hair had splayed out over the pillow, making her delicately boned face seem, somehow, even younger and more vulnerable; of the pale golden loveliness of her limbs and the sweet upward curve of her breasts; and, most vividly of all, of that look of startled wonder that had briefly illuminated her dark eyes as he had possessed her completely.

Interposed over memories of that girl in his bed, however, were those of another woman: a poised, elegant creature in a high-necked silk gown who had stood beside him at the altar, her lovely face cool and closed to him, her dark eyes remote. And of the icy-faced stranger who had faced him defiantly in her bedroom, her eyes filled with loathing, her voice jeering. It was that woman he had wanted, in a burst of rage, to destroy. Yet, aferwards, shocked and ashamed at his own brutality, he gazed down into his wife's face and saw, beneath the glint of fear in her wide, staring eyes, that the aloof stranger was still there, still defiant, still rejecting him.

When he had stormed away from the Babcock house that day, he told himself that he was well rid of Captain Babcock's daughter, that as far as he was concerned the travesty of a marriage had never happened. But the closer the *Louisa* had come to Honolulu, the more the truth had been rammed home that he couldn't wait to see his wife again. And the child, he thought, a half hour later as he climbed into the carriage that was waiting for him at the dock and turned the horses toward the Nuuanu Valley. Was it a son or daughter? he wondered, surprised by his own depth of feeling for this child he had never seen.

At least that was one thing he had settled in his own mind during the cruise. Despite the girl's outrageous insinuation, Morgan was convinced the child was his. He might not understand how a woman charted a course, he thought grimly, but he knew men. Captain Amos Babcock was too honest a man. He would never have practically forced Morgan into marriage with his daughter if he believed for one moment that the child was bred by some other man.

At the Babcock house, Lani answered the door, her face paling when she saw the man standing on the veranda. For a moment, he was afraid she was going to turn and flee back into the house.

"I'm here to see my wife," he said firmly.

Lani gaped at him, then stammered, "Your—your wife? Oh, you mean Jasmine. She's—she's gone."

Morgan felt fear like a knife thrust between his ribs. Had something happened to Jasmine? Women did die in childbirth.

"Gone? Gone where?" he rasped so that Lani took a frightened step backward into the house.

"I'll—I'll fetch Mother."

Impatiently Morgan grabbed her arm, his eyes narrowing angrily until he realized he was only frightening the girl more. He said gently, "Never mind Mrs. Babcock. Tell me. Where has Jasmine gone?"

"To the beach," Lani blurted. "She's at our beach house at Waikiki."

It took Morgan little more than an hour to locate the beach house. The road gave out, and he was forced to leave the carriage and walk the rest of the way toward the ocean. As he came over a rise of land, he could see a thatched house surrounded by coconut palms and heard in the distance, over the sound of the surf rushing to shore, a man's voice calling and a woman's laugh, childlike with excitement. Jasmine, he thought at once, although it occurred to him that he had never heard his wife laugh. He saw in one swift glance that there was no one at the beach house, and his gaze swung out to sea. There was a heavy surf beyond the reef, blue green waves with white crests like smoke flying in the air above them. Even within the reef area, the surf was high enough, he saw, for two surfers paddling their surfboards furiously toward shore. The next second a wave caught and lifted the boards, and the two surfers were standing, balancing their bodies lightly on the boards and soaring like young, brown gods over the water. No, not two gods, Morgan saw, his eyes narrowing against the sunlight flashing against the ocean, a god and goddess. He recognized his wife on the second board. She was wearing a *pa'u*, and her long, black hair flew out behind her as she raced toward shore on her board. The man reached the shore first, the waves breaking in a burst of foam, making a tumultuous rushing sound as the breaker fell, spent, on the beach. The man stepped easily from the board to the sand. Halfway to shore, however, Morgan saw Jasmine's board suddenly twist out from beneath her and go flying into the air, while the girl flew in the other direction, disappearing into the wave cresting at her feet. For a heart-stopping moment Morgan lost sight of her, then he saw her dark head come to the surface. She was laughing as she swam toward shore then splashed the rest of the way to the beach, silver drops of water breaking around her long, tawny legs.

"Rather strenuous activity for a new mother, isn't it?" Morgan asked.

Neither Kale nor Jasmine had heard him approach, and they both whirled, startled. Morgan shot Kale a furious glance. "She could have been badly hurt when she fell off the board."

Kale shrugged his broad shoulders, amused. "Jasmine has been using a surfboard since she was eight years old. She's almost as good as I am." He glanced indifferently at the waves piling rhythmically into the shore at their feet. "Besides, these are only *wahine* waves; a child could ride them. As for the new mother . . ." He gave his sister a quizzical glance.

Jasmine stepped forward. "It's all right, Kale. I'd like to speak to Captain Babcock alone, please."

Kale glanced suspiciously at the captain, then muttered, "I won't be far away, if you need me."

Jasmine waited until her brother had gone a short distance down the beach then turned to Morgan, her face pale but composed. "There was no child," she said.

Morgan was conscious of a sharp sense of loss, even as his eyes raked her face coldly. "So it was a trick, after all."

He saw an answering anger leap into her eyes, but her voice was as cold as his as she answered, "It was no trick. I did think I was pregnant, but it was a fever. I was sick for several weeks. I'm sorry if you think I deceived you on purpose, but, of course, it is better this way."

"Better?"

A note almost of menace in Morgan's voice brought a startled look to Jasmine's face, but she stood her ground. "Surely you're no more eager than I am to continue this farce of a marriage."

With an effort, Morgan controlled the sudden, wild

anger that flared in him. So it was that simple for her, was it, to marry him then just as quickly to discard him when he had served her purpose. And to think he had been fool enough to think, once or twice, aboard the *Louisa* that he might be in his wife's thoughts as much as she had possessed his. For a long moment, he studied Jasmine. The sun had darkened her skin so that she was almost the same tawny gold shade she had been that first night he had met her, and the wet scarlet *pa'u* hugging her breasts and hips showed that she was not as thin as she had been on her wedding day. But the cool, supercilious look on her face as she stared at him was the same, as if he were a stranger whose presence she was just barely, politely, enduring.

Damn it, she was his wife, child or no child. Morgan did not question the unexpectedness of his decision. Aboard the *Louisa* he was used to making split-second life-and-death decisions and to not looking back once he made them. He did not look back now. Jasmine Babcock Tucker was his wife and she would remain his wife. There was no way he could live with the idea of another man possessing her, arousing her, placing that look of startled wonder in her dark, lustrous eyes.

Then, glancing over her shoulder at Kale, glowering in the background, he decided prudently that this was neither the time nor the place to put his decision into action.

He gave his wife a mocking half smile, murmuring, "I quite agree. However, marriages are not dissolved so easily. I'll drop by your home this evening and discuss the matter with your father. Now, if you'll excuse me, I have business concerning the *Louisa* to attend to."

He turned and strode away without a backward glance. If he had, he might have noticed a look of pained surprise on Jasmine's face as she stared after him. It wasn't that she wanted Morgan to protest the dissolution of their marriage, she thought irritably that evening when her husband arrived promptly at the Babcock home and closeted himself with her father for several hours then left without even a word to her. But he could have at least had the common decency to pretend disappointment, even a touch of regret, at losing her.

For the next weeks, Morgan turned up regularly at the Babcock home in the evenings, several times staying for dinner at Malia's insistence. He was always punctiliously polite to Jasmine on these occasions, but he spent more time talking to her parents and the rest of the family than he did to her.

Captain Babcock was interested in the latest whaling news that Morgan brought with him and delighted in telling tales of the days when he had captained his own whaling ship.

Morgan listened, apparently absorbed, while Jasmine's father told of his crew's chasing one particular sperm whale off the Marquesas and harpooning it. Then a storm had separated them from the mother ship. "It was four weeks till we found them again," the captain said proudly. "And not a soul aboard had been lost, nor the whale either. She had the iron still in her." He chuckled. "Though the sharks had taken most of her, and the men were a mite skinnier, too." He turned to Jasmine. "That was when you and your mother were sailing with me. Of course, you were just a wee lass then and probably don't remember."

"I didn't know your daughter had sailed with you, Captain," Morgan said.

"My wife and daughter made several cruises with me. The men doted on Jasmine, and she was all over the ship if her mother didn't keep an eye on her."

Morgan gave Jasmine a thoughtful glance, but there was something else in those narrowed eyes, resting lightly, possessively on her face, that made Jasmine vaguely uncomfortable. Then Morgan turned his attention back to his host. "I'm afraid you'd find the crews aboard the whalers are much changed today. In your day, they were the sons and nephews of whaling men, eager to learn the whaling trade. Now they're either greenies, farm boys from Vermont looking for adventure, or men who are the dregs of the waterfront or deserters fleeing the law or worse. The best men a skipper can find these days for his crew are the *kanakas*, Hawaiian lads." Morgan gave his brother-in-law a questioning glance. "I understand you shipped for one cruise on a whaler with Captain McNally."

"Once was enough," Kale retorted grimly. "The forecastle was filthy, twenty men sleeping in a room not big enough for five. The food was garbage that even the cockroaches rejected, and if the behavior of the crew didn't satisfy the captain, the seaman was hung by his thumbs in the rigging, his shirt stripped off, and he was given a taste of the cat." Kale grinned mirthlessly at Morgan. "No doubt you're acquainted with the many-tailed, knotted whip they call the cat, Captain. It can tear a man's back to shreds; and when the man passed out from the pain, a bucket of saltwater was thrown on his raw back to bring him screaming to life."

Almost in an aside, he added, "And, oh, yes, the captain was a church-going man, well liked, I understand, ashore."

Jasmine gazed, horrified, at her brother. Kale had never spoken of his life aboard the whaler, and now she understood why. She was sure her father had never used the whip on his ship, but what of Captain Tucker, she wondered suddenly. Would he hesitate to use the cat aboard the *Louisa*? Shifting her gaze across the table, her eyes met her husband's. Although the impassive expression on Morgan's broad-boned face did not change in the slightest, she was sure he knew what she was thinking. A muscle beside his mouth jerked, but when he spoke, his voice was quiet. "I'll not deny there are whaling captains like McNally, shore saints and sea devils. But I've seen the bloody results of a mutiny aboard a ship when a captain is too soft. It's not a pleasant sight either."

Lani, sensing the tension at the table and as always anxious to preserve the peace, said in her soft, sweet voice to Kale, "Not all captains are like Captain McNally.

The Seamen's Bethel in Honolulu is supported by donations from whaling captains, as well as the church. Without the Bethel, the poor forgotten seamen would have no church or hospital or meeting place to turn to when they're sick or alone in port." She gave Morgan a shy smile. "Captain Tucker had made a sizable donation to the Bethel."

Jasmine frowned, annoyed, at her sister. It wasn't enough that Morgan Tucker had her father and stepmother fairly eating out of his hands, but now, apparently, he had captured the affection of Lani, too. And, of course, the captain had had no need to try and win Lilikoi's favor. Her sister bestowed her smiles on Morgan endlessly, always conspiring, somehow, to be seated next to him with her arm or leg accidentally brushing against his. And the dress Lilikoi was wearing for dinner this evening, Jasmine thought, gazing irritably at her sister. The dress was cut so low that if Lilikoi leaned over any further, the captain could see straight down to her navel, and Morgan didn't seem to be avoiding the attractive scenery available to him.

Well, at least she and Kale were still able to see through the captain's charm, she fumed, stabbing at the piece of fish on her plate with her fork as if it were her mortal enemy.

Then, several nights later, on the captain's last night in port, Jasmine unhappily discovered that Kale, too, was deserting her.

The captain had dropped by the house to say his farewells. Her father had brought out his best imported French wine and, since it was a pleasant evening, the family sat on the veranda as the captain poured the wine into cut-crystal goblets and passed them around.

"They say the young princes, Alexander and Lot, have developed a taste for French wine since their trip abroad with Dr. Judd." Captain Babcock laughed, adding, "Although I can't imagine the good doctor letting the young princes within smelling distances of spirits."

"Dr. Judd treats Prince Alexander and Lot like

children," Kale said, glowering at his father. "But all that will change when Alexander takes over the throne. Americans like Judd, and the other merchants and traders, will discover they can no longer run these islands as if they belonged to them. Prince Alexander told me that when he was in Washington, he was roughly ordered off a train by the conductor because the man took the prince for a Negro. Alexander knows now how Americans treat men of a color different from their own. He has seen in America how black men are treated like dogs, to come and go at an American's bidding, while in England an African may sit next to Queen Victoria. Prince Alexander will not forget what he has learned when he comes to the throne."

Captain Babcock's brows bristled warningly at his stepson. "I'll remind you that Captain Tucker is an American and a guest in our home. You owe him an apology."

"There's no apology needed," Morgan said quickly. "I've no liking for slavery, or to see a man or woman mistreated because they have a different color skin. My mother, as well as other New Englanders, is active in a society that is working to abolish slavery in the United States. For myself, I have a free black, Hamish Walker, as a cooper on my ship, and I've never met a finer gentleman at sea or in port."

He lifted his glass of wine to his host and smiled. "Anyway, I hate to have an argument spoil this excellent wine, Captain." He turned toward Jasmine, noticed that her glass was almost empty, and before she could protest that she'd had quite enough, said, "Let me fill your glass."

It was a delicious wine, Jasmine thought, sipping at the pale rose liquor. For the first time since the captain's return, she could feel herself relaxing, smiling happily at her family, enjoying the delicious night scents from the garden. All in all, despite the presence of Morgan Tucker, it was a most pleasant evening.

"Would you care to accompany me, Jasmine?"

Startled, Jasmine realized that her mind had drifted dreamily away from the conversation on the porch and that Captain Tucker had risen to his feet and was leaning over her, obviously waiting for an answer to a question.

She saw her stepmother and father exchange glances, then her father cleared his throat and said loudly, "The captain would like to take you for a carriage ride, Jasmine, if, of course, you are willing."

Morgan leaned closer so that she could see the teasing golden lights in his hazel eyes, the half-taunting smile on his lips. "Or are you afraid to be alone in a carriage with me?" he asked softly.

Jasmine stared haughtily at the man. Did he really believe she was frightened to be alone with him?

She pulled herself with careful dignity to her feet, giving him a cool, gracious smile. "A spin in the night air sounds delightful, Captain Tucker."

Malia rose to her feet. "You'll need your shawl, *keiki*." She hurried away to fetch it herself, and when she placed it around Jasmine's shoulders, she gave her stepdaughter a quick hug.

Captain Babcock walked with Morgan and Jasmine to the carriage, helping Jasmine inside, then turned abruptly to Morgan. "You'll drive carefully, now. Those horses look skittish to me."

"I'll be very careful, Captain," Morgan assured him gravely. "You needn't worry about your daughter."

Jasmine settled back in the carriage seat, pulling the shawl closer around her, thinking, amused, that the way her father was fussing over her, you'd think she was still a child. Then Morgan had climbed into the seat beside her and picked up the reins, urging the horses forward.

All at once, Jasmine felt embarrassingly drowsy. It was the wine, she thought. She never did have a head for wine. It was too bad, too. She had a few choice things to say to the captain before he left, but suddenly she felt too tired even to talk. She would rest a moment, she decided, her head nodding against Morgan's broad shoulder, surprised at how comfortably it fitted there. . . . That was the last thing she remembered thinking before sleep, like a white-crested breaker, pulled her under.

Chapter 10

Even before she opened her eyes, Jasmine knew she wasn't in her own bedroom at home. The bed she was in seemed to be rolling slightly beneath her, and it wasn't lavender-scented bed linen that she smelled but the sharp tang of tobacco and saltwater and . . . yes, Jasmine thought, still half asleep, her nostrils twitching . . . raw fish.

All traces of sleep fled as she jerked upright in the bed, staring around her incredulously. She was only too familiar with the cabin and the bed in which she found herself. She was aboard the *Louisa*. Pushing aside the coverlet, she hurried to the port, little more than a slit in the thick timbers, and looked out on a patch of open sea.

How had it happened? she wondered, confused, aware of a dull throbbing in her head and the ocean stretching before her as far as her eyes could see. How had she come here? The last thing she remembered was drinking wine on the veranda with her family, going for a carriage ride with Morgan Tucker, and feeling oddly drowsy.

Of course. Anger started a frantic pounding in her chest so that she forgot her headache. Morgan must have drugged her wine. And when she had passed out in the carriage, he had simply carried her aboard the *Louisa*. Well, he wouldn't get away with abducting her a second time, she thought furiously, reaching for her wrapper, which was lying across the foot of the bed. As soon as her father learned what had happened, he would . . . Jasmine's thoughts ground to a halt as she gazed, bewildered, at the wrapper. It was her own robe, and the white cambric nightgown she wore was hers, too. Morgan might have kidnapped her, but how had he gotten his hands on her nightclothes? A second more embarrassing question followed hard on the first. Who had undressed her, placed the nightgown on her, and put her to bed in the captain's cabin?

Then her eyes fell on a small, familiar trunk shoved against the wall of the tiny quarters. She could see her initials painted in blue and gold on the lid as she knelt and opened the trunk. Inside, neatly packed were her own dresses, undergarments, shawls, and shoes, along with her toilette articles—all the personal necessities she would need on a trip.

She was still staring, puzzled, at the trunk when a knock came at the door of the quarters. Tying the robe around her, she walked into the adjoining cabin and pulled open the door.

The cabin boy stood in the doorway with a tray of food, a little taken aback by the appearance of the captain's wife, her face flushed, her dark eyes flashing fire.

"I'm—I'm sorry if I woke you, ma'am," he apologized, blushing, as he quickly looked away from the woman still in her nightclothes. "The captain thought you might want breakfast in the cabin this first morning."

Carefully Daniel edged past Jasmine and placed the tray on the captain's table then retreated swiftly to the door again.

Jasmine's icy voice stopped him in his tracks. "Where is Captain Tucker?"

"He's having breakfast with the first mate in the mess room."

The woman's eyes narrowed, studying the boy standing before her. "I've seen you before?"

Daniel's face burned an even brighter red. "Yes, ma'am." He remembered vividly the night he had first met the captain's wife here in this cabin, her hair hanging down in tangles around her shoulders, wearing one of those skimpy little gowns that the native women wore. At first, he had assumed she was an island girl from one of the grogshops on Fid Street until he had taken a second, closer look. Even as inexperienced as he was with women, Daniel still recognized a lady when he saw one. And he was sure of it now when, sensing the boy's embarrassment, the woman didn't pursue the matter any further.

"Thank you for breakfast," she said, smiling faintly at the boy.

"The name's Daniel, ma'am," he blurted. "And I'm . . . all the crew are happy to have you aboard." He grinned, a wide, boyish grin. His eyes, Jasmine saw, were a clear, innocent blue, his body still thin, lanky, and growing. "Some of the men think having you aboard will change our luck for the better, but the first mate says if nothing else, having you sail with us will put the captain into a better humor!"

Then he darted out the door, leaving Jasmine to her breakfast. She had thought she wouldn't be hungry but, instead, discovered she was starving. She quickly ate the eggs and biscuits and drank coffee laced with molasses. Then, going to the trunk, she pulled out a striped blue-and-white gown, several starched petticoats, a chemise, and drawers. There was warm water in the washbasin and scented soap, and after she had bathed herself, she slipped into her clothes, feeling grateful that the gown fastened up the front so that she could manage the buttoning by herself.

She had found her brush and was putting her hair into some semblance of order when a second knock came at the door. By the peremptory sound of this knock, she knew at once who it was. She put down her brush and turned to face the captain as he entered the cabin.

Morgan stood at the doorway of the small cabin, glancing quickly around the room before turning to her. "I see you've found everything you need. There's another trunk of your clothes below. There wasn't enough room for them in the cabin. You can go through it later and get anything else you might want."

How dare he, Jasmine thought, the rage returning and rolling over her in waves so that she had to clench her hands to keep them from trembling. How dare he sound so—so complacent!

"You shanghaied me!" she exploded.

Morgan walked into the outer cabin and seated himself on the horsehair couch, his legs stretched out before him. "You might say that," he agreed. "It seemed simpler than dragging you kicking and screaming aboard the ship."

"You won't get away with it!" She could hear her voice rising childishly, shrilly, despite her firm intention to treat the man with the icy contempt he deserved. "Father will send a ship after us. He'll drag you back to Honolulu and see you hanged."

Morgan lifted an amused eyebrow. "Oh, I doubt it. In the first place, if a captain wants to take his wife with him on a whaling cruise, there's no law against it. In the second place, hasn't it occurred to you by now that I have your parents' approval?"

For a few seconds Jasmine was speechless, then she gasped, "I—I don't believe it. Father . . . Malia . . . they wouldn't . . ."

Morgan shrugged. "How else do you suppose your belongings were packed and sent aboard late last night?" At the stunned look on Jasmine's face, his voice softened. "If it makes you feel any better, I'm sure it wasn't an easy decision for them to make. It took a lot of persuading on my part to convince them that we deserved the chance to have a real marriage. They agreed to give me a year. If at the end of that time you still want a divorce, I promised them that you should have it."

"A year!" Jasmine stared at him with loathing. "A year or a hundred years—do you think that it will make any difference? You must be out of your mind!"

"Perhaps, but the fact remains that we are married, husband and wife, whether you like it or not. And there's no way you can get a divorce without my consent. So I suggest you make the best of the situation for the good of everyone concerned."

"I won't!" She glared at him mutinously. "I won't be kept a prisoner on this ship for a year."

"You won't be treated as a prisoner but as my wife," he corrected her. "That is, as long as you conduct yourself like a proper wife." He smiled thinly. "Here in the cabin you can scream at me like a fishwife if you wish, but outside this cabin I'll expect you to give me the same respect and obedience that I receive from every member of the crew. I'll not tolerate insubordination aboard the *Louisa*."

Although his calm voice did not alter in the slightest, she caught the underlying threat in his words, and her mouth set rebelliously. She was well aware that the master of a whaling ship had absolute power over every man on the ship and that his word was law, to be obeyed instantly. But she wasn't one of Morgan's crew, she thought, enraged. She had been drugged and dragged aboard the ship against her will. "And if I don't agree?" she asked coldly.

He got slowly to his feet. "Then you'll make yourself at home inside my quarters. The crew will be told that you're indisposed." He glanced, almost indifferently, around the tiny cabin and adjoining stateroom. "It's a small world. I'd find it boring myself after a while, but suit yourself." He inclined his head toward her. "Now, if you'll excuse me, I have work to do."

The door closed quietly behind him before she could make a suitable, biting retort. She stared, exasperated, at the door, then around the two small rooms, whose

stout walls she could feel—or was it only her imagination?
—closing in upon her. Finally she began to explore her
surroundings. She took her time, but in half an hour she
had examined every inch of space.

She was surprised to discover that there was a small
room off the cabin that held a privy, a luxury she knew
was not found on most whaling ships. She also found the
captain's clothes in a small trunk under the bed. The
only personal item of his she found in the chest was a
small, beautifully done oil portrait in a gold frame of a
young woman. The woman had brown eyes and hair,
and although she was not beautiful—her nose was a
little too long—there was an appealing vitality in the
expression on her face. No doubt one of the captain's
conquests, Jasmine decided, though evidently more long
lasting than the others if he kept her portrait. Then,
feeling suddenly ashamed, as if she were prying where
she didn't belong, she pushed the portrait back beneath
the clothes, shoved the trunk under the bed, and rose,
frowning, to her feet.

The front cabin revealed little of interest. The table-
top was covered with charts, and a binnacle hung above
the table, holding a compass and lantern much like the
one Jasmine remembered from her father's cabin, so
that even in his quarters the captain could quickly plot
the location of the ship.

She glanced finally through the books on the shelf
above the horsehair sofa. She had enjoyed reading at
the academy, although the books at the school had been
carefully and unimaginatively selected so as not to in-
flame the delicate female mind. A few of the books by
Charles Dickens she had already read. The other au-
thors were unknown to her, and she was vaguely surprised at the captain's wide range of taste in books. She
pulled out a slim volume by a man named Herman
Melville, titled *Typee*, and to take her mind off her
unhappy circumstances, she sat on the sofa and began to
read.

She became so engrossed in the book that she was

startled when the cabin boy appeared again, this time with a lunch of hot stew, plum duff, and coffee.

"I'm sorry you're not feeling well, Mrs. Tucker," he said, his glance sympathetic. "Seasickness can be miserable, but if you can keep some food down, it will help."

So that's what Morgan had told the boy, Jasmine thought, her pride stung. Why, she had never been seasick a day in her life!

Swallowing her protest, she said instead, "Thank you, I'll try. The stew smells delicious." And was delicious, she discovered after taking a taste.

"Lijah's the best cook on any whaling ship anywhere," Daniel said enthusiastically. "Of course, after we're at sea a few months and run out of fresh vegetables and eggs, we'll be down to eating salt pork and hardtack," he said cheerfully. "Still, even then the food aboard the *Louisa's* better than the slop they serve on most whalers."

Jasmine couldn't resist smiling at the young man's pride in his vessel. "Have you been on many whaling ships, Daniel?"

The boy flushed. "No, ma'am. The *Louisa's* my first. It's what I always wanted to do, though, go to sea on a whaler, so as soon as I turned twelve, I signed aboard. I won't always be a cabin boy, either. The captain's promised that as soon as he thinks I'm able, he'll put me in the fo'c'sle."

Jasmine stared at the young man who looked, with his fair hair falling over his forehead and shining, innocent eyes, as if he should be in a schoolroom. "What did your mother say about your going to sea?"

A shadow crossed the young face. "She tried to talk me out of it. My oldest brother was a harpooner on a whaler. He was killed when the line caught his leg as he was putting the iron into a whale, cut his leg off as neatly as if a surgeon had done it. He might have lived, but blood poisoning set in. I have another brother on a whaler, the *Seneca*. The *Louisa* raised the *Seneca* last month, and Sam and I had a good gam together. His ship was headed for the Marquesas, so maybe I'll see him again."

"Is that where the *Louisa*'s bound, the Marquesas?" Jasmine asked curiously.

If the boy was surprised that the captain's wife didn't know where her husband's whaling ship was heading, he gave no sign. "Yes, ma'am, and if our luck's good, then maybe we'll be heading home. We've been away for more than three years."

Uneasily the boy glanced at the door. "I'd best be getting back to the galley, ma'am. Lijah doesn't like my wasting time when I should be helping him."

Jasmine, perforce, returned to her book. Once again she became so absorbed in the young whaling hero, Toby Green, and his adventures among the South Pacific cannibals in the valley of Typee that she hardly looked up when Daniel brought in her evening meal. As she read further into the book, she felt her face growing warm and was guiltily sure that the book would never have been allowed at Miss Ander's Academy. Young Toby described with too much intimate and exuberant detail his love affair with the dusky, beautiful, and uninhibited native girl, Fayaway.

She had regretfully turned the last page of the book and was still pensive over the sad ending of the romance between Toby and Fayaway when the door opened and Morgan stepped inside. "I thought you'd be in bed by now," he said brusquely. Then he glanced at the book she held in her hand. "I see you've been reading Mr. Melville's story."

Jasmine, who had been sitting with her feet tucked under her on the sofa, rose quickly to a more dignified position.

At the note of amusement in his voice, she said defensively, "It's a beautiful book."

"Oh, it's well written," he agreed, "but considerably overromanticized. The cannibals of the Marquesas, where I gather young Melville jumped ship and got the material for his book, are hardly the lovable natives leading the idyllic, unspoiled lives that he describes." He smiled grimly. "And although the Fayaways are quite willing to share their charms, unfortunately they also share their lice and certain unmentionable diseases they received from previous lovers who jumped ship."

The last remark, Jasmine suspected, was meant to shock her and determinedly she kept her face composed, although she felt a growing alarm as she watched her companion remove his jacket and hang it on a hook on the door.

Silently she fumed at her own stupidity. Instead of sitting, reading all day, she should have been trying to plan her escape. Surely there was one gentleman aboard the *Louisa*, she thought desperately, who would have helped her, if she had explained her predicament. But even as she thought this, she knew such a plan was futile from the beginning. No one aboard a whaler would raise his hand or voice against the captain. It would be the same as mutiny, and whaling captains were not noted for dealing leniently with mutineers.

The bitter truth was Morgan could do what he wished with her, just as he had the night of the *luau*, and there was no one to stop him. Especially now that he had a marriage license to legalize his ruthless behavior.

Remembering what had happened between the last time she had been in this cabin, she cringed inwardly, a terrible, enervating despair creeping over her, as if she could already feel his rough hands on her body arousing sensations that both frightened and appalled her.

Morgan turned and saw her staring at him, her hands clenched in her lap, her face drained of all color so that the dark eyes were enormous in her paper-white face. Irritably, because suddenly he felt damned foolish, he growled, "Well, don't you plan to go to bed? Or are you going to stay up all night reading?"

She took a deep, ragged breath. "I'm—I'm not tired. I think I will read for a while."

He shrugged indifferently. "As you wish, but would

you mind not reading in my bed? It's been a long day, and I'd like to get some sleep."

"Your bed?" She glanced around her, bewildered.

He indicated the sofa. "I'll be sleeping here. I'm often awakened during the night by the watch, so it's better that you take the cabin bed."

He saw the relief flooding her face and felt a quick jab of anger. Or was it wounded pride? he wondered wryly. In any case, he had no cause to complain at the position he found himself in. It was his own doing. "I gave my word to your parents," he said harshly. "I wouldn't . . . force myself upon you but would wait until you came to me of your own free will."

Jasmine still did not move, bewildered even as she was relieved at this unexpected turn of events. Why? Why should he agree to such a condition? she wondered, perplexed. She had no illusions about Morgan Tucker. He would never have gone to all the trouble he had gone to, tearing her from her home and family and bringing her aboard his ship, so that he could lead a celibate life. Of course, she thought suddenly, her face flaming. With his cocksure male arrogance, no doubt he expected it would only be a matter of time before she eagerly crawled into his bed. It was obvious that the only women he had known were wanton and abandoned native girls who delighted in giving their bodies to men. Why should he expect her to be any different?

She got swiftly to her feet, staring with cold loathing at her husband. Quite clearly he hadn't shaved since that morning, and there was a dark growth of beard on his broad face. The shirt he wore was old and dirt stained, and his dark hair was windblown, in need of a good brushing. She remembered how faultlessly groomed Jeremy had always been, with never a trace of a beard on his handsome face.

"Am I supposed to thank you for not brutally manhandling me as you did before?" she asked contemptuously. "Do you think I'll ever willingly share your bed? I'd sooner take a knife and shove it between your ribs!"

Then, at the darkness that suddenly flooded his face and the dangerous glitter in the dark, narrowed eyes staring at her, she realized she had gone too far, and she beat a hasty retreat to the cabin door. But not quickly enough. Her chin was caught in a powerful hand, the fingers forcing her to look up into a face that was filled with menace before his mouth descended on hers, ruthlessly forcing her lips apart as his hands moved over her body so that she could feel their warmth and persuasion through the cloth of her gown. When he abruptly pushed her away from him, she was breathing rapidly, her dark eyes wide and shining behind her lashes.

"I warned you once that I don't like being threatened," he said, his voice a low, angry growl. "And unless you want me to forget my promise to your parents, I suggest you retire to your cabin right now."

She didn't wait to be told twice. Quickly, with an indignant flounce of her skirt, she went into the cabin, closing the door loudly behind her.

It was late, though, before she fell asleep that night, so the sun was high above the horizon the next morning when she awoke and dressed. In the cold light of day, she realized how foolishly she had behaved the night before, losing her temper and deliberately baiting her captor. She should have had enough sense to know that she could never win a battle by pitting her slender strength against the captain's brawn. In the future, she must use her wits and a calm, indifferent composure that she sensed would protect her better than any insulting words she could fling at the man.

When Daniel brought her her breakfast, she noticed that the boy was distracted, and she asked, "Is something wrong?"

"Nothing to bother you, ma'am," he said quickly. "Just a little trouble in the forecastle, a new man we brought aboard in Honolulu."

Then he darted out the door, in his hurry not closing it securely, so the door swung open and Jasmine could hear the excited sound of men shouting and an odd thudding noise. Curious, she got to her feet and, passing through the adjoining stateroom and saloon, she climbed the companionway to the deck. The sounds seemed to be coming from between the forecastle and the quarterdeck, where she could see men gathered in a circle.

As she approached the waist of the ship, an older man turned and saw her approach. Quickly he left the circle and joined her. "I'm the first mate, Mrs. Tucker, Henry Gibbons. I'm glad to see you're well enough to come on deck, but I think, for just now, you'd best return below."

Where he had broken the circle she was able to see her husband and another man, both stripped to the waist, fighting with their bare fists. The thuds she had heard was the sickening sound of bone striking flesh. Although both men were broad-shouldered and burly, it was Morgan whose fists smashed expertly again and again into his opponent, turning the man's face into a bloody pulp. Morgan's own face, she saw, held no expression at all as his fists continued to inflict their punishing blows into the man who was staggering on his feet.

Jasmine heard her own voice, crying aloud as she struggled to get to the men to stop the carnage she was witnessing. "What are you doing? Stop it! For God's sake, you'll kill him!"

Chapter 11

She saw several seamen turn in surprise at hearing a woman's voice. Then she felt the first mate's hand on her arm as he escorted her down the companionway and back to the cabin. At the door of the cabin, she whirled upon the man. "How could you just stand there?" she cried. "Why didn't you stop them?"

Henry Gibbons frowned unhappily. "The man the captain was fighting, Mrs. Tucker, had refused to obey a direct order. Ever since we took him on in Honolulu, he's been surly and disobedient. The captain gave him a choice this morning. He could be put in irons the rest of the trip or he could fight it out with the captain. If he won, he could have a whaleboat to go wherever he chose; if he lost, he would turn to and pull his weight with the rest of the crew." At the horror he still saw in Jasmine's eyes, he sighed and said, "I know it seems hard, Mrs. Tucker, but I can tell you another captain would have flogged the man till he couldn't walk for a week. This way, at least the man had a chance of winning."

A chance, Jasmine thought. What chance did the man have against Morgan Tucker's fists?

The first mate hesitated a moment, then said, "You don't remember me, do you, Mrs. Tucker?"

She stared into the man's face. His hair was completely gray, although she guessed he was still in his thirties, his face sunburned, with deep-set, kindly eyes. "No, I'm sorry . . ."

"I sailed with your father. I was a harpooner then, and you were just a tiny tyke." He smiled. "I gave you a bit of scrimshaw for your fifth birthday."

Jasmine laughed, pleased. "I do remember. It was a beautifully carved box. I still use it as a jewel case. . . ."

Their conversation was interrupted by the sound of footsteps coming down the companionway. The next second, Morgan swung into view, carrying his shirt. A trickle of blood ran from one corner of his mouth, and there was a cut over one black, slanting brow. He scowled, glancing from Jasmine to his first mate.

"Why aren't you on deck, Mr. Gibbons? Your station's not in my quarters during this watch, is it?"

"No, Captain." The first mate quickly disappeared up the companionway.

Morgan brushed past Jasmine into the stateroom. Pouring water into the washbowl, he cleaned the blood from his face and hands, then, taking a bottle of whiskey, poured some of the alcohol into the cuts on his face, letting out a resounding oath as he did so.

"A gentleman," Jasmine said reprovingly, "wouldn't use such words in the presence of a lady."

Morgan toweled himself dry and slipped into his shirt, tucking the tail into the waist of his trousers before he turned to face her. "I never claimed to be a gentleman," he growled balefully. "And don't expect me to measure my words for you."

Stung by his brusqueness, she lifted her chin haughtily and turned to walk into her cabin when his voice stopped her. "One minute, madam. I have a few words to say to you."

She turned warily at the grim note in his voice. "I saw you on the deck," he said, "so I assume you've changed your mind and don't plan to spend the entire cruise in the stateroom. I have no objection to your going above deck, but you will walk only as far as the skid beams amidships, no farther. I shouldn't have to remind you that you are no longer a child roaming as you please on your father's ship. I'll not have the crew, officers or seamen, distracted from their jobs by your presence. You may speak to my officers and, if necessary, to the crew in the steerage. But you will hold no conversation with any of the men in the forecastle."

Jasmine bit back the angry words that sprang to her lips, grudgingly realizing that Morgan's words made a kind of sense.

"One more thing. I've no doubt the first mate told you to go below when you came on deck this morning. In the future, when you are given an order while you're above decks, by myself or my officers, you will obey instantly. Is that understood?"

When she did not answer, her chin thrusting out mutinously, his voice became ominously quiet, his straight dark brows lowering over narrowed eyes. "I asked you a question, madam. I want an answer."

"No!" she blurted. "I won't jump every time you snap your fingers. I'm not a member of your crew and I didn't come aboard your ship willingly. You can't brutalize me with your fists the way you almost killed that man on deck."

Listening to the defiance in her voice, Morgan's face darkened. Damn it, she had lived on a whaling ship. She should know that the deck of a whaler wasn't as safe as strolling the streets of Honolulu. There could be times when if she didn't obey a command immediately she could be badly hurt, even lose her life. "I've never raised my hand to a woman—yet," he said grimly. "But I can confine you to these quarters until you learn some sense." Deliberately he let his gaze roam in a leisurely fashion over her body, smiling tightly. "And there are other ways that I can enforce my authority, if necessary. Do I make myself clear, madam?"

Reluctantly Jasmine remembered the decision she had made when she had awakened that morning. She would win nothing by antagonizing the man. It was far wiser, for the moment, to at least pretend to give in gracefully.

She forced herself to swallow her anger, even as it threatened like a stone to choke her. She shrugged in cool disdain. "Very clear, Captain. There's no need to threaten me further. In the future, I'll obey your commands, above deck."

She added the last deliberately and had the satisfaction of seeing a muscle at the corner of Morgan's mouth twitch, although later she wasn't sure if it was from exasperation or amusement.

As it turned out, it was several days before she was able to venture above deck again. The seas turned rough, and the rain was heavy enough so that there wasn't a seaman posted in the topgallant crosstrees to keep a lookout for whales. Jasmine once more turned to Morgan's library for her entertainment. This time she struggled through one of James Fenimore Cooper's sea novels, which was much heavier going than Toby's adventures among the Typee tribe. She had already noted that most of the books were well worn, as if they had been read and reread. By whom? she wondered. The captain? If so, it presented a side to his character with which she was not acquainted, she thought bitterly.

She now ate her meals with her husband and his officers in the saloon, a small mess room off the captain's quarters containing a table with the stump of the mizzenmast rising through its center and fiddles around the edge of the table to keep the plates from sliding off in rough weather. The first mate, Mr. Gibbons, was always pleasant, but the second mate, John Turnbull, was a dour, taciturn New Englander who seldom spoke. The third mate, Harry Otis, was always too busy shoving food into his mouth to talk, although occasionally Jasmine caught a slyly amused look on his face when he glanced her way.

A few days out of Honolulu, the weather cleared, and as the *Louisa* drew closer to the equator, the cabin soon became too warm for comfort. Jasmine spent more of her time on deck, sitting under an awning that Mr. Gibbons had rigged for her, usually with a book in her hand, although she seldom turned a page. She was much too fascinated watching the activities going on around her.

She discovered that the crew on watch were never allowed a moment's idleness. If the men weren't scrubbing down the decks, fore and aft, they were wielding paintbrushes, checking and tightening the rigging, mending sails, or twisting the interminable yards of spun yarn that she remembered was used to wrap whalebone.

The harpooners, cooper, and blacksmith, who were neither foremast hands nor officers, lived in their own quarters in the steerage, and they also had no time for idle chatter. The harpooners never stopped polishing and sharpening the harpoons, lance points, and blubber tools hanging in racks around the ship; the boatsteerers painstakingly coiled whale line into tubs; the blacksmith plied his bellows; and the carpenter built the wooden barrels for the whale oil that would, it was hoped, be stored in the hold.

Although Jasmine kept her promise to Morgan and didn't talk to the seamen, she began to recognize certain faces among the crew: a high-cheekboned Narraganset Indian; several dark-faced Portuguese and Hawaiian men; three fresh-faced young men who looked as if they had just come off the farm; an elegant, sad-eyed man who, she learned from Mr. Gibbons, was a failed Shakespearean actor. There were a few men with grizzled beards and lined faces who seemed too old to be seamen but who climbed the rigging with an agility that put the younger men to shame. And there, too, were those burly men with unshaven faces and hard eyes who returned to a whaling ship because they had nowhere else to go.

Each day she watched as Morgan and the first mate conducted whaleboat drills. Every crewman was assigned to a station, and the whaleboats, hanging in iron davits on the port and starboard side of the ship, were hoisted quickly, on command, over the side. The last crew to get their oars in the water received an ear-scorching lambasting from the captain.

For hours at a time, the men bent at the oars, their muscles straining in the equatorial sun as Morgan shouted and swore at them, "Spring, boys, on your oars. Spring hard, I tell you. Now starn all!" Within a split second, the trim wooden whaleboats, pointed at both ends so that they could move more swiftly through the water, reversed course, turning almost in their own shadows. No matter how well they did, though, Morgan was never satisfied, working the men until the sweat ran down their backs and the blood dried on their raw hands and stuck to the oars.

"He'll kill them," Jasmine complained to the second mate, appalled at his cruelty.

For a second, the reticent look disappeared from John Turnbull's face as he replied tartly, "Better now than when they're facing a sperm whale head on."

Miffed, Jasmine returned to her cabin, yet she was aware over the next days of the grumbling among the crew, never loud enough, though, for the captain or officers to hear. Sometimes it seemed to Jasmine, as the *Louisa* moved gently over the rolling, even swells of the ocean, a trade wind ruffling the surface of the sea and filling the sails, that she could never get away from the sound of Morgan's bellowing voice.

One afternoon as she sat on deck, she watched one of the Hawaiian boys who had joined the ship at Honolulu being sent into the rigging for the first time. Halfway up to the double lookout hoops and fifty feet above deck, the young man froze, clinging terrified to the rigging as the mast swung in slow circles over a somnolent sea.

One of the men offered to climb up and bring the boy down, but Morgan, appearing on deck, said sharply, "Belay that!" Standing at the foot of the mainmast, he reared back and roared, "If you don't climb up to the lookout in ten seconds, *kanaka*, I'm coming up and dragging you down. If I do, you'll spend the rest of the cruise in the hold on bread and water." Jasmine made a sound of protest, and Morgan turned to glare icily at her before returning his fierce gaze upward. "Do you hear me?"

Evidently the boy did hear and was frightened enough

of the captain's threat that painfully, inch by inch, he pulled himself the rest of the way to the narrow platform and the waist-high double hoops one hundred feet above deck. After his two-hour watch searching for whales in the broad, empty sea, the lad swung down from the rigging to the deck. Jasmine saw that he looked slightly green, but he walked with a confident, almost swaggering step toward the forecastle.

That evening, she sat on the horsehair sofa reading while Morgan worked at his charts. She waited for him to say something about that afternoon. When he made no effort to speak to her, she finally snapped her book shut and demanded hotly, "Would you really have put that boy in the hold?"

Morgan turned, gazing absently at her. "Of course. A man who won't go into the rigging is useless on a whaler, as worthless as a captain whose crew won't obey his commands." Then, as if he had already forgotten her presence, he turned back to his charts.

Jasmine frowned at the back of his dark head. She knew he was concerned because the *Louisa* was still a clean ship, without a single whale having been spotted since they had left Honolulu. Still, he needn't act as if she didn't exist. He hadn't spoken a word to her all evening.

Pretending to stifle a yawn behind her hand, she got to her feet. "It's late. I'm going to bed."

Morgan did not look up, but as she went into her cabin and started to close the door behind her as she did every night, he said gruffly, "It's going to be a hot night. You'll get more air if you keep the door open."

She gave him a wary look, then said stiffly, "I prefer the door closed."

As it turned out, it was a hot night, without a breath of air stirring through the open port. The little cabin was stifling. After several hours of tossing and turning, the high-necked cambric nightgown Jasmine wore was damp with perspiration. Lighting the whale lamp, she shed the gown and had just slipped into a much cooler chemise when she felt something crawl across her bare foot. Her scream of pure horror brought Morgan crashing through the door just as the shiny black insect went scuttling off into a corner of the room.

"I—I can't endure cockroaches!" she wailed.

She had roused him out of a sound sleep over a cockroach, Morgan thought, aggravated until he saw that the slender body was trembling and the wide dark eyes were bright with unshed tears.

"I'll have Daniel put sulphur around the room tomorrow. Sometimes that helps, though you'd best get used to the creatures," he warned gruffly. "The hot weather always brings the vermin from below decks."

Then as she stared at him, he saw her eyes widen with dismay.

"Now what's wrong?"

Her face grew rosy pink, and she averted her eyes quickly. He remembered then that he had been sleeping nude and hadn't stopped to put on any clothes when he'd heard Jasmine scream.

"Great Jehoshophat, madam," he growled. "We're married, aren't we?" Then as she continued to keep her face turned away from him, he pulled a coverlet from the bed and wrapped it, toga fashion, around him.

He studied the girl standing before him in the sheer chemise, which barely covered her breasts and exposed a length of well-turned thigh and leg. "For myself, I find your own lack of attire most fetching," he murmured, amused.

She whirled to face him, crossing her arms across her breasts and glaring at Morgan, but he could see the fear gathering in her eyes.

"You needn't worry," he said curtly. "It's too hot a night for what you have in mind."

The words were a lie, though, for he could already feel the desire stirring in him, seeing her in that sheer bit of gown. Perspiration gleamed on her skin, giving her body a soft, burnished glow in the lamplight, and her black hair, hanging disheveled around her shoulders, reminded him of the way she had looked when he had first taken her in this room. He groaned silently to himself. It had been hellish enough these last weeks living in such close proximity to his wife and never touching her, but fully clothed, she was at least less of a temptation than she was now. The urge to forget his promise to her parents, to simply push her down on the bed and quickly possess her, was almost overwhelming.

As if she sensed what he was thinking, she reached hastily for the door. "I'm sorry I bothered you. It won't happen again. Good night, Captain."

His fierce gaze met hers like a blow, and she felt her breath stop in her throat. Time seemed to hang, suspended, between them. Her fate, she sensed, balanced precariously between his desire for her and the promise he had given her parents. At last, reluctantly, the narrowed eyes turned away. As she began to close the door, though, he swung back and kicked the door violently open.

"I'd like some air, madam, even if you don't," he snarled. His eyes flickered coldly over her. "Do you think that if I wanted to have you a door would stand in my way?"

Then he was gone into the darkness of the stateroom and Jasmine hastily climbed back into bed. Strangely enough, though, it wasn't the heat that kept her awake now or made her skin prickle. It was the memory of Morgan standing before her without his clothes, an indelible picture printed in her mind of broad, sloping shoulders, wide chest with the mat of black curly hair, narrow waist and hips and muscular thighs. She remembered how the muscles in his back and arms were not bunched but smoothly flowing beneath the skin. Even with a jagged scar that slashed across one hip, Morgan was a fine figure of a man, she thought almost grudgingly. Then she quickly pushed such an outlandish thought from her mind and tried to concentrate on sleeping. She wondered vaguely if she were coming down with a fever, feeling a formless, indefinable ache in her legs and arms.

The heat continued the next day and the next. The sun was a bright red ball caught in a pearl-colored sky. The men found excuses to work in the tiny patches of shade thrown by the masts and sails on the deck, and in the pen the last remaining pig squealed and grunted in the heat until a seaman took pity and threw a bucket of seawater over him.

Jasmine sat under the shade of her awning, trying to read, but the glaring reflection of the sun on the smooth sea made her eyes burn and the letters dance on the page. Yesterday she had been aware that the wind had been slowly diminishing, and this morning the breeze died completely. The ship was caught in a death-still calm. Aloft, the sails hung slack, the reef points barely moving.

The silence aboard the ship was so complete without the normal creak of the ship's timbers and the splash of her bow that when the call came suddenly from the lookout aloft, Jasmine jumped and dropped her book.

"Land, ho!"

She went to the rail, but all she could see was the ocean looking like a sheet of glass so that ship, clouds, and birds were reflected on its surface. On the quarter-deck, Morgan shouted to the lookout, "Where away?" She saw him look up through the tangled network of rigging to where the lookout was pointing.

"On the port beam!" the man called.

Morgan swept the horizon with his telescope then snapped the glass shut. The men crowded at the rail, pointing and talking loudly. Jasmine turned to the third mate, who had come up beside her, his eyes squinting against the sun, and she saw his eyes held the same uneasiness she was feeling. "Is something wrong?" she asked. "Won't it be cooler when we get near land?"

"There's a lot worse than being inconvenienced by a little heat," he replied, gesturing toward the shimmering horizon. "Those are the Gilberts, cannibal islands, we're drifting toward. If the wind doesn't get up, we can pile up on the reef and the cannibals will swarm all over the ship in a matter of minutes. Or their warriors will come out in canoes even before we reach the reef and try and take the ship. They got a special hankering for man-meat, boiled or baked or just raw—don't matter to them. I hear tell how the chiefs always get the favored parts, the eyes and the intestines, or bash in a man's skull like it was a coconut and eat the brains."

Jasmine felt the sour taste of nausea rising in her throat, and though she longed to look away, it was as if the man's eyes had crept underneath her bonnet and she was trapped by his loose-lipped grin.

"Belay that talk, Mr. Otis." The first mate came up beside them. "You want to spook the men?" Then he saw Jasmine's face and said quickly, "No cause for alarm, Mrs. Tucker. The wind will rise by tonight, and if not, more than likely the natives will just want to barter."

However, the ship was still becalmed the next morning when Jasmine arose early, but not as early as Morgan, who had already eaten and was on the quarterdeck, studying the sky and horizon for any sign of a breeze, when she came on deck.

She could see the coast of land now in the distance as the sun climbed steadily in the pearly sky. Gradually she was able to make out an island, green vegetation, and water breaking on the beach. The seamen had seen the island, too, and were once again lining the rail, pointing, but their voices were subdued now. Jasmine noticed that they kept glancing to the quarterdeck, where Morgan stood, surveying the horizon with his glass. Their faces, she saw, were not resentful now. They watched the captain anxiously, as if they knew that their very lives could depend on the decisions he made in the next couple of hours.

Then a murmur ran through the men. Jasmine saw an arm pointing, then another, toward the shore, where a number of black specks moved between the island and the reef. Despite the blazing heat beating down on her head, she felt suddenly cold, her mouth dust-dry. She could see the canoes more clearly now, fanning out toward the ship and reminding Jasmine of black waterbugs skimming the surface of the ocean.

She moved away from the rail toward the quarterdeck, looking wildly around her as if for somewhere to flee. But where? There was only the tiny ship and the ocean stretching like a glass wall all around her. She heard the bosun's whistle sounding, mustering the men, who assembled quickly in rows facing aft, toward the captain.

Morgan spoke quietly, but his voice carried across the deck. "The natives coming in their canoes may or may not be friendly. We'll take no chances and allow none of them aboard." He glanced toward the cabin boy and the steward. "Bring on deck all the guns from below, load them, and stack them against the mizzenmast. They will be used by the officers. The rest of you men will be given cutting knives, lances, and axes and will be stationed in the bow and stern and amidships. Any loose ropes dangling over the sides of the ship will be pulled on deck. If the savages look like they're coming alongside, threaten them with your weapons. Then if they try to climb aboard, jab at them with the lances; if necessary, slice off their hands. No guns will be fired unless I give the command. Once the savages see we don't fear them, they'll clear off."

Morgan's narrowed gaze passed along each row of men, touching each man's face in turn. Jasmine, watching, was startled to see a devil-may-care twinkle in his eyes. His voice was almost jovial as he added, "If you do exactly as your officers tell you, you'll all live to have a fine yarn to spin at the next gam."

A murmur of laughter ran through the assembled men. Then as if suddenly remembering Jasmine, Morgan took two quick strides to her side. "You'll wait below, Mrs. Tucker," he ordered, his dark eyes searching her face, although she had no idea what he was seeking there.

Jasmine ran her tongue over her dry lips, wondering

if the panic she was feeling showed in her eyes. She was aware of the glances of the men watching her curiously. To see if the captain's wife was afraid? she wondered, a fear that she sensed could be contagious. She forced herself to stiffen her shoulders. She was a whaling captain's daughter, wasn't she? Her father would never forgive her if he learned his daughter had turned out to be a coward.

She inclined her head graciously toward Morgan and walked, her chin held high, toward the companionway as slowly and calmly as if she were going down to the cabin for her afternoon nap.

Once she reached the quarters, though, she hurried into the cabin and looked out the port. At first all she could see was the sea, with an oily sheen, dazzling in the sunlight. On the deck above she could hear the hurried footsteps of the steward and cabin boy, running up and down the companionway, bringing guns on deck, and of the men taking their stations around the ship.

For fifteen minutes then, it was quiet. She could hear the water washing alongside the ship. Suddenly there was a new sound that she recognized as paddles dipping into water as slender canoes filled with savages pulled closer to the *Louisa*. Five and six deep, the canoes gathered on either side of the ship. From her vantage point, Jasmine could glimpse an occasional canoe close enough now so that she could make out blue-black bodies, tattooed faces, and frizzy black hair. The savages were swinging war clubs and spears, and a particularly frightening weapon: a row of shark's teeth edged to a strip of coconut wood that could swipe through a man's face.

Jasmine stared as if hypnotized at the faces of the cannibals, the dazzling whites of their eyes, the grotesque tattoos on their skin, their glittering teeth as they yelled excitedly and brandished their weapons threateningly toward the ship. It was an hour before the savages were gathered in an armada around the ship. The bloodthirsty yells and shrieks of the warriors rose to a crescendo, sending tremors down Jasmine's spine and making her flesh crawl.

She put her hands over her ears and left the cabin for the saloon. The hatch closed over the companionway muffled the frightening sounds. Then she heard a crashing, bumping sound as the attack on the ship commenced, and the savages dropped their paddles and reached out for the chain plates attempting to board. She could hear the shouts of the men and imagine them jabbing with their lances at the cannibals swarming up the sides of the *Louisa*. And she heard the shrieks of the savages as they splashed back into the water, minus hands and arms.

Jasmine sat clutching at the fiddle on the table in the saloon, her eyes fastened on the companionway. It sounded like mass confusion above deck. Had the savages managed to climb aboard? she wondered. Were they even now slaughtering the men of the *Louisa*? How soon would they find the hatch, tumble down the companionway, and find her?

The noise seemed to slacken somewhat and then she heard the explosion of a gun, making her jerk her head upward. Then as she sat, frozen with fear, she saw the hatch rising, a sliver of light falling down into the saloon, and feet descending the companionway.

Chapter 12

For a second longer Jasmine sat, numb with fear. Then she leaped to her feet, panic-stricken, her eyes searching the cabin looking for some weapon, any weapon, to defend herself. She remembered that there were knives in the pantry off the saloon. When Daniel swung the rest of the way down the companionway, he found the captain's wife waiting for him, her face bleached white, but with a knife clutched in a very businesslike fashion in her hand.

"The captain sent me to tell you it's all over," he said, looking a little nervous until Jasmine let the knife fall from her suddenly nerveless hand to the floor.

She sank down in a chair then asked anxiously, "Is anyone hurt?"

"A couple of men were wounded. The second mate got a bad cut in his arm, but he'll be all right. We drove them off twice," he said proudly. "Then the wind started rising, and I guess the savages knew it wasn't any use. We weren't going to drift onto the reef."

"I thought I heard a gunshot."

Daniel laughed. "That was the captain. One of the savages—he looked like a chief—stood up in his canoe before they left and showed his backside . . . begging your pardon," he said, flushing, remembering to whom he was talking. "Anyway," he finished hastily, "the captain's musket was loaded with buckshot. I don't suppose that chief will be sitting down comfortably for a while."

Jasmine laughed, too, and if there was a touch of hysteria in the laughter, she hoped the cabin boy didn't notice. She was surprised that Morgan had even thought to send the boy to tell her the battle was over. It was obvious he had forgotten all about her when he had been making plans to defend the ship. Not that she should have expected anything else, she thought later that evening as she took the air on deck before retiring for the night.

The breeze that had fortunately risen that afternoon still hummed through the rigging above her, while the mast tops seemed almost to spear the multitude of stars hanging low in the mild Pacific night. She leaned over the ship's side and watched the phosphorescent spangles dance upon the water, the sea fires flashing along the hull and gilding the wake.

Caught up by the tranquil beauty of the night, she forgot her irritation with Morgan. She didn't even hear the footsteps come up behind her until his voice interrupted her reverie. Her nerves still on edge, she whirled, her hands outflung.

In the bright starlight, she could see the laughing golden flecks in Morgan's eyes as he teased, "You weren't planning to pull a knife on me the way you did on poor Daniel?"

So he thought it was funny, did he? Jasmine thought irritably. Did he even care that she had spent the afternoon huddled below deck, scared half out of her wits?

"I fail to see the humor in knowing that I might have been murdered by those savages," she said icily.

The laughter faded from his eyes as he scowled down at her. Did she really think he would have let those savages touch her? But he sensed his anger was with himself rather than Jasmine. It was, after all, his doing. She wouldn't have been in any danger at all if he hadn't forced her aboard his ship. At the time, it had seemed the only thing to do, partly because his pride would not let him admit that any woman had bested him and partly to slake his desire for her, which had never left him, even when she most infuriated him.

Now, as he stared down into her face, the starlight placing a cool, silver patina across her delicate features, he had the uncomfortable feeling that he had been hoist with his own petard. His wife was as remote from him at this moment as if he had, in fact, left her behind in Honolulu. Only, at least, in Honolulu she would have been safe from the horror of a cannibal attack. For the first time, he considered how frightened Jasmine must have felt, trapped below deck with the noise of the battle going on overhead. Yet she hadn't complained afterwards or had womanly hysterics, as he might have expected.

Awkwardly groping for the words, because apologies

were alien to him, he said slowly, "I'm sorry you were frightened." He reached out to tuck a curl that had been pulled free by the evening breeze back beneath the shawl she wore over her head. "I suppose I thought you knew that I would never let any harm come to you."

Jasmine was caught and held by the piercing intensity of that gaze on her face, by the way the starlight etched the strong curve of Morgan's mouth, by remembering, suddenly, disturbingly, the feel and shape of that mouth on her own.

Searching for a conversational topic to fill the odd, breathless silence that had fallen between them, she glanced up at the sky and said, "When I was a little girl on my father's whaler, on a night like this he'd take me on deck and tell me the names of the stars. He always promised that when I was older, he'd teach me how to navigate." Her voice became wistful. "Of course, when he left the sea, he never did."

"I can teach you something of navigation," Morgan said cautiously, "if you'd like."

"Oh, yes, I would," she said eagerly, and then, smiling, she reached out and touched a tear in his shirt. "In return, I'll mend your shirts." It was time, she decided, that someone other than an indifferent cabin boy looked after the captain's apparel.

"Tending my clothes is a chore I'm sure Daniel will give up gladly," Morgan said. He added absently, "Since we've several wounded men on our hands, Daniel will have to move to the forecastle, anyway. We'll need another hand in the whaleboats."

"He's too young for such work," Jasmine protested at once.

Then she fell silent as Morgan slanted a stern brow at her. "I was Daniel's age when I went into the forecastle."

Reluctantly Jasmine made no further protest. She was beginning to recognize the danger signals when she pushed her husband too far: the tightened lips and the dark brows slanting angrily above hazel eyes. If she objected anymore, she was sure he would remind her sharply that running the ship was his business, not hers.

The next week, despite her unhappiness about Daniel's move to the forecastle, she and Morgan maintained a wary truce. He kept his promise and gave her daily lessons in navigation. Jasmine proved an apt pupil and was soon methodically taking observations, peering at the chronometer with painstaking care and marking the latitude and longitude exactly as Morgan did, without the deviation of a second.

She, in turn, mended his torn shirts and trousers and even washed his clothes with hers on deck, occasionally stopping to watch, delighted, a porpoise leap playfully through the water or a silvery flying fish with gauzelike wings skim the snowy crests of a wave.

It was one morning while she was hanging her wash on a makeshift clothesline—the spanker boom—and watching an albatross lazily circling the ship by drifting along the wind currents without moving a wing that she was startled to hear a cry from the masthead. "There she blows! There, there!"

Immediately, the ship exploded into action. Men off duty came bursting from the forecastle and headed for the rail to look for the whale while others, on watch, stopped work to join them.

Morgan appeared at the foot of the mast and shouted up to the lookout, "Where away?"

"On the starboard bow, three points alee!"

"How far? What does it look like?"

"Less than a mile. It's a sperm whale coming right this way." Then, in a bellow, "She breaches! She breaches!"

Jasmine could not see the wispy spout of mist that the whale exhaled from its blowhole several feet into the air as it surfaced to breathe. But she could see that the creature seemed to leap out of the water, then crashed back into the sea so that a wall of water rose behind it.

Morgan was rapidly giving orders calmly, not shouting. "Call all hands, Mr. Gibbons," he said. "Stand by to run down to him. Bring me my glass, steward. Get the boats ready. Little more to starboard. Little more. Hustle with those boats, but quiet now."

Jasmine retreated to the quarterdeck, out of the way of the whaleboat crews, who were rushing to put all the necessary equipment aboard. The men completed their tasks in a few short minutes, removed their shoes, then eagerly stood alongside the whaleboats, swinging in their davits.

Morgan was continuing his steady stream of orders to the helmsman. "Keep her steady, I say. Steady. Stand by to brace round the yards. We don't want to run down into her. Helm a little more to starboard. Steady now. Not too close. Don't want to gally her till the iron's fast. Ready with those yards. Main topsail aback!"

As the men hauled at the yards and the big sail eased around, Morgan gave the last order, "Clear away your boats. . . ."

Four whaleboats swung down onto the water with Morgan standing, spread-legged, in the stern of the lead boat. The wind whipped his hair back from his face, his shirt billowing around him. For just a moment, Jasmine saw his face, which was filled with a dark, brooding intensity that she had never seen before, and she knew with a stab of resentment that he had forgotten her again. His whole being was concentrated on that point in the ocean where the whale had been and was no more. But at least she was pleased to see that Daniel was in Morgan's boat.

Mr. Turnbull ordinarily would have commanded one of the whaleboats, but because of his injured arm he had been left behind in temporary command of the ship, with the cooper acting as helmsman. The mate handed Jasmine a telescope. "You can see better with a glass."

Gratefully she placed the spyglass to her eye, but even with the glass, the four whaleboats, pulling farther and farther away from the ship, looked tiny and fragile in the immense ocean. She could see Morgan holding the steering oar and facing forward while the rest of the men rowed, facing him.

She remembered her father telling her years before that the men always went shoeless in whaleboats so that they wouldn't make any noise and frighten the whale away. By the same token, the men always rowed facing the steerer so that they wouldn't be thrown into a panic by the sight of the whale rising from the ocean within a stone's throw of the boat.

"Do you suppose the whale's still there?" she asked Mr. Turnbull as the boats reached the site where the whale had made his dive. The boats hove to, rolling gently in the Pacific swells, waiting for the whale to surface again.

"Could be," the man said dourly. "Or he could be racing off miles in another direction before coming up for air again."

But even as the man spoke, Jasmine saw a gigantic, glistening black mass, like a mountain breaking the surface of the water, a boat's length away from one of the whaleboats. She stared, awestruck, at the whale, which was almost half the length of the whaler on which she stood. Its great tail, fanning the air and churning the water, was itself as large as a whaleboat. In the boat, the harpooner stood poised, holding the heavy harpoon, which was raised like a child's toy over the gigantic beast, with both hands.

Then the harpoon flashed downward deep into the whale's blubber. The shock of the iron entering his body sent the enormous creature rearing half out of the water; Jasmine could see the immense teeth and huge jaws viciously snapping the air. When its flukes struck the water, she could hear a distant boom, like thunder roll across the sea. The water around the struggling, pain-maddened whale was churned into a fury of splashing white water. The tiny whaleboat was caught in the foaming maelstrom.

Behind her, she could hear the second mate, sounding excited for the first time, carrying on a running commentary. "The boat's fast, now stern all, lads! Back away hard! Careful, he's coming up. There goes flukes . . . white water . . . watch it, boys. Wet the line!"

Finally the animal began to weaken, plunging, but not as deeply as before; its body rolling, exhausted, in the swell. The second mate said almost crooningly, "Now lay her close, boys. Ahead now, ahead!" The tiny whaleboat was almost nudging the beast, which was floating on the surface. "Now, Skipper! Set the lance. Give him a good dance!"

Morgan had changed places with the harpooner in the gunwale of the boat. At the last second, as the whale lifted his head, his massive jaws opening as if he meant to crush the boat to splinters, Morgan hurled a lance with deadly efficiency at a point near the whale's eye. A second lance quickly followed the first.

The whale bellowed like a distant foghorn. In its death throes, the creature spouted into the air a fountain of steam, first pink then bright red, showering the men in the boat with blood and staining the sea. Petrels danced over the water, their wings fluttering as they fed on the blood.

"They have him now," the second mate said triumphantly. "His chimney is afire."

He turned to his companion and discovered, chagrined, that the captain's wife was swaying, her face alarmingly pale.

The second mate snorted disapprovingly. "I thought from what Mr. Gibbons told me you were raised on a whaler. Surely you've seen whales killed before, Mrs. Tucker."

Jasmine shook her head. "Mother would never allow me to watch." Now she knew why, she thought, shuddering. Always before, she had thought of a whale as simply a large-sized fish. Now, watching the animal being coldly murdered, she realized it had been a breathing, feeling creature, as magnificent in death as it had been in life. The dizziness passed, and she gave the second mate an imploring glance. "You won't tell the captain?"

The second mate shook his head. He remembered suddenly the first time he had commanded a whaleboat and given the mortal thrust to his first whale. As the whale had wallowed in its own blood, writhing in its final agony, he remembered uncomfortably how he had plunged the iron deeper into the wound, twisting it until the whale blew its blood, a terrible, almost human groan coming from the head of the animal. When the rain of clotted blood had descended over him, he had felt all at once sick to his stomach, not just at having murdered the creature, but with the guilty knowledge that he had found a shocking, savage pleasure in the killing.

He gazed somberly out to where the men in the whaleboat were now beginning the weary business of securing the whale. Since the breeze had almost died away, they would have to break their backs at the oars towing the giant carcass back to the whaler for cutting up and trying out. "Don't be forgetting," he said to the captain's wife, "that there's many a whaling man who's died with a whale. The whaleboat can be smashed to kindling by one sideswipe of the fluke, every soul aboard drowned, or crushed in the whale's jaws. Once a whale even sunk a whaler, the *Essex*. You've heard the tale?"

Jasmine nodded. She had heard the story from her father years before of how the whaler, rammed by a whale, had sunk immediately. The men who survived had drifted for months in their tiny whaleboats; finally, when their food was exhausted, they had turned to cannibalism, eating the bodies of their shipmates to stay alive.

The thought sent a wave of dizziness through Jasmine making her unsteady on her feet again, and she decided she had had enough of whales for one day and retired to her cabin.

She stayed below deck for the next two days while the whale was lashed to the side of the ship, causing the *Louisa* to groan and tilt at a sharp angle. The blubber was cut from the whale's body in great strips with a ripping, cracking sound by men perched dangerously on a wooden platform slung over the side of the ship; the platform was dangerously slippery with the whale's blood and oil. Afterwards, the blubber was cut into still-smaller pieces and slowly cooked in the trypots. Thick black smoke rose from the pots, blackening the sails and the men who worked in the ankle-deep gore and grease around the pots. The foul odor from the boiling blubber enveloped the whole ship so that even below deck Jasmine could not get away from the stench.

Once at night she ventured onto the deck, but the sickening smell from the blubber, the booming sheets of flame shooting upward into the yardarms, the black, greasy smoke, and the suddenly illuminated faces of the half-naked men around the trypots reminded her of a charnel house and sent her quickly below again.

She saw very little of Morgan, for he was kept busy night and day supervising the cutting up and trying out of the whale, hardly taking time to snatch a bite to eat. When he did sit down with his officers at the saloon table, all they talked about was how many barrels of oil the whale would make. "Ninety barrels, I'll wager," Mr. Gibbons said. "Not forgetting the four hundred gallons of spermaceti and the whalebones that will bring us a tidy sum in New Bedford. Too bad, though, we found no ambergris in him."

Jasmine knew the smooth, waxy spermaceti was especially valuable, burning brighter than any other whale oil, while ambergris was a much-sought-after fixative for perfume. But she also remembered that spermaceti was dripped like melted butter from the head of the whale and that ambergris formed only in the intestines of sick sperm whales. Suddenly she no longer felt hungry and, pushing her plate away, retired again to her cabin.

She told herself that she was being foolish. After all, it was the purpose of a whale ship to catch and kill whales. Whatever money the whale oil brought in New

Bedford was split among the owner of the ship, the officers, and the men, as their pay, or lay, for the voyage. And without whale oil, homes would be back to using primitive, sputtering candles for illumination.

Nevertheless, even after the trying out ended and what was left of the whale was tossed to the sharks who had been circling the *Louisa* for days, the memory of the whale's death, Morgan's lance thrusting into the writhing body, and the bright red gushing fountain of blood stayed with her. Just as the smell of oil turning rancid in the casks remained with the ship. Determinedly she tried to hide her feelings from Morgan and was sure she had succeeded. She could not have known that Morgan was well aware that Jasmine's glance no longer met his directly and that there was a subtle difference in her attitude toward him and not for the better.

She still kept the door open, though, between her stateroom and the outer cabin. Sometimes at night, unable to sleep, he would stand quietly in the doorway, listening to the sound of her soft breathing. When there was enough moonlight filtering through the port, he would study hungrily the pale curve of breast and thigh he could just glimpse through the chaste white nightgown; Jasmine's mouth, half parted, temptingly; her face, relaxed, without the guarded look that he usually saw in her eyes when she glanced at him. Then, feeling vaguely guilty at violating her privacy, he would dress and go up on deck, where he would pace back and forth until the aching need within him subsided or until dawn streaked the horizon pink and gold.

It was on one such night, when the *Louisa* had been zigzagging up and down along the Line for a month, that he made his decision. He couldn't go on this way. It was clear that Jasmine had no interest in sharing his bed, and, after giving his word to her parents, he would not bed his wife by force even if, he thought grimly, the idea did have a certain appeal.

He had planned to cruise to the Marquesas and then follow the coast of California to the offshore grounds near the Galapagos Islands before setting a course for New Bedford. Now he decided that after stopping at the Marquesas for wood and supplies, he would take the *Louisa* directly around the Cape and home, ending this ridiculous farce of a marriage once and for all.

The next day in his cabin, he told Jasmine of his decision. "Once we reach New Bedford, you can start divorce proceedings," he said brusquely. "I'll take care of your return passage to Hawaii, of course."

Jasmine had been mending a pair of his trousers. Now she looked up, startled, at his words. "But the year won't be up till . . ." Then she felt her face grow warm at his appraising glance and she changed tack quickly. "If you cut your cruise in half, won't you end up in New Bedford with your hold only half full?"

Although the *Louisa* had taken three more whales, they had been small and female, yielding only thirty barrels each. She knew the men would be disappointed if the cruise were cut short. Their percentage of the lay was small to begin with. They could end up back in New Bedford with only a few dollars in their pockets to show for their years spent at sea aboard the *Louisa*.

But, of course, she supposed that how the men felt didn't matter to Morgan. It was evident that all he cared about was getting rid of her as soon as possible. "I'll pay my own way back to Hawaii," she said coldly. "As you may recall, this sea voyage was not my . . ."

"She blows! There she bloooows!"

The cry brought Jasmine to her feet. It couldn't be, she thought, surprised, even as she raced after Morgan up the companionway. A storm had risen early in the morning and the *Louisa* had been lying to under shortened canvas, drifting on a slanting course before the wind.

When Jasmine stepped out on deck, the wind, filled with salt spray, struck her full in the face, blinding her for a moment before she saw the seamen at the starboard rail jumping up and down with excitement and pointing out toward the sea. Holding tightly to the bulwark, her skirt whipping around her, she edged forward until she, too, saw the quarry. Not one whale but a school of them, and not more than a hundred yards away. They were gamboling, like children at the beach, climbing to the crests of the great green waves and then sliding down into the troughs. The storm might not even have existed as far as they were concerned.

The second and third mates joined Morgan with Mr. Otis cursing softly. "There's thousands of dollars just waiting to be harpooned. I say we go after them."

Mr. Turnbull frowned at the man. "We can't put boats out in this storm."

Mr. Gibbons joined them, squinting at the sky to windward, where black and gray clouds clashed and separated. "The wind's dropping, sir," he said to Morgan. "And the sky's clearing a little to the southeast. If we lowered the boats to leeward, we might harpoon one of them and keep him alongside until the wind drops."

The crew in their oilskins huddled together, turning their gaze toward Morgan and waiting eagerly for his reply.

Morgan's gaze swept the faces of the men thoughtfully, then he announced, "Volunteers only. No one will be blamed for staying behind. And all boats are to stay close together."

Jasmine gazed at her husband, shocked. It was madness going after a whale with the sea this high. But already a dozen men had eagerly stepped forward and were dashing for the boats. To her dismay, she saw that Daniel was one of the volunteers, flashing her a brief boyish grin of excitement as he helped ready the captain's whaleboat.

Impulsively she reached out and tugged at Morgan's sleeve. "Not Daniel, please, Morgan."

His scowling look quelled her, his voice curt. "He's a man. Would you have me shame him before the rest of the crew by refusing to take him with me?"

Then at the stricken look in her dark eyes, the salt spray like tears on her eyelashes, he reached out and brushed her cheek with his hand. "You're not to worry," he ordered gruffly. "With the oil we take from these whales, we'll have a full hold when we reach New Bedford."

Then he was gone, shouting orders as the boats were launched and men sprang into them even as they were being lowered over the side.

This time it was the first mate who was left behind to command the ship. He stood beside Jasmine and watched as the school of whales, with lazy strokes of their great tails, tacked and swam away from the ship, with the three whaleboats in close pursuit. In the great, mountainous waves, the whales and the tiny boats were soon hidden from sight by a nearly vertical wall of green.

The first mate turned to Jasmine. "You'd be more comfortable waiting below," he suggested. "It'll be several hours before they return."

But looking into the man's kindly face and seeing the strained tightness around his mouth, she knew the same worried question was echoing in his mind, too. In that terrible sea, would the boats return at all?

Chapter 13

Jasmine stayed in her cabin for an hour, and then, unable to endure the suspense of waiting any longer, she wrapped a scarf around her hair and went above deck. The sky was still gray black, but the wind had died a little, although it still pulled her skirt around her and tugged at her scarf. When Mr. Gibbons saw that the captain's wife was determined to stay on deck, he arranged a place for Jasmine in the small room where vegetables and extra gear were stored.

Every ten minutes, she left her shelter to walk across the slanting deck to the rail, her eyes narrowed against the wind, scanning the ocean, as if willing the boats to appear. It was two hours before the first whaleboat arrived back at the ship, and another hour before the second, incredibly towing a whale alongside, appeared. Each time, as the wet, exhausted men scrambled back aboard the *Louisa*, the first mate questioned them closely. Had they seen the captain's boat?

The second and third mates, glancing toward Jasmine, lowered their voices as they spoke to Mr. Gibbons. The fear that had been locked inside of Jasmine now clawed at her like a tiny animal trying to escape a cage. When the first officer returned to her side, she said before the man could speak, "The captain's boat is lost, isn't it?"

"We don't know that for sure, Mrs. Tucker," the man said quickly. "Mr. Otis said he saw the harpooner in the captain's boat set his iron into a whale almost the same time they harpooned their own whale. He said he saw the whale turn upon the captain's boat; he thought its fluke whipped against the stern, but he isn't sure. Their own boat was dragged for half a mile before Otis managed to lance her. By the time they got back, the captain's boat was gone. They searched for about an hour, but the waves were too high. They thought that perhaps the captain had returned to the ship, and since it was growing dark, they decided they'd better head back, too."

"We have to send boats out right away to look for them," Jasmine cried, her hand clutching unconsciously at the arm of the first mate.

Mr. Gibbons shook his head. "It won't do, Mrs. Tucker. It'll be dark in an hour. We'll have to wait till morning."

Morning, Jasmine thought frantically. By morning it could be too late. No crippled boat could survive in that sea, and if the men aboard had already been swept overboard . . .

"You musn't give up hope, Mrs. Tucker," the first mate said. "It's a good sign that Otis didn't see any floating debris. We'll light the lanterns along the bulwarks and at the masthead so that the captain can find the ship."

Jasmine's agitated gaze roamed the deck. Surely there was something more they could do than just light lanterns. Her glance was caught by the brick tryworks. "We could start a fire in the tryworks," she said eagerly. "The blaze could be seen farther than the lanterns."

Mr. Gibbons frowned and shook his head. "In this wind, there's too much danger of the fire spreading, of a spark getting into the rigging. The captain wouldn't want us to gamble the *Louisa* against his safety, Mrs. Tucker," he said gently.

Frustrated, Jasmine turned away but knew that he was right. It was odd, the way he kept calling her Mrs. Tucker, she thought irrelevantly, her eyes straying back to the empty, storm-tossed sea. She supposed he had always called her Mrs. Tucker, but somehow she had never thought of the words before in connection with herself. Jasmine Tucker. She sounded the words quietly to herself. The wife of Captain Morgan Tucker, out of New Bedford. The words fit her tongue as if they belonged there.

Perhaps, though, not wife but widow, she thought suddenly, and a pain like she had never felt before slammed into her body like a gale-force wind, tearing the breath from her lungs. How could she be a widow, she thought wildly, when she'd never been a wife? And now, angrily, she knew it was too late. Too late to be a real wife to Morgan. She thought of the times when she had watched Morgan working in the cabin, or when he would join her in the evening on deck, and she had thought: now . . . now if he would make some tender, loving gesture toward her, but she was always too stubborn and proud herself to make the first move. And because of her stubborn pride, for the rest of her life all that unspent love would be there, festering inside of her. The pain struck at her again. If Morgan's officers hadn't been there watching her, she would have screamed aloud with the pain. But she knew that Morgan wouldn't want his wife breaking down, having hysterics before his men.

She tightened the knot of her scarf beneath her chin and straightened her shoulders. "You're right, Mr. Gibbons. A fire in the tryworks wouldn't be a good idea in this wind." She forced herself to smile faintly, reassuringly, into the man's worried face. "I'll—I'll wait below."

At least in the privacy of her own cabin she could allow the tears to come. Except, she discovered, she couldn't seem to cry. She sat, dry-eyed, on the sofa with an open book in her hand, but the words blurred and slipped away. Morgan seemed to fill the cabin with his presence: his dark head bent intently over the charts; the breadth of his shoulders filling the chair; his quick, impatient movements that tore the seams of his shirt no matter how often she mended them; the hazel eyes that lightened, gold-flecked, when he smiled and darkened when he scowled.

She didn't want to go to bed, but finally she lay down on the sofa and realized, with a new sense of guilt and self-reproach, how hard and uncomfortable the sofa, —too short, really, for the length of his body—must have been for Morgan, sleeping here all these months. Exhausted, she dozed, then jerked awake when she saw the first faint pink light of dawn coming into the room; almost at the same moment, she heard shouting on deck and a horn being sounded over and over.

Without bothering to tie on her scarf, she rushed up the companionway, almost running headlong into Mr. Gibbons, who was coming to fetch her. "The lookout's spotted a boat to the starboard." He thrust the glass into her hand. "See for yourself."

At first she could see nothing but the empty sea, the waves quieter, a paler green. Now that the wind had died and the storm had passed, the horizon was shot with pink and gold. Then she saw the boat, a tiny chip tossing in the swells like a child's plaything. The men were slumped, exhausted, at the oars, and the boat was not so much making its way toward the *Louisa* as the whaler, its sails still furled, was drifting toward the whaleboat.

It was another hour before the whaleboat was nosing the ship's side. The men gathered, talking excitedly among themselves at the rail as they saw the hole in the bow of the boat covered with a makeshift canvas. Mr. Gibbons began to snap orders. "Stand aside, there. Watch that hoisting tackle! Can't you see there's injured men aboard her?"

The men were carefully hauled onto the deck of the *Louisa*: first, the two injured men, one who could walk, though unsteadily, and the second, Daniel, hauled aboard in a sling. There was a blood-stained cloth tied around his head; his blond hair was also blood-stained, so the hair looked black against a blue-white face. The boy's eyes were closed, and Jasmine, rushing to his side, thought for one terrifying moment that he was dead. Then she saw the slight movement of the chest beneath a torn and soaking-wet shirt.

Then Morgan was beside her on the deck, and her relief at seeing him was so great that she almost threw herself into his arms, but he was already bending over Daniel, gently covering the boy with a blanket that the first mate had handed him. "Get the lad to the fo'-c'sle," he commanded. "And fetch the medicine chest."

"No!" Jasmine ignored the startled glances cast in her direction. She faced Morgan, her dark eyes blazing. "Take him to the captain's cabin," she ordered. She wouldn't have Daniel in that dark, airless forecastle, she thought indignantly.

A tired grin tugged at the corner of Morgan's mouth. He nodded at the first mate. "You heard Mrs. Tucker."

As soon as the boy was placed on the sofa in the captain's cabin, Jasmine undressed him quickly then tenderly toweled the shivering young body dry and wrapped him in another blanket. Only then did she carefully remove the stiff, blood-soaked cloth from around the boy's head, and she gave a small gasp of dismay when she saw the deep, jagged cut in the flesh. "What happened?" she asked Morgan as she bathed the boy's wound and wrapped a fresh bandage around his head.

"We put the iron in the whale, but he turned and stove in our boat then took off, with our line still in him. Daniel grabbed a knife and managed to cut the line, but he was thrown overboard. He must have hit his head when he went into the water. I think he may have a couple of broken ribs, too."

"How long has he been unconscious?"

"A few hours. At first I thought it was a blessing, but he should have come around by now." Morgan frowned as he gazed down at the boy. "I'll get the medicine chest."

"I'll take care of Daniel," Jasmine said, studying Morgan's face, which was gaunt with exhaustion, the white lines by his mouth standing out like scars and salt caking the dark lashes. "You get out of those wet clothes," she said firmly, "and into bed."

Morgan shook his head groggily. "They'll be cutting the whale. I'll be needed on deck."

"Mr. Gibbons can handle the trying out. You need rest."

Morgan looked around him. "I could sling a hammock in here."

"Don't be foolish," Jasmine said, exasperated. "Use my . . . the bed in the cabin." She could already hear the sounds on deck, that told her the cutting of the whale had begun, the men going about their butchering work as if nothing had happened. After all, she thought, suddenly furious, men died all the time on whaling ships; the medicine chest was useful for only the simplest of ailments. She looked down at Daniel. He probably hadn't even begun to shave yet. And there was his mother waiting for him in New Bedford, she thought bitterly. Jasmine could imagine her agony if she lost another son to whaling. She gave Morgan an angry glance, speaking without thinking. "How many barrels of oil will the whale make? Fifty? Sixty? How many barrels of oil is Daniel's life worth?"

Then she was instantly ashamed of her outburst when she saw the bleakness in Morgan's face. He touched the boy's blond hair gently, without speaking. When he turned to her again, his face held no emotion at all as he said in a level voice, "Wake me at once if there's any change."

But there was no change. For the rest of the day, Jasmine sat beside the sofa, sponging Daniel's face, changing the bandage, trying to get the boy to swallow a little of the spirits she held to his lips. Every now and then she would call him by name, trying to coax him back from wherever he had gone to in his mind. His eyelids did not quiver; his face remained still. She had no idea whether he heard her or not.

The steward brought her food on a tray and offered to sit with the boy, but Jasmine shook her head. She knew how busy every man aboard was during the trying out, even the steward. By late afternoon, they began boiling the blubber in the huge try-pots. The stench crept into the cabin, reminding Jasmine guiltily of the bitter words she had flung at Morgan earlier.

She was wrong to accuse Morgan, she thought unhappily. She was sure it wasn't money for himself but for the crew that had made him decide to go after whales in that deadly sea. In a way, she was as much to blame. It was because of her that Morgan had decided to cut the cruise short. The whale being tried out now would help fill the hold with oil to make up for a shorter voyage.

Later, when she heard the steward strike eight bells calling the watch, she bent over Daniel again, sponging the boy's face. She was wrong about Daniel, too, she thought. He might look like a boy, but he was a man, with a man's right to make his own decisions. He must have known the danger of cutting a running line, but if he hadn't cut the line, the whale would have undoubtedly capsized the boat and everyone aboard would have been killed, including Morgan.

She took the boy's hand in her own and squeezed it, placing a kiss on the pale cheek. "I think your mother would be very proud of you," she whispered.

Then, so faintly she thought she had imagined it, she felt a slight return of the pressure on her hand holding Daniel's. When the boy spoke, she had to lean forward to hear what he said.

"Mother?" The eyelids opened and the blue eyes, dazed, fastened upon the woman beside the bed.

Jasmine blinked back tears as she said swiftly, "It's Mrs. Tucker, Daniel. You're safe aboard the *Louisa.* How do you feel?"

He lifted a hand to his head and winced. "My head hurts."

"Do you remember what happened?"

For a moment longer, the blue eyes were clouded over, then, his voice stronger, he said slowly, "I remember cutting the line, then something hit my head and I was in the water." Terror flooded the wide blue eyes, remembering. "The water . . . the waves, they smashed into me, so I couldn't breathe. I thought I was going to die. Then the captain was in the water with me, holding me up, dragging me back to the boat. Afterwards, the boat didn't seem to move no matter how hard the men rowed. The wind was against us; it was like putting an oar into the same patch of water, over and over again. And the water kept seeping in around the plug they'd put in her hull. The men wanted to give up, but the captain wouldn't let them. One man went crazy, I guess. He tried to throw himself over the side. The captain knocked him down. He never stopped telling us we would make it." A grin touched the boy's wide mouth. "I remember he yelled that he'd see us in hell before he let us make Jasmine Tucker a widow. After that, everything went black. The next thing I remember was my mother kissing me, the way she used to do before I fell asleep at night when I was a boy at home." He gazed, bewildered, at Jasmine. "Have I been here long? Am I all right?"

"You'll be fine," Jasmine assured him, tucking the blanket closer around him. "Sleep now. You need rest."

The boy sighed, and his eyes closed again, but this time Jasmine saw it was a natural sleep, and that there was the beginning of color in his face.

She got to her feet, stretching, her limbs cramped from sitting so long, and discovering she was tired herself. Going into her cabin, she found that Morgan was still sleeping heavily, his body taking up almost all of the bed. Jasmine gazed longingly at the little space that was left on one side of Morgan's sprawled body. It was better than sleeping on the floor, she decided as she slipped quickly out of her clothes and into a clean nightgown. Despite the tiny space left for her in the bed, the moment her head hit the pillow she fell sound asleep.

Chapter 14

Morgan was dreaming, a by-now familiar dream. Jasmine was lying in his arms, the soft curves of her body pressed against the length of him; her eyes, gazing at him, blurred with love; the fragrance and warmth of her so real that when he awoke and found his wife snuggled next to him in bed, at first he thought he was still dreaming.

Then Jasmine murmured in her sleep. She curled

closer to him as she sought a more comfortable position,
and the movement of her body brushing against his
brought an instantaneous response within him. And he
knew he was only too wide awake. It was still night, but
in the pale, mistlike moonlight streaming through the
port, he could glimpse the pink-tipped breasts through
the white cambric nightgown with insets of revealing
lace across the bodice.

The compulsion to touch those proud, upthrust peaks
was overpowering. Almost against his own volition, Morgan found himself undoing the pearl buttons that ran
from neck to waist, his hand slipping inside the gauzy
material to stroke the silken flesh. Then, as his hand
caressed the velvet-soft nipple, Jasmine's eyelids flew
open.

She did not gaze at him with the love-blurred eyes of
the woman in his dreams, but neither were the dark
eyes as cool and distant as they usually were. And she
did not immediately pull away from his touch but lay
very still, hardly breathing.

Emboldened, with neither of them speaking, he bent
his dark head over her and caressed the other breast
with his tongue until it, too, matched its mate in
excitement, and he could feel her heart racing, hear her
breathing become more rapid. When his hand impatiently pushed aside the cambric gown so that he could
find and stroke every part of her with his fingertips, he
felt her stiffen but only for a second. Then, as his hands
moved downward to touch the dark, inviting area between her thighs, he felt all resistance leave her. Her
body twisted toward him, as if to draw closer to those
questing hands.

He had meant to possess her slowly, lovingly, with
infinite care, so that there would be no reminder for her
of their last encounter in this bed, but he had denied
himself too long. As he felt her responding to him, her
hips moving beneath him, he swiftly sought a deeper
and deeper pleasure within her, his passion cresting
suddenly, without warning.

When he finally rolled away from her, lifting himself on his elbows to look down into her eyes, dark and unfathomable between the thick fringe of lashes, he realized that he had no idea what she was thinking or feeling.

Then, suddenly remembering, he asked abruptly, "The boy?"

"Daniel came around," she said quietly. "He's sleeping."

He swung over her and out of bed, padding into the outer cabin to discover, relieved, that the boy was indeed asleep, his mouth half open, snoring a little.

Looking at the boy, though, he was suddenly reminded of earlier that evening when Jasmine turned upon him demanding scornfully, "How many barrels of oil is Daniel's life worth?"

Did she really think so little of him? he wondered and then thought wryly that the truth was, at the moment, he hadn't too high an opinion of himself. Oh, he had kept his word to Jasmine's parents. He had not physically forced their daughter into his bed. But by deliberately arousing the girl's untutored passionate nature, had he really given her a choice? Would she have come to him willingly if he hadn't already begun his seduction of her while she was still off guard, half-asleep.

He went back into the small cabin. Jasmine's eyes were shut, and she had moved to the edge of the bed near the bulkhead. He suspected, though, that she was only feigning sleep, and he remembered the way she had stared at him afterwards, that strange, unreadable look in her dark eyes. Well, it was done, he thought gloomily, and he would not lie and pretend that he regretted it had happened. Overhead, he could hear the sounds of the men still working at the try-pots, the smell of gurry wiping out the remembered fragrance of Jasmine in his arms. He picked up his clothes and went into the outer cabin to dress. His place was on deck, not mooning down here in his quarters.

Jasmine heard Morgan return to the cabin and waited for him to come back to bed, to take her in his arms and hold her, not with passion but with tenderness, while they talked. There was so much they had to say to each other. Most important would be the words of love Morgan would whisper to her, assuring her that he needed her as much as she loved and needed him.

When he did not come to her and she heard the cabin door close behind him, her eyelids flew open, and she sat up in bed, hugging her knees to her chest, feeling suddenly bereft and cold.

When she saw Morgan later at breakfast, his hazel eyes touched her face for only a moment before looking away. He spoke of the successful trying out of the whale. To the crew's delight, ambergris, a large, spongelike lump, had been found in the whale, letting out a sweet stream of heavenly perfume that had enveloped the entire ship and would bring a small fortune in New Bedford. Morgan also spoke of setting a course for the Marquesas as soon as the trying out was finished.

So nothing had changed, Jasmine thought dully, playing with the food on her plate so that she would not have to look again into Morgan's face. She and Morgan were still two strangers sharing the same quarters.

Except that night, even though Daniel had been moved to the first mate's quarters, Morgan did not return to his bed on the sofa. Without a word, he threw aside the coverlet and slipped into bed beside Jasmine.

When his arms reached out for her, she drew back, resentment at his casual high-handedness flickering within her, but as his hands moved surely, persuasively, over her body, she knew as well as he that it was only a token resistance. And in spite of the bitter knowledge that it was only his male need that she was satisfying—any other personable woman in his bed would have done as well—nevertheless, she found herself responding to him as ardently as she had the night before.

Over the next weeks, their bodies became accustomed to each other, learning each other's special needs and how to give each other the greatest pleasure. She discovered that on the nights when Morgan did not peremptorily reach over and pull her into his arms, she lay awake sleepless with an aching void inside of her. Their lovemaking, however, was always performed without words, although once she heard Morgan murmur against her hair, "Sweet . . . sweet." And afterwards, her own throat felt raw, stifling back the words of love she wanted to pour out.

It was December when the *Louisa* reached the Marquesas Islands. When she anchored at Magdalena Island, canoe-loads of naked, tattooed men swarmed aboard. Remembering the experience with the cannibals off the Gilberts, Jasmine watched them warily. These men, though, despite their savage appearance, simply wanted to trade and were as curious to see a white *wahine* as she was to see them. They brought pigs and fowls, coconuts, breadfruits, bananas, and potatoes, all badly needed to replace the *Louisa*'s depleted stores.

The ship stayed at the Marquesas over Christmas, anchoring Christmas Day off Dominica Island, where a missionary, the Reverend Mr. Kekela and his family from Hawaii, had a small church. For the first time in months, Jasmine attended church services, and in honor of the occasion, she brought out from her trunk a blue silk dress, its high lace collar fastened with a scrimshaw brooch that Daniel had made for her. She wore white silk gloves and a blue-and-white flowered bonnet tied with long satin ribbons under her chin.

Several merchant and whaling ships were cruising the Marquesas at the same time, and the captains and officers also attended the church service. Morgan noticed, with an unexpected stab of jealousy, that the men's eyes were more often on Jasmine than they were on the preacher in his makeshift pulpit. He was sure that his wife was aware of the flattering glances. She kept her eyes sedately enough on the preacher, but he could see the color in her cheeks, the lustrous gleam in her eyes. Afterwards, the ships' captains and officers gathered at the minister's house for tea. The minister's wife was an older woman, her face wrinkled and worn, serenely indifferent to the hardships of the life around her. Her eyes, when they rested on her husband, glowed with a pride and affection that made Jasmine wonder wistfully how it would be to be able to show your love for your husband openly and not to carry it hidden, like some dark, terrible secret, inside of you.

Still, it was pleasant being with another woman, even being with men that she could flirt with mildly, as if she were the belle of the ball again surrounded by admiring swains.

When Captain and Mrs. Tucker returned to the *Louisa*, Jasmine's cheeks were still flushed with pleasure as she said, smiling happily, "What an enjoyable afternoon."

"Aye, it's plain you were enjoying yourself," Morgan growled.

Jasmine's smile wavered, and Morgan felt a spasm of remorse. Why should he begrudge her the pleasure of a tea party? It was difficult enough for a woman on a whaling ship—the cramped quarters, heat, vermin, and the constant stink of rancid whale oil—yet he had never heard Jasmine complain.

Wanting to make amends for his sharpness but unable to put it into words, he took a carved, narrow wooden chest from his trunk and thrust it awkwardly into her hands. "A Christmas gift."

"I have one for you, too," Jasmine said, "though it's not very grand, I'm afraid." It was a neck warmer that she had knitted. "I thought it might come in handy when we round the Cape."

While Morgan was assuring her that it was just what he needed, she opened the box he had given her and, with a gasp of pleasure, drew out a rope of perfectly matched pearls. Each pearl was a lustrous ivory that gleamed softly, as if lit from within.

"How beautiful," Jasmine breathed, fastening the pearls around her neck. "Where did you ever find them?"

"I bought them off a whaling captain I met while cruising the Japan grounds in the fall of forty-eight." He grinned. "How he got them I never asked."

So he had bought the pearls before he had ever met her, Jasmine thought, wondering to whom Morgan had originally meant to give them.

Then she saw that her husband was watching her, a golden warmth in his eyes, his glance lingering on the pearls nestled against her breasts. "I've heard that pearls are best displayed when a woman wears a low-cut gown." He locked the cabin door that led into the saloon and walked slowly toward her, smiling. "Or, better still, no gown at all."

Jasmine gave him a startled glance. "But, Morgan, it's the middle of the afternoon!"

"So?" He shrugged impatiently. "Is there some law against a husband taking his wife to bed in the daylight? The men have all been given an extra tot of rum for the holiday, and they'll not be disturbing us." His hands were already at the high ruffled lace collar, ripping the lace a little as he removed the scrimshaw brooch, awkwardly trying to unbutton the tiny, silk-covered buttons that ran up the front of her bodice.

Afraid that he might ruin the gown, she stepped back. "Let me," she said softly, her own hands trembling a little as she unbuttoned the gown and, stepping out of it, folded it neatly. Still completely covered by her lacy drawers, petticoats, corset, and chemise, nevertheless, she felt vaguely embarrassed with Morgan, his eyes narrowed, watching her every movement.

She turned quickly and picked up her wrapper from the bed. With the lack of privacy in the small cabin, she had become quite proficient at undressing beneath her robe.

"No," Morgan said sharply, scowling as he saw Jasmine attempt to cover herself with the wrapper. Damn it, she was his wife, wasn't she? Why should she hide her loveliness from him? The slippery silk buttons might have been a hindrance, but he had no trouble at all removing the undergarments, which drifted in a white cloud to the floor.

Jasmine made no move to stop him. She stood as

quietly as a statue as he undressed her, but as he gazed at her with pleasure, he saw there was nothing stone-like about the softly gleaming flesh and lissome curves of the woman who stood finally revealed before him. The glowing, peach gold tones of her skin rivaled the luster of the rope of pearls that, dipping into the dark hollow between her breasts, was all she now wore.

Proudly she did not turn away from Morgan's raking glance. Her dark hair was still piled on top of her head, giving her an air of dignity that matched the cool, aloof darkness of her eyes.

Suddenly, uncomfortably, Morgan was reminded of that first night they had been alone here in this cabin; how he had impatiently torn away the nonsensical strip of silk wrapped around Jasmine's body and forced her into his bed, thinking only of his own pleasure. Looking into his wife's still face, he knew, with an icy feeling of despair in the pit of his stomach, that she was remembering those moments, too. Would it always be there between them? he wondered, the memory of that night like a barrier impossible for him to surmount.

He knew that if he took Jasmine to bed now and made love to her, she would respond with a passionate eagerness and warmth, satisfying him in a way he had never found with any other woman. Yet, always, he was aware that there was some essential part of Jasmine that eluded him, no matter how closely he held her. And that afterwards, her beautiful face, wiped clean of passion, would once again be coolly remote; her eyes, like now, staring at him, unfathomable, holding their own secrets.

For the first time in his life, Morgan faced a disturbing truth. He wanted more than just the body of this woman he held in his arms, seductive as that body was. He wasn't even sure what more he did want. After all, he thought, bewildered, what more could a man want from a woman?

Gazing at Jasmine's face, all he knew was that he had cruelly and clumsily managed to humiliate her, as if she were his whore instead of his wife. Sickened at his own loutish behavior, he turned blindly and strode from the cabin.

In the saloon, where his officers were gathered enjoying their rum, Morgan's sudden entrance brought looks of surprise to their faces.

Morgan snarled at the assembled men. "Is no one taking the watch on deck? Do you plan to have the natives steal us blind while you sit on your duffs, guzzling your rum?" Then, turning to the first mate, he ordered, "I want you to finish loading those potatoes and hogs this afternoon. We'll be hoisting anchor the first thing in the morning."

The men exchanged startled glances. They had expected to spend several more weeks off the Marquesas before sailing for the coast of California. It was the first mate who had the temerity to ask, "And where will we be heading next, Captain?"

Morgan scowled at the man. "I'll be setting a course for the Cape and then, the sooner the better, home."

The minute Morgan left the cabin, Jasmine tore off the rope of pearls from around her neck, returned it to its box and shoved the box deep inside her trunk where she needn't look at it again. Tears of helpless fury burned her eyes. How dare Morgan treat her like one of the cheap trollops with which he was no doubt well acquainted! Did he think a necklace of pearls gave him the right to do as he wished with her, as he had the first night he had taken her? Would he ever accept the fact that she was his wife and forget that he had been forced into an unwelcome marriage? She had hoped that in time his feelings toward her would change as hers had toward him, that he might just once murmur words of love to her when they lay together. But he never had.

Jasmine straightened from kneeling beside her trunk, brushing away the tears from her eyes with her hands. She was being foolish again, she thought, as foolish as she had been when she had been shocked by the brutality of the whale's death. Morgan would not change. If she were to accept this marriage, then she must accept

Morgan as well, for what he was, not for something she wanted him to become.

Despite the constraint almost visibly palpable in the air between Morgan and her during the following weeks, Jasmine continued to play the role of the dutiful, loving wife as the *Louisa* fairly flew through the waters with all sails set, seemingly as anxious to return to New Bedford as her captain.

Morgan did not return to his bed on the sofa. He continued to share Jasmine's bed, and although for several nights their bodies lay carefully apart, inevitably there came the morning when they woke up in each other's arms. With a groan breaking from his lips, Morgan drew his wife even closer, and Jasmine, her own desire mounting uncontrollably, made no protest as his hands and mouth brought waves of pleasure sweeping over her. It was only afterwards that she felt a faint, guilty shame that she should find such profound delight in the arms of this man, when she knew that any other woman in his bed would have served him just as well.

Then the *Louisa* reached the southernmost tip of South America, and as she began to round Cape Horn, Morgan spent very little time in bed at all. The ship had been carefully prepared for her dangerous passage around the Horn. All rigging had been repaired, new sails had replaced old, the royal mast had been sent down, hatches had been barred and caulked, and warm clothes for the men had been brought up from the hold.

Nevertheless, Morgan spent most of the daylight hours, and much of the night, on deck, keeping a close eye on the barometer, cautiously laying to when a gale sprang up suddenly with the wind seeming to come every ten minutes from another point on the compass. The *Louisa* ran into almost daily squalls of wind, rain, hail, and even snow, but she continued to make steady progress in the unpredictable Cape weather. Then one night the wind shifted around to the southward. By morning, the ship was hit by a screaming snow squall.

In the cabin, Jasmine, dressed in her warmest wool

dress and a heavy shawl pulled tightly around her, rubbed her hands together and walked back and forth in a vain attempt to keep warm. Morgan had offered to have the cabin stove set up for her, but he had warned her that its heat would attract the cockroaches, so she had elected to do without. She was beginning to wonder if perhaps the repulsive vermin might be preferable to chilblains when she felt the *Louisa* suddenly go over on her side and she was flung to the floor. The ship heeled even further as Jasmine struggled to her feet, clutching at the horsehair sofa for support. She could feel the ship tremble in every timber at the shock of the heavy swell of water crashing over her lee rail, and she watched, terrified, as water, running down the gangway and through the skylight, poured into the cabin.

She fought her way into the saloon, and above the roar of the wind she could hear Morgan's bellow through the closed hatch. "Put the wheel hard up. . . . Take in the foresail."

The ship bucked under her like a wild horse, then rose onto a more or less even keel and fell off safely before the wind. After mopping up the floor as best she could, Jasmine removed her wet clothes and climbed, shivering, into bed. For the rest of the night, she slept fitfully, if at all, and would wake up, her heart pounding, to the sound of the howling wind. The ship reeled under mountainous waves, burying the deck under tons of green water. As the ship labored and rolled violently, Jasmine worried about how Morgan and his men were faring above deck. Still, she consoled herself, if anything happened to Morgan, someone would surely come and tell her.

It wasn't until the next afternoon, when the wind died off, that Morgan returned to the cabin. As she had waited through the night, clinging to the sides of the bed to keep from being pitched to the floor, Jasmine's temper had risen, along with her discomfort. Morgan could at least have sent someone to check to make sure she was all right, she thought, sitting up in bed and glaring at her husband as he stumbled through the cabin door.

Then she saw Morgan's ashen face, the snow on his eyelashes, his jacket and trousers stiff as a board with ice. He gazed blankly at Jasmine, his voice harsh, forced through raw, chapped lips. "One of the Portuguese . . . he lost his hold on the weather rigging . . . went overboard."

Jasmine knew, without his saying, that there was no way the captain could turn the *Louisa* back in weather like this to search for a man overboard. She went to Morgan and rubbed his icy hands gently between her own. "I'm sorry," she said softly.

She found the steward and got some hot coffee, liberally laced it with rum, then, since his hands were too swollen to hold the mug, she held the drink to Morgan's mouth. While she had been gone, he had removed his ice-stiff clothes and wrapped himself in a blanket.

He gestured toward the chest. "Get me some dry clothes," he said hoarsely.

"You can't go back on deck again," she protested indignantly. "The wind's dying. Rest awhile. You haven't slept in two days."

As she spoke, she was coaxing him firmly toward the bed. She breathed a tiny sigh of relief as, too exhausted to object, he slumped into the bed.

She piled blankets on top of him, then slid in beside him, flinching with shock when his body, as if invisibly coated with ice, touched her flesh. She pressed closer to him, using her own body heat to warm him until he finally stopped shivering and fell asleep in her arms.

When she awoke, two hours later, he was gone. The wind was no longer howling through the rigging, and, although the ship was still rolling and the room was clammy cold, she managed to dress and make her way up the companionway. The deck was covered with snow, the canvas sails frozen stiff. Ice turned the rigging into glittering crystal cobwebs in the moonlight.

On the afterdeck, she found the first mate with the helmsman.

"If it's the skipper you're looking for," Mr. Gibbons said, "he's checking the damage to the ship."

"Is it bad?"

"Aye, aside from the poor soul we lost, one of our boats was stove in, the mizzenmast needs repair work, and part of the galley was washed away."

Jasmine gazed out at the dark gray swells, the color of the sky so like that of the water that it was impossible to tell where the sea ended and the sky began. "Will we be much longer rounding the Cape?"

"The captain thinks we're off the Diegos," he said. "That means one more day and we'll have passed the Cape and reached the Atlantic." He smiled in anticipation. "Another two months, if all goes well, we'll be raising Gay Head and Mrs. Tucker will be waiting on the dock at New Bedford, the way she always is when the *Louisa* comes home."

Mrs. Tucker? For a moment, Jasmine stared at the first mate, puzzled. She was Mrs. Tucker. Then she realized. Of course, Morgan's mother. All at once, it occurred to her how little Morgan had told her about his family, or about himself, for that matter.

"Do you know Mrs. Tucker?" she asked Mr. Gibbons, hugging her shawl closer around her, not sure whether the movement was against the cold or the thought of her unknown mother-in-law.

"Everyone in New Bedford knows Louisa Tucker," the man said, chuckling. "She's what outlanders call a slab-sided New Englander, shrewd as they come. After her husband's ship was lost, when Morgan was only a baby, everyone expected her to move out of the fine house that Matthew Tucker had built for her. But not Louisa. She took what money the captain left her and turned it into a fortune. She owns a half-interest in this ship, and some say she owns half the commerce in New Bedford. There's not many that can outsmart Louisa

Tucker. She's harder than most men that I know, but she fair dotes on her son."

Uneasily Jasmine wondered what Louisa Tucker would think when her son unexpectedly came home with a bride. Perhaps she had already chosen a young woman to be Morgan's wife, someone from New Bedford, perhaps even the young woman in the oil portrait Morgan kept carefully wrapped in his chest.

Or would she still be Morgan's wife after they reached New Bedford? she thought suddenly. Morgan hadn't spoken anymore about the divorce, but since he was so anxious to return to New Bedford, it was undoubtedly on his mind. Jasmine felt a sudden, odd pain, like a stitch in her side.

Mr. Gibbons saw the young woman's face grow pale. "Are you all right, Mrs. Tucker?" he asked, concerned. "You're not ill?"

Jasmine took a deep, steadying breath. The pain passed, leaving only a dull ache behind. She smiled at the first mate. "I'm fine, Mr. Gibbons. I was just thinking, how—how nice it will be to be home again."

Chapter 15

The first mate's predictions proved amazingly accurate. It was May, almost exactly two months later, when the *Louisa*, her tattered rigging replaced, her decks scrubbed till they shone, the ugly brick tryworks dismantled and tossed overboard, glided past Palmer's Island and raised Clark's Point Light. A whaleboat was dropped into the water to take the lines ashore, and the ship was warped alongside the wharf at New Bedford.

As Mr. Gibbons had also predicted, Louisa Tucker was waiting on the wharf when Morgan and Jasmine left the ship and stepped ashore. Morgan swiftly embraced his mother. At first glance, all Jasmine could tell about the woman was that she was tall and slender and dressed in widow's weeds, from black boots to the black bonnet that was tied with a bow of black ribbon beneath a square chin.

Then Morgan stepped back and said firmly, "My wife, Jasmine, Mother."

No doubt Louisa Tucker was startled at the news, but her face revealed none of her emotions as she turned her head, and Jasmine saw framed within the black bonnet a face that was vaguely familiar. The face was older, the dark hair now a silver gray, but the dark blue no-nonsense eyes still looked directly at Jasmine as they had in the small oil portrait tucked away in Morgan's chest.

So the girl in the portrait was not a rival after all, Jasmine thought, in her relief giving Louisa Tucker a radiant smile of greeting. The smile was not returned, but Morgan's mother did lean forward and place a cool cheek against Jasmine's, murmuring, "You're welcome to the family, Jasmine."

Then they were in the carriage, heading away from the docks. While Mrs. Tucker questioned Morgan closely about the voyage—how many barrels of oil and spermaceti, how much ambergris and whalebone he had brought home—Jasmine glanced curiously around her. It was easy to see that New Bedford was a bustling whaling port, the largest and busiest since a series of sandbars had been swept across the entrance to Nantucket. Whaling ships filled the harbor with a forest of masts. Barrels of oil and stores for the ships lined the streets, and the noise of the iron-rimmed wheels of the carriage rolling over cobblestones mingled with the deafening clang from the smithies and the pounding of mallets in the cooperages along the road.

As they passed a row of warehouses, Jasmine caught the fragrance of sandalwood and tea, along with the odor of ambergris and the heavy scent of spermaceti from the candlemaking factories, almost hiding the more prosaic odors of fish, hemp, and tar. The men swarming through the streets all seemed to be carrying something on their shoulders, and their faces were not only those of rugged whaling men but those of Quakers in flat hats, dark South Sea islanders, Africans, and Portuguese.

Twisting in the carriage to look behind her, Jasmine caught a glimpse of Daniel, in a neat pea jacket, walking from the dock, an older woman, evidently his mother, striding proudly beside him. How I will miss Daniel, Jasmine thought wistfully, and Mr. Gibbons and even dour Mr. Turnbull and the *Louisa* herself. She was a good ship, Jasmine thought fondly, not beautiful like the graceful clippers but strong and dauntless.

Like the woman the *Louisa* was named after? she wondered, turning her thoughtful gaze back to Morgan's mother and recalling the coolness in the woman's manner. But then she remembered from her schooldays that cautious New Englanders were not immediately welcoming of strangers into their midst.

The carriage had left the wharf area now and was climbing the hill behind the waterfront where wide streets were planted with avenues of towering maples and bordered by two-story stone mansions. The carriage finally stopped before a broad swatch of green lawn and a hedge of purple-blooming lilacs. The mansion that sat back from the street was built in the Greek Revival style and resembled its neighbors except for a cupola built on the roof.

Although it was not as large as the Babcock home, Jasmine decided that the Tucker home was just as beautiful. As she walked in the front door, she glimpsed a paneled library to the left and a drawing room papered with rich yellow China silk. There was a Brussels carpet on the floor and curtains in a deep buttercup yellow brocade covering high windows. She gazed around her, a little startled. Somehow she would not have guessed that her husband came from such gracious surroundings.

Then before she had time to mull over the matter, her mother-in-law said crisply, "I'm sure Jasmine must be tired, Morgan. Why don't you show her to your room?"

Jasmine started to protest that she wasn't tired. Then she realized it had not been a question but a command. And, she suspected, in this house, Louisa Tucker wasn't accustomed to having her orders ignored. She followed Morgan meekly enough to a large room on the second floor with windows overlooking the town of New Bedford. There was a carved four-poster bed in the room covered with a white woven cotton spread, and through a half-opened door, Jasmine saw a huge white clawed bathtub sitting on a platform in a small adjoining room.

Following her glance, Morgan suddenly grinned. "That was Mother's idea. She shocked half of New Bedford when she installed inside plumbing in the house."

Jasmine returned her gaze to the bed, running her hand lightly over the woven coverlet, and thought, delighted, how wonderful it would be to sleep in a full-sized bed again that didn't pitch and roll beneath you.

Watching her, Morgan frowned, wondering what she was thinking, wondering if he would ever know what was going on behind his wife's composed face. Was she thinking hopefully that this bed was to be hers alone. "We'll have to share the bed," he said harshly. "Mother would think it . . . strange otherwise."

Jasmine did not answer, simply nodding.

"I'll have to return at once to the wharf and start settling the *Louisa*'s accounts," he said. "I'll see that your trunks are sent up here to the house if you want to start unpacking."

Jasmine nodded again, but as Morgan started for the door, she asked suddenly, "Do you intend to tell your mother about our . . . that we plan to be divorced?"

Morgan's face darkened. "Yes, of course. But not right away. Great Jehoshaphat! We just arrived."

The door slammed shut behind him. Jasmine sighed and walked to the window, when she saw Mrs. Tucker already waiting for her son in the carriage. Impatiently, no doubt, Jasmine thought. And it occurred to her that perhaps she had been mistaken: Louisa Tucker might be a rival after all, and a formidable one at that. As she watched the carriage drive away, she wondered just how much Morgan would tell his mother about his marriage.

Morgan was wondering the same thing as he gazed out absently from the carriage, yet very conscious of his mother's presence beside him, knowing she was waiting for him to tell her about this unexpected marriage of his.

It was Louisa who finally had to speak first. "Your wife is very beautiful, Morgan. You met her in the islands?"

"She's the daughter of Captain Amos Babcock. You met him years ago when he sailed from New Bedford."

"I remember him and Mrs. Babcock," Louisa said after a moment. "The girl has something of her mother in her face." She gave her son a curious glance. "How did you happen to meet Jasmine?"

Morgan felt an embarrassed flush rise to his face, something that hadn't happened to him with his mother since he was ten. He had no intention of telling his mother the real circumstances surrounding his meeting with Jasmine, not because she would be angry with him but because she might think less of Jasmine.

"We met through mutual friends," he said.

Louise glanced thoughtfully at her son. She was well aware that there was something he wasn't telling her. Had the girl perhaps tricked him into marriage? No, she thought, Jasmine was much too lovely to have to resort to tricks to catch a husband.

"I hope, Morgan," she said slowly, "that your wife has the courage to be a whaling captain's wife."

"What do you mean?" Morgan asked sharply. "Jasmine's not a coward." He remembered the courage she had shown during the cannibal attack. If she had been afraid aboard the *Louisa*, she had never once showed it.

His mother shook her head. "I wasn't thinking of that kind of courage. I was thinking of the fortitude a whaling wife needs to bear the long separations from her husband when he's away on a voyage for three or four years at a time. You won't always be able to take Jasmine with you, you know, especially when the children start coming."

When her son didn't answer, his face setting into a familiar, stubborn scowl, she sighed to herself and changed the subject. She talked about the testing and selling of the oil aboard the *Louisa*, about how soon the ship could be refitted for another voyage. "I was planning on sending her into the Atlantic on a short cruise," she said. "However, Captain Hennessy's wife is gravely ill, and he doesn't want to leave New Bedford. What do you think about Captain Jenson?"

Morgan was only half listening, lost in his own thoughts. He regretted now that he hadn't told his mother right away about the real state of affairs between Jasmine and himself. She was bound to find out anyway, as soon as Jasmine started divorce proceedings. Unless . . . His mother's words suddenly sunk in, and he grinned to himself. Unless he wasn't in New Bedford. It would be difficult for Jasmine to take legal action against him if he were away. "Why don't I take the *Louisa* into the Atlantic?" he asked abruptly.

His mother glanced at him, her voice shocked. "But you've just returned. Surely Jasmine won't want to go to sea again so soon."

"Jasmine will stay in New Bedford with you," Morgan said. At his mother's questioning glance, he added hastily, "It will take a month before the *Louisa* can be refitted, so I won't be leaving right away. And while I'm gone, it will give Jasmine a chance to find out about the separations you were talking about."

And give his wife time, perhaps, to change her mind about the divorce, he thought hopefully. Wasn't there an old saying that absence makes the heart grow fonder?

He'd tell Jasmine that very night about the trip, he decided, but that evening when he came into the bedroom and found his wife waiting in bed for him, he forgot everything else. Her dark hair tumbled around her shoulders, and the long-sleeved white bastiste gown she wore was demure, yet sufficiently sheer so that he could glimpse the gentle curve of her breasts. When he took her in his arms, her skin was still warm from her bath and lightly scented, her face in the lamplight holding the fresh-scrubbed innocence of a child. But there was nothing childlike or innocent about the way she molded her body against his, or the pinpricks of fire he saw deep in the wide, dark eyes, burning brighter and brighter as his hands and lips and finally his own body possessed hers.

Somehow, after that night, there never seemed a proper time to tell Jasmine about his impending trip until the week before he was to sail, when he made the announcement at dinner.

"It's a plum-pudding trip," he said cheerfully. "I'll be back within six months."

So she wasn't to go with him, Jasmine thought, her hands hidden beneath the table and curled together in her lap, her nails digging into her soft palms to keep the pain and fury from showing in her face. How naive she had been to hope that those nights spent in his arms in that heavenly soft, wide bed upstairs would make him never want to leave her side. She cast a quick, suspicious glance across the table at her mother-in-law. Was this her doing? Jasmine sensed that for all of Louisa Tucker's outward acceptance of her son's marriage, she still had reservations about the suitability of her new daughter-in-law. With an almost physical effort, Jasmine swallowed the angry words that she wanted to fling at Morgan. Probably that was exactly what Morgan's mother expected, she thought, that she would make a scene about her husband's leaving so soon.

"When will you be leaving?" she asked.

"The *Louisa* should be ready by the end of the week."

For a moment, in her husband's narrowed gaze studying her face, Jasmine thought she saw a question, a waiting for some unknown response from her, but then the look was gone as if it had never been there and Morgan returned his attention to his food.

The next months after Morgan left were the longest and loneliest Jasmine had ever spent in her life. The days dragged and the nights in that wide, now-empty bed stretched interminably. Her sleep was restless, and several times she awoke to find herself hugging a down-stuffed pillow to her, its embroidered linen case damp with her tears.

She always saw her mother-in-law at the evening meal, but during the day Louisa was busy in town or at the wharf. She had given her daughter-in-law the use of a carriage, and Jasmine spent her days driving around town, becoming acquainted with New Bedford. Whaling had made the town one of the richest in the country, and its wealth could readily be seen in the gracious homes and well-stocked shops with the latest fashions from New York and Paris.

But when Jasmine stopped one day at the Seamen's Bethel on Johnny Cake Hill, with its prow-shaped pulpit and its many memorial plaques to lost seamen on the walls, she knew that whaling had brought tragedy to the town, too. She read the sad inscriptions: "Killed by a sperm whale," "Towed out of sight by a whale," "Fell from aloft off Cape Horn," "Lost at sea with all her crew." Suddenly terrified for Morgan, she knelt within a pew and prayed that he would come home safely.

But as the days passed and summer drifted into autumn, Jasmine discovered that it wasn't only Morgan that she missed. She longed to see the islands and her family: her gruff-voiced father, loving Malia, gentle Lani, darkly handsome Kale, and even Lilikoi with her mocking smile.

She hadn't written to her family since she had left Honolulu. At first she had been too furious with her father and step-mother for allowing Morgan to abduct her aboard the *Louisa*, then there had been nowhere she could mail the letters.

The next morning she sat down and wrote a long letter, telling her parents almost everything that had happened to her since she had left the islands. It was too difficult to write of the divorce, and she said simply that Morgan was well and sent his love.

To her surprise, toward the end of November a whaling captain only recently arrived in New Bedford from a Pacific voyage brought to the house a letter for her from Hawaii. She knew that her own letter could not possibly have arrived yet and saw that the date on the letter she received was seven months earlier. It was written in Malia's hand.

My dearest daughter,

I hope this letter finds you happy and well, and you have found it in your heart to forgive your father and me for allowing your husband to take you with him aboard the *Louisa*. We did what we thought was best for you, and I pray that we were not mistaken about Captain Tucker.

Auwe, my dearest Pikake, now I must tell you some sad news. Your sister, Lani, has grievously sinned with her brother, Kale. They were married, following the Hawaiian custom of *Niau Pio*. When your father heard, I was sick with fear that he would kill Kale. Instead he has ordered that the names of Lani and Kale never again be mentioned in his household. I obey him because he is my husband, and I know the terrible pain he must be feeling. I grieve, too, but they are my children and I cannot stop loving them. I have told you this terrible news because I did not want you to hear of it by chance, from a stranger.

Your father and I speak of you often with much *aloha* and pray for the day when you will return to the islands and our loving arms. . . .

Shaken, Jasmine read and reread the letter. How could Kale and Lani do such a thing? she thought, heartsick. She had heard of the custom among the Hawaiian *alii* of brother marrying sister, a custom that the missionaries had quickly banned. She had even read at the academy that the ancient Egyptian royal families had followed the same custom, but the knowledge made the news no easier to accept. And worse even than the anger and shame and shock she was feeling was the painful realization that two people she loved dearly and thought she knew as well as she knew herself had suddenly become strangers that she didn't know at all.

The letter still clutched in her hand, she had turned, almost automatically, to the wooden ladder that led to the small room on the roof of the Tucker home. She had discovered the entrance to the cupola shortly after Morgan left, and it had become her escape and retreat. There was a powerful spyglass mounted in the room, and through it she could look out across the New Bedford harbor and watch for the return of the *Louisa*.

When she mounted the ladder into the room, she was startled to discover Louisa Tucker at the spyglass. The woman turned at her entrance. Her mother-in-law was dressed as usual all in black, and not a gray hair was out of place.

"I'm sorry," Jasmine said. "I didn't mean to intrude."

Louisa Tucker snapped the telescope shut, her voice wryly crisp as she glanced around her. "Sometimes I feel as if I've spent my whole life in this room; first, watching for Morgan's father to return." For a moment, her voice faltered, then continued firmly, "And more years watching for Morgan's ships." She broke off as she suddenly became aware of the unhappiness in Jasmine's face and the letter the girl clutched in her hand.

"Is something wrong? Have you had bad news from home?"

Jasmine hesitated a moment, then shook her head and thrust the letter in her pocket. She could not bear talking about Lani and Kale to her mother-in-law.

Mrs. Tucker did not press her. "We'll have some tea," she said.

Jasmine followed Mrs. Tucker into the parlor, where a fire had been lit in the grate. As always, Jasmine felt a great delight in the parlor and with the exotic beauty that met her eyes wherever she looked. Before the fireplace sat a pair of old rose Canton vases filled with dried grasses. Ribbon-backed Chippendale chairs stood next to a rosewood spinet and a highly lacquered Chinese sewing box. In the center of the room was a rich, reddish brown table, its top inset with a glorious peacock designed entirely of iridescent mother of pearl.

"My husband brought back these pieces for me," her mother-in-law said proudly, her hand gently brushing the pastel-shaded peacock. "He wanted me to have the finest house and furnishings in all of New Bedford. We moved into the house just before he left on his last voyage."

"You never sailed with him?"

"I wanted to, but my husband felt it was too dangerous." Pain laced her voice. "Matthew and I were married ten years. In all those years, we had little more than a year's time together between his voyages."

She lowered her head to pour the tea, but not before Jasmine caught a suspicious brightness in the dark eyes. When she spoke again her voice was once again crisp. "There's a tea party at the McPherson home this afternoon. Would you like to go?"

Jasmine shook her head. "Thank you, but I'd rather stay home."

A smile briefly touched Louisa's stern face. "I never cared much for hen parties myself," she admitted. "With so many of our men away at sea, that's about the only kind of party we have in New Bedford. Of course, when my husband didn't come back, I was too busy working and raising Morgan to have time for gadding about."

"I'm surprised that after what happened to Captain Tucker you allowed your son to go to sea."

Her mother-in-law gave her an amused glance. "You

should know your husband better than that. I tried everything, short of chaining him in his room, to keep Morgan from the whaling ships. I did manage to enroll him in the academy at Fairhaven for a few years, but then he signed aboard a whaler as a cabin boy when he was twelve. By the time he came home, three years later, he had worked his way into the forecastle."

She smiled in memory. "After he paid the owners back for what he'd bought from the ship's slop chest during the voyage, he was paid a lay of 1/180, or the grand sum of twelve dollars for three years' work. I talked him into returning to the academy. Then, one year later, he was offered the position of harpooner on a whaler and came back after that four-year trip as a third mate." She paused a moment, then said slowly, "He was twenty years old and a second mate when he survived a mutiny aboard the *Corolla*."

"A mutiny?" Jasmine put down her teacup so abruptly it clattered on the tray.

"The captain of the *Corolla* was a hard man, but he used the cat on his men too often. The crew turned on him when the ship was off New Zealand. All the officers were killed, and Morgan was left for dead. The mutineers took the whaleboats and sailed for New Zealand, leaving Morgan aboard the ship with the cabin boy, the steward, and three men from the forecastle, who refused to join the mutineers. Morgan not only survived but tracked down the leader of the mutiny. They fought, and the man was killed. It was a fair fight, but Morgan was tried for murder and acquitted. Afterwards, he refitted the *Corolla*, took on a new crew, and sailed her back to New Bedford, but not before filling her hold with sperm oil," Mrs. Tucker finished. She gave Jasmine a thoughtful glance. "It was five years before Morgan returned from that voyage, and during part of those years, I believed my son had died with the officers aboard the *Corolla*."

Although Jasmine was fascinated, learning more about her husband, she couldn't help wondering why her mother-in-law was telling her these stories about Morgan. Was she trying to prepare Jasmine for the separations she would face as Morgan's wife?

Jasmine's chin set stubbornly. She would never lead the life that Louisa had led, married and not yet married, pacing endlessly in that tiny glass room on the roof, waiting long, lonely years for the return of her husband. She would insist on sailing with Morgan. She wouldn't become one of New Bedford's whaling widows.

Then, suddenly, she remembered how casually Morgan had left her to take the *Louisa* on the Atlantic cruise. Why would it be any different in the future? Before he had left, Morgan had said nothing more about the divorce, but she was sure if she wanted one, he wouldn't stand in her way. As much as she loved Morgan, did she want a marriage that would, in its own way, be even lonelier than that of a whaling widow? For even when Morgan made love to her and she clung shamelessly to him, she knew that afterwards she would be once again as alone in that wide bed as if their bodies had never touched.

Wouldn't a clean break be less cruel? she thought the next morning, after another sleepless night. It had begun to snow during the night, and she stood at her bedroom window, watching the topography of the front yard change into an icy, trackless sea, with banks of snow curling over the low stone fence like the crests of waves.

Jasmine shivered and drew her flannel robe more closely around her. She had always dreaded the coming of winter when she had attended school in Connecticut. No matter how warmly she dressed, all winter long she was chilled to the marrow of her bones and gripped by a dark depression. Now, staring at the dead white, bleak landscape, her sense of hopelessness, of despair about her marriage to Morgan, became overwhelming.

She had to attend to some shopping that morning, and as she drove into town, on an impulse she stopped by an office where gold letters printed discreetly on the door announced the office to be that of Elijah Wincomb, Attorney-at-Law.

An elderly man was warming his hands at a pot-bellied stove when she entered. He looked up, surprised, at his visitor. Flakes of snow were caught in Jasmine's dark lashes and glittered in her hair, which had the rich sheen of the black seal muff she held in her hands.

The lawyer hastened to her side. "May I help you, madam?" he asked politely. It was unusual for a woman to come into a law office alone, much less the woman he immediately recognized as Captain Tucker's young, beautiful bride.

Jasmine was suddenly struck speechless. Something about the man's bright blue eyes, the grizzled, heavy beard, reminded her of her father. How disappointed the captain would be, she thought, if he knew what she was doing. She could imagine him shaking his head at her, his eyes bright with anger. What was it he had always told her? "Fight like the devil for what's yours, no matter what the odds. Even if you don't win, you'll still have the fun of a good scrap!"

Mr. Wincomb was becomingly increasingly alarmed at the girl's silence. "Would you care to sit down, Mrs. Tucker?" he asked gently.

Startled that the lawyer should know her name, she stepped back abruptly. "No, no, thank you," she said, and before the man could question her further, she turned and fled into the street.

It was snowing harder now, the snow stinging her face like tiny bits of glass, but Jasmine no longer felt the cold. She was warmed partly by her embarrassment at her behavior in the lawyer's office and partly by a sense of conviction that had taken hold of her like a fire running through her blood. She wouldn't give Morgan up, not without a fight, she thought fiercely. It would be like giving up a part of her own flesh and blood and bone. Somehow she would find a way to make Morgan need her as much as she needed him.

A half smile quirked the corners of Jasmine's long,

lovely mouth as she returned to the waiting carriage. She climbed into the driver's seat, tucked a blanket over her legs, and picked up the reins, her eyes sparkling. There was, after all, one sure way she knew for a wife to hold on to a husband. . . .

Chapter 16

When the Louisa returned to New Bedford, in February, Morgan found both his mother and his wife waiting for him on the snow-covered quay. He gave Louisa a quick hug, and when Jasmine lifted her face demurely for his kiss, he swept her instead into his arms in a bear hug, which left her eyes softly shining into his and made Morgan decide smugly that he had been right. A six months' absence had made his wife's heart grow fonder. It would be different tonight when he took Jasmine in his arms in that wide feather bed. There would be no holding back between them, no feeling that there was any part of his wife that he did not possess completely. And there would be no more talk of divorce.

At dinner that night Jasmine wore a gown of crimson velvet with shirred, short, puffed sleeves and a scooped-out neck that showed off to perfection her rounded shoulders and the slim, proud column of her throat. Morgan smiled to himself when he saw that she was wearing the long rope of gleaming pearls he had given her the Christmas before aboard the *Louisa*. It was, he thought, a sign that she had forgiven him for his behavior that day.

His mother had asked friends to join them to celebrate Morgan's homecoming after dinner. There was hot mulled wine and fruitcake, and later in the evening one of the guests sat down at the spinet and played a gay waltz, which was the latest rage among the young people of New Bedford. When Jasmine discovered that Morgan didn't know how to waltz, she insisted that she must teach him, to a great deal of teasing and laughter from the guests. Finally, though, Morgan got the hang of the step and swung Jasmine furiously around until her skirt swung high above her ankles and the Canton vases before the fireplace were in danger of being toppled to the floor.

It was late when the last guest left, and after Jasmine, yawning, had excused herself, Morgan and his mother were left alone in the parlor. Morgan, his eyes following his wife impatiently, would have followed after her immediately, but his mother asked quietly, "Could we talk for a moment, Morgan?"

"What is it?" he asked, concerned by the gravity in her voice.

Louisa moved to the yellow-and-white striped brocade couch and straightened the pillows absently. For the first time, Morgan sensed that his mother, usually so calm and unruffled, was nervous. She spoke in spurts. "It's Jasmine, Morgan. . . . It's none of my business. . . . I hate to say anything, but everyone in town knows. . . . She was seen coming out of his office. . . ."

"Knows what?" Morgan asked quietly, but a warning bell sounded in his mind, the same way it did when he was aboard the *Louisa* and the sea and sky were deceptively calm, yet he sensed there was a storm building somewhere near.

"Your wife was seen visiting Mr. Wincomb's office," Louisa said unhappily. She knew as well as Morgan that no respectable young married woman visited a lawyer's office without her husband except for one reason. If her marriage was in trouble; if the woman was contemplating divorce. Louisa was not blind. She had long suspected that there was something wrong between her son and his new wife. During these last months, Jasmine had not just been a lonely woman wandering around the house, waiting for her husband's return. Louisa had seen the fear in those wide, dark eyes, the tension in the lines of that young face, when Jasmine thought no one was watching. As if, Louisa thought, the girl had been wondering whether her husband was coming back to her at all.

Louisa gave her son a searching glance. "Do you love Jasmine?"

"Of course," Morgan answered, startled, although he had never put the thought into words before. "I married her, didn't I?" he growled, exasperated. "I took her with me aboard the *Louisa* and I haven't touched another woman in the last six months. It's Jasmine who won't ever forget. . . ." He fell silent, a darkness settling over the hardness of his face.

Louisa waited for him to continue, and when he didn't, she sighed to herself and felt suddenly old. She should know better than to expect Morgan to confide in her. Even as a child, he'd always kept his own counsel. Perhaps it was because his father's death had made him grow up too quickly, turned him into a man before he'd had a chance to be a child. Or perhaps, she thought guiltily, it was her fault. It had always been difficult for her to express her emotions openly, even to her husband and son, just as difficult, she suspected, as it was for Morgan to express them to his wife.

Morgan saw the sadness clouding his mother's face. He reached out and touched her shoulder, his voice gently brusque. "It'll be all right, Mother. Don't worry."

But he felt her eyes following him anxiously as he climbed the staircase to his bedroom. Jasmine was waiting for him, not in bed but standing by the small fireplace, where applewood logs burned, scenting the room. She was wearing a nightgown he had never seen before. Unlike her usual prim, high-necked gowns, this one was of a gauzy pale pink material. With the firelight behind her, he could see clearly the slender outline of her body, the rose satin ribbons caught at her shoulder and waist, almost the same shade as the pink tips of her breasts. She still wore the rope of pearls around her neck, and they gleamed a soft pink in the firelight, in contrast to the snowy white curve of her bosom, against which the pearls nestled.

For the last six months, Morgan had been waiting in a fever of impatience for this moment, but all at once staring at his wife, he was filled with the heat of anger—not desire. First she had made a fool of him before the eyes of the town by running off to visit a lawyer, and now here she was, dressed like a high-priced harlot, waiting for him, as if she couldn't wait to entice him into her bed.

He tore his eyes away from her, shrugging off his jacket as he frowned and said, "That's a damn silly gown to wear on a cold night like this. Do you want to catch pneumonia?"

He had turned away from her so that he did not see the hurt bewilderment that leapt into the wide dark eyes, only heard the softly mocking note in her voice as she replied, "How odd. I don't recall your complaining about my lack of clothing before, aboard the *Louisa*."

It was cold in the room, he realized as he tossed his clothes onto a chair, the fire doing little to dispel the chill. He turned back and studied his wife. Beneath the sheer gown, he saw that her skin was not just pale but almost blue white with cold. And that low-cut scarlet gown she'd worn at dinner, he thought suddenly, couldn't have been very warm either in that great, drafty dining room with its high ceilings.

"For God's sake, at least get into bed, where it's warm," he grumbled.

She hesitated, looking suddenly uncertain. "Aren't you coming?"

"In a moment." He made a pretense of yawning vigorously. "It's been a long day. I feel as if I could sleep for a week."

He went into the bathroom and took his time preparing for bed. When he returned to the room, Jasmine was in bed and the lamps were extinguished; the only light was from the flames dying in the fireplace.

When he slipped into bed, he stayed as far away from her as possible, not trusting his instincts as he felt desire knotting inside of him, the urgent need to possess her even after what his mother had told him. But it had been a long, hard day, and with the sheets warmed by a hot-water bottle, he finally slept.

It was Jasmine who remained miserably awake as the hot-water bottle lost its warmth, and she curled in a tight little ball trying to ward off the chill within and without her. She would have edged closer to Morgan's warmth, but suppose he should awaken and find her lying next to him? No, she thought, wincing in memory, he had made it very clear that he did not want her. She wouldn't throw herself at him again. It would be better if she got up and restarted the fire.

She threw back the covers and slipped out of bed as quietly as possible, but when the freezing air in the room hit her, it was like stepping into ice water and she gave a little gasp.

"What is it?" Morgan asked, coming instantly awake, the way she remembered he always had aboard the *Louisa.*

"The fire's going out," she said, trying to keep her teeth from chattering.

"Stay in bed," he growled. "I'll take care of the fire."

Gratefully she crawled back beneath the covers, but even after Morgan had coaxed the banked flames into burning and returned to bed, she could not stop shivering convulsively. Her hands and feet felt like lumps of ice.

When Morgan suddenly loomed over her in the darkness, she no longer cared what he might think. She reached greedily for his warmth with both arms, snuggling, shivering, against him. When, shocked, he felt how cold her flesh was, he began to chafe her arms and legs, at first roughly then more gently, her skin tingling painfully as the blood returned to her limbs. Gradually, inevitably, his caressing hands stirred memories of past pleasure when her body had quivered beneath those hands, not with cold but from another much more agreeable sensation.

In the flickering firelight, she saw his face above hers so close that she could see the muscles pulled taut by his mouth, the golden light in his eyes staring down at her. His hands continued to evoke their magic, and her body responded mindlessly, obeying unspoken commands, as if their bodies were moving through the intricate steps of a dance without music. She pulled his mouth down to cover her parted lips, their tongues caressing languorously, their warm breath mingling.

Then his mouth left her lips, lingered at the dark hollow in her throat before covering the rosy peak of her breast, teasing the softness with his tongue, and she stopped thinking, only feeling, drowning in waves of ever-deepening sensation. Her body was on fire, and she no longer felt the chill of the room. Deliberately she closed her eyes and gave herself up to pure sensation, postponing as long as possible the final moment when she knew the dance would end and she and Morgan would pull apart, their bodies spent, and once again become strangers.

This time, though, she was the one who afterwards fell immediately into a sleep that was troubled and restless, filled with nightmarish dreams of frozen, snow-drifted fields through which she stumbled endlessly. In the unreasoning manner of dreams, she was dressed only in her sheer nightgown, and the icy cold so numbed her body that it was agony to force herself to go forward. Always in the distance before her, moving across the frozen landscape, was a tall, dark figure that she was struggling toward and who remained, tantalizingly, out of reach.

Then, in her dream, she stumbled and fell, a snowy drift closing slowly over her, and she awoke with a cry, drenched in perspiration. It was daylight, bright sunlight without warmth streaming into the bedroom window. Morgan was dressed and standing beside the bed, looking down at her.

"What time is it?" she muttered hoarsely.

"It's almost noon." He placed a hand on her forehead. "You don't look well."

"That's because I don't feel well," she said petulantly.

"You've probably caught a cold," he said, his voice irritable. "You should have more sense than to wear so little clothing in the dead of winter."

"Oh, shut up," she whispered, annoyed. She was in no mood for a lecture. Her throat was sore, her head was pounding, and every bone in her body ached.

A smile quirked one corner of Morgan's mouth. "Well, at least your disposition hasn't been affected," he said more cheerfully. "Would you like breakfast brought up to the room?"

"No." Even the thought of food made her stomach flip-flop. "I just want to be left alone. I'll feel better in a day or two."

But it was several weeks before she fully recovered from her cold, which had turned into a mild form of pneumonia. For two days, her temperature climbed. The doctor came and gave her medicine, which made her drowsy, so she was only vaguely aware of Morgan and his mother taking turns sitting beside her bed as she drifted in and out of sleep.

Once she heard the doctor speaking in a low, worried voice to Morgan. "Must take care it doesn't settle into her lungs. . . . Her system isn't accustomed to the severity of our winters. . . . Fortunately, she has a strong constitution."

The islands, Jasmine thought, tears suddenly burning her eyes, the homesickness so bitter in her mouth that it was like biting into a persimmon. If only she could be lying in the sunshine at the beach with the golden heat pouring over her aching body, the ocean murmuring at the shore as the waves crested over the coral reef. Then, afraid that Morgan would see the tears, she turned her face away, ashamed of her weakness. New Bedford was Morgan's home. If she were to remain his wife, she would have to learn to live here, to endure the long winters and cherish the brief summers.

February turned into March, and winter kept its grip on New Bedford, the snow cover never leaving the ground. Jasmine was able to sit up now and move around, but the doctor cautiously forbade her to leave the house until the days grew warmer.

Then one day as she roamed the house restlessly, she decided to climb the ladder to the cupola. Halfway up the ladder, the room began to spin dizzily around her and she had to grab at the ladder to keep from falling.

As quickly as it had hit her, the dizziness passed and she almost forgot to mention it to the doctor during his next visit except that he was asking her very explicit questions about her health. "I feel fine, doctor, really I do," she assured him, sitting up in bed. April had at last arrived, a trace of pale green appearing here and there between melting patches of snow. "I can go out for a carriage ride now, can't I?" she asked anxiously, dreading the thought of being shut up in the house any longer.

"I don't see why not," the doctor said, his eyes twinkling behind steel-rimmed glasses. "I've always found fresh air very healthy for young women in your condition."

"My condition?" Jasmine blurted before understanding broke over her.

"From what you've told me, I'd say the baby will be born in November," the doctor said, putting away his instruments and snapping his bag shut. Then seeing the alarm in his patient's eyes, he said quickly, "There's no reason to be concerned, my dear. It's a natural process, having babies, and you're in splendid condition. I'm sure Captain Tucker will be very pleased to hear the news."

Jasmine wished she were as sure as the doctor that Morgan would be happy with the news of his impending fatherhood. Still, it was what she had planned for, wasn't it? she reminded herself, ever since the day she had left

the lawyer's office. It was why she had worn the flattering scarlet gown and the embarrassingly filmy nightgown the night of Morgan's return, to lure him into her
arms in the hope that his seed would be planted within
her, tying him to her in the way women had tied men to
them from time immemorial—with a baby.

As the doctor rose to leave, she said, trying to hide
the panic in her voice, "I'd like to tell my husband the
news."

"Of course. That's a wife's prerogative," he assured
her, then added jovially, "but I wouldn't wait too long. I
noticed yesterday at the wharf that the *Louisa* was
being fitted out again, ready for another voyage very
shortly, no doubt."

So that was why Morgan had been away from the
house so much lately, Jasmine thought. He was getting
the *Louisa* ready for another whaling trip. How soon,
she wondered, would he be sailing? And was he planning to leave her behind again as he had on his last trip?

Not this time! Jasmine thought as she walked to the
front door with the doctor. She would not endure a life
of loneliness like the one her mother-in-law had spent.
When the *Louisa* left New Bedford, she would be aboard
her even if she had to stow away. And she would have
her baby in Hawaii, in her old room, not in this great,
cold house.

At the door, she asked the doctor off-handedly, "Would
it be possible for me to sail with my husband?"

The doctor frowned. "Decidedly not! I know it's been
done by some whaling wives, but I certainly don't approve of such a dangerous course of action. Nor would
Captain Tucker, I'm sure."

At the growing look of concern in the doctor's eyes,
Jasmine said hastily, "Oh, I quite agree, doctor." She
gave the man a brave smile beneath fluttering eyelashes.
"That's why I want to tell my husband myself about my
condition in my own time. Captain Tucker will just
worry and perhaps even decide not to make the trip,

and I wouldn't want that to happen. You must promise me that you won't say anything to my husband."

"As you wish," the doctor agreed reluctantly and a little enviously, thinking how fortunate the captain was to have such a beautiful, as well as brave, wife.

That night when Morgan came to bed, he found Jasmine waiting for him, the covers pulled up around her but her frilly nightgown flung across the foot of the bed.

At Morgan's quizzical look, she smiled sweetly. "The doctor said I'm quite recovered. Of course, if you're too tired . . ."

Laughter flashed behind Morgan's eyes for a moment, then he shed his clothes and was in the bed beside her. He had not bothered to extinguish the lamp in his haste to join her, and just for a moment, looking into his wife's face, which was framed by a black cloud of hair against the pillow, he thought he glimpsed a look of frightened defiance in the dark eyes, reminding him of the girl he had first met aboard the *Louisa*.

Then Jasmine had pulled his face down to hers, her lips moving softly, invitingly, under his, her velvet tongue darting in his mouth as her hands stroked the short, crisp black hair at the nape of his neck.

It was the first time she had approached him in their lovemaking deliberately, openly seeking to arouse him. He could feel his pulse pounding as her mouth left his to nibble teasingly at his earlobe, her fingertips trailing over the muscles in his shoulders and back, pulling him closer and yet closer to her.

Then as he pulled her beneath him, unable to postpone any longer the pleasure she was offering him, she whispered, "Take me with you, Morgan."

Startled, he drew back, his dark brows slanting together across the broad bridge of his nose as he demanded, "How did you know?"

She shrugged. "What does it matter?" She arched her body so that the tips of her breasts brushed against his chest, her hands moving boldly downward to caress the hard-muscled thighs. "Please, take me with you," she whispered again. "I swear I'll be no bother. You can leave me in the islands while you search for your whales. Please, Morgan . . ."

So that was what this was all about, he thought, a cold perspiration of rage and desire glistening on his face as he stared down coldly at his wife. All her seductive smiles and beguiling ways were only ploys to get him to agree to take her back to Hawaii. Undoubtedly the lawyer had told her of the difficulties of a wife gaining a divorce without her husband giving her sufficient cause. Back in the islands, while he was away on the *Louisa*, she could be free of him without the necessity of a divorce. Damn her devious, scheming little mind, he thought savagely, that like her heart and affection would forever elude him. Well, if she wanted to barter with her body, if that was all she had to offer him, then he would be a blind, lovesick fool no longer.

Jasmine gasped as Morgan suddenly pulled her hands free and imprisoned them above her head. His mouth crushed hers cruelly again and again as he entered and took her quickly, not thinking of her pleasure but only of his own desire to finish the act, to be free of her. Unbelievably swiftly, he had achieved a sort of satisfaction and was out of bed, pulling on his clothes, while she stared at him, her mouth still trembling from his bruising kisses, her body trembling with unfulfilled desire.

When he headed for the door, she cried, "Morgan, wait!"

He half turned. She sat up in bed, the covers falling away from her, her hair tumbling in wild disarray over her shoulders. He saw her swallow hard before she asked uneasily, "You haven't said, will you take me with you?"

His mouth half twisted in a sardonic smile, his eyes flicking contemptuously across her face. "You needn't have bothered with your little charade. I'd always planned to take you with me."

Then the door closed behind him, and for Jasmine it had the ominous finality of a thunderclap.

Chapter 17

"What island is that, Mr. Gibbons?"

Jasmine stood at the rail of the *Louisa*, looking across the water at cliffs plunging to the sea and clouds drifting around dark blue peaks.

"Más Afuera, Mrs. Tucker. We're off the coast of Chile."

"Will we be stopping there?"

"The captain says not. We can't afford to take the time."

The first mate eyed the captain's wife sympathetically as Jasmine returned slowly to her chair near the tiny deckhouse and picked up her book. But then Mrs. Tucker wasn't the only one disappointed that the *Louisa* wasn't stopping at Más Afuera, Mr. Gibbons knew. He had heard the men grumbling at the pace the captain had set for the *Louisa* and her crew ever since they had left New Bedford, two months before. Even after they had rounded the Horn and reached the Pacific whaling grounds, instead of poking along under light sail, hoving to and furling the topsails at night, the usual custom among whaling ships, the *Louisa* kept all sails set day and night, catching every breeze that sent her speeding before the wind.

"The captain must think the old tub's a clipper," the first mate had heard one of the men from the forecastle complaining. "We'll have a clean ship all the way to the Sandwich Islands at this rate."

Mr. Gibbons, having three children of his own, had already guessed the reason for the captain's haste to reach the Hawaiian Islands. Not that the skipper had mentioned his wife's pregnancy to any of his officers. Gazing speculatively at the young woman trying to make herself comfortable under the rigged awning, Mr. Gibbons wondered how far along she was. It was impossible to tell with the way she always kept herself swaddled in layers of clothing.

As he came up from the companionway, Morgan saw the way Jasmine walked slowly to the chair and the sheen of perspiration on her face from the July sun beating down upon the deck and the heavily clothed figure. Morgan frowned, and when Jasmine made her way down to the cabin, he waited a few moments then followed her.

She had removed her dress and was laving water on her face from the washbasin when he entered the cabin. He closed the door behind him and, crossing his arms, leaned against the door, surveying Jasmine coldly as he asked, "How long had you planned to wait before telling me I was to become a father?" One dark eyebrow slanted upward. "I assume there is no question this time that it is my child?"

A flush ran up to Jasmine's hairline. She clutched her gown to her and cried, "You know very well it's yours!" And then, she said sulkily, "How long have you known?"

"Since shortly after we left New Bedford. You're a good sailor. When you became seasick every morning, naturally I got suspicious." He scowled at her, his voice impatient. "Why else do you think we've been under full sail? And why I slung a hammock in the cabin?"

Knowing very little about expectant mothers, he had been concerned that, sharing the small bed with Jasmine, he might turn over in the night and accidentally hurt the child. And with the nights growing warmer, he was sure that Jasmine would sleep better alone.

"I thought . . ." Jasmine bit her lip and fell silent. After the humiliating way he had stalked out of her bedroom that night in New Bedford, what was she to think? That he couldn't bear to be near her, so he had moved into the outer cabin. Or was it that her pregnancy made her unattractive to him? She felt unattractive with her thickening waistline, and, to her surprise, she felt miserable most of the time. She was almost as ignorant about having babies as Morgan. When she had so blithely decided to have Morgan's child, she hadn't realized she would spend her mornings feeling nauseous or that she would become stupidly clumsy on her feet. Or that she would feel so bloated and ugly that she hated for Morgan to see her. She had no illusions about what had drawn Morgan to her in the first place and still held him despite everything. Without her beauty, she felt defenseless and vulnerable.

When Morgan came to stand before her, she lifted her eyes, trying to read in his face what he was thinking, and was surprised to see a glint of humor in the hazel eyes staring down at her. "Did my mother know about the baby?" he asked curiously.

"No, of course not." Or had Louisa known? Jasmine wondered suddenly. She remembered the suspicious shine in the woman's eyes as she had embraced her daughter-in-law for the last time aboard the *Louisa* and murmured, "I wish I had had your courage years ago, my child. God be with you."

"I would have told you sooner," Jasmine said, "but I was afraid you'd leave me behind."

"You're damn right I would have," Morgan said tersely. "Do you think I would have endangered you or the child had I known?"

A sudden chill engulfed Jasmine, a frightening thought that she had determinedly pushed out of her mind all these months. What if the baby should come before they reached the islands? There would be no doctor to help her.

Her dark eyes were charged with fear as they clung to Morgan's face. "My mother died in childbirth," she said tremulously. "I was in the next room. I heard her screaming. . . ."

"Listen to me, Jasmine Tucker!" Morgan's hands dug painfully into her shoulders, his eyes glaring fiercely down at her. "You won't die! I won't let you!"

She was still clutching the shapeless, heavy woolen gown before her, and he jerked it from her hands and tossed it on the bed. "Unless you die of heat stroke," he said, scowling at the garment then at her. "Don't you have anything cooler to wear?"

The scowl faded as his narrowed gaze traveled slowly over his wife's body, the new soft swell below her waist clearly visible. Suddenly embarrassed, she started to turn away, but he wouldn't let her, holding her gently but firmly by the shoulders. With a sharp thrust of desire, Morgan thought that Jasmine had never looked lovelier. Her skin had lost its wintry paleness and was once more a warm peach gold shade, her breasts fuller than he remembered, her eyes shimmering like the glow on the sea just before sunset.

His hands left her shoulders and trailed downward over the deep breasts, lingering on the miraculously rounding belly; his voice was shaken, hoarse, as if the words were torn out of him. "Dear God, how I love you!"

To his amazement, his wife immediately began to laugh then cry hysterically, her fists pushed against her mouth as if trying in vain to hold back the laughter while tears streamed down her face. "Now!" she gasped. "Now you tell me when you've never told me before!"

Alarmed by her odd behavior, he sat down on the bed and pulled her into his arms, cradling her as if she were a child. "Hush," he said gruffly, smoothing her hair away from her face. "You'll make yourself sick. Of course I love you. You're carrying my child, aren't you?"

When she finally grew quiet in his arms, he laid her on the bed and pulled a coverlet over her. When he started to leave, she reached for his hand. "Stay with me," she said softly.

It was almost three months since they had lain together, and Morgan remembered only too vividly her trembling softness in his arms a few moments before. He could still feel the heaviness of her breasts against him. Damn it, he thought helplessly, if only he knew more about pregnant women. If he took her now, would he hurt her and the baby? He supposed he could ask Henry Gibbons for advice, but it went against the grain for Morgan to admit ignorance of anything, especially to his officers. Determinedly, he tore his eyes away from Jasmine and pulled his hand free. No, he didn't dare take the chance of harming her or the child. And there was no way he could lie down beside her without wanting to possess her completely.

His sense of frustration roughened his voice. "You're forgetting I've a ship to run, madam, and you need your rest."

After he had left, though, Jasmine consoled herself with the thought that he had said he loved her. Even if it was said only because she was carrying his child, still it was a beginning. And once the child was born and she had regained her figure, she was sure that she could entice him back into her arms. If only she weren't so tired, she thought drowsily. All she seemed to want to do was sleep.

As the weeks passed, she was glad that Morgan continued sleeping in the hammock in the outer cabin. She slept restlessly these nights and the baby's kicking often woke her. And every day the child grew larger and heavier within her, so walking was an effort, but sitting for long periods was equally uncomfortable.

She did wear lighter clothes, which helped as the *Louisa* crossed the equator. The sun became fiercer overhead, the pitch on the deck softening and oozing under her feet when she climbed up on deck. The cotton dresses she wore now didn't hide her pregnant condition. At first she felt embarrassed when she saw the men look at her then quickly look away, but she soon got over it. And the first and second mate were always somewhere near, she noticed, when she was on deck, to help her down the companionway. The third mate, Mr. Otis, had not sailed with them on this trip, and Jasmine was glad, but she still missed Daniel, who was in the forecastle again on this voyage. He had made a piece of scrimshaw for Jasmine, presenting it to her shyly after first obtaining permission to present himself on the quarterdeck. It was a baby's teething ring, its handle intricately carved. He had flushed a bright red with delight when Jasmine had praised the gift to the skies.

The ship stopped briefly at the Galápagos, only long enough to take on fresh water and one of the giant terrapins that the islands were famous for and that would feed the crew for days. The water was rough, though, and Morgan would not allow Jasmine to leave the ship to go ashore. She objected, having looked forward to a few hours of steady land beneath her feet, but Morgan was adamant.

"You care more for the baby than you do for me," Jasmine said petulantly, gazing longingly at the land. She felt hot and sweaty and unattractive with the perspiration gathering beneath her swollen breasts and running down her back.

She did not see the amusement in Morgan's face. "The baby is an unknown quotient," he said calmly, "while you, madam, are not."

And what was that supposed to mean, Jasmine thought irritably, walking away from her husband with as much dignity as she could manage, although she was sure she must look from the rear like a waddling duck.

Five weeks later, the *Louisa* raised the island of Hawaii, and Jasmine eagerly completed her packing. While she was folding gowns into her trunk, she heard a rustle in the skirt of a gown and pulled out the letter from Malia she had received in New Bedford. She realized guiltily that she had never told her husband the shocking news about Lani and Kale, partly because she still could not bear to think, much less talk, about it and partly because she could not bear it if Morgan would think the less of her and the child. Well, he would find out soon enough when they reached Honolulu, she thought, pushing the letter quickly back into the skirt pocket, hating herself for being a coward but hating more the moment when she must tell Morgan the truth.

When the *Louisa* laid off the port of Honolulu the next week and Jasmine was carefully escorted ashore by her husband, she found her father waiting for them. He hugged Jasmine, smiling and holding her away from him so that he could admire her obviously pregnant condition. "So it's a grandfather you're making me," he boomed, pleased. The blue eyes searched her face. "You're happy, then, lass?"

Jasmine hesitated for only a second before answering, "Very happy, Father."

If he was aware of his wife's slight moment of hesitation, Morgan's face did not show it as he shook Captain Babcock's hand and gestured toward the harbor. Although it was only October, almost two hundred whaling ships already crowded the docking space. "It looks like a good whaling year," he said. "I've never seen so many ships in port before."

His father-in-law nodded as he handed Jasmine into the carriage. "It's a good year for Honolulu, too," he said. "The seamen spend their money like it was water." He frowned as he saw several sailors who had staggered out from a grogshop, trying to pick a fight with a native policeman. "I'd be happier if the men were a better disciplined lot, though. The police have their hands full, and the jail's already overcrowded."

The carriage drove slowly past the wharf area, often stopping for whaling men swaggering across the streets, rum bottles in their hands. Groups of men, Jasmine noticed, were gathered around buildings where music could be heard streaming out of the doors.

At her startled glance, her father smiled a little sheepishly. "Aye, they're public dance houses, just started a few months ago. The missionaries are furious, but I say if it keeps the men from tearing up the town, what's the harm in it?"

"Not to mention it's good business if you happen to own a dance house," Morgan said dryly, well aware of his father-in-law's shrewdness in investing in money-making concerns. He glanced at the captain curiously. "How is your sugar plantation doing these days?"

"Well enough, though there's a dozen planters who have gone into bankruptcy with the collapse of the California market now that the gold boom's passed. The biggest problem for the plantations, though, is the lack of laborers."

"What about the Hawaiians?"

The captain shrugged. "Oh, there are *kanakas* that make good workers, but most of them don't like field work. No, the planters think the answer will be found in those. . . ."

He pointed with his whip to a group of men coming down the street. Jasmine could not see the men's faces, their heads were bent submissively, but she could tell they were Chinese by the pigtails swinging down their backs. Two men on horseback rode alongside the shuffling group of men, herding them along. Something about the men made Jasmine feel vaguely uncomfortable, the way they walked almost in lockstep like prisoners.

Morgan cocked a surprised eyebrow at the captain. "Coolies?"

"They're brought in from China under contract," the captain said. "Then they're sold to the planters as workers under the Masters and Servants Act."

"Why, that's the same as slave labor," Jasmine said, shocked.

"Not at all," her father replied, his heavy eyebrows bristling. "The coolies are indentured to a planter for five years. When their time is up, they can return to China if they wish. I have a dozen of them at my plantation, and they're fine workers. Most of them live much better here on the plantations than they ever did in China."

Then as if to change the subject from an unpleasant one, he said quickly, "Of course, the real answer to the problem of the planters is to have a steady market for our sugar in America without having to pay import duty."

"You're talking about the annexation of these islands to the United States, aren't you?" Morgan asked quietly.

"Oh, it's been talked about for years, but that's all it is, talk," Captain Babcock said glumly. "I think the king is willing, but the young princes are dead set against it."

As the talk between her father and husband turned to politics, Jasmine's attention drifted away. How beautiful Honolulu was after the stark black, gray, and white of New Bedford, she thought happily, taking in the scarlet hibiscus spilling over a low, white-stone wall, the sky a dazzling blue overhead, the gentle warmth of the sun on her face.

Then suddenly the child she was carrying kicked hard against her. As if, Jasmine thought, laughing aloud, the baby was telling her that it, too, was happy to be here.

Morgan heard his wife's burst of pleased laughter and, turning, saw that Jasmine's eyes were dancing with merriment, her face holding a passionate, tender warmth that he had never seen before, even in those moments when she cried out with rapture in his arms. Perhaps, he thought hopefully, it would be better between Jasmine and him here in the islands. After the baby was born, that laughing, bright-eyed, passionate young woman in the carriage would give herself completely to him, without the smallest part of her eluding his desire for her.

Then they were turning into the Babcock grounds, and Malia and Lilikoi were waiting on the front veranda. Malia's eyes grew softer, her smile more welcoming, if that were possible, when she saw Jasmine's condition.

She held her stepdaughter close, and when the child kicked again so that she could feel it, she smiled happily. "It is a *kane*, I think, the way it kicks so hard."

Lilikoi glided gracefully forward to embrace Jasmine,

but her kukui brown eyes moved quickly to Morgan as she murmured, "We've missed you."

Jasmine saw that her sister no longer had the sylph-like figure she once had, but the ripe fullness of Lilikoi's body was still eye-catching, as the silken folds of her loosely shaped *holoku* clung to heavy breasts and voluptuous hips.

Later, as Jasmine undressed and slipped into a robe, tightening a satin sash around her extended abdomen, she frowned unhappily at her reflection in the mirror. Even Lilikoi wasn't as fat and ungraceful as she was at this moment. She could hardly remember the slim, tiny-waisted figure that had once been hers. Nine months was too long, she thought irritably, averting her gaze from the swollen stranger in the mirror. Pushing open a window overlooking the garden, she took a deep breath of the fragrance from the jasmine shrub growing beneath her window, the blossoms as fragile as tiny stars scenting the air with their sweetness.

Then she saw Morgan in the garden standing in the shadow of a lauhala tree, its twisted, ropelike roots growing half out of the soil. She started to call to him when she saw that Lilikoi was with him, their dark heads bent closely together.

Afraid they might see her, Jasmine backed away from the window. Deliberately, not wanting to think about the somehow clandestine scene she had just witnessed, she turned her gaze to the four-poster bed. Well, at least the bed was large enough so that Morgan would have no excuse to sleep elsewhere tonight, she thought. Malia had insisted that Jasmine and her husband stay at the Babcock home until the baby was born. And, naturally, Morgan would be expected to share his wife's bed. And after the baby was born? Jasmine wondered suddenly. The *Louisa* would be sailing with the rest of the whaling fleet in November for the Japan grounds. And Captain Tucker's wife, with their new baby, would most certainly be left behind.

Hurriedly Jasmine pushed that dismaying thought

aside. She would worry about that later. Right now, she realized, she had a more pressing problem on her hands. With Morgan staying here in the house, she would have to tell him about Lani and Kale. He must already be wondering why her sister and brother hadn't been at the house to greet them when they arrived.

When Morgan came into the room a few minutes later, she took a deep breath and spoke quickly, "There's something I have to tell you, Morgan."

"I already know about Lani and Kale," Morgan said, scowling, as he closed the door behind him.

"How?" she asked, startled. Then, remembering the scene she had witnessed in the garden, she said, "Lilikoi told you?"

He nodded grimly. "She also informed me that ours won't be the first grandchild for Captain Babcock and Malia. Lani had a child, a daughter, three months ago."

"Oh." Jasmine sat down abruptly on the bed, her knees suddenly weak.

Morgan gave her a sharp, worried glance. "Are you all right?"

"Yes, it's just . . . poor Lani." She tried to imagine her little sister having a baby when Lani was little more than a baby herself. And suddenly it no longer mattered, the shameful thing that Lani and Kale had done. All that mattered was that they were her brother and sister, and she loved them both. "I have to go to Lani," she said, her hands twisting unhappily in her lap. "She must be so . . . alone."

"It's out of the question," Morgan said flatly. "Lilikoi isn't even sure where Lani and Kale are, at the moment."

In any case, Jasmine thought, gazing regretfully down at her swollen abdomen, she was in no condition to travel, with the baby due in only a few weeks. Or sooner, she thought as an odd, pressing pain pushed down in her abdomen. "I think you should get the doctor," she whispered, frightened, to Morgan.

Dr. Cary arrived promptly. Large, bluff-spoken, and red-faced, he assured Jasmine that she was experiencing false labor pains, that the baby probably wouldn't arrive for another two weeks. However, to be on the safe side, he suggested that she remain in bed for the remainder of her confinement and move about as little as possible. Although he didn't press the point, he glanced meaningfully at Morgan, and once again Jasmine found herself alone in bed while Morgan moved into Lani's old room across the hall.

The next few weeks dragged by, each day so much like the one before that Jasmine lost track of the time, only aware of her mounting discomfort. She grew more and more short-tempered and impatient, even with Malia, and her disposition wasn't helped by the fact that Morgan seemed to be spending all his time in town, returning to the house for dinner then disappearing again. She supposed he was busy getting the *Louisa* ready for her next cruise. As if he couldn't wait to leave, she thought bitterly one night as, unable to sleep with an aching pain in her back, she shifted her body clumsily in bed, trying to find a comfortable position.

It was a warm night and she had thrown aside the covers, thankful for the faint breeze that stirred the curtains at the window with a rustling sound. Gradually she identified other familiar night noises in the house: the branch of the lauhala tree brushing against the dining-room window below her bedroom, a wooden step creaking, a door opening softly. Jasmine turned her head toward the latter sound. It seemed so close, as if it were the door to Morgan's room across the hall. Where would he be going at this hour?

Curious, she pulled herself awkwardly out of bed and, crossing the room, opened her own door a crack to peer out into the hall. Morgan's door was opened halfway. In the yellow lamplight that spilled out like a ribbon through the doorway, she saw Lilikoi leaving Morgan's room.

Her sister's shining black hair swung long and straight to the pointed, rose brown crests of deep breasts. A drowsy, self-satisfied smile was all that Lilikoi wore. The door to Morgan's bedroom closed softly, plunging the hall into darkness. Through the darkness, Jasmine listened to the padding sound of Lilikoi's bare feet as she walked unhurriedly to her own bedroom at the far end of the hall.

Chapter 18

When Jasmine awoke the next morning, she thought at first that the odd heaviness she felt in her chest had to do with the child she was carrying. Until she remembered. Then the heaviness became a black weight pressing down upon her as she saw, in her mind's eye, the burnished brown body of Lilikoi, not in the hallway as she had seen her last night but lying in Morgan's arms. She saw his hands, whose strength and touch her own body knew so intimately, caressing the lush curves of Lilikoi's soft body, finally burying himself in that softness and placing that pleased, satiated smile on Lilikoi's lips.

After all, she thought, as if she were deliberately teasing an aching tooth with her tongue, it wasn't as if Morgan and her sister hadn't lain together before, aboard the *Louisa*. He had as much as said so the first night they had met. No doubt her husband found Lilikoi a much more exciting, certainly more experienced, bed companion than Jasmine.

A tortured groan escaped from her lips and immediately the bedroom door opened and Malia hurried in. "Are you all right, child? Is it the baby?" she asked, worried.

Jasmine shook her head, fighting back the tears of

rage and humiliation that threatened to overflow and deluge her. She glared down, frustrated, at the rounded bulge in her middle. "I'm tired of being fat and ugly and clumsy," she complained bitterly. "I'll never have another child."

Malia clucked soothingly. "Hush, *keiki*. Of course you will. And afterwards, when you hold the child in your arm, your happiness will make all the waiting worthwhile." She smiled mistily. "And my happiness, too, for this grandchild, at least, I will be able to hold in my arms."

So Malia knew that Lani had had a child, Jasmine thought. Although Malia never spoke of Kale or Lani, Jasmine had always suspected that her stepmother still kept track of her son and daughter.

"Have you seen Lani and her daughter?" she asked eagerly.

Tears flowed down Malia's plump face. "I have never seen my granddaughter, nor my precious Lani since she left this house," she cried, anguish in her voice. "But Lilikoi saw her sister on Maui. She said that the child, named Ulimi, is as beautiful as her mother."

"And Kale? How is he?"

A smile broke through the tears. "Causing much *pilikia*, as usual. He goes from village to village, island to island, speaking against the *haoles* and the Masters and Servants Act. The newspapers call him a rabble-rouser and troublemaker, but the people flock to hear him." Then, remembering Jasmine's condition and that the doctor had warned that she must not be upset, she said quickly, "Let me get you something to eat. You slept right through breakfast."

"I'm not hungry," Jasmine said, then turned her head toward the window. She could hear church bells tolling, as if for a funeral, and even more faintly, the sound of shuffling feet, mourners following the coffin in a procession to the cemetery. She glanced curiously at Malia. "Did someone of importance die?"

Malia hesitated, then said, "It was a sailor, Henry Burns. Nothing to concern yourself about, my dear."

But Malia's face was too open for deception, and why should there be so many mourners for a common seaman? Jasmine wondered.

"What did he die of?" she asked. When Malia didn't answer at once, she said petulantly, "You might as well tell me. If you don't, you know one of the servants will."

"It happened two nights ago," Malia said reluctantly. "The man was in jail for drunkenness. A prison guard tried to quiet him, and when the prisoner became unruly, the guard hit him with a club. Unhappily, the poor man died from the blow."

Not wanting to upset Jasmine, she did not add that news of the seaman's death had spread swiftly through the harbor area. Boatload after boatload of men had come pouring off the whaling ships into Honolulu, demanding vengeance on the guard, threatening to tear down the fort. And of course, Malia thought, sighing to herself, the fact that most of the men were drunk and getting drunker didn't help matters any.

Still, she thought hopefully, her husband and Captain Tucker, along with other merchants and shipmasters, had gone into town trying to calm the men by talking to them. Surely, the *pilikia* would be over by evening.

But the trouble did not end that evening, Malia learned. The hundreds of seamen who had gone directly from Henry Burns's funeral to the grogshops had turned into a drunken, uncontrollable mob. Armed with axes and clubs and any other murderous weapon they could lay their hands on, they began to roam the streets of the town, destroying anyone and anything that stood in their way.

A male servant whom Malia had sent into town to discover what was going on returned with blood running down his face from a cut on his head and fear in his voice. "The men are *pupule*," he cried. "They've set fire to the police station and the flames have spread to many more buildings. If the fire spreads to only one ship in the harbor, the whole fleet will go up in flames. The police can do nothing to stop them. The seamen are forcing their way into private homes, threatening to burn the houses of the merchants, saying they've been cheated for years by the Honolulu shopkeepers."

"Shhh!" Malia said, casting an anxious glance up toward Jasmine's room. There was no need to alarm the child. An hour ago, Malia had sent Lilikoi and most of the servants to stay with friends farther up in the valley, but she didn't dare to take the chance of moving Jasmine. The girl was too close to her time.

Now as she hurried up to Jasmine's bedroom, she wondered, worried, if she had done the right thing. When she entered the bedroom, she found Jasmine sitting up in bed, her voice irritable as she demanded, "Where is everybody? The house is as quiet as a tomb."

Malia went to the window and pulled the curtains shut, but not before she saw how strangely light the sky looked near the harbor area. If the oil-soaked timbers of the whaling ships caught fire, she knew that no one could stop the holocaust that would follow.

Then her eye was caught by flickering lights, like fireflies; coming up Nuuanu Street. Torches, she recognized at once. Were the drink-maddened seamen coming this far up into the valley? Trying to keep the fear from showing in her face, she turned with a smile to the young woman in the bed.

"Your father and husband went into town on business," she said. "And I warned the rest of the household to be quiet so you could sleep."

"I'm not sleepy," Jasmine protested, trying to adjust the pillows behind her aching back. Suddenly she reached for her stepmother's hand, holding it with a death grip, her voice brittle. "When Morgan returns, I don't want to see him."

Malia stared at her, bewildered. "But he's your husband."

Jasmine's hand tightened its grip. "You must promise me, Malia. I don't want to see him."

Alarmed at the girl's pallor, the feverish brightness in the dark eyes, Malia said soothingly, "If you wish, of course. Now you must try to rest."

When she returned to the first floor of the house, she was aware, too, of the thickness of the silence around her, as if she could reach out and touch it. A palm branch scraping at a window made her jump. Or was it a branch? she wondered nervously. Was it perhaps someone trying to break into the house? She grasped one of her husband's heavy oak walking sticks and lifted it firmly in her hand; her body, for all its weight, glided without a sound through the dining room, a dark, fierce look on her usually placid face.

"I'd appreciate your not using that stick on my head."

"Captain Tucker!" Relieved, Malia lowered the stick to her side as the captain stepped out of the shadows. "Is my husband with you?" she asked anxiously.

"No. The merchants have formed a citizens' guard patrolling the streets of the town. I came back to see how Jasmine was."

He had started for the stairs when Malia's voice stopped him. "Jasmine's resting, Captain. I—I wouldn't bother her." When he turned, giving her a questioning look, she asked hastily, "How bad is the fire in town?"

"The wind's shifted, so the ships are saved," Morgan said. "I don't know about the rest of the town. The mob's tearing the wharf area apart." His glance probed sharply at Malia's face. "You're sure Jasmine is all right?"

"Yes, but I think the baby will come soon. Perhaps you . . ."

Both Malia and Morgan heard the sound at the same time, a low cry coming from Jasmine's room. As quickly as Malia moved, Morgan was there before her. Jasmine was out of bed, standing beside a bureau, its drawers pulled open. Her glance flew to Malia. "My gown's all wet," she said. "I was getting a dry one when . . ." Another pain caught her, and she doubled over with a startled cry.

Morgan quickly carried her back to the bed, standing

by helplessly while Jasmine bit savagely at her lower lip to keep from screaming aloud with the incredible pain tearing at her body.

Malia smoothed the dark hair back from Jasmine's damp forehead. "Don't fight the pain, *keiki*," she murmured. "And scream as loud as you want if it makes you feel better."

She pulled Morgan out into the hall, her voice urgent. "Fetch Dr. Cary. Hurry!"

Morgan gazed blankly at her. "But I thought the doctor said the first baby could take hours before it comes."

"Not this baby," Malia said impatiently. "I think this one will come *wikiwiki*."

Morgan frowned. "I saw the doctor in town an hour ago, patching up a wounded constable. But I'll find him. . . ."

He broke off at the sound of feet stumbling loudly up the veranda steps of the Babcock home. Fists pounded at the front door, then drunken voices bellowed, "Open the door and hurry up about it, or we'll break it down!"

Malia clutched at Morgan's arm. "*Auwe!*" she wailed softly. "It's the men from the ships. They'll burn the house over our heads!"

"Does Captain Babcock have any guns in the house?" Morgan asked quietly.

Malia shook her head. "Only at the store."

Morgan thought a moment, his eyes narrowing, his face growing very still. "Are there any servants left at all?"

"Just the gardener. He refused to leave."

The pounding at the door grew louder. Morgan gave Malia a gentle shove toward the bedroom. "Stay with Jasmine. Keep the door locked. I'll send the gardener for a doctor." He started down the steps, then stopped and swung back. "Where does the captain keep his liquor?"

"In the sideboard in the dining room," Malia said, surprised. "But what . . ."

"Never mind." Morgan flashed her a grim smile. "I'll take care of the men. You take care of Jasmine."

By the time he had sent the gardener into town to look for a doctor and returned to the front hall, the men on the porch had smashed in several of the windows in the front parlor. They were ready to take an axe to the door when Morgan pulled it open and stepped back, smiling hospitably. "Come in, gentlemen, come in. Sorry to keep you waiting."

A half-dozen men crowded into the front hall, all in various stages of drunkenness and all glaring suspiciously at Morgan. "We was told one of those damn cheating merchants lives here," the ringleader muttered ferociously.

"I'm a whaling captain," Morgan said. "Captain Tucker of the *Louisa*."

A startled silence fell over the men. Several of the seamen shuffled their feet uneasily. None of them had served on the *Louisa*, but they all knew of Captain Morgan Tucker's reputation. The ringleader, feeling his support falling away, blustered, "Well, you're not on the quarterdeck now, Captain, and we men aim to be treated fairly for a change, not like a lot of scum kicked up on the beach."

"I quite agree," Morgan said. He gestured amiably toward the dining room. "Would you gentlemen care to join me? I was just about to begin celebrating. My wife is upstairs having our first child at this very moment." He winked broadly. "A man hates to drink alone at a time like this."

As he was talking, he was taking bottles of Captain Babcock's prized rum and brandy from the sideboard, handing out delicate Waterford glasses to the men, who gazed around them as if bewildered by this unexpected hospitality.

Then Morgan was filling the glasses, and their surprise changed to pleasure as they eagerly swallowed the liquor. Only the leader still stood warily to one side. "How do we know that you ain't lying, that you haven't gone and sent for the constables while we're standing here?"

But he had no sooner finished his accusation than a woman's cry of pain could be heard from an upstairs bedroom. One of the men, startled, almost dropped his glass, while another, a gray-haired, older man, jabbed the ringleader in the arm and chortled, "Plain you ain't had any kids, Maloney. I've had a half dozen myself, and my wife yells like a stuck pig, just like that, every time." He turned and lifted his glass to Morgan. "The first one's always the hardest, mate. Myself, I respect a man who doesn't just lay the keel but stays around for the launching."

At the sound of Jasmine's scream, Morgan's knuckles had turned white, his hand tightening on his glass. Damn it, where was the doctor? he thought helplessly.

One of the seamen had found the spinet in the front parlor and was banging away at it happily. The other men were enjoying second helpings of Captain Babcock's liquor, their voices boisterous enough so that upstairs, between contractions, Jasmine turned her head weakly on the pillow and gave Malia a surprised glance.

Malia wiped her face with a cool, wet cloth and murmured, "Just some friends dropped by." As the pain once again held Jasmine in its torturous grasp, she grasped Malia's hand. "The doctor?" she gasped.

"No time for a doctor now," Malia said quietly. "No need, either. Women have had babies long before there were doctors." She leaned over the bed, smiling encouragingly. "Now, you must do as I say. Bear down hard when I tell you. I see the head already. Push down, child. Push."

Downstairs the sound of a baby's cry brought a stunned silence to the men gathered in the parlor. Their drunken revels were forgotten for a moment, their rough faces softening as they turned toward the sound. Morgan stood for a moment as if frozen, then he bolted for the door.

The gray-haired seamen caught his arm, chuckling.

"I'd wait a few minutes before you check the cut of the new brig, Captain. I recollect there's always some tidying up to do before the launching's finished."

Morgan scowled, but deciding that the man might be right, he paced nervously at the bottom of the stairs for another ten minutes before the bedroom door opened, and Malia, smiling proudly, came down the steps, cradling a blanket-wrapped bundle carefully in her arms. Ignoring the men, she went directly to Morgan and lifted a corner of the blanket so that he could see the wrinkled red face of his son. The small arms were flailing furiously in the air and, to Morgan's mind, an amazing volume of noise was coming from the tiny mouth.

He gingerly touched the cap of hair, as black and silken as Jasmine's, he thought, and asked quickly, "Jasmine? Is she all right?"

"She's fine. Tired, that's all."

Morgan's gaze returned to his son, to the tiny, increasingly red face as his wails of protest grew louder. "Is something wrong?" he asked Malia, worried.

"He's a fine, healthy boy," Malia assured him, "with a fine, healthy set of lungs." Her black eyes sparkled, amused. "And from the way he started using them the minute he arrived, I'd say he was going to take after his grandfather."

"What are you going to christen him, Captain?" one of the men asked, a silly, bemused look on his bearded face as he edged closer to the squalling infant.

Malia glanced at Morgan then said quickly, "Your wife thought to name him after his two grandfathers, Matthew Amos Tucker."

"It's a fine handle," the gray-bearded seaman said, lifting his glass. "Here's to the future Captain Matthew Amos Tucker. May he have greasy luck and a long life."

The rest of the men lifted their glasses with equal enthusiasm. Morgan lifted his glass, too, but he hardly noticed what he was drinking.

The leader of the group put down his glass and turned to the bleary-eyed men, his voice booming, "I think it's time, mates, to leave the happy couple alone." He bowed with elaborate courtesy toward Malia, somehow managing not to fall on his face. "We thank you for your hospitality, ma'am, and wish you good evening."

Morgan waited until the last man had straggled out the door before starting hastily up the stairs. He wanted to see Jasmine for himself, to make sure she was all right.

Malia hurried up the stairs after him. "Captain Tucker, please wait. You mustn't. . . ."

Morgan turned at the bedroom door, scowling blackly at his mother-in-law, his voice ominously quiet. "I'm going in to see my wife, Mrs. Babcock. Were you planning to try and stop me?"

Malia sighed, remembering her promise to Jasmine, but looking into Morgan's face, she knew there was no way she, or an army of men, could keep Captain Tucker away from his wife.

Jasmine appeared to be sleeping as Morgan silently approached the bed. Her eyelashes lay feathery black against her pale cheeks; she hardly seemed to be breathing. But when he lightly kissed her lips, her eyelids opened drowsily.

"The baby?"

"Matthew Amos is fine," Morgan assured her. He studied the lines of exhaustion still etched in her face, and yet she had never been so radiantly beautiful and more precious to him. A feeling of love and humbleness welled up inside of him, choking him so that when he spoke his voice was gruff. "I should have been with you when our son was born. Next time, I promise. . . ."

For a moment, a warm, glowing softness filled Jasmine's eyes as she looked at him, then suddenly, inexplicably, the softness was gone and there was only a cool, remote darkness effectively shutting him out. "It doesn't matter," she said coldly. "I'll not give you another child."

Then her eyelids lowered, and she turned her face away from him.

Malia had come into the room behind Morgan. She saw the look of shocked pain in the man's face, and as she placed the still-crying child beside his mother, said gently, "Jasmine doesn't know what she's saying, Captain. In a few days, she'll forget."

But a few days and then a few weeks passed, and Morgan knew his wife hadn't forgotten. The dark eyes remained cool, aloof, when they met his gaze. It was only when she was adoringly tending their son that he saw that shimmering, loving warmth back in Jasmine's eyes. Although he knew he was being irrational, Morgan found that he was jealous of the child held so closely against his mother's breast.

Even when Morgan told Jasmine, six weeks after Matthew's birth, that he would not be sailing on the *Louisa*, that he had given the command of the ship to Henry Gibbons, only for a second did surprise wipe that coolness from Jasmine's eyes before she asked almost absently, "What will you do, then? Will you give up whaling?"

"Not completely. When the *Louisa* returns from her present whaling cruise, I plan to have her refitted into a brig. She'll be the start of a shipping fleet I hope to own someday. The whaling grounds in the Pacific will soon be fished out. In the future, whalers will have to go more and more into the Arctic Ocean to fill their holds."

And he had no intention of being away from his family for the years at a time that such long voyages would entail, he thought, gazing longingly at his wife's newly slim yet distractingly mature figure, which motherhood had brought her, and then proudly to his son, gurgling happily in her arms. Nor would young Matthew grow up without a father, as he had. Of course, he could take the fortune he had made in whaling and retire comfortably in New Bedford, as other whaling captains had done before him. Only he was sure that Jasmine would never be happy living anywhere other than the Hawaiian Islands.

Practically, Morgan's Yankee shrewdness had also influenced his decision to remain in the islands. Despite the sailors' riot that had burned part of the town, Honolulu was still booming. New buildings were springing up all the time: a marketplace, chandleries, shops, hotels, mercantile buildings.

"These islands lie across one of the most valuable trade routes in the world," he said thoughtfully to Jasmine. "They're bound to prosper over the next years and a man with his money invested in the right place—in shipping, trade, cattle, and sugar plantations—is bound to prosper with them."

A faint smile touched Jasmine's lips as she murmured, "Somehow I can't imagine you as a planter."

"I already am a planter." Morgan grinned. "Over a month ago I bought a sugar plantation near Waianae. I've hired a manager to handle the daily operations, but we'll probably have to spend several months of the year at the plantation. The rest of the time we'll be living here in Honolulu. There's a house on Beretania Street that's for sale. If it meets with your approval, we can move in next week."

He waited expectantly for Jasmine's response, but she said nothing. She had been seated, feeding the baby, half turned away from Morgan so that he could only glimpse his son's tiny hands and mouth pressing eagerly at his mother's breast. Now she got to her feet and carried the child to the wide bed, deposited him in the middle, and tucked the covers carefully around him.

"Well?" Morgan asked impatiently. "I thought you'd be pleased with my news."

Jasmine straightened, tugging the bodice of her gown up over her breast, her glance barely skimming his face. "I'm sure if the house pleases you, it will satisfy me," she said indifferently.

Morgan's frown deepened at that calm, noncommittal voice. And his feeling of frustration wasn't helped by the sight of the softly swelling breasts that he could just glimpse above the bodice of her gown.

He had continued to occupy the room across the hall

from Jasmine's after Matthew's birth in deference to his wife's delicate condition, but it was more than time, he decided now, that his life of celibacy come to an end.

He crossed over to the bed, grinned down at his sleeping son, and said, "You're going to have to find a bed of your own, young man. Your father plans to occupy this one tonight."

Jasmine was standing very still watching him, and he said hastily, "I've spoken to Dr. Cary. He said there was no reason why I couldn't . . ." Annoyed, Morgan felt a flush rising in his face. "There was no reason why we couldn't . . . Damn it, Jasmine . . ." He broke off, exasperated. "You know what I mean."

"Oh, yes," she said quietly. "I know what you mean."

He frowned uncertainly, his eyes searching her face. "Is it because you're afraid of having another child?" he asked. "There's no need to be. The doctor says you could have a dozen children without any problems. And it'll be easier the next time."

A faint pink stained Jasmine's cheeks. Her chin lifted, annoyed. "I'm not afraid of having another child."

"Well, then . . ." In one long stride, Morgan closed the distance between them, his arms closing around her as if he could not get enough of the feel and scent of her, as if trying to slake a long-endured thirst. There was a momentary resistance, but as his hands moved insistently over her body, he felt her lips open, curving to the shape of his mouth, as her body melted against him.

Finally, reluctantly, he released her, but he still held her within the circle of his arms so that she had to tilt her head back to look up at him. Her voice was without a hint of emotion as she asked, "How do I compare to Lilikoi?"

His arms abruptly fell away, and she stepped away from him. Her face was composed, but her lips were trembling childishly. "Don't bother to deny it. I saw my sister leave your room the night before Matthew was born."

Desperately Morgan wished he could deny it, to swear

that nothing had happened between Lilikoi and him that night. And in a way nothing had. He had been sound asleep when Lilikoi had climbed into his bed and plastered herself against him. Coming slowly awake, he had been vaguely conscious of bare, silken flesh warm against him, of hands caressing him, but it had seemed only part of the same frustrating dream he'd had so many nights in his celibate bed. Dreams of Jasmine, warm and yielding, cloud-soft in his arms; of her pink tongue darting, warm and moist, into his mouth; of her hands exciting him until he would reach out to take her, and awake alone in his bed, soaked with perspiration. This time, though, when he had turned, still half-asleep, and pulled her soft, yielding body beneath his, seeking immediate entry into that softness, the fantasy did not disappear. And by the time he was fully awake and aware that it was Lilikoi, writhing in ecstasy beneath him, making soft, guttural noises in her throat, it was too late.

Afterwards, Lilikoi had laughed at him, her eyes shining triumphantly, before he'd lit the lamp and sent her on her way with a few well-chosen words.

Now, staring into Jasmine's dark, accusing eyes, he knew, helplessly, that there was no way he could explain what had happened. How could he expect her to understand?

When he made no attempt to defend himself, her white face filled with contempt. "How could you? My own sister, and while I was carrying your child."

So she had already judged and convicted him, Morgan thought grimly, feeling anger flare up inside of him as he studied his wife, his eyes narrowing speculatively. He had no doubt that if he were to take her now, she would fight him off at first, but he was sure, in time, her body, with the proper coaxing, would respond with all the passion of which he knew she was capable. And it would start all over again, he thought wearily. He would possess her body and nothing more. Jasmine herself would forever escape him.

He glanced toward the bed, and his wife followed his

gaze to where their son lay asleep. For a moment, she saw pride and love soften Morgan's harsh features. When he turned back to her, though, his voice was cold, almost menacing. "I'll not let you go, nor my son either."

Jasmine felt a trembling start in her stomach and spread through her body so that she was sure Morgan could see. And suddenly she knew that she hadn't expected it, after all, to end this way. She had hoped that Morgan would sweep her into his arms and assure her that she was mistaken, that he had never lain with Lilikoi.

It took all her strength to keep her voice from shaking as she said, "I don't plan to leave you. I'll move into your house, entertain your friends, be everything a wife should be except . . ." She fell silent, knowing there was no need to put it into words, that he understood only too well what she meant by her silence.

"I see." She watched as the eyes narrowed and grew cold, the long, hard mouth twisting into a cruelly mocking smile. "As you wish, madam. But just so we understand each other, I have no intention of living the life of a eunuch!"

Then he turned and was gone, the door slamming shut behind him so that the walls trembled, and on the bed Matthew woke up, startled, and began to cry.

Chapter 19

"*It's been a lovely evening, Jasmine. Thank you so much for inviting us to your housewarming.*"

Jasmine, who had been moving from one group of guests to another, making sure that everyone was enjoying himself, turned to Emily Palmer with a smile of regret. "Oh, must you go so soon?"

But the protest was perfunctory, because Jasmine could already hear the musicians tuning their instruments for the dancing that was soon to begin, and mission families like the Palmers always left a party when the dancing began, even at royal soirées.

Mrs. Palmer gazed around the spacious drawing room, with its crystal chandeliers and pale green damask-covered chairs, the windows opening onto a colonial-columned lanai and the gardens magically lit with kukui torches and lanterns hanging in the trees. "You've done wonders with this house, my dear," Mrs. Palmer said. "In six months, you've turned it into one of the handsomest homes in Honolulu. Your husband must be very proud of you."

Jasmine followed Mrs. Palmer's gaze across the room to where Morgan stood talking with a group of merchants and planters. How handsome he was, Jasmine thought with an odd wrench of her heart, noticing how Morgan's dark head towered above the other men and how he always stood with his feet braced, his hands locked behind him. He might look like any other merchant planter, with his elegantly cut, black broadcloth suit and fine white ruffled handkerchief-linen shirt, but he still carried himself as if his feet were planted firmly on the quarterdeck of a whaler.

Emily Palmer, who missed very little, saw the shadowy look of pain darken Jasmine Tucker's eyes as she glanced across the room at her husband. Surely the young couple weren't having problems, she thought, dismayed. Naturally she had heard the gossip that Captain Tucker had been seen in the company of beautiful, but not so proper, *hapa-haole* women. Emily had refused to give credence to such stories.

Glancing at her hostess standing beside her, Emily couldn't imagine why Morgan Tucker would seek elsewhere for feminine companionship. Motherhood definitely agreed with Jasmine. She had never looked more beautiful than she did that evening in a dark rose brocade gown that embraced her tiny waist and fell in velvet-edged flounces to a pair of small matching kid slippers.

"How is young Matthew?" she asked.

Maternal pride instantly lit Jasmine's face as she said happily, "Oh, he's fine. The *lomilomi* masseur Malia hired for young Matthew says she has never seen a more perfectly formed baby."

For a moment, the engaging grin on her hostess's face reminded Mrs. Palmer of the mischievous schoolgirl she had once known. "But then I don't suppose you approve of *lomilomi*?" Jasmine murmured.

Mrs. Palmer refused to rise to the bait. "My husband has studied the ancient Hawaiian art of massaging the body," she said calmly, "and has found that, like some other old Hawaiian customs, *lomilomi* can do a great deal of good in some cases."

But not the traditional Hawaiian custom of *Niau Pio*, Emily thought suddenly, thinking of Jasmine's sister: gentle, kind-hearted Lani. How could it have happened? she wondered sorrowfully. The girl had seemed sincerely dedicated to the church, a true believer. Emily sighed to herself. After almost thirty years in the islands, it still pained her; the converts to the church who fell away, those who professed Christianity but still prayed in secret to their ancient gods. Even the king himself, she thought. His heavy drinking and numerous mistresses were common knowledge, for all that he sat in a church pew on Sundays. And it was whispered that he still visited, grief-stricken, the tomb of Nahienaena, the sister he had married.

There was the even more disheartening awareness that those natives who did bother with Christianity were turning more and more to the other religions that had taken hold in the islands these last years—Mormon, Catholic, even the English Episcopal Church—since Prince Alexander's visit to England. Emily felt a great sadness welling inside of her as she thought of the hardships and sufferings the early mission families had endured to bring the Hawaiian people out of paganism. Had any of it been worthwhile? Had it all been in vain?

"Mrs. Palmer, is something wrong?"

Emily heard Jasmine's worried voice and shook herself mentally. She was becoming a foolish, old woman. Of course it had not been in vain. If only one soul had been saved, had been brought to accept God's word, then it had all been worthwhile.

The music was growing louder now. People were gathering with partners, waiting for their host and hostess to lead the first dance. Emily glanced over at her husband, who was deep in conversation with a man whose back was toward her. "Nothing's wrong," she assured Jasmine. "But I really must collect Mr. Palmer."

Jasmine accompanied her across the room. Even before they reached the minister's side, they could hear his deep voice lifted in righteous indignation. "And I tell you the Masters and Servants Act is an abominable law. It delivers the Chinese workers and the Hawaiians, who sign such contracts, into virtual bondage to the plantation owners."

"Come now, Reverend Palmer. You surely know that the men sign the contracts of their own free will," his companion answered.

There was something familiar about that unctuous voice, Jasmine thought, although she could see only the back of the man's head.

"And how many of them, unable to read, know what they are signing?" Mr. Palmer demanded tartly. "Or that they'll be forced to work from sunup to sundown at a pittance of a wage, and that if they run away, the law permits them to be arrested, forced to serve double time on the plantation or be sent to prison."

"The planter is entitled to an honest day's work for his money. And a prosperous sugar industry will be the salvation of these islands once they are annexed to the United States."

"There'll be no annexation," Mr. Palmer protested hotly. "The king and Dr. Judd will never allow it."

Mr. Palmer's companion gave a shrill laugh. "The king will do as he is told, and if certain people have their way, Brother Judd won't be strutting around much longer either."

Jasmine recognized the voice then. She stood to one side while Mrs. Palmer attempted to catch her husband's eye and thought, surprised, how Micah Beale had changed. The man was almost attractive in his expensively tailored Prince Albert suit coat and discreetly embroidered vest. Working outdoors had added weight and muscle to the tall, lanky frame, and the sun had bronzed the once sallow skin so that the smallpox scars were hardly visible, the now neatly trimmed sandy hair streaked with gold. Only the oddly shaded pale gray eyes, strikingly light against the long, tanned face, were the same, as was the grating, high-pitched laugh.

Jasmine was aware that other guests were turning, glancing curiously at the two men and their raised, angry voices. Morgan stepped between the two men and spoke quietly. "Perhaps you gentlemen would prefer to continue your conversation in my study. The dancing is about to begin."

Mrs. Palmer took the opportunity to place her hand on her husband's arm, murmuring, "Thank you, Captain Tucker, but my husband and I must be leaving." At the same time, she was firmly ushering her husband toward the door.

Micah Beale turned to Jasmine, the gray eyes lingering a moment longer than necessary on the rose bodice before making her a stiff bow. "I haven't had a chance to extend to you my best wishes on your marriage, Mrs. Tucker." The light gray gaze swung to Morgan. "And my congratulations to you, of course, for capturing such a charming wife." Listening, Jasmine thought she heard a derisive note in the man's voice, as if, she thought uneasily, he somehow knew of the circumstances behind her hasty marriage to Morgan.

She saw a muscle twitch in Morgan's jaw, but his face remained impassive as he nodded and said, "Thank you,

Mr. Beale. Now if you'll excuse us, sir, my wife has promised me the first dance."

Since the waltz was so popular these days in Honolulu, Jasmine had decided for her first party in their new home that she would eliminate the traditional quadrille for the opening dance, and the strains of one of Mr. Strauss's waltzes now liltingly filled the drawing room.

The next moment Morgan had swung Jasmine out onto the cleared floor. Even though his hands rested lightly on her back and waist, it was as if her nerve ends had an atavistic memory of their own, and the touch of those hands brought back an instant flood of memories. Her teaching Morgan to waltz in the Tucker home the night he had returned to New Bedford and how they had laughed together at his stumbling awkwardness. And later that same night, when she had been freezing cold in bed, Morgan's hands had warmed her. Those same hands touching her so lightly, so indifferently now, had caressed her intimately, bringing a tingling warmth to every part of her body.

Deliberately, to dispel the treacherous weakness that was fast taking hold of her, Jasmine forced herself to remember Lilikoi. Those hands had caressed her sister's body, too, she thought bitterly. And how many other women in the last months? Mrs. Palmer was not the only one who had heard rumors of Morgan's being seen with certain beautiful young women in the wharf area.

Quickly she slammed the door shut on such thoughts and, placing a hostess smile on her lips, glanced around the dance floor. It was a nice party, she thought proudly, although there had been more rejections to her invitations than she had expected. There would be tons of food left, she thought absently; then glancing across the dance floor, she saw Micah Beale watching Morgan and her as they danced. Something about the man's intent, pale gray gaze reminded her of those embarrassing moments aboard the *Jeremiah* when the minister had tried to force her to her knees to pray with him, even though his hands on her had seemed more of a clammy, awkward embrace. She was certain she hadn't sent the man an invitation to her party.

"I didn't know you were acquainted with Mr. Beale, Morgan," she said. "Did you ask him to the party?"

"I know his reputation better than the man. His sugar plantation, Bonniville, is very successful, although I gather Beale's methods of handling his workers is frowned upon in some quarters." He smiled mockingly down at Jasmine. "I ran into the man in town a week ago. He as much as intimated that you and he were old, close friends, so I felt the least I could do was invite him to our party." Morgan frowned as he saw how Beale could not seem to keep his eyes away from Jasmine. "Is he an old or a new conquest?" he taunted.

Jasmine was female enough to detect the note of jealousy in Morgan's voice and decided that there was no need to let her husband know that Micah Beale's presence made her feel uncomfortable rather than amorous.

"Mr. Beale did me the honor of asking me to marry him," she said stiffly.

"Oh?" Morgan lifted an amused eyebrow. "I didn't know that I wasn't the only suitor willing to make a respectable woman out of you."

Jasmine glared at her husband. How dare he remind her that he had been forced into matrimony, as if it weren't his fault in the first place that she had had to marry him.

"At least if I had married Mr. Beale, he might have proven to be a faithful husband," she said bitingly and felt an unholy glow of satisfaction as she saw Morgan's hazel eyes darken dangerously, his hands tightening on her soft flesh.

Before he could reply, though, the waltz ended, and Jasmine withdrew quickly from Morgan's arms as she murmured sweetly, "You will excuse me? I must see to the enjoyment of our guests."

Still scowling, Morgan watched her, her flounced skirt swinging provocatively as she walked away from him directly across the floor to Micah Beale. Well, two could play at that game, he thought savagely, spotting Lilikoi happily stuffing herself at the food table. Lilikoi was wearing a white satin *holoku* with a scarlet hibiscus tucked into her black shining hair. The tightly fitting *holoku*, clinging to Lilikoi's ample curves, flattered the plump, supple body more than any tight bodice and billowy skirt could have done.

For the rest of the evening, Morgan and Jasmine carefully avoided each other's company, Morgan escorting Lilikoi into the midnight supper and Micah Beale escorting Jasmine.

Lilikoi was delighted at Morgan's sudden attention to her. He had hardly spoken two words to her since the night she had slipped into his bed. As for Micah Beale, he was too dazzled at having Jasmine at his side, hanging on breathlessly to his every word, smiling up at him with her shining eyes, to care how the miracle had come about.

How many long, lonely nights had he dreamed of having this lovely creature beside him? Of course, in his dreams she was not smiling. Her beautiful face was bruised and tear-stained, because he had finally avenged himself upon her for the humiliation he had suffered at her hands aboard the *Jeremiah* and for her summarily rejecting his offer of marriage. In his fantasy, her beautiful body, whore-naked, writhed beneath his hands as he forced her to confess her sinful lusts, to scream for forgiveness, finally forcing her abjectly to her knees, knowing that only then could she be cleansed and he find peace.

"Mr. Beale . . ."

With a start, Micah realized that this was not a dream after all. Jasmine was actually walking beside him across the lanai and out into the garden, where torches glowed like flowers in the darkness.

Jasmine glanced uneasily at the man beside her and, louder this time, repeated, "I think we should go back inside, Mr. Beale."

To her surprise, his hand tightened on her arm and

she found herself being yanked off the path into the darkness, the branches of an algarroba tree forming a black tent overhead. "I must speak to you," he whispered urgently.

Angrily she tried to pull free. "Mr. Beale . . . my husband . . ."

"I know all about your marriage," he said in a frantic rush. "I know that the captain would never have married you if your father hadn't threatened him into the ceremony."

Jasmine gasped. "How do you—how could you know?"

"Your sister Lani told me."

"Lani?" In her surprise, Jasmine stood still, staring at the man. "When did you see Lani?"

"Not long ago. She was living at the time in a grass hut not far from my plantation. I'd heard of the terrible sin she had committed with her brother. I had met her when she taught at the mission school, and I considered it my Christian duty to visit her, to try and save her lost soul."

"How is she?" Jasmine asked eagerly. "Is she all right?"

Micah frowned. "How could she be all right?" he demanded. "Your sister is condemned to eternal damnation for choosing to live in sin with her brother. I tried to talk to her, to pray with her. Day after day I tried. For a short time the Lord touched her heart, and she prayed with me. It was then she told me about your relationship with Captain Tucker. She was worried about you, about your marriage, about whether you were happy. So you see, I know everything and it makes no difference. I want to help you save your immortal soul. Your sister, unhappily, is doomed, but there is still hope for you."

As he talked in feverish spurts, Micah's hands on her shoulders moved downward to caress the breasts that were hidden from his view and yet were as clear to him as the fragrance in the woman's hair mingling with the scent of the jasmine growing in the garden. With a groan of despair, he buried his face in that tempting swell above the rose brocade, tasting her flesh with his tongue. Kicking and squirming, Jasmine fought against him.

Then suddenly, large and powerful hands pulled Micah away from her. Jasmine gave an inward sigh of relief until she saw her husband's face, black with a deadly fury, in the flickering torchlight. With one hand, Morgan held Micah Beale while his other hand, curled into a stonelike fist, was poised ready to smash into the man's terrified face.

He'll kill him, Jasmine thought, appalled. Without thinking, she thrust herself between the two men, protecting Micah with her own body as she cried, "Morgan, don't!"

She saw the darkness in her husband's face drain away slowly, the terrible rage leaving his eyes, to be replaced by an icy contempt as he shoved the planter, sprawling, into the shrubbery. He turned to Jasmine and growled, "If you must cuckold me, madam, at least do it with a man!"

Then he turned and disappeared down the path toward the house, toward the candlelight and music streaming out onto the lanai as the musicians played a polka more loudly than well.

Chapter 20

Jasmine slept late the next morning. The party had not broken up until the early hours, but even after she had fallen, exhausted, into bed, she did not immediately fall asleep. She kept remembering the look on Morgan's face when he had found her in Micah Beale's arms. But even more sleep-destroying was the almost maniacal look of hatred she had glimpsed in Micah's flat gray eyes glaring at her before he pulled himself to his feet and she heard him stumbling through the garden to the street.

It was an hour after she had gone to bed that she heard Morgan come up the stairs with a heavy, uneven tread, and she knew he had spent the last hour drinking in his study. She heard his footsteps stop outside her door and she stiffened in her bed—in dread or anticipation, she wasn't sure which—until she heard the footsteps continue unsteadily down the hall.

When she did finally fall asleep, she slept too heavily and awoke with a headache. As she pulled on her morning robe, she thought gratefully that with all the noise of the polka the night before, none of the other guests had heard or witnessed the ugly scene between her husband and Mr. Beale.

She pulled her robe more tightly around her, wishing that Morgan had never invited the man to their party, except that if he hadn't, she remembered suddenly, she wouldn't have heard about Lani. At least she knew now that her sister was on the island of Oahu.

She walked into the dining room and saw, surprised, that Morgan was seated at the table. He usually had his breakfast and went to his office down at the wharf before she arose.

As she slid into a chair across from him, she studied his face cautiously, wondering if he was still angry with her. With her head pounding the way it was, she couldn't face a scene, too, she thought miserably. But there was no trace of last night's fury in her husband's expression as he carefully folded his newspaper and said almost absently, "I think it would be a good idea if you and young Matthew stayed at the plantation for a while."

So he *was* still angry, Jasmine thought, and she was being sent away like a naughty child to an isolated sugar plantation on the other side of the island where, presumably, she couldn't get into any more mischief. Anger pulled sharply at her nerves. Why should she be punished, banished, for a minor indiscretion, while Morgan's pecadillos with his lady friends went unnoticed.

She opened her mouth to protest, but her head was pounding too painfully and she thought wearily, what difference did it make? She had never been to Palekaiko, as Morgan had named the plantation. It might be well for Morgan and her to be apart for a while, instead of rubbing each other raw by the very fact of their sharing the same house.

When she said nothing, merely nodding her agreement, Morgan got quickly to his feet, tucking the newspaper under his arm.

"I'll see to your boat passage to Waianae," he said. "The trail over the Waianae Mountains would be too hard for young Matthew." He saw Jasmine press her fingers to her forehead and asked sharply, "Are you feeling all right?"

"I will after I have my coffee."

"How is Matthew?"

"He's fine," she said, surprised. "I looked in on him before I came down." She gave Morgan a puzzled glance. "Why do you ask?"

He shrugged. "No reason." So she hadn't heard about the new cases of smallpox discovered in Honolulu yesterday, he thought, relieved. In February, a merchant ship flying a yellow flag had come into Honolulu Harbor with smallpox aboard her. The passengers had been quarantined, and when no new cases developed, the ship was allowed to leave. Then, in May, two families on Maunakea Street had come down with the disease. Now, according to the newspaper, the disease was spreading through town, and a general vaccination of everyone in Honolulu was being called for.

Morgan knew that Jasmine had been inoculated as a child, but the doctor had told him that Matthew was too young to be vaccinated. Morgan wasn't taking any chances. Jasmine and Matthew would be safer at the plantation if a full-scale epidemic should develop in Honolulu.

At the door, he stopped a moment and looked back at his wife, who was sipping a cup of coffee and staring out into the garden. With her black hair hanging loosely over her shoulders and her soft mouth drooping at the corners, she did not look at all like the beautifully coiffed and polished coquette who had lured that poor fool, Micah Beale, into the garden and into her arms and then had flung her own body in front of the man to protect him from Morgan's wrath. Did she care that much for Beale, then? Morgan wondered. Were they perhaps even lovers? Somehow he could not believe it, even as he thought wryly how ironic it would be if his wife could take other men into her bed while he had sent Lilikoi home last night without so much as touching her.

Sensing his eyes on her, Jasmine turned to him. "Was there something else, Morgan?" she asked with cool politeness.

"No," he growled. "Be sure you and Matthew are packed and ready to leave by tomorrow. I should be able to arrange your boat passage by then."

As it turned out, he was fortunate to be able to secure passage for his family the next day. The day after Jasmine and his son left Honolulu, frightened people began to flee the city any way they could as word of more and more smallpox cases began to circulate through the city. The health commissioner, in order to stop the disease from spreading to the neighboring islands, forbade all boats from leaving Oahu. Stealthily, by night and day, however, boats departed with sick and well families for what they hoped was the safety of the outer islands, only to take the deadly illness with them.

Throughout the summer, the disease raged while natives lined up for the required vaccinations. Many more, afraid of the white man's medicine, scratched themselves with a pin, pretending vaccination marks, and instead visited their local *kahunas*.

For thousands of Hawaiians, the inoculations were

too late. Yellow flags hung in doorways on every street of Honolulu. A pall of smoke hung over the contaminated houses that had been burned while volunteer drivers went from house to house picking up the dead. The carts, stacked with corpses, made their way to Kakaako, where the dead were buried on their sides, three feet deep, to save space.

Business in the town ground to a halt. Markets were empty of food, and servants disappeared. Instead of going to his office, Morgan helped at one of the local vaccination stations, trying to talk fearful men, women, and children into taking the vaccine when he wasn't even sure himself how much good the inoculations did. At night he would return to his empty house, where he would find himself listening for the quick step and laughter of Jasmine, the romping noises of his son, and finally fall asleep. . . .

"Mrs. Tucker, wait a moment, please."

Jasmine had just started to mount her horse for her early morning ride when she saw the plantation manager come hurrying into the stableyard. She stopped at once, turning to smile at the young man. She had liked James Scott from the first moment they had met, when she had arrived at Waianae.

With his fine blond hair, which kept falling boyishly across his forehead, his round, beardless face, and clear, guileless blue eyes, he looked too young to be managing a plantation the size of Palekaiko. But Mr. Scott had proved to be very competent, unobtrusively making sure that she and Matthew were comfortable in the frame, gabled house called the "big house," though it was much smaller than the Tucker home in Honolulu. The Hawaiian woman, Nakeli, he had selected as a nursemaid for Matthew had turned out to be a jewel whom young Matthew adored and Jasmine trusted completely. But most of all, Jasmine liked the way Mr. Scott handled the Chinese workers employed on the plantation, even learning to speak a little of their language so that he could talk to them.

"What is it, Mr. Scott?" she asked, one hand still resting on the saddle of her horse. She was wearing her dark green riding habit, which fell in long, graceful folds from her waist to her feet. She had tucked a pale apricot hibiscus blossom into her hat, and to James Scott's already smitten gaze, the color of the flower exactly matched the flawless complexion of the lovely face beneath the hat.

When the *luna* didn't answer at once, Jasmine moved restively. The west coat of Oahu was dryer and much warmer than Nuuanu Valley, and she liked to take her morning rides early, before the heat became oppressive. "Did you want me to take a message to the field *luna*?"

"No, I just wanted to tell you I'd rather you wouldn't ride off the plantation."

"Was there some reason why I shouldn't?" Jasmine asked, wondering for a moment if Morgan had ordered the plantation manager to spy on her, but then she quickly pushed the thought aside as unworthy of Morgan and Mr. Scott.

The manager had the type of fair skin that burned and peeled and never tanned, but she could have sworn that his sunburned face was flushing as he blurted, "There's smallpox in the village."

Shortly after Jasmine had arrived at the plantation, she had learned about the smallpox epidemic in Honolulu. Worried about Morgan and her family, she had wanted to return at once to Honolulu, but James had dissuaded her.

"Your husband sent you and the boy here to keep you away from the pox, Mrs. Tucker," he said earnestly. "In his letter, he gave me explicit instructions that I was not to allow you to return to Honolulu until all danger had passed." He had grinned sheepishly at the wife of his employer. "You know Captain Tucker, ma'am. It'd be my neck if I disobeyed a direct order from him."

"I thought the smallpox was only in Honolulu," Jasmine said, troubled.

James Scott shook his head. "Not anymore. It's all over the island. I had a letter from my parents last week. My father's a mission doctor at Waialua. Mother says they've both been working night and day with the sick and the dying."

"Your parents are missionaries?" Jasmine asked, surprised.

He nodded. "They came to the islands in thirty-two." Once again the open, boyish grin flashed across his face. "I know some people think all missionaries made a fortune out of these islands, but I'm living proof that mine never did. They were barely able to afford sending me back to Boston to college. Father wanted me to follow him into the ministry, but I prefer working the land. Someday I hope to own my own place and raise cattle. The Hawaiians may not make good field workers, but they make good *paniolas*."

Jasmine accepted James's hand up into the saddle, settling her long skirt around her as she smiled down at the young man. "Well, you needn't worry about me, Mr. Scott. I've been vaccinated against smallpox."

As she rode away from the stable, Jasmine's smile faded. If smallpox was spreading through the countryside, even here into this remote corner of Oahu, who knew how long she'd have to remain here at the plantation? Or how many more weeks before she saw Morgan again? Not that she supposed he was missing her, she thought with a pinched sense of loss. He had been quick enough to send her away and, no doubt, despite the epidemic in town, was finding ways to amuse himself.

But as she rode through the plantation, it was much too beautiful a day for her to remain depressed for long. The sky was a sparkling blue overhead, with the misty green of the cane fields melting into the pale bluish purple of the distant Waianae Mountains. She followed her customary trail leading past the whitewashed sugar mill with its towering chimney. In the courtyard, workers were unloading cartloads of sugarcane, which would be fed into the grinding wheels of the mill, and other workers were spreading the crushed cane stalks out to dry in the sun. The mill was busy, as usual, the air filled with the continuous rumbling sound from its massive rollers crushing the cane stalks. Jasmine wrinkled her nose at the almost-too-sweet molasses odor from the sugarcane juice being boiled in the furnace of the mill.

After she had passed the mill and the plantation buildings clustered around it, she followed a road that wound around and through the fields of sugarcane, some fields newly scorched and harvested, others with tiny stalks just beginning to flourish, and still other fields where the ripened stalks rose several feet high, the tassels a sea of waving pale violet feathery plumes.

In one of the tasseled fields, the men had started harvesting the burned-over cane, and Jasmine stopped her horse a moment to watch them. She had learned enough about the cultivation and milling of sugarcane from James Scott to know that the cane when ripe had to be cut immediately, and fed into the mill within three days or the sugar soured.

The field *luna*, patrolling on horseback, lifted his hat to Jasmine when he saw her, exposing a great deal of thick yellowish gray hair. When he brought his horse closer to Jasmine's and she felt his small, deep-set eyes on her face, she had the same crawling sensation as when the cockroach had run across her foot aboard the *Louisa*.

She glanced with distaste at the blacksnake whip coiled at the man's saddle. "Why do you carry that, Mr. Hanes?" she asked coldly. "Mr. Scott doesn't allow the workers to be flogged."

The man laughed genially. "It is my little joke, Mrs. Tucker. I know Mr. Scott's orders, but the coolies . . ." He glanced contemptuously at the workers in the field. "They don't know I won't use the whip. That way they work harder and I don't have to worry about finding a machete in my back."

"Why should they attack you?"

The man shrugged. "You don't know these coolies, Mrs. Tucker. Most of them are criminals who managed to escape hanging in their own country by signing work contracts and coming here. A man's a fool to turn his back on them."

Jasmine found herself gazing uncertainly at the laborers, each man with a wicked-looking hooked machete in his hand as he lopped off the soft top and threw the stalk behind him, all in one rhythmic movement. Most of the men wore only baggy trousers or a loincloth, and their golden muscular bodies twisted and glistened in the sunshine as they bent to their back-breaking task.

The *luna* edged his horse closer to Jasmine's so that his leg brushed hers. "If I was you, Mrs. Tucker," he said with a wolfish smile, "since your man's not with you, I'd sleep with a revolver beside me at night."

Jasmine jerked at the reins so that her horse side-stepped quickly away from the man, her voice icy. "Thank you for your advice, Mr. Hanes. Good day."

Jasmine was annoyed with herself for even listening to the man. Mr. Scott had told her that most of the Chinese workers were dispossessed farmers facing famine in their own country who had come to Hawaii to work to send money to their starving families in China. The plantation manager had spoken highly of the laborers.

"They're clever people, and hard-working when they're handled properly," he said. "The trouble is most of the workers we bring here are young men, and there aren't any Chinese women in the islands. It isn't normal for a man to go without—" James Scott had blushed furiously, stammering, "Sorry, ma'am. Of course, you wouldn't understand."

Jasmine smiled to herself, remembering the *luna*'s embarrassment. She wondered wryly why men seemed to assume that women didn't have longings and hungers, too, that their bodies didn't ache with needs and desires the same as men. And she couldn't help thinking that if the celibate life the Chinese coolies were forced to live was unnatural, wasn't the life she lived with Morgan just as unnatural?

Deep in her unhappy thoughts, she didn't notice that she had left the plantation grounds until she saw how close to the sea she had come. There were no protective reefs here as there were in Waikiki. Foam-crested waves tumbled freely onto the shore along a jagged coastline. Occasional clumps of palm and kiawe trees leaned with the wind toward the ocean; otherwise, the beach stretched wide and empty as far as she could see.

Primitive bamboo huts were clustered together like a pile of haystacks not far from her, but she could see no people. The village seemed to be deserted, and, remembering Mr. Scott's warning, she stopped on the outskirts. Probably the villagers had already fled up into the hills, she decided, when a loud, piercing wail cut through the eerie silence: a baby crying. For several minutes, the crying continued, grating on Jasmine's nerves. Finally she could stand it no longer, and, slipping off of her horse, she approached the hut nearest her.

When she pushed aside the *tapa* cloth that hung in the doorway and stepped inside the hut, she could see nothing but darkness. Gradually, though, as her eyes became accustomed to the gloom, she made out several figures lying on matting on the floor: an elderly man and woman together and a young woman by herself. Their eyes were wide open, staring blankly up at the thatched ceiling.

Although the morning had already grown warm, a chill of horror caused gooseflesh to rise on Jasmine's arms as she gazed at the blotched, disfigured bodies. Ugly smallpox pustules had swollen the faces almost beyond recognition, and on the arms and legs the yellowish eruptions had run together so that the skin appeared blistered and burned. Then the stench in the tiny hut, of human excrement, vomit, and death itself, caused Jasmine to gag. She snatched up the baby, who was crawling near its mother's body on the mat, and fled from the hut into the sunlight.

The sky, mountains, and ocean all swung in a bright blue, dizzy arc around her as she clutched the baby to her with one hand and the saddle of her horse with the other. When the world finally stopped spinning, she examined the baby—a girl—and discovered, relieved, that there were no eruptions on the soft skin, although from her crying, Jasmine judged that she was hungry. How long had those bodies lain in that fetid-smelling hut? Jasmine wondered with a shudder.

Then from another hut at the end of the dirt-packed trail, she heard a sharp, desolate cry that wrenched her head around.

"*Auwe! Auwe-ee-e!*" The Hawaiian wail of grief split the air. Suddenly a man burst out of the hut, his body so disfigured with the yellow pustules and inflamed skin that it was impossible to tell his age. He raced toward the beach and flung himself into the ocean. For a few seconds, half-delirious from the fever consuming his body, he flailed at the water as if he were trying to swim. And then suddenly he lay very still, floating facedown, while from the hut the moaning continued incessantly.

Jasmine did not wait to see any more. Panic broke over her. She mounted her horse and, holding the baby in the saddle before her, raced back to the plantation, her heart pounding in her throat. She did not even see the startled glance of the field *luna* as she flew by, stopping, at last, a short distance before the big house, where Nakeli was playing with young Matthew on the veranda.

Seeing his mother, her son gave a happy gurgle and began to crawl toward her. "Don't let Matthew near me, Nakeli!" Jasmine ordered sharply. "Take him inside the house and keep him there."

The Hawaiian woman gave her a startled glance but obediently scooped up the child and retreated hastily inside the house.

James Scott came cantering up the circular drive and stopped beside Jasmine. He had been out in the fields

when he had seen Mrs. Tucker racing through the cane
fields.

"What is it?" he asked, glancing from the baby in
Jasmine's arms to her pale, frightened face. Then,
alarmed, he exclaimed, "You didn't go into the village?"

She nodded helplessly, her eyes still glazed with horror.
"The baby was crying. . . . They were dead—all dead.
Only the baby . . ." She heard the hysteria mounting in
her voice and forced herself to speak more slowly. "We
have to help them. We must do something."

"We don't dare bring the pox onto the plantation,"
James Scott said unhappily. "The Chinese have no immu-
nity against the disease, and your own son, Mrs. Tucker
. . ." He broke off, gazing at the woman on horseback.
"You have to get out of those clothes and burn them at
once."

Jasmine was not listening. "There's a frame shed at
the edge of the plantation," she said quickly. "I think
farm equipment is kept there. We can turn it into a
hospital. If nothing else, we can isolate the sick from the
well. You'll have to fetch a doctor."

"There is no doctor within miles, Mrs. Tucker," James
said quietly.

"Then we'll have to manage by ourselves," Jasmine
said, frowning. "You've been inoculated, haven't you,
Mr. Scott?"

James nodded, wishing nervously that he had more
experience with handling women, especially beautiful,
headstrong women like Mrs. Tucker. He made his voice
firm. "It's out of the question, Mrs. Tucker. Your husband would never approve of my allowing you to go
near smallpox patients."

Jasmine curbed her impatience and gave the young
man a soft, pleading smile. "But I've been vaccinated,
so I'd be in no danger. Of course, if you don't want to
help me, I'll manage somehow alone."

James sighed unhappily. No doubt this would cost
him his job, but Mrs. Tucker was right. He had too

much missionary upbringing not to do what he could for those poor people in the village.

"I'll see to clearing out the building," he said. "And if it's as bad as you say in the village, the huts will all have to be burned."

"We'll need clean linen and water," Jasmine said. "Nakeli can bring them from the house and leave them on the veranda."

James made one last valiant effort. "Please, Mrs. Tucker," he begged. "Give me the baby and let me handle this by myself. I promise I'll do everything I can."

He might, he thought, resigned, have been talking into the wind for all the good it did him. He had been through a smallpox epidemic as a boy, though, and remembering the horrors he had seen, the grotesque disfigurements, the terrible stench as the pustules broke, he was sure Mrs. Tucker wouldn't last more than a few hours working with such patients.

To his surprise, however, Jasmine never once faltered as August turned into September and she worked beside James in the stagnant heat of the building, which had been scrubbed clean and had fresh mats placed on the floor. The mats were quickly covered with the sick and dying from nearby villages. There was medically little enough that they could do for their patients except to try to make them comfortable, sponging their fevered bodies with tepid water, feeding those who could still swallow around the pustules that had formed in their throats and air passages, restraining those who wanted to rush out to the ocean to cool their burning bodies. Each night the mats and linen and pieces of clothing from dead victims were burned, Jasmine taking her turn with James in thrusting the articles into the bonfire.

"If there were only more we could do," she complained one morning as she sat at breakfast with James under a hau tree. They took turns sleeping but ate their meals together. The servants from the big house brought them baskets of food and drink, then quickly fled from the pesthouse, as they called the makeshift hospital.

James's young face was lined and weary, his eyes red-rimmed with exhaustion. "Maybe someday they'll find a cure," he said. "Now the strong survive. The old and the weak die."

And the young, he thought, remembering the baby girl Mrs. Tucker had found in the hut in the village that first day. They had hoped the child had escaped the disease, but yesterday she had developed the first symptoms of smallpox, and that morning the baby had died of convulsions in Jasmine's arms.

Worried, he studied the young woman seated across from him. Mrs. Tucker's gown hung loosely on her, and her skin was like thin white parchment stretched tightly over fragile cheekbones. Yet she was still beautiful, James saw, his senses stirred in spite of himself, even if it was a drawn, shadowy sort of beauty.

"Why don't you try and get some rest?" he urged. "I can handle the patients for the next couple of hours."

Jasmine hesitated, then said, "Well, perhaps, if you don't mind, I will ride up to the big house for a few moments. Nakeli brings Matthew out on the veranda, so I can see him and . . ."

Her voice died away suddenly. Then, abruptly, she sprang to her feet, her tray of food spilling to the ground. As James watched, too startled to move, she ran across the yard and into the arms of a tall, husky Hawaiian man.

Chapter 21

"*Kale! Is it really you?*"

Jasmine flung her arms around her brother, then, remembering, stepped back quickly. "You shouldn't be here. We've smallpox patients. . . ."

He smiled down at her. "I know." He cupped her face gently in his hands, his dark eyes searching her face. "How are you, little Pikake?"

Jasmine stared, shocked, into her brother's face, at the deep knife cut that slashed across the right side from his ear to his nose. The wound still looked raw, only recently healed. "Kale!" she gasped. "What happened?"

"What are you doing here, Kale?" James Scott's usually pleasant face was set in grim lines as he glared at the intruder. "If you're planning to stir up trouble with my workers . . ."

Jasmine interrupted quickly, her hand resting lightly on Kale's arm as she said, "Mr. Scott, I'd like you to meet my brother, Kale. Kale, this is James Scott, the manager of Palekaiko Plantation."

"Your brother!" Something in the Hawaiian's expression, a dangerous flash in the intense dark eyes, made James amend his outraged tone of voice. But how was it possible, he wondered, bewildered, staring from Mrs. Tucker to the man's obviously Polynesian features.

Jasmine turned eagerly back to Kale. "Tell me, how is Lani? And your daughter, Ulimi?"

"My wife is dead. And so is my daughter."

Jasmine swayed. "Oh, no," she whispered. "How? How did it happen?"

Kale glanced coldly at James Scott. "My sister and I will talk alone."

The arrogant bastard, James thought, annoyed. He acts as if he owned the plantation and I were his servant. There was something unnerving, though, about that unblinking, icy stare, and he heard himself muttering, "I'll look in on the patients, Mrs. Tucker."

Jasmine slipped her arm into Kale's, and as if they could read each other's minds, they turned and walked the short distance to the shore, where the surf breaking over the fawn-colored sand made a soft, soughing sound like a low, mournful sigh. For several minutes, they walked along the beach without speaking. Jasmine was only dimly aware of the sand burning through the thin soles of her slippers, the sharp scent of seaweed, and a fisherman wading out into the surf, throwing his kukui-bark-stained net into the aquamarine sea. All her senses seemed numbed, blunted by the shock of Lani's death.

Near a clump of short, thorny kiawe trees, she stopped and turned to Kale. "Was it the smallpox?"

She could see her own pain reflected in Kale's face, but he spoke quietly. "The smallpox took Ulimi. Then Lani became sick. At first I thought it was grief at our daughter's death, until the symptoms of smallpox appeared." At Jasmine's low gasp of dismay, he said quickly, "She was never disfigured. Her face was untouched. My Lani was as beautiful in death as in life. When she grew steadily weaker, I fetched a *haole* doctor. Afterwards, he said it wasn't the smallpox that killed her. Her heart had given out."

"But it wasn't her heart that killed her," Kale said, the raw, savage anger burning in his voice making Jasmine flinch. "It was the *haole* preacher Beale. He *kahuna*ed my Lani; he prayed her to death."

"Micah Beale?" Jasmine asked, bewildered. "I don't understand."

"We were living near Nanakuli at the time. I was away for a week on the windward side of the island when Beale came to see Lani. He had met her when she worked at the mission school." Kale's bow-shaped mouth twisted scornfully. "He'd heard of Lani's fall from grace. He came, he said, to save her soul from damnation. She tried to send him away, but he kept coming back, day after day, kneeling and praying before her door so that all in the village could hear him. He described the tortures waiting for my wife, told her that she was already dead and doomed in the sight of the *haole* god. And not just her soul but that of our child would burn forever in the afterlife."

Kale's angry voice softened, his dark eyes filled with tears. "My sweet Lani. How frightened she must have been by the man's prayers. She was happy with me, but there was a part of her that believed Beale; she believed he had the power to pray her to death. At first Lani didn't tell me about Beale's visits. When I found out, I tried to convince her that my love for her was stronger than any *mana* that Beale possessed. Then Ulimi died of the smallpox. Lani believed that it was her sin in marrying me that had killed our daughter and that her precious Ulimi was burning in hell because of the curse Beale had put upon her. Each day she grew steadily weaker. She had so little strength, my Lani. She died, at last, in my arms."

Jasmine felt tears streaming down her face, salty in her mouth. Sweet, gentle Lani, she thought, so loving and giving, trying to live in two worlds, the ancient Hawaiian world of the husband she loved and the *haole* world of her father, and finally torn helplessly apart between them.

Looking into her brother's mutilated face, she remembered then the traditional custom of the Hawaiian people of mutilating themselves in mourning after the death of a loved one. She touched the jagged scar on Kale's face. "You did that—to yourself?" she asked.

"I covered Lani's body with scented maile leaves befitting the granddaughter of the *alii*, then I mourned for her, keeping watch beside her body, placing the knife to my face. I am ashamed," Kale said sadly, "that I could not force myself to knock out my teeth, as my ancestors would have done. Afterwards, I took the bodies of Ulimi and my precious Lani and buried them high in the hills where no *haole* can ever find them and disturb their rest. Then I went looking for Micah Beale."

At the look of alarm in Jasmine's face, he shook his head. "No, I did not find him. He was not at his plantation." Kale's hand crept to the knife thrust into the *malo* at his waist, and speaking softly, his eyes burning, he said, "One day I will find him, and he will pay with his blood for Lani and Ulimi."

Jasmine's face paled at the cruel, primitive fury in Kale's face. He reached out and caught her arms, concern taking the place of the murderous anger in his voice. "I am sorry, Pikake. I should not be upsetting you this way. You're not ill?" he asked, studying her face, worried.

"No, just tired. I haven't slept much these last weeks."

"That is why I came," Kale said, taking her hand and walking back again across the beach. "I heard what you were doing here, taking care of the sick. I thought you might need help."

A smile suddenly lightened his face, so for a moment he looked like the brother she remembered, teasing her mercilessly, as quick to laugh as to rage. "That is, if your *luna* will accept my help. From the look on his face, I'd say he'd prefer to throw me off the plantation."

"You'll like Mr. Scott when you know him better," Jasmine assured him. "And we'll both be happy to accept your help." She gave her brother an unhappy, sidelong glance. "You can't believe all *haoles* are like Micah Beale."

Kale gazed broodingly at the fisherman they were passing, his catch a flash of silver caught in his net. "All I know is that when the white men first came to our islands, they said they only wanted to trade their rum for our sandalwood, to teach us about their god. But little by little they forced their foreign god and laws upon us. Then when we were securely caught like a fish in their net, the *haoles* sharpened their knives and chose which part of the fish they would take for themselves: one the side piece, another the belly, another white meat, another red. And so the land that had once been ours to cherish was cut up between them.

"Taro patches that had fed and sustained whole Hawaiian families since the days of our forefathers have been drained, the water sent to their sugarcane fields. And when our people refused to work on their plantations, bound and goaded like oxen, they brought cheap labor from China, selling coolies at auctions like so many bags of jute, binding them to the planters with their Masters and Servants law."

Kale turned his fierce gaze upon his sister. "And now there are men in Honolulu calling themselves the Committee of Thirteen. They threaten to bring in paid mercenaries from California and start a revolution unless the king hands his country over to the United States—to a country where black men, women, and children are bought and sold and our own Prince Alexander was treated like dirt beneath the white men's feet." Kale's mouth twisted with the taste of bitterness. "The *haoles* say it is for the good of the Hawaiian people, this annexation, but it is only for the good of the traders and planters. And I say it will not be allowed to happen!"

"What can you do? What can one man alone do?"

"I am not alone," Kale said proudly. "There are many who feel as I do, who will fight to stop the Hawaiian people from becoming outcasts in their own land."

They had left the beach and reached the dirt trail, where burned-out huts and shallow graves bore mute witness to the smallpox that had swept through the village like a scythe. Jasmine imagined that she could still smell the stench of the pox in the air and, guiltily, she remembered the patients she had left in the cramped, dark shed.

"I must get back. I've left Mr. Scott alone too long."

Kale nodded. "I'll go with you."

As her brother had warned, James Scott wasn't pleased at Kale's staying on at Palekaiko. As the days passed, though, and Kale worked long hours beside James and Jasmine, the plantation manager began to feel a reluctant respect for the tall Hawaiian man who never seemed to tire. From his pallet on the floor where he would try to snatch a few hours' rest, James could hear Kale moving quietly among the patients: speaking soothingly in Hawaiian to a frightened, sick child; restraining gently but firmly a man whose fevered body had sent him into convulsions; coaxing an elderly woman who would surely be dead by morning to drink a little water.

By the end of the third week after Kale had come, the number of sick and dying streaming into the whitewashed frame hut began to lessen. One morning at breakfast James announced, "There's been only one new patient in the last two days. I think the worst is over."

"Let's hope so," Kale said, stretching and grinning wryly as he felt his tired muscles complaining. "If I had known nursing was such hard work, I wouldn't have been so quick to offer my services."

"I've some other news, too," James said, pulling a newspaper out of his pocket. "One of the servants dropped this off with the food. It arrived by boat from Honolulu. Dr. Judd has been asked to resign as prime minister. There was a public meeting at which he was attacked for mishandling the smallpox epidemic. That's poppycock, of course," James said, frowning. "Judd is a good doctor. I'm sure he did everything he could to control the epidemic, and he's worked very hard all these years for the Hawaiian people."

Kale lifted one charcoal black eyebrow, his voice contemptuously amused. "Like trying to persuade the king to sell the kingdom for five million dollars to an American millionaire?"

A flush crept up to James's receding hairline. "That's only a malicious rumor. Dr. Judd may have his faults, as every man does, but he's certainly preferable to Wyllie, who will undoubtedly get Judd's job. Wyllie and the young princes are too much under the influence of the British," he said gloomily. "If we aren't careful, England will own these islands one day."

Kale rose to his feet, towering over the shorter plantation manager, his voice a low, angry roar. "These islands belong to the Hawaiian people. Our forefathers fought beside the great Kamehameha in Wailuku Valley; the bones of our ancestors lie buried in our red soil. What have you foreign traders and merchants and planters ever done for the kingdom, except trying for years to trick and cheat the people out of their land?"

Jasmine saw the blood rushing angrily into James's face as he rose, too, squaring off against Kale. She got quickly to her feet and, turning to James, smiled ingratiatingly at the young man. "Was there anything in the paper about the smallpox in Honolulu?"

Slowly James turned his gaze away from Kale. "There's been a drop in new cases in Honolulu, too," he said. "The authorities hope the epidemic has finally run its course."

Casting a last disdainful look at James Scott, Kale took Jasmine's hand and pulled her to one side. "I must be leaving, Pikake," he said. "The news from Honolulu means I still have much work to do, and you no longer need me here."

"Can't you stay a little longer?" Jasmine pleaded, walking with him to the footpath that wound past the plantation. "Or better yet, come with me to Honolulu. The family will want to see you."

Kale shook his head, his voice stiff with pride. "My father and mother turned their backs on Lani and me when she was alive. I'll not go to them now that she's dead." At the unhappy look on Jasmine's face, he brushed her cheek lightly with a kiss. "It's all right, little sister. Perhaps someday, when the pain is not so bad, I will come to Honolulu and we will sit on the veranda at night laughing and talking, the way we used to, Malia and the captain and Lilikoi." He laughed suddenly. "How is my sister? Still causing as much *pilikia* as ever?"

For a moment, Jasmine was tempted to tell Kale about Morgan's taking Lilikoi to his bed, but she could not. She had never been able to speak of that night to anyone, not even Malia. She had even invited Lilikoi to parties at her house because she knew Malia would become suspicious if she didn't.

When she didn't answer at once, Kale's eyes on her face became too probing, too knowing. "Has Lilikoi caused trouble between you and the captain?" he asked shrewdly, well aware of his sister's desire for Jasmine's husband. "Is that why there is sadness in your eyes?"

Jasmine shook her head without speaking.

Kale frowned at her, his voice gently chiding. "If you love the captain, Pikake, forget your *haole* blood. Give yourself to him like a Hawaiian *wahine* gives herself to a *kane*, freely, from the pure *aloha* and joy of giving."

Jasmine forced herself to smile. "You mustn't concern yourself about me, Kale. It's you I'm worried about. You will be careful, won't you? I couldn't bear it if anything happened to you, too."

Then one last hug, and she watched her brother stride off down the road, an uneasy feeling that she would never see him again taking hold of her as she watched him go. The frightening premonition stayed with her as she returned to James Scott, who was waiting outside of the hospital for her.

"I'm sorry, Mrs. Tucker," he said, shamefaced. "I didn't mean to argue with your brother. There are many mission families who feel as he does about the annexation." He broke off, flustered by the sight of tears suddenly pouring down the young woman's face, her throat working convulsively. It was the weeks of nursing without enough sleep, Jasmine thought wretchedly, then hearing of Lani's death, and now Kale's leaving. Suddenly it was all too much for her, and she couldn't stop the tears from flowing helplessly.

"Do you have a handkerchief, Mr. Scott?" she asked,

digging in vain into her own skirt pocket. "I'm sorry to make such a fool of myself."

It was too much, too, for the plantation manager, all the weeks of working beside Jasmine Tucker and forcing himself not to think about her slim, white body, so sweet and enticing beneath the work-stained cotton gown, watching the tender smile on her lips when she tended one of the children, catching her fragrance through the stench of sickness around them.

And now, unbelievably, here she was mopping her eyes with his handkerchief, and it seemed so natural that his arms should fold around her and draw her close, her head resting on his shoulders, her tears dampening his shirt front while she sobbed with childish abandon.

Neither of them heard the sound of approaching hoofbeats. James was too ecstatically happy; Jasmine too wrapped up in her own misery.

They both sprang apart guiltily when a man on horseback suddenly appeared in the clearing beside them.

Chapter 22

Morgan Tucker remained in the saddle for a few seconds, staring impassively down at his wife and plantation manager standing carefully apart now. He looked at Jasmine's face streaked with tears and at James Scott, with his youthful, ingenuous features looking more like a boy caught with his hand in the cookie jar than a man caught in a compromising position with his employer's wife.

It was Jasmine who broke the awkward silence with a

startled exclamation. "Morgan . . . we weren't expecting you."

Morgan slid off his horse, his voice dry. "That seems obvious."

"But when . . . how did you get here?" Jasmine was annoyed at how flustered her voice sounded, at the color she felt rushing into her face.

"I came on the boat from Honolulu this morning." Morgan's glance fastened on James Scott with a deceptively mild look that many a seaman had learned, to his sorrow, boded no good. "I placed my wife and son under your care, Mr. Scott, and you allowed her to expose herself to the danger of smallpox infection. You have a lot of explaining to do."

"The hospital was my idea, not Mr. Scott's," Jasmine objected. "He wanted me to stay away, but I refused."

"No, Mrs. Tucker," James said quickly. "Your husband is right. You and your son were my responsibility, and I abused that trust. I'll submit my resignation, sir, whenever you wish." Then casting an unhappy glance at Jasmine, he added, "As for what you saw . . . I assure you, Captain Tucker, your wife is blameless."

Something almost like pity briefly touched Morgan's face. He had seen enough men dazzled by Jasmine's beauty not to recognize the familiar symptoms in the young man standing before him. There was no pity in his voice, though, as he said curtly, "We'll discuss your responsibilities later, Mr. Scott." Then he turned to Jasmine, his hand grasping her arm so tightly that she winced. "As for Mrs. Tucker," he said grimly, "her nursing days are over."

Before she could protest, Jasmine found herself being bundled onto Morgan's horse, riding sidesaddle in front of her husband, his arm pinioned around her so tightly that she could not have found the breath to speak, much less break free.

When they reached the house and dismounted, Morgan's grip didn't loosen. "You're hurting my arm," Jasmine gasped indignantly.

Ignoring her protest, and still without speaking, he practically dragged her up the stairs of the front veranda and into a sunny bedroom at the front of the house, where he thrust her into a large wicker chair.

Jasmine opened her mouth to protest such high-handed behavior, but when she looked into Morgan's face the protest died in her throat. She had seen her husband angry with her before, but never like this. The hazel eyes looked almost black with rage, the muscles beside his mouth pulled into taut, white ridges.

"You will stay quarantined in this room," he said through clenched teeth. "I've sent for a doctor from Ewa. When he tells me that the danger of your having been infected with smallpox is past, we will return to Honolulu at once. Until then you will see no one. Particularly, you will not go near Matthew."

She drew in her breath sharply. "You can't think that I would expose Matthew to the pox. I haven't been near him since I started nursing the people from the villages. Anyway," she said, with a flash of her old defiance, "I've been vaccinated against smallpox."

"So had dozens of people in Honolulu who still died of the disease," Morgan said pitilessly. "And they had less exposure to the disease than you've had."

He saw the defiance fade from her face and a shriveling fear take its place as the truth of his words sank home. She should be afraid, he thought as fear for her squeezed his own throat with an iron hand. He had been half mad with rage and despair when he had learned of Jasmine's quixotic nursing of the smallpox victims. Anger at his own helplessness, that he could do nothing now for her but stand by and wait, flared in his voice as his glance flicked over the disheveled gown she wore. "Get out of those clothes. I'll see that they're burned."

He did not leave the room but waited as she undressed. The momentary flash of defiance had taken the last of her strength, and she was suddenly too weary to protest any further. As she unbuttoned her gown and undid her petticoats, she caught a glimpse of herself in the mirror and stared, shocked. How thin she was! She could see her rib cage beneath her breasts, and her skin was dull and lifeless.

She saw a nightgown and wrapper lying across the foot of the bed and hastily drew them on, hating that Morgan should see her looking so unattractive.

He didn't even glance at her, however, as he gathered up her clothes without speaking. At the door, he paused and said, "I'll have the servants bring hot water. They'll leave the pails outside the door. There's a tub behind that screen, and soap and towels on the washstand. Someone will knock at the door when they leave the trays of food." A wintry smile touched his lips for a moment. "There are books on the table. I seem to recall you enjoyed my library aboard the *Louisa*."

As the door closed behind him, Jasmine was reminded of her first night aboard the *Louisa*, when she had been locked in Morgan's cabin. Well, she wasn't locked in now, she thought ruefully, glancing around the room, but she might as well be. She was not going to be allowed to leave until the doctor gave her a clean bill of health. If, she thought, suddenly shivering, she were given a clean bill of health. Suppose during these last weeks she had been infected with smallpox. What if she were carrying death inside of her? She remembered the terrible suffering of her patients so that death, in the end, had been a release. No, she thought quickly, she mustn't think of that. She must believe she was all right.

Soaking in a warm bath made her feel better. She scrubbed herself until her skin felt raw, then washed her hair and fell, exhausted, into bed.

For the next week, all she did was eat and sleep as her body slowly regained its strength and the weight she had lost. The second week she started reading the books Morgan had left in the room, but by the third week, she was too restless to read. She prowled around the bedroom or sat at the window and watched young Matthew playing on the veranda with his nurse.

How handsome he was, she thought proudly, and how quickly he was growing. In another month he would be a year old. Watching him toddle after his nursemaid, her arms ached to hold him.

Heartsick, she turned away from the window and began to pace the room in earnest. She was furious with Morgan for keeping her here in this room, even though the doctor who came to see her each week warned her that her being inoculated against smallpox was no guarantee that she would not contract the disease. In some cases, the vaccine was faulty or too many years had passed.

She remembered bitterly that Lani had been inoculated and must have thought herself safe. Or was Kale right? Was it Micah Beale who had literally prayed Lani to death like some ancient evil *kahuna*?

Several times Jasmine had sat down to write to Malia and her father of Lani's and their granddaughter's deaths, but she had never been able to get past the first line. Just as she had never been able to speak to Morgan about her sister's death. Putting it into words would make it final—that she had forever lost her sister.

At the end of the third week, she awoke to find the moonlight pouring in through the curtained window, making the room almost as bright as day. And she knew she couldn't stand her confinement a moment longer. She slipped into a loose *holoku* and flung a towel over her shoulder, the window groaning slightly as she opened it wider and stepped out onto the veranda.

There was no one at the stable, and she didn't bother to saddle her horse. She slipped a bridle over the mare's head and mounted her astride, as she had ridden as a young girl, heading the horse toward the shore and feeling pleasantly guilty as if she were playing hooky from school.

She trotted the horse along the water's edge until she found a secluded cove, although there was hardly any need for privacy. There wasn't a soul in sight at this hour of the night, and the only houses were the burned-out huts a half mile down the beach. As she tossed the reins around a coconut palm, she was sure that she could have her swim and be back at the big house without anyone being the wiser.

Disposing of her *holoku* in one swift motion over her head, she let it drop on the sand a safe distance from where the tide was curling inwardly over the beach, the foam silver white in the moonlight. Then she walked slowly across the damp sand and out into the water. A gentle breeze rustled the coconut palms and slid like teasing, familiar hands over her nude body. The water lapped higher and higher at her legs, the surf stronger, tugging at her, until finally she dived head first into a breaking wave. The shock of the water after the warm night air snatched her breath away. She came up, gasping, tossing her wet hair from her face, treading water for a moment before she found her stroke and swam away from the shore.

For a half hour she swam, then floated, letting the water lift and carry her as it willed, her mind blissfully blank, her body completely relaxed. Finally, reluctantly, she swam back to shore. As she started to splash from the water to the beach, she saw a darker shadow separate itself from the shadow of the coconut palms where she had left her horse and *holoku*.

Morgan cast a long, black shadow in the moonlight, his face dark and expressionless as he walked to within a few feet of her and stopped. Looking into that dark, somehow menacing, face, she had an impulse to flee, to dive back into the sea.

Morgan, his eyes narrowed against the brilliant moonlight, saw the slight stiffening of the slender body and felt his throat go dry, sensing her turning away from him. *She looks like a sea nymph,* he thought; her body glistening silver in the moonlight; the wet, shining hair falling over one shoulder; the long strands curling around, framing a perfectly formed breast. She was no longer painfully thin, and the flesh covering her delicate bones was softly gleaming. Her hips gently swelled downward to the silken thighs that smoothly tapered into long, graceful legs. Silver drops of water ran slowly down between her breasts, over the taut belly, and were caught in the dark hair curling damply between her thighs.

Cold perspiration broke out on Morgan's face as he forced himself to remain still while every instinct urged him to seize her before she could slip away from him again. Except he knew, in that one bit of cold, logical reasoning left to him, that if he did, he would gain nothing. She must come to him of her own free will, or he would lose everything.

Her voice was wary when she finally spoke. "How did you know I was here?"

"I followed you from the house. I couldn't sleep either."

She tossed her head rebelliously. "I couldn't stand being cooped up in that room any longer. And I'm sure if I had the smallpox, I would have developed the symptoms by now."

He nodded. "The doctor agrees with you. He told me today that we could return to Honolulu whenever we wanted."

A breeze stirred the palm branches. Jasmine shivered, not from a chill but from the thought of their returning to that sprawling house in Honolulu, together but always apart.

And suddenly it was as if Kale were standing beside her, whispering, "If you love the Captain, Pikake, forget your *haole* blood. Give yourself to him like a Hawaiian *wahine* gives herself to a *kane*, freely, from the pure *aloha* and joy of giving."

Hardly breathing, legs braced, Morgan waited, as if sensing Jasmine's indecision. Then all at once a smile pulled at the corners of his wife's mouth, her eyes bright as starshine as she lifted her arms to him and said teasingly, "Why don't you join me? It's a beautiful night for a swim."

Then she turned and plunged back into the surf. He caught a flash of silver as she cut the surface of the water before she disappeared from view. When she did not immediately surface again, he searched uneasily the dark, rolling ocean for a glimpse of her dark head. The surf was heavier now, roaring deep in its throat as it attacked the shore. Then swiftly he tore off his clothes and dived into the water.

He had only gone out a short distance when he felt hands circling, tightening around his ankles, catching him unawares and pulling him beneath the water.

He felt warm lips cover his mouth. A soft, supple body pressed against the length of his body in the water, slender arms and legs entwining so closely with his limbs that they seemed one entity, one body taking breath and life from the other.

When they drifted slowly to the surface, their bodies were still entangled. Laughing, Jasmine tried to break free and swim away, but it was Morgan's arms that held her fast now. Her body arched in his arms as his tongue licked the saltwater from one high, peaked breast, teasing the nipple to hardness, while his free hand glided possessively over her body, her flesh as satiny smooth as the sea itself.

Suddenly she gave a soft, shuddering cry, and he saw that her eyes, flecked with moonlight, were shimmering with desire. They swam back to the shore, to the towel she had dropped on the sand. His eyes never left her face as his hands continued to caress every part of her body until she was no longer a silver-gilded sea nymph in his arms but a woman, with a woman's warmth, her skin flushed and glowing, her breasts taut and proud.

When he lowered her gently to the towel, her own hands, shyly at first, then more boldly, rediscovered the shape and feel of his broad, muscular back and lean, hard flanks. Her eyes were softly glowing, filling with joy as their pleasure mounted with exquisite slowness. But their passion had been too long denied. They could no more prolong their lovemaking than the silver-crested waves could be slowed from crashing into the shore behind them. When Morgan swung himself above her,

Jasmine's body arched upward eagerly, and their bodies found each other in an immediate, simultaneous explosion of joy and fulfillment so complete that afterwards, as they lay in each other's arms, Morgan knew exultantly that this time there was no part of his wife that had eluded him. This time he had possessed her completely.

Later as they rode back to the plantation and crept quietly into the house, laughing softly and foolishly, like children returning from a night's lark, Morgan followed her into the bedroom, closing the door behind him.

"You'll never know how many nights I wanted to break down that blasted door," he growled as Jasmine slipped out of her *holoku* into a wrapper. "Though I confess," he said, grinning, "that when I thought of bedding you, it wasn't on the beach but in a nice, comfortable bed."

All at once, Jasmine remembered something Lilikoi had once said, bragging about the captain who had made love to her in the sea.

"Did you ever . . . ?" she blurted then fell silent, knowing, of course, that she could never bring herself to ask the question.

"Did I ever what?"

"Nothing." She turned her gaze quickly away.

"You're thinking of Lilikoi, aren't you?" Morgan asked quietly.

She nodded, knowing it was useless to lie.

Morgan cursed silently. Would the ghost of Lilikoi always be there, lurking at the edge of their happiness?

"I make no excuses for the life I led before I met you," he said roughly. "I'm a man, not a saint. As for what happened that night in your father's house . . ." He searched awkwardly for words then shrugged helplessly. Damn it, even if Lilikoi had been the seducer that night, he couldn't place the blame on her. The responsibility, the guilt, was his, not Lilikoi's.

"Did you love her?" Jasmine asked in a small voice.

He gazed at her, startled. "Love Lilikoi?" A mocking

smile curved his lips. "No more than I assume you loved that popinjay Beale, or James Scott, whose embrace you were sharing that day I arrived."

Now it was her turn to look startled, her eyes widening, annoyed. "You surely can't think that Mr. Scott and I . . . that we . . ."

Morgan shook his head, amused. "No, I don't believe you and Scott were lovers." His voice hardened. "If I did, Mr. Scott wouldn't have gotten off with just a tongue-lashing. But you must admit it was hardly prudent, your sleeping under the same roof with the man for so many weeks."

"I slept in a small room in the back of the shed," Jasmine protested. "And we weren't always alone. Kale was with us part of the time."

"Your brother was here?" The surprise in Morgan's face made Jasmine realize she hadn't yet told her husband about Kale—and Lani.

At the thought of her sister, the pain surged back. How could she have been so selfishly, deliriously happy only a short time ago? she thought guiltily. How could she have forgotten Lani?

The tears blinding her, she stumbled into Morgan's arms, whispering, "Kale came to tell me that Lani and her child—they're dead."

Morgan's arms crushed her against him as if he were trying to absorb her pain into his own body. "I'm sorry, my love. I'm so sorry," he murmured, holding her close until she grew quiet in his arms and was able to tell him the rest—about Micah Beale and how Kale believed that the man had prayed his wife to death.

"Is it possible, do you think, Morgan?" Jasmine asked, her voice trembling, her eyes wide with horror.

Morgan scowled blackly, cursing Kale beneath his breath for adding to Jasmine's anguish with his superstitious nonsense. "Of course it's not possible. Your sister died of smallpox, as thousands of others have." Then to get off the subject of Kale, he asked, "Have you written to your parents yet?"

She shook her head. "I—I couldn't. I thought it would be easier when we get back to Honolulu, telling them in person."

"We won't be leaving Palekaiko," Morgan said, frowning. "Not right away. I'll have to stay and oversee the plantation until I can find a new manager."

"You let Mr. Scott go?" Jasmine asked, shocked. "But I told you the hospital was my idea, not James's. And you'll never find a better *luna*. Mr. Scott knows everything about growing sugarcane. He was even experimenting with cultivating deeper, so the cane would give a better yield."

If Jasmine had not been so incensed at the injustice done the plantation manager, she would have noticed the storm clouds gathering in Morgan's eyes. "I had no idea you had become such an expert in raising sugarcane, madam," he said coldly. "You and Scott must have spent more time together than I thought." The black, straight brows slanted ominously across his face. "I'd prefer that you find more suitable ways to occupy your time here at the plantation than meddling in plantation matters that don't concern you."

"Why?" Jasmine retorted. "Because I'm a woman? Your mother runs successful businesses in New Bedford, and she's a woman."

Morgan scowled, partly at her defiance and partly because he sensed uncomfortably that what she said made a kind of sense.

"My mother was forced to enter a man's world after my father died," he said pointedly. "But you have a husband to look after you." His narrowed gaze traveled over her with that familiar possessive look she remembered so well. All at once Jasmine felt her heart pounding, as if those precious moments at the beach that had brought them so close were slipping away from her. In another moment they would be strangers again.

Then Morgan had roughly pushed aside the satin robe, his hand cupping her breast, his thumb caressing the soft peak as he murmured, "Or have you forgotten?"

Jasmine closed her eyes, blotting out that narrowed, possessive gaze touching her face, letting the waves of pleasure sweep over her like the cresting surf lifting her helplessly. All that mattered, she thought, was that she and Morgan were together. She didn't dare put that closeness into jeopardy again.

She felt her wrapper being removed and sliding to the floor, then she was being carried to the bed. She kept her eyes closed as she heard Morgan removing his clothes, then the bed creaking.

"Look at me, Jasmine," he said quietly.

When she opened her eyes reluctantly, the possessive arrogance was gone from his gaze. There was a need in his face as desperate as her own, as if he, too, sensed how fragile the tie that bound them was. "I didn't dismiss James Scott," he said. "It was his own idea. He has a chance to go into partnership with a friend, raising cattle on Hawaii."

"Who will you get to replace him?" she asked, worried. "The grinding gears in the mill are always breaking down, and James is the only one who knows how to repair them."

Morgan covered her mouth with his own and when he finally pulled away, she was silent, her face flushed, her mouth still half parted.

"I don't know who'll run the mill, and at the moment I don't care." Morgan laughed softly as he pulled her into his arms again. "At the moment, all I care about is making up for all those nights we've lost. . . ."

Chapter 23

The Tucker family didn't return to Honolulu until spring.
It took longer than Morgan had thought to find a competent plantation manager to replace James Scott. Although he grumbled about the time he was spending away from his other business interests in Honolulu, Jasmine enjoyed their stay at the plantation, while young Matthew thrived under the care of Nakeli and the loving attention his mother and father showered upon him.

Knowing now how Morgan felt about her becoming involved in plantation matters, Jasmine stopped visiting the mill and the sugarcane fields as she had done with James Scott and carefully refrained from offering Morgan any advice on how the plantation should be run.

Then one evening over dinner Morgan casually mentioned that, unable to find any better candidates, he was thinking of offering the manager's job to the field *luna*, Walter Hanes. Jasmine's cup clattered as she replaced it hastily on its saucer, her voice outraged as she exclaimed, "But, Morgan, you mustn't!"

"Why not?" Morgan asked, annoyed. He had had a long, frustrating day. As Jasmine had warned, the gear shaft on the grinding wheel had broken down in the mill, requiring arduous hours of repair work. The coolies had stubbornly refused to work when they were fed poi instead of rice, and an insect was found boring into several cane stalks that could threaten the cane crop.

Ignoring the simmering anger in her husband's eyes,

Jasmine said, "Because you won't be able to trust Mr. Hanes not to mistreat the workers."

"I'm running a plantation, not a Sunday School," Morgan growled. "Any man who has the job of managing other men has to be hard, or the work will never be done properly."

Jasmine remembered how Morgan had never tolerated laziness or slackness among his men aboard the *Louisa*, and that he hadn't hesitated to use his fists to punish the seaman who had disobeyed his orders. Yet she knew that for all his hardness, Morgan had expected nothing of his men that he wasn't prepared to do himself. And she was sure that while he was present at the plantation, he would not allow Mr. Hanes to brutalize the workers. But what would happen when they left Palekaiko and returned to Honolulu?

"Have you any other objection to Mr. Hanes?" Morgan asked coldly.

Jasmine remembered the way the man had put his horse next to hers so that he could brush her leg with his own, and a flush rose on her face before she lowered her eyelids quickly, but not quickly enough.

Morgan got to his feet and came to stand beside her at the table. "Has the man annoyed you?" he asked quietly.

As much as she disliked Mr. Hanes, Jasmine had no wish to have him incur Morgan's wrath. "No, of course not," she said quickly.

Morgan drew her to her feet, his eyes never leaving her face. "You're a very poor liar, my sweet," he said softly.

"It's just that I don't like the way he looks at me," she stammered.

To her relief, Morgan threw back his head and laughed. "If I were to thrash every man who looked at you, madam, I'd have no time for anything else!" He drew a finger gently across one delicately arched cheekbone, traced the uptilted curve of her mouth, the hardness in his eyes softening as he murmured, "You may have noticed that I have a hard time keeping my own eyes away from you."

His fingers were undoing the tiny pearl buttons that ran down the front of her pale blue muslin gown until he exposed the tempting, scented hollow in her throat, where he dropped a warm, lingering kiss. But when, smiling, he began to undo the remaining buttons, Jasmine cast a nervous glance toward the door. "One of the servants might come in," she murmured.

"Nakeli has gone to visit her family, and I told the cook she could have the rest of the night off," he replied calmly, continuing his determined assault on the tiny pearl buttons. And then he groaned, exasperated, when he discovered the beruffled and beribboned chemise that still stood guard between him and the soft flesh beneath. His large hands fumbled impatiently with the lacy chemise, trying to locate the tiny, hidden fasteners beneath the ruffles, until, laughing a little breathlessly, Jasmine whispered, "Let me."

Deftly she began to unfasten the clasps, then halfway through she paused, her thick lashes shadowing her dark, lustrous eyes as she murmured sweetly, "I'm sorry for what I said about Mr. Hanes, dear. Of course you mustn't pay any attention to how I feel about him, if you think he's the proper man for the job."

Unhurriedly then, her small hands resumed their task until the pale blue cotton gown and chemise lay open to her waist, and Morgan could just glimpse the tempting peaks of velvet breasts.

"The hell with Hanes," he muttered hoarsely as he impatiently freed the silken mounds from the confines of the material binding them, the palms of his hands moving then to flatten on her back, lowering, pressing her hips and thighs against his hardness. "I'll find someone else for the job."

Two weeks later, Morgan hired Robert McTavish from Maui as the new *luna* of Palekaiko Plantation. He made the announcement to Jasmine at breakfast, wry amusement in his voice as he asked, "Unless, of course, you have some objection to Mr. McTavish, too?"

Jasmine felt tips of flame touch her face under Morgan's suddenly too astute gaze. Was it possible, she wondered uncomfortably, that he had known all along that she had deliberately tricked him into not hiring Mr. Hanes? The thought was disconcerting and somehow infuriating. Hastily she rose to her feet and went to the sideboard, pouring herself a cup of coffee, keeping her face carefully turned away from her husband.

"Mr. McTavish seems very well qualified for the job," she said coolly. As a matter of fact, she had been very favorably impressed with the man, who, with his gruffly kind manner, had reminded her of the first mate on the *Louisa*. And she had been equally impressed with Mr. McTavish's middle-aged, comfortable wife.

If Morgan was aware of a certain chill in the air, he gave no sign of it as he threw down his napkin and said cheerfully, "Well, it's settled, then. I'll make arrangements for us to return to Honolulu on the coastal schooner next week." He added, as if in afterthought, "It seems we'll be able to accept the invitation to the king's birthday levee, after all."

Jasmine spun around, startled. "You never told me we were invited to the palace."

Morgan grinned in mock surprise. "Didn't I? Well, I suppose I didn't mention the invitation because you seemed so contented with life in the country that I didn't think you'd be interested." He hesitated a moment and then said casually, "I've even been thinking that perhaps you'd prefer to live here permanently at the plantation rather than returning to Honolulu."

"But your business concerns are in Honolulu," Jasmine said, surprised.

Morgan shrugged. "Naturally, I'd have to spend some time in Honolulu, but you and Matthew could . . ."

"Stay here without you?" Jasmine finished indignantly. "I'd never do that!" She studied Morgan's face, a formless, uneasy impression taking hold of her that there was something he wasn't telling her. Some reason why, perhaps, he didn't want her to return to Honolulu with him? Another woman? she thought jealously for a moment before Morgan smiled and admitted, "The idea doesn't appeal much to me either."

"Well, then, it's settled," Jasmine said firmly and then frowned a little. "But I haven't a thing to wear to the levee. I'll need a new gown." Then, suddenly remembering, she lifted her eyes guiltily to Morgan. "I forgot. I can't go to the levee. I'm still in mourning for Lani."

"I remember your sister as a warm, loving person," Morgan said slowly. "I can't believe she'd want you to wear sackcloth and ashes as some sort of tribute to her dying." He shrugged, his eyes twinkling. "For myself, if you droop around in black for me after I'm gone, I'll come back and haunt you."

Jasmine flew into his arms, placing her hand over his mouth, her eyes bright with alarm. "You mustn't ever talk of your dying. It's bad luck! I'd die myself if anything happened to you."

Morgan gave her a bear hug, his voice roughly soothing. "You needn't worry. If a sperm whale couldn't finish me off, no doubt I'll live to a ripe, cantankerous old age. Now, dry your eyes, my sweet, and start thinking about what dress you'll wear to the levee. . . ."

The captain and Malia met Jasmine, Morgan, and young Matthew at the wharf when they arrived in Honolulu, Malia immediately grasping her grandson to her pillowy breast, where he nestled contentedly. Jasmine embraced her father, hoping that the dismay she felt didn't show in her face. She was shocked at how old her father looked, his grizzled hair and beard completely white now. And there were deep lines gouged into his face that had not been there before.

Morgan had convinced her that she should write her parents of the death of Lani and Ulimi, that it would be cruel to wait any longer before telling her parents the sad news. She knew that Lani, the baby of the family, had always been a special favorite of her father's, and she could see the weight of grief in his eyes, although he made no mention of either Lani or Kale as they rode in the carriage to the Tucker home.

Later that afternoon, though, when the captain and Morgan had gone to their offices in the wharf area, and Malia and Jasmine sat together on the lanai enjoying a cool fruit drink and watching young Matthew half walk, half crawl, around the lanai, Malia's face suddenly crumpled, tears glistening on her eyelashes as she cried softly, "*Auwe*, it breaks my heart that I never held Ulimi in my arms. And Lani, my baby . . ."

The tears rolled down her cheeks. Quickly Jasmine went to her side and embraced her stepmother, her own tears mingling with Malia's as they shared each other's grief.

It was only when young Matthew, alarmed by the strange actions of his mother and grandmother, began to cry, too, that the two women dried their tears. Malia settled her grandson on her lap, soothing him gently until he fell asleep in her arms.

Only then did she look across the table at Jasmine and ask, "Is it true? Did that man, Micah Beale, pray my Lani to death?"

Jasmine glanced up, startled. In her letter to her parents, she had not mentioned anything about the role that Kale believed Mr. Beale had played in Lani's final illness. "How did you know about that?" she asked.

"Lilikoi has been visiting friends on Maui for the last month. She saw Kale at Lahaina, and he told her the terrible thing this *kahuna* has done, putting a curse on my Lani."

"Micah Beale isn't a *kahuna*," Jasmine protested. She frowned uncertainly at her stepmother. "And you don't really believe that a person can be prayed to death?"

"Of course I believe it," Malia said calmly. "As a young girl on Kauai, I saw it happen many times."

Was it possible? Jasmine wondered, feeling suddenly

chilled, as if the sun had gone behind a cloud. Could Lani have lost all will to live because she believed that Micah Beale had the power of life and death over her? But the thought was too disturbing and she thrust it from her mind, asking instead, "How is Kale? Did Lilikoi say?"

Malia frowned unhappily. "You know Kale. He is like a calabash of poi, fermenting until it explodes, especially with all this talk of annexation. No one speaks of anything else these days in Honolulu. There is even a rumor that an annexation treaty has already been secretly given to the new American commissioner, Mr. Gregg."

Jasmine was surprised at the anger she felt at Malia's news. "How could the king allow such a thing to happen?" she demanded.

Malia sighed. "King Kauikeaouli is not strong, like his father, the great Kamehameha. And since his mistress died of the smallpox, he is drinking too much again. And the foreigners keep pressing him, demanding annexation. They threaten that if the king does not turn his country over to America, then rough men, filibusters, will be imported from California who will take the government by force. Already there are such men seen in town, bragging that soon these islands will be a republic."

Malia rocked her grandson in her arms, her voice a low wail of despair. "I fear the days of our beloved kingdom are over."

"What of the young princes?" Jasmine asked hopefully. "Prince Alexander will never give up his throne willingly."

Malia nodded agreement. "The young prince is unhappy with his uncle for listening to the *haoles* preaching annexation. I wonder if Alexander will even be at the king's birthday levee." She gave Jasmine a questioning glance. "Will you and the captain be there?"

"We have an invitation," Jasmine said. "I'm going to have a new gown made from a piece of gold brocade I've been saving." She giggled. "It's going to be cut very décolleté." She was almost positive that it wasn't because of a woman that Morgan hadn't wanted her to

271

return with him to Honolulu. Just the same, she wasn't taking any chances of his attention wandering elsewhere at the levee. The conversation turned away from politics to fashion, but at the king's birthday levee the subject of annexation was on almost everyone's tongue.

Jasmine had taken her time dressing for the ball, and when she finally came down the stairs to a waiting Morgan, who was pacing the floor impatiently, she was wearing a long, dark red cloak that swept down to her ankles and covered her gown completely.

She paused at the gold-framed mirror in the entrance hall, fussing with her hair, which was piled in gleaming curls on top of her head under a tiara of plumeria blossoms. Morgan came up behind her, his hands resting lightly on her shoulders as he dropped a kiss amidst the scented curls, and growled softly, "We're already late, madam, and if you make yourself look any lovelier, we'll never get to the levee at all."

Jasmine smiled innocently up at him. "I didn't know we were late, Morgan. You should have told me."

When they reached the outer square before the palace, they found the area crowded with the carriages of late-arriving guests. They walked up the road to the palace, black sand crunching beneath their feet, past uniformed members of the King's Guard and flaming kukui torches.

In the entrance hall, brilliant with feathered capes on the wall and tall, colorful *kahilis* held by the minor chiefs of the royal court, Jasmine disappeared for a moment into a small room set aside as the ladies' retiring room. Morgan was waiting for her when she returned. He was talking to a fellow merchant, and when he heard a slight hush fall over the hum of voices around him, he turned and saw Jasmine, smiling, walking toward him. The gold brocade flounced skirt swirled gracefully downward from her tiny waist, the rich brocade catching and reflecting the light from the crystal chandeliers overhead. But it was not the skirt of the gown on which Morgan's gaze fastened but on Jasmine's bosom. The combination of a low-cut pleated neckline and a boned waistline caused

Jasmine's breasts to rise perilously above the bodice of the gown. She wore no necklace or even flowers to detract the eyes from, at least to Morgan, an unnerving expanse of softly gleaming flesh.

In two strides he was at his wife's side, growling, "Damn it, Jasmine. What possessed you to wear that gown tonight?"

Jasmine unfurled her fan, made of the same gold brocade as the gown, and fluttered it before her while she laughed teasingly up at her husband. "What's wrong with my gown?"

"You know damn well what's wrong." Morgan was suddenly aware that his voice had risen and curious glances were being cast in their direction. "We'll talk about this later at home," he said, a tightly controlled smile on his face, but his eyes were still narrowed and angry as he escorted Jasmine through the receiving line.

When Jasmine curtsied before the king, she was startled to see the lines of dissipation in the once-handsome face, the deep weariness in the dark brown eyes. When she rose from her curtsy, the king leaned forward, smiling, as he spoke in Hawaiian to her. "We've missed your charm and beauty at our court, Mrs. Tucker. It's good to have you back." Then he added somberly, "I was saddened to hear of the death of your sister and her child. I know the pain of losing someone you love."

Sorrow cast a shadow across his face, and Jasmine wondered if he was thinking of the mistress he had just lost or of the beloved sister he had married as a young boy and also lost to death.

Then the ceremony of presentations was finished, and the dancing began with a quadrille, followed by a polka. Jasmine did not lack for dancing partners, but as she whirled gracefully around the floor, first in the arms of the French consul, then the governor of Oahu, and a naval commander from one of the U.S. warships recently arrived in port, she became aware of the icy stares of some of the women on the dance floor.

She stared back indifferently. What did she care what some jealous old biddies thought about her gown? Morgan's reaction to the dress, though, had surprised her. Her husband was hardly straitlaced or prudish. She had expected him to be, if not pleased, at least amused by the scandalous cut of her gown. Certainly she had thought he would remain at her side all evening.

Instead she realized after several sets had passed that she hadn't seen Morgan for over an hour. It wasn't very flattering, she thought irritably, that he should prefer other company to that of his wife, particularly if that company should turn out to be feminine and pretty.

"Mrs. Tucker, I believe this next dance is ours."

John Brooks, an attorney and marine insurance agent, was bearing down upon her, smiling eagerly.

"Yes, of course." She glanced absently around the ballroom, trying to find Morgan's dark head. "I would like to speak to my husband first. You haven't seen Captain Tucker, have you?"

"He was out on the lanai the last time I saw him," the man said, his eyes roaming greedily over Jasmine's bosom barely restrained by the brocade, as if he were hoping the delightfully unexpected might happen.

They were several groups of gentlemen on the lanai, Jasmine saw, smoking their cheroots and talking politics. She could hear snatches of conversation as she walked by. "Something has to be done to push the annexation through. . . ." "Wyllie is playing the commissioner for a fool, always putting new terms in the treaty. . . ." "Now that Admiral Perry has opened Japan to American commerce, it's vital that we keep our trade routes to the Orient secure. . . ."

Then she saw Morgan standing with about a half-dozen men at the edge of the lanai. As she approached, she heard one man announce indignantly, "Did you hear that Wyllie has included a clause in the treaty that Hawaii must enter the union as a state? He knows the senate would never approve of these islands becoming a state, giving the natives the same rights as American citizens."

"It's outrageous," agreed another man that she recognized as a friend of her father's. "When you think of all America has done for these people . . ."

Jasmine's low, musical laugh drifted across to the men, her voice softly jeering. "How ungrateful of the Hawaiian people not to be thankful to the *haoles* for taking their land, killing them with their diseases, and forcing their laws upon them!"

The man's face reddened angrily, then, recognizing Captain Tucker's wife, he recovered his composure and bowed toward her. "I would never argue with a beautiful woman, Mrs. Tucker," he said, smiling, "but, surely, you, as an American citizen . . ."

Jasmine stiffened, her dark eyes flashing in the light from the torches placed around the lanai. "I'm a citizen of Hawaii." Her scathing glance swept the assembled men. "And, as I recall, so are most of you gentlemen, since you rushed to take out citizenship papers so that you could own fee-simple land in these islands." Her voice trembled with contempt. "Do you think the Hawaiian people will sit meekly by and let their country be stolen away from them?"

"The natives? You're very mistaken, Mrs. Tucker, if you think they care who runs these islands."

A third man cleared his throat. "I wouldn't be too sure of that, Gordon. When Dr. Judd spoke for annexation the other night, he was roundly hissed by the audience. And there's that young firebrand, Kale. They say he draws crowds whenever he speaks against the annexation."

Then the man speaking fell silent as he recalled that the young firebrand was Jasmine Tucker's brother. An odd, awkward silence fell over the entire group, broken only when Morgan quietly left the group and took Jasmine's arm. She turned to face him, angered by his silence. Why had he just stood there? Why hadn't he spoken up in her defense?

"I believe this is our dance," he said calmly.

Before he could edge her away from his friends, though, John Brooks appeared. "Oh, there you are, Mrs. Tucker," he said with a glad cry. "I've come to claim my dance."

Jasmine pulled her arm free from Morgan's grasp, deliberately turning her back on her husband to give the lawyer a ravishing smile. "Of course. I haven't forgotten, Mr. Brooks. How could I?"

As she allowed Mr. Brooks to lead her across the lanai and into the ballroom, she did not see the anger narrowing Morgan's eyes to glittering slits that followed her into the ballroom. Mr. Brooks turned out to be a surprisingly graceful dancer, for all that he was portly and old enough to be her father, Jasmine thought, amused and then annoyed, as she felt a damp hand tighten on her waist and noticed the way her partner's glance kept dropping to her bosom. When the dance finally ended, she withdrew as tactfully and quickly as she could, but Mr. Brooks came hurrying after her. "You'd do me a great honor, Mrs. Tucker, if you'd take supper with me," he pleaded.

Jasmine smiled politely. "I'm afraid I can't. My husband and I are to dine with the royal family. And after all, it is the king's birthday."

The plump, moist lips turned sulky. Her partner cast a disdainful glance toward the king, who was escorting his wife into a side room set aside for the private dinner of the royal family and their friends.

"That sooty sprig of royalty," he sneered. "No one knows for sure on what day he was born, so how can they celebrate his birthday?"

"Still, he is the king," Jasmine said coldly.

"Not for long." Mr. Brooks gave his companion a broad, knowing wink. "The white men in these islands won't endure being ruled much longer by a black man who can barely speak English. Mark my words. It's only a matter of time now before a beautiful woman like you will no longer have to suffer the indignity of bowing before a savage dressed up in fancy clothes."

Jasmine gazed coldly at the puffed-up little man standing before her, her face as frozen as her voice as she replied, "I can assure you, Mr. Brooks, the only indignity I've suffered tonight is having to endure your company!"

Mr. Brooks's mouth fell open, the heavy-jowled face splotching an ugly red as he stared at Jasmine. Then the moist lips twisted into a smile that was more like a disagreeable smirk, his voice thickened with venom. "I'd forgotten how fond your family is of the native customs, Mrs. Tucker. Tell me, was it just the one sister your brother took to his bed, or all of you?"

Chapter 24

Anger flashed through Jasmine, a shock wave that left her for a moment feeling faint. Then, furious, her hands half lifted to claw that obscene, sly smirk from the man's face when Morgan appeared beside her. He captured his wife's wrists in an iron grip, jerking them down to her side while his other arm circled her waist, pulling her tight against him in what, to the other couples around them, appeared to be a loving, husbandly embrace.

Morgan then turned his gaze upon John Brooks, his voice deceptively mild. "I believe you were just about to apologize to my wife, Mr. Brooks?"

John Brooks took one look into Morgan's face, into eyes honed to a razor's edge slashing at his face, and his own face drained to a chalky white, his Adam's apple bobbing frantically in his throat. "Yes, yes, of course," he stammered, gazing desperately around him as if looking for help. "I—I meant no insult. Please accept my most sincere apology, Mrs. Tucker. Now, if you'll excuse me, I have friends waiting."

He scuttled away while Jasmine was still trying to struggle free from Morgan's grip on her waist and wrists. She glared after the man, then at her husband. "You should have let me scratch his eyes out!"

Morgan released his grip on her wrists a little so that the blood could once more circulate through her arms. "Don't you think your wearing that gown has caused enough gossip for one evening?" he asked dryly.

While he was talking, he was drawing her away from the dance floor toward the door leading to the outer reception room.

"Where are we going?" Jasmine asked, trying in vain to pull free of the hand still encircling her wrists.

"Home."

"We can't leave now. We're expected to join the royal party for supper."

"I've already informed the king that you are indisposed," Morgan said. He stopped in the now-empty outer reception room to smile grimly down at his wife. "A sudden headache from too much excitement."

Almost, Jasmine was tempted to protest being hauled off so unceremoniously from the party, but when she saw the ominous set to Morgan's jaw, the seething anger behind that tightly controlled smile, she decided that for the moment, discretion was the better part of valor. Haughtily she allowed him to place her cloak around her shoulders and hand her into the victoria. She didn't, however, speak a word to her husband all the way home. When the carriage stopped before the Tucker home, she descended swiftly, ignoring Morgan's outstretched hand, and without a glance in his direction swept imperiously across the lanai and up the stairs to the bedroom, slamming the door behind her.

She expected Morgan to come storming into the room

after her. When the door remained closed, she frowned uncertainly, then opened the door a crack, wide enough so that she could hear Morgan's footsteps in the downstairs hall, the door to his study, just below the bedroom, opening and closing.

Jasmine stalked across the room to her dressing table. Her maid came sleepily into the room to unclasp Jasmine's gown, but after that was accomplished Jasmine sent her back to bed and removed the rest of her clothes by herself. Still angry with Morgan, she kicked off her slippers so that they flew against the wall. He could at least have apologized for his atrocious behavior, first standing by and letting that boorish Mr. Brooks insult her, then dragging her away from the party like a fractious child.

She sat down at the dressing table, removing the pins from her curls so that her hair tumbled down around her shoulders. As she brushed furiously at her hair, though, her anger slowly faded away. The pull of the brush against her hair reminded her of Morgan's hands gently stroking her hair, even as she could still feel the rough imprint of those same hands on her wrists. She remembered other times, too, when those hands had held her a willing prisoner, and those narrowed eyes, which at the palace had burned into her face, had roamed over her body with a fierce, devouring passion.

Jasmine's lips parted in a soft, half smile, her brushing forgotten. She got to her feet and went to her bureau drawer, taking out a pale yellow lacy nightgown that was a special favorite of Morgan's. Then after she touched jasmine scent to her temples and the hollow of her throat, she settled herself into bed, fluffing the pillows behind her, her gaze fastening in anticipation on the door.

He would have to come to bed sometime, she thought confidently. She could wait.

In the study, Morgan's wrath did not dissipate so quickly. He had poured himself a stiff drink and then a second one as he prowled back and forth from desk to window, trying to calm the fury raging inside of him. The more he thought about the evening, the more incensed he became, not sure with whom he was the angriest: his wife, for wearing that deliberately shocking gown, or John Brooks. Remembering the man's vicious taunt, Morgan's hands balled into fists, his body still aching from the frustration of depriving himself of the pleasure of smashing his fists into the man's face. Captain Morgan Tucker of the *Louisa* would have done so without a second thought and not felt a moment's regret afterwards.

Morgan picked up his glass and scowled at the delicate crystal brandy snifter. But then Captain Tucker hadn't moved in respectable social circles with the reputations of a wife and a young son to protect.

If he had given Brooks the beating he deserved, the man's vile insinuations would have spread all over Honolulu by morning. And Morgan was well aware that it was only Captain Babcock's respectable standing in the community and, he thought grimly, a certain fear of his own swift retaliation that had kept the Babcock and Tucker families from being immediately and completely socially ostracized after Kale and Lani's scandalous behavior.

Morgan once more began to prowl restlessly. He didn't give a damn for himself what people whispered behind closed doors, but he wasn't about to allow Jasmine to suffer for the actions of her brother and sister. And there was young Matthew to think about, too. His son and, he hoped, one day, Matthew's brothers and sisters would be growing up in these islands. He didn't intend for their futures to be clouded by any hint of scandal.

He took a last swallow from his glass, knowing he was only postponing the inevitable as he cocked his head toward the ceiling of the study. Earlier, he had heard the door to the bedroom slam shut, a thudding sound of something being flung against the wall, but now all was quiet. Had Jasmine gone to bed? A softness touched his face at the thought of his wife in bed, remembering the warmth in that soft, silken body curling against his. Then he took a deep, steadying breath, chiding himself for his own weakness. Was he going to allow his love for that black-eyed vixen upstairs to blind him to her capricious, often reckless, behavior, which could only add more fuel for gossip?

Morgan straightened his shoulders and strode determinedly through the hallway and up the stairs. No, the question simply was: was he to be master of his own house or not?

When he opened the bedroom, though, and saw Jasmine, the bedcovers pushed to the foot of the bed, the transparent slip of a nightgown somehow making the pale pink gold flesh beneath more alluring than if she had worn nothing at all, he was almost undone, his resolution fast slipping away.

Except, he thought, frowning, there was something about the scene that reminded him painfully of another night in New Bedford, when his wife had been waiting in bed for him dressed in the same fashion and for her own reasons.

From the bed, Jasmine was watching him warily, but her voice was meek enough. "I'm sorry you didn't like my gown." She smiled, her eyes bright with amusement. "The other gentlemen didn't seem to find it so objectionable."

Morgan gazed at her coldly. "The other gentlemen aren't married to you. I prefer my wife to dress like a lady, not a high-priced whore."

While waiting for him to come upstairs, Jasmine had promised herself that she would be sweet and forgiving, but it was a promise that was swiftly forgotten now as she straightened in bed, color running along her arched cheekbones. "I don't recall your being so high-minded about whores when we first met," she said tartly.

So she hadn't forgotten after all, Morgan thought. Even after what they had come to mean to each other, she hadn't been able to put their first night together out of her mind. He had even been foolish enough to hope that she had finally forgiven him. Well, he was wrong. He saw that now. Perhaps she would never be able to forget that night. Perhaps a woman never could. Nevertheless, matters still had to be settled between them.

He came to stand beside the bed, frowning down at her. "It's not only the gown. It's what you said, the way you behaved, with my friends. As for John Brooks . . ."

Jasmine interrupted, her eyes blazing. "You'd stand up for that—that vile man!"

Morgan shook his head. "No, I have no liking for Brooks. He's a fool and worse. But there are men, respected, honorable men like your father who aren't interested in starting a revolution but who still feel that America's annexation of these islands is necessary and inevitable."

"Well, I don't believe it!" Jasmine slipped out of bed to stand defiantly before Morgan. "I'll never believe it." Her eyes searched Morgan's face unhappily, a sinking sensation in her stomach. Somehow it had not occurred to her that Morgan might feel different from her about the islands keeping their independence. "What about you, Morgan? What do you believe?"

Her husband shrugged. "I'm a practical man. The king means well, but these islands have become too valuable, like precious jewels sparkling in the sea. Someone is sure to come along and scoop them up. And, frankly, I'd prefer it to be America, rather than England or France."

"What about the Hawaiian people? What about what they want?" Jasmine demanded. "Don't they have the right to govern their own country as they see fit, to follow their own customs and traditions?"

Morgan's mouth twisted wryly. "Which Hawaiian customs? Not thirty-five years ago it was the tradition in these islands to kill a man if his shadow fell across the king, to bury unwanted babies alive, and for priests to sacrifice human victims at their *heiaus*. It was also the custom for the king and high chiefs to drive men and women up into the hills to collect sandalwood, which they would exchange for fancy trappings from sea captains while their slave laborers died by the hundreds and the hills were stripped bare." He slanted a mocking eyebrow at Jasmine. "Or didn't your brother explain any of those quaint customs and traditions to you?"

"Kale only wants what's best for the people," Jasmine protested stubbornly. "I won't have you speak against him."

"I haven't spoken against him up to now, but the truth is your brother seduced a young, innocent girl," Morgan said brutally. "Oh, I've no doubt he loved her, but if he did, then he should have known that your sister had neither the temperament nor the strength to endure the sort of life he expected her to share with him. Nor," he added bitterly, "did your brother seem particularly concerned about the effect his actions would have on his family—on you."

"What do you mean?" For the first time, Jasmine's voice held a note of uncertainty.

Morgan scowled. "Do you really think that Brooks is the only one, that there haven't been others in Honolulu with their sly innuendos and nasty gossip about you and Lilikoi and Kale?"

Jasmine flinched. "That's despicable," she whispered brokenly. "How could people believe . . . ?" She could not put it into words, could not even allow herself to think about it, because it hurt too much. It was the pain twisting cruelly inside of her that made her lash out at Morgan. "It's not true. You have no right to say such things." Then she said furiously, "If you'd only been man enough to stand up to John Brooks and stop his foul mouth . . ."

Morgan's hands tightened on her arms, his eyes roving over the slim gold-and-rose body so visible under the cobweb-sheer gown. "I can assure you, madam," he said. "There are more pleasant ways of proving my manhood to you than beating a man to death."

Her dark eyes stared not at him but through him, her

face cool and remote. "Let me go," she said haughtily. "We have nothing more to say to each other."

"You're mistaken," he growled. "I have a great deal more to say to you, and I plan to say it only once, so you had better listen. There'll be no more scandal touching this family. In the future, you'll dress and behave so circumspectly that there won't be a hint of gossip connected with your name. And you'll treat my friends and associates with civility, whether or not you agree with their political opinions. As for your stepbrother, you are not to see him again or have any communication with him."

"You can't ask that of me!" Jasmine tore herself free, her dark eyes flashing with disdain, her lovely body taut, so that Morgan couldn't help thinking regretfully how anger only intensified his wife's beauty.

"I wasn't aware that I was asking," he said coldly. "I was telling you how matters are going to be handled in this house from now on."

Jasmine studied that implacable face. "And suppose I don't choose to go along with your demands?"

Morgan shrugged and began to undress. "Well, then, there's always Palekaiko. Mr. and Mrs. McTavish would prove excellent chaperons for you, and the plantation's far enough from Honolulu so that any indiscretions on your part wouldn't reach the ears of society here. Of course, you'd miss young Matthew's company. . . ."

"You'd keep our son here?" Jasmine's face paled. "How can you even suggest such a thing? You know how much I love him."

Morgan smiled grimly. "You have an odd way of showing your love, recklessly exposing yourself to a deadly disease when young Matthew was in your care and now refusing to have any thought for your son's future in these islands."

Gazing into his wife's stricken face, he drew her gently into his arms, his lips brushing lightly over her eyelids and then exploring the softness of her mouth while he felt her skin grow warm beneath his hands. His mouth moved downward and caressed the hollow in her throat as he murmured, "I want your word, my sweet. You'll do as I ask."

He heard her sharp, indrawn breath as his tongue found the down-soft peak of her breast and coaxed it to tautness. "Promise me, my love," he whispered.

Waves of sensual delight swept through Jasmine. She thought how cold and empty her bed at Palekaiko would be without Morgan. She sighed, her voice a thin whisper as she murmured, "Yes . . . I promise."

Perhaps it was the hint of laughter in Morgan's gold-flecked eyes gazing down at her, or the memory of her own behavior that day at the plantation when she had persuaded Morgan not to hire Mr. Hanes as head *luna*, that made her eyes flare wide, her voice indignant, as she thrust Morgan away from her. "You tricked me!" she said accusingly.

Morgan grinned down at her. "You didn't think that only the female of the species could perform that maneuver?"

He turned away and began removing the rest of his clothes, discovering when he turned back that Jasmine had slipped into a wrapper and was tying the sash around her.

At his quizzical look, she said coldly, "I'm going downstairs to read for a while."

As she walked by Morgan on her way to the door, she did not even see his arm reach quickly out to enfold her until she felt herself being lifted in his arms and carried to the bed. When Morgan dropped her abruptly amidst the pillows, she attempted to roll away, but she did not move quickly enough. The next second, Morgan was in bed beside her, holding her fast. She struggled against that gentle but firm embrace; then, realizing it was futile, she lay still in his arms, her breasts rising and falling rapidly from her exertions, but her eyes stared at him coldly indifferent.

Morgan shook his head warningly. "Oh, no, my sweet," he growled. "There's one more matter to be settled between us. I'll not return to that hell I endured after Matthew was born. And that ice-maiden act of yours no longer deceives me. You want me as much as I want you."

As he was speaking, he was opening her robe, his hand almost casually caressing her body while his eyes probed her face deeply and possessively. Then his hand moved downward to caress the silken black hair that clung to his fingers, softer than the dark hair spilling in disarray over the pillow.

"No!" she gasped, trying to twist away from him, to ignore the treacherous, pleasurable excitement building inside of her, sensing that in another moment it would be too late. "Let me go!"

"Are you sure?" he asked, his face so close to hers that she could see the dancing golden glints in his hazel eyes, feel the warmth of his breath against her skin, as his tongue caressed her lips lightly before moving downward, warm against the slender column of her throat, to claim the already taut peak of her breast. At the same moment, she felt his hand slide inexorably between her thighs, and passion stabbed upward through her with a knifelike thrust. It was already too late, she realized helplessly as he guided her soft curves to fit against his hardness. Then, as she gave a soft cry of pleasure, he deliberately, tantalizingly, pulled himself away from her silken thighs, poised above her as she writhed and arched beneath him trying to reach the fulfillment he was denying her.

He only laughed softly as her fingernails clawed at his back and her eyes blazed up at him while he continued his gentle, knowing assault on her body with his mouth and hands, as if he were making very sure that she knew how much she wanted him, how powerless she was to resist him. At last there was nothing left in her world but the consuming, aching desire to become part of him, the emotions lifting, carrying her almost painfully in their intensity, unable to be endured another moment. She called out his name, her body clinging to him. The laughter faded from his eyes, his need now as great as hers. He took her quickly in a union so complete that for one frightening moment, she felt as if her heart had stopped beating and she had died and been reborn in his arms.

When she awoke the next morning, she saw that the sunlight was already halfway across the floor of the bedroom. A drowsy half smile curved her lips. Although she couldn't have had more than a few hours' sleep, she had never felt more gloriously alive, she thought as she stretched luxuriously.

"You look like the cat that swallowed a whole bucket of cream," Morgan said, amused.

He was standing beside the bed, smiling down at her. She saw that he was already dressed for the office, in a black suit coat and trousers, crisp white shirt, and black cravat. His hair was neatly brushed, and as he leaned down to kiss her good morning, she caught the spicy scent of his shaving soap. Illogically she suddenly found herself missing the torn shirts, colorful kerchiefs, and gilt-buttoned jackets Morgan had worn so casually aboard the *Louisa*. When he had kissed her then, she had always caught the scent of the sea, and his hair had always been tousled by the wind.

"Must you go so soon?" she murmured.

He sat down on the bed beside her, almost absently reaching out to stroke the long, slim column of her throat. "I'm already late. The *Louisa* docked yesterday, and I have to see to transferring her cargo."

All memory of last night, except for the last, lovely hours, had been blocked from Jasmine's mind. Now, in a sobering cold rush like a dash of ice water in her face, she remembered the argument with Morgan, the ultimatum he had laid down. But of course, she assured herself, remembering the fiery intensity of their lovemaking before they had fallen asleep in each other's arms, that had only been Morgan's temper talking.

Her hands lifted, looping around Morgan's neck as she smiled up at him through half-lowered eyelids, her lashes casting dark fanlike shadows over her cheeks. "You didn't really mean what you said last night, did you, darling?"

Morgan got to his feet, pulling her out of bed and hard against him, kissing her with such thoroughness that when he released her suddenly, she clung to him to keep her balance.

Then he said flatly, "I meant every word I said, madam." He picked up his high silk hat, tipped it to Jasmine, and added, his dark brows slanting menacingly together, "And I intend to hold you to your word, my love."

Then the door closed behind him. Jasmine thought she heard the sound of his laughter, the last thing she heard before she picked up the porcelain figure of a shepherdess and flung it, with a most satisfying crash, against the door.

Chapter 25

The noise of the porcelain splintering to pieces against the door was loud enough so that in the nursery next door Matthew awoke and let out a lusty cry. Snatching up her robe, Jasmine hurried into the nursery. She gathered her son into her arms, talking to him soothingly until the tears dissolved into hiccups, and Matthew's sunny smile played across features that were startlingly like Morgan's, even to the broad forehead and squared chin. Only his eyes were his mother's, large and dark and luminous with a fringe of long, thick lashes that would make him the envy and despair of any sisters he might have.

When Jasmine placed him on the floor, he immediately pulled himself to his feet and made a determined beeline for his favorite toy, a carved wooden model of the *Louisa* that his grandfather had made for him. He dragged the ship back to his mother and held the toy up to her, crowing triumphantly, "Papa?"

"Yes, dear, that's Papa's ship," Jasmine answered, still fuming with anger at Matthew's father. Let him ship her off to Palekaiko, she thought. She wouldn't be bullied into meekly submitting to his outrageous demands.

As if sensing his mother's unhappiness, Matthew pushed the toy into her hands, wanting to make amends, his dark eyes, round with concern, lifted to her.

Looking into her son's face was like seeing his father staring up at her, and Jasmine sighed and knew that of course she couldn't do it. She could no more leave Matthew than she could leave Morgan. And as for defying her husband, hadn't last night taught her how powerless she was to resist him? Memory of their wild, bittersweet coupling returned, bringing a flush to her cheeks as she remembered how she had behaved like a mindless, wild creature in her husband's arms, biting and clawing and begging Morgan to take her.

Quickly she put the memory aside and, kneeling down beside her son, hugged the sturdy little body to her. What hurt the most, though, was Morgan's accusing her of not caring enough for their son. Suely he must know that she would do anything to protect Matthew from harm.

She frowned uneasily as a traitorous thought slipped into her mind. Wasn't that exactly why Morgan had made his demands upon her—to protect their son?

She got to her feet, her robe making swishing, agitated sounds as she strode back and forth in the tiny nursery. Was that the real reason why Morgan had hinted that she and Matthew should stay behind at Palekaiko, because of the gossip swirling through Honolulu about the Babcock family? She remembered her housewarming, the unusual number of guests from prominent families who had turned down invitations to her party for no apparent reason. And the sly, knowing glances she had seen on the faces of several women at the levee last evening. How could she have been so blind not to realize the damaging effect that her brother and sister's scandalously living together would have on her and her family? Why hadn't Malia said something to her, warned her?

Except she knew that Malia seldom bothered to attend social activities, and wouldn't have cared anyway what *haoles* whispered about her children. Well, I care, Jasmine thought coldly and angrily as she swept her son up into her arms.

No one was going to snigger behind her back or cast aspersions on her son's background or close doors in his face when he became old enough to venture out into the social and business world. Not if she had anything to say about it, Jasmine thought, her chin setting stubbornly.

She carried young Matthew down the steps and out onto the lanai, where he could play safely while his nursemaid gave him his breakfast and kept a fond eye on him. At the last moment, Matthew clung to her, not wanting her to leave, but she carefully pulled herself free, giving him a last hug and kiss as she murmured, "Your mother has to go now, darling. She has a lot of work to do."

For the next three months, while the annexation and antiannexation factions in Honolulu fought bitterly in the legislature, on street corners, and in the newspapers, and the Committee of Thirteen made what many suspected to be its own more secret, violent plans for taking over the island kingdom, Jasmine determinedly went about mending her social fences.

She dressed decorously but in the very latest fashion as she carefully cultivated the friendship of wives who controlled Honolulu's social life. She attended women's sewing circles and mission society meetings; visited church services faithfully each Sunday and donated heavily to the funds for carpeting the Seamen's Bethel and for improving the lot of the natives in the Marquesas. She gave charming teas and dinner parties, carefully selecting those guests that were invited, until gradually a lively, jealous competition developed for invitations to the gracious Tucker home and to one of Jasmine Tucker's delightful dinner parties.

There were times when she had to bite her lip to keep from retorting angrily to some of the political opinions she heard at her dinner table, but she managed to smile and keep quiet, aware of Morgan's dark, narrowed gaze on her. Whether he was amused or wary of her silence she wasn't sure.

By the fourth of July, the Tuckers had returned sufficiently to the good graces of Honolulu society, so they were invited by the American consul, as his guests, to observe the parade always held in Honolulu in honor of America's natal day. This year the parade was especially elaborate, with floats for each state of the union gaily decorated with young *haole* girls dressed in white. These floats were followed by another float carrying a company of young *haole* men in uniform, a float representing "Young Hawaii" bringing up the rear.

Mr. Gregg gave a stirring speech on the power and glory of America and her manifest destiny to spread the wonders of democracy among the lesser nations of the world, as well as to protect such weaker countries from those powerful nations who would oppress them.

"Mr. Gregg sounds as if the annexation were an accepted fact," Jasmine said indignantly to Morgan as they made their way through the crowds to their carriage after the parade. "I doubt that Mr. Wyllie agrees with him."

"I think Wyllie is more concerned with the filibusters in Honolulu," Morgan said thoughtfully. "The legislature has already granted him funds to raise an army for the protection of these islands."

"Against whom?" Jasmine asked uneasily.

Morgan hesitated, then said, "Of course, it's only rumors, but for weeks now ships have been noticed standing off from the island of Oahu, and every vessel from the West Coast seems to bring an unusual number of able-bodied men from California." He glanced around him toward the fort with its useless guns, the wooden shacks, and grass huts. "It wouldn't take many well-trained men to set a torch to this city and take over the government."

Jasmine suspected unhappily that he was right. Hadn't the French stormed ashore and captured the city in only a few hours? And she remembered as a child watching the British take over the island kingdom. She gave her husband an uncertain glance. Was it possible that Morgan could be part of the conspiracy to bring about a revolution?

As if reading her thoughts, Morgan smiled and shook his head. "No, my dear, as long as there is a chance for annexation, I prefer a peaceful solution to open warfare." His face grew grim as he said gruffly, "But if not annexation, then I'm afraid it will be revolution."

The carriage had pulled up to their house, and Morgan pressed Jasmine's hand warningly when he saw the anger bright in her eyes. "We have guests arriving, remember?"

Of course she hadn't forgotten, Jasmine thought, annoyed, as she swept from the carriage into the house. Did Morgan still think he had to remind her not to upset his friends with her antiannexation remarks? After all, the fourth of July party they were giving was her idea; even to the red, white, and blue bunting wrapped around the columns of the lanai, and the red-skirted gown that she wore, with its striped white-and-blue bodice and bright red sash.

She had to grit her teeth, though, as she moved among her guests later, listening to their pleased comments about Mr. Gregg's speech.

"Did you see the British consul general's face during

the speech?" one man chortled. "I thought old Miller was going to have an apoplectic attack."

His companion nodded. "It's time Gregg let Miller know that we Americans are tired of kowtowing to British arrogance and of their trying to prejudice the minds of the natives against annexation to the union."

"It's not only Miller," the other man replied, sipping at his rosy fruit punch liberally laced with rum. "I hear there have been meetings on the other islands, native agitators talking against annexation. One of the meetings on Maui last week ended in a brawl, with the police coming in and having to knock a few *kanaka* heads together."

It was halfway through the party when Jasmine, her jaws aching from keeping a gracious smile on her face, retreated for a few moments upstairs to her bedroom. And found Lilikoi there before her, stretched out on the bed.

Her sister smiled and stretched lazily. "*Aloha*, sister. Is the *ho'olaule'a pau*?"

"Not yet." Jasmine moved to her dressing table, fussing with her hair to hide her annoyance at finding Lilikoi making herself at home in her bedroom. She remembered how while they were growing up Lilikoi would often slip into her sister's bedroom and borrow her clothes without asking permission. She smiled wryly to herself. She should know by now that her sister had little regard for the possessions of others, including other women's husbands.

"Don't be *huhu*, Pikake." Lilikoi got to her feet and came to stand behind Jasmine, smiling coaxingly at her sister in the mirror. "I had to speak to you alone." Her dark, kukui nut eyes sparkled mischievously. "And surely you don't still begrudge me my one little taste of your *pua'a* when you can feast whenever you wish!"

Jasmine sat, startled, then began to laugh helplessly, although she doubted that Morgan would appreciate being compared to the main entry at a *luau*.

"What is it?" she asked. "Why did you want to see me?"

Although the two sisters had met occasionally in the months since Jasmine had returned from the plantation, and Lilikoi had turned out to be a surprisingly doting aunt to Matthew, this was the first time Lilikoi had sought Jasmine out for a private visit.

The sparkle faded from Lilikoi's eyes as she said abruptly, "It's Kale. He's in some kind *pilikia*."

Jasmine remembered the conversation she'd heard downstairs about the fight on Maui between agitators and the police. "Kale's not hurt?" she asked anxiously.

"No, but there was a big *mokomoko* when he was giving a speech on Maui. One of the policemen had his head bashed in. They blame Kale. But after they arrested him, he managed to escape. Now the police are looking for him. He needs money." Lilikoi shrugged. "I have none. You know what a *u'uki* allowance the captain gives me."

"What will happen when they find Kale?"

"He'll be put into prison, although he swears he didn't touch the policeman. And you know our brother would die, locked up in a cage like a mad dog," Lilikoi said fiercely.

Lilikoi was right, Jasmine knew, troubled. Kale couldn't stand being penned up. With money he could at least hire a good lawyer to defend himself. She found her purse and scrambled through it, but she had only a few coins. Morgan took care of the household accounts, so she had no need to carry money around with her.

"What about your *kane*?" Lilikoi asked. "Won't he give you money if you ask?"

Jasmine was sure Morgan would, but he might also wonder why she needed the money. And she doubted that her husband would approve of her sending money to Kale.

Impatiently Lilikoi began to rummage through the scrimshaw jewel case on the dressing table. "Don't you have any jewels? What about this?" She held up the gleaming matched strand of pearls.

"I couldn't sell those," Jasmine said, shocked.

Lilikoi frowned. "Not sell, little sister. I know a Chinaman, Lee Tai. He'll lend me a good sum for these. That way you can buy them back later."

When Jasmine still hesitated, Lilikoi shrugged her shoulders toward the hallway, to the sound of voices from the party drifting up the stairs. Her voice filled with scorn. "Of course, if you care more for your *haole* friends than you do for your own brother . . ."

Jasmine took the pearls in her hands, remembering when she had first placed them around her neck aboard the *Louisa*, that day off the Marquesas when Morgan had undressed her and there were only the pearls between her and his warm, caressing glance.

"You're sure I can buy them back?" she asked, worried.

"Of course." Lilikoi's hand closed once more around the pearls and slipped them into a pocket of her voluminous loose *holoku*. "*Mahalo*, Pikake," she said softly, and then she was gone.

Jasmine returned to the dressing table and closed the jewelry case quickly, guiltily. There was no reason for concern, she told herself, frowning at her pale face in the mirror, pinching her cheeks to bring color into them. She would have the pearls back before Morgan even noticed they were gone.

The Honolulu newspapers the next day carried the story of the wounded policeman and of Kale's daring escape from the law.

At the lunch table, Morgan twitched his newspaper irritably. "Your brother should turn himself over to the authorities. He'll do himself no good running and hiding."

"Kale didn't hurt that policeman," Jasmine protested.

Morgan turned his quizzical gaze upon her. "How can you be so sure?"

Jasmine felt color flame in her cheeks, and she lowered her eyes hastily. She only knew what Lilikoi had told her, she realized.

"Jasmine, my love, look at me," Morgan said quietly.

Reluctantly she lifted her gaze to meet Morgan's narrowed gaze. "I won't have you involved in your brother's troubles," he said. "If you know where he's hiding . . ."

"I don't know," Jasmine said quickly. And that was the truth, she thought, relieved.

Morgan stared at her for a long moment, then, apparently satisfied, returned his gaze to the newspapers, while Jasmine continued eating, trying to ignore a sharp feeling of guilt like a fish hook caught in her throat, remembering her promise to Morgan.

The twinge of guilt returned during the following weeks, every time she looked at her jewel box. It took longer than she thought it would to put aside the sum of money needed to redeem the pearls, saving a little each week from her household allowance so that Morgan would not become suspicious. It was late September before she made her way on horseback to lower Fort Street. Although Lee Tai's shop was only a few blocks from Morgan's office, it was in a part of town that a respectable matron seldom visited. Almost every other building was a grogshop, bowling alley, poolroom, or dance hall. And since the whaling fleet was making its fall visit to Honolulu, the streets were crowded with seamen in various stages of drunkenness, with native women in skimpy gowns hanging on to their arms.

Several of the men turned to stare at Jasmine as she found Lee Tai's shop, next door to a fishmarket. The shop was little more than a crudely thatched hut, and Lee Tai himself was a man of indefinite age with a wrinkleless face and eyes devoid of any expression.

He listened with a smoothly blank face as Jasmine explained her errand. When she had finished, he shook his head and said, "No have."

"But you must have the pearls," Jasmine said, thinking that the man hadn't understood her. "My sister—the woman who brought you the pearls—said you would hold them until I redeemed them."

The man held up eight fingers, as if it were Jasmine

who didn't understand English and said slowly, "Eight weeks. I told the *wahine* eight weeks."

Jasmine looked around the cluttered shop as if somehow the pearls would miraculously appear. Then her voice rose accusingly. "I have the money." She held out her hand with the gold coins. "Where are my pearls?"

The man shrugged. "Gone. Sold."

"To whom?" Jasmine asked, so desperate now that her voice shook. "Who did you sell them to?"

The blank look turned to her was like a wall. "Many come to my shop," he said indifferently.

"Please. You must remember," Jasmine pleaded. "Was it a man or woman?"

For a second, she thought she saw a chink in the wall, a flash of sympathy in his eyes, but the next moment it was gone. "I do not remember," he said and disappeared through a calico curtain that separated his living quarters from the shop.

Jasmine stared after him, too stunned to move. She would have followed the man, but she suddenly realized she was no longer alone in the shop. Two seamen, one redheaded, the other skinny as a nail, had followed her into the shop, the smell of gurry and cheap rum preceding them. They eyed Jasmine appreciatively as the redheaded man, smiling to show a lot of yellowed teeth, muttered, "That's a nice horse you got there, lady. But me and my friend think you're too pretty to be riding alone."

Jasmine gave him an icy glare. "Excuse me."

She started to walk around the two men, but the redheaded man shot out a surprisingly strong hand that clamped like a vise on her arm. "What's your hurry, little lady?" he said, leering and pulling her into his arms so that she got the full impact of his rum-laden breath in her face.

Chapter 26

Jasmine was more angered than frightened by the seaman's rough, dirty hand on her arm. She debated calling for help but doubted that the shopkeeper would interfere. In any case, she didn't dare call attention to herself by causing a scene. Morgan might somehow hear of it and would naturally wonder what she had been doing in a pawnbroker's shop in the first place.

With a sudden movement, she freed her hand from the man's grip and tossed several gold coins, still clutched in her palm, to the dirt floor. The coins rolled a short distance, the gold gleaming dimly in the poorly lit shop.

The skinny seaman made a dive for the coins at once while the redheaded man turned, startled, long enough for Jasmine to pull herself away and dart out of the shop. By the time the seamen followed her, she had already mounted her horse. When the redheaded sailor made a grab for her reins, she brought her whip down across his hand, bringing a startled oath to his lips. Then she wheeled her horse around in the narrow street and trotted swiftly away.

It wasn't until she reached the cool, shadowy house with the palm branches shading the lanai that she began to tremble. Suddenly her legs would no longer hold her, and she sank down into one of the large wicker chairs. What was she to do now? she wondered numbly. How was she going to explain the missing pearls to Morgan? If she told him they had been stolen from her jewel chest, suspicion would fall unjustly on the servants in the house. Anyway, the thought of trying to deceive Morgan, with that golden, narrowed gaze searching her face, was too unsettling to contemplate.

An hour later, when she stiffly pulled herself to her feet and climbed the stairs to her bedroom, she still had not found any solution to her problem. All she could do was hope and pray that Morgan wouldn't discover the pearls were missing until she could come up with some plausible reason for their disappearance.

For several days, she lived on the knife edge of fear and trepidation waiting for the ax to fall. As the days turned into weeks, though, and Morgan never mentioned the pearls, the fear began to ebb. There were days at a time when Jasmine forgot the missing pearls altogether.

Certainly there was enough going on in Honolulu to occupy her attention. Even though summer had passed without any armed insurrection, more and more rough-looking men were arriving in town on ships from California. Rumors circulated that there were hundreds more such men waiting on the West Coast ready to leave for the islands at a moment's notice, and that hundreds of foreign residents were prepared to join in an uprising against the Hawaiian government.

When a store of weapons being smuggled into the islands was discovered, alarms were sounded up and down the coast, and Wyllie's small army, which drilled daily in the streets, was hastily increased in size. By November tension had flared to the point that the American consul and the captains of the American warships, which had arrived recently in Honolulu harbor, warned the prime minister that the only chance to escape violence and the burning of Honolulu was for the kingdom to immediately surrender its sovereignty to the United States.

"It's the same as blackmail!" Jasmine complained bitterly to Morgan one evening when they had returned from a dinner party where Mr. Gregg's warning to Mr.

Wyllie had been the heated topic of conversation at the dinner table.

"I believe in politics it's called diplomacy," Morgan said dryly.

"You can call it what you like," Jasmine said indignantly, "but the American commissioner knows that Mr. Wyllie's small army can't stand off the threat of warships, much less an insurrection."

Morgan stood behind his wife, watching as, seated at her dressing table, she began to pull the pins slowly from her hair. "I wouldn't be too quick to give up on a canny Scotsman like Wyllie," he said. "Gregg's a fool if he underestimates the man."

Jasmine glanced up, startled at the undercurrent of anger she heard in her husband's voice. "I thought you were for the annexation."

Morgan's chin jutted out belligerently. "I don't take kindly to bullies or to being threatened by any man or government." He himself had been surprised at the indignation he had felt at the American consul's veiled threats against the tiny Hawaiian kingdom, which threats were backed up with the might of American warships. He had never before questioned how closely his love for Jasmine had become part of his deep affection for the islands, so he could not have told where one began and the other left off, only knowing that he could not bear to see harm come to either of them.

He studied his wife closely in the dressing-table mirror, the lamplight highlighting the pale apricot gold of her skin, the dark, proud arch of her eyebrows, the soft, full curve to her mouth. He hadn't realized he could ever love anyone as deeply as he loved this woman, and yet, although she came willingly, ardently, into his arms at night, there were times when he noticed a tightness at the corners of her mouth, a shadow that would appear and then quickly disappear in her luminous eyes. He knew how hard she had worked to restore the Tucker family to a prominent position in Honolulu society. Too hard? he wondered, frowning a little as he noticed a disturbing pallor beneath the glowing skin.

"How would you like to take Matthew and visit Palekaiko for a while?" he asked.

A coil of long, shining hair fell over one shoulder as she turned to him, her voice worried. "Then you think there will be trouble if Mr. Wyllie doesn't agree to Mr. Gregg's demands?"

"I think Gregg is running a bluff," Morgan said quickly. He doubted that even the most convinced Manifest Destiny politician in Washington would approve of the United States government taking over the Hawaiian kingdom at gunpoint. Still, with tempers running high and the filibusters from California just waiting in the wings to stir up violence for their own cause, he would be happier knowing that Jasmine and Matthew were away from Honolulu.

"You'll be coming to the plantation, too?" Jasmine asked.

"As soon as I can," Morgan assured her, dropping a kiss onto the gentle sloping curve of her shoulder exposed by the scooped-out scarlet bodice of her gown. "Isn't that the gown you wore in New Bedford my first night home from the Atlantic cruise?" he asked curiously. "I remember how good your pearls looked with the dress. Why didn't you wear them tonight?"

Jasmine jerked to her feet and moved away from the too-revealing lamplight on the dressing table. "I—I couldn't," she stammered. "The clasp is broken."

She stood, hardly breathing, her heart turned to stone, as her husband reached his hand toward the jewel case on the dressing table. "I'll bring the pearls into town tomorrow and have the clasp repaired," he offered.

"Don't bother," Jasmine said quickly. "I'll take care of it." Then she murmured softly, smiling up at Morgan, "Would you mind unhooking me, dear? I told the maid not to wait up."

Morgan moved behind her, and as she had known would happen, after he had deftly unclasped the back of her gown and then untied her frilly undergarments so that they fell in a scarlet and snow white cloud to her feet, his strong hands still encircled her waist.

"You've become a much more skilled lady's maid than you were aboard the *Louisa*," she said, laughing softly, leaning lightly against him.

"Oh, have I?" Morgan growled, kissing the nape of her neck while she watched in the mirror his suntanned hands moving slowly over her pale, gleaming body until her own eyes grew heavy-lidded and filled with desire. And she knew, half triumphantly, half guiltily, that there would be no more mention of the pearls that night.

The next day as she said her good-byes to Morgan at the dock, clinging to him tightly even though she knew that it was not proper to display such open affection for a husband in public, she whispered urgently, "You'll come as soon as you can?"

For an answer, he crushed her in an embrace that left her breathless. When he released her, he frowned down at her teasingly. "And you'll cause no *pilikia* at the plantation?" Although his voice was light, she was conscious of the intensity of his gaze fastened upon her face. Was it possible, she wondered uneasily, that Morgan had somehow learned about her sending money to Kale? But how could he know? She hadn't even told Malia. Only Lilikoi knew, and she was still on Maui.

Nevertheless, the feeling of unease stayed with her, even after she and Matthew reached the plantation. She would wake up in her sun-splashed bedroom at the Big House with a worrisome darkness crouching in a corner of her mind, thinking of Kale and the missing pearls.

Matthew, however, enjoyed himself thoroughly at the plantation, and since he was at the age where he was into everything, it took the combined attention of both Jasmine and his nursemaid to keep an eye on him. When he tired both his nurses out, the overseer's wife, Martha, was always happy to help out. In addition, she kept a motherly eye on Jasmine, insisting that she should nap in the afternoons and coaxing her into eating the delicious breads, pies, and cakes that she baked and brought daily to the Big House.

"At this rate, I won't be able to fit into anything but a *holoku*," Jasmine protested in vain one morning when Mrs. McTavish brought her yet another delicious home-baked confection, a rich banana cake with a creamy coconut icing.

It was Martha McTavish's considered opinion that Jasmine Tucker could do with a bit more flesh on her bones. "She doesn't eat enough to keep a bird alive," she had commented to her husband. "Something's bothering that young woman. She's as skittish as a colt in a high wind." Still, it wasn't her place to criticize the wife of her husband's employer, and she reached instead into the copious pocket of her skirt and said to Jasmine, "I have a bit of mail for you and the latest newspaper from Honolulu."

The latest newspaper was several days old by the time it reached the plantation, but Jasmine was happy to have any news at all. She gladly accepted Mrs. McTavish's offer to watch Matthew while she curled up on the lounge and read her mail. Most of the mail consisted of invitations to teas and parties and receptions. Whatever the worries about violence breaking out in Honolulu, Jasmine thought, it apparently hadn't interfered with the social life of the town.

There was a brief letter from Lilikoi, over two weeks old. Her sister's anxiety came clearly through the hastily written letter. "I have much *maka'u* for our brother. He has left Maui, and I do not know where he has gone. All he talked of was returning the land to our people and seeking revenge upon the *haole* who killed Lani."

Jasmine frowned as she carefully destroyed the letter. Surely Kale, a hunted man himself, wouldn't be so foolish as to hunt another man. But the worrisome darkness was there again, nagging at a corner of her mind, and the newspaper did little to dispel her gloom.

Mr. Gregg was still rattling his sabers and threatening dire consequences if the king didn't sign the annexation treaty. Several British and French warships had arrived in Honolulu harbor, and the editor of the newspaper hinted that the king was weakening. Jasmine remembered the last time she had seen King Kauikeaouli at his birthday levee, how sad-eyed and tired he had looked. How much longer, she wondered, could he withstand the pressures to hand his kingdom over to a stronger, foreign power?

She was about to put the newspaper with its discouraging news aside when her eye was caught by a tiny item on the back page of the paper. A small plantation owner near Nanakuli had reported to the authorities that he thought he had seen a man resembling the escaped prisoner, Kale.

Mrs. McTavish, looking up from chasing Matthew across the veranda, saw that Jasmine's face had gone as white as the muslin *holoku* she was wearing.

"What is it?" she asked.

Jasmine's thoughts were racing feverishly. Micah Beale's plantation was near Nanakuli, she remembered. Hadn't Morgan even once pointed it out to her on a horseback ride they had taken? And if her brother were in the vicinity of Beale's plantation, it could only be for one purpose.

Jasmine became aware of Martha McTavish's worried voice, and she set the paper carefully to one side, smiling at the woman. "I thought I might take a ride while it's still cool. Would you mind watching Matt until Nakeli arrives?"

Mrs. McTavish assured her that she wouldn't mind at all. Jasmine went to her room and changed quickly into her dark green riding habit. At the stable, she waited impatiently while her horse was saddled, and a few minutes later, she rode by the sugar mill. She was so deep in her thoughts that she didn't notice Mr. McTavish waving a greeting to her as he directed the unloading of cartloads of cane stalks. The overseer turned and stared after Jasmine, surprised. It wasn't like Mrs. Tucker to be unfriendly, and where was she off to in such a hurry? He cocked an eye up at the sky. Well, she wouldn't be going far. It would be raining in another hour if he didn't miss his guess.

Once away from the plantation grounds, Jasmine began following a trail that was little more than a footpath paralleling the coastline and curving south. The path was too narrow and rocky to urge her horse to any speed, and she had to content herself with allowing her mare to pick her way cautiously past kiawe trees and spiny shrubs that snagged at her riding skirt. She remembered taking this path on a horseback ride with Morgan last spring, and after an hour or so, Morgan had pointed to a side trail that branched off into a valley planted with sugarcane and said that it led to Micah Beale's plantation.

Thinking of Morgan, her hands tightened on the reins as she imagined the icy anger in his face if he should ever discover the reason for this ride. But even more vivid in her mind than Morgan's disapproval was the frightening look she remembered on her brother's horribly mutilated face that day on the beach when he had told her that Micah Beale had killed his beloved Lani.

She had had no doubt then, and she had no doubt now, that Kale would kill Micah Beale if he had the chance. And it would not matter to her brother that he would inevitably forfeit his own life for murdering his enemy. Or had he perhaps already murdered Beale? Jasmine wondered, despair squeezing her chest. The Honolulu newspaper had been several days old. Kale could have reached Bonniville, the Beale plantation, and by now have taken his revenge on the plantation owner. She might already be too late.

Dear God, please let me be in time, she prayed soundlessly. Even Morgan must understand that she couldn't sit idly by and let her brother commit murder, without lifting a hand to try and stop him.

She had been riding for more than an hour and was beginning to worry that she might have missed the turnoff to Bonniville when she saw a break in the kiawe trees that grew alongside the road. And beyond the short, spiny woods, she could see the beginnings of cane fields, some reaching to the ocean's edge.

Fortunately, the path that veered to the left through the fields was wider than the rocky path along the shore. Her mare was able to make better time. Soon, she began to see workers in the fields, a *luna* on horseback. The coolies did not look up as she rode by. She noticed that the overseer held a black snake whip coiled in his hand, and she saw, repelled, the angry red welts on the backs of the workers.

Then a sudden clap of thunder overhead made her mare toss her head and sidestep nervously. Jasmine glanced up at the sky, surprised to see the dark clouds that were sweeping in quickly through the valley. It would be pouring rain in a moment, she realized, and she wasn't sure how much further the main house was. She put her knee to the horse, urging her forward. The mare needed little encouragement.

They followed the road for another ten minutes through the cane fields, and she could see the house in the distance when the first raindrops began to fall. At almost the same moment, lightning flashed overhead, followed by a crash of thunder. The startled mare lost her stride, stumbled, and almost plunged to the ground but at the last moment righted itself.

Jasmine was not so fortunate. She felt herself sliding from the saddle, her heel catching in the stirrup, her skirt entangled around her foot so that she could not pull free. Then the ground came flying up at her, and she felt herself being dragged, helplessly, alongside the frightened, galloping horse.

Chapter 27

The mare dragged her mistress along in this undigni-
fied fashion for several seconds before stopping, whinny-
ing nervously, and turning to stare down at her mistress,
an aggrieved expression in the large brown eyes.

Jasmine managed to release her foot from the stirrup
and cautiously pulled herself to her feet, clutching at the
saddle for support. Aside from a few bruises on certain
tender portions of her body and an uncomfortable throbbing pain in her left ankle, which had been caught in the
stirrup, she determined that she had come to no great
harm. Speaking softly, stroking the mare's silken mane,
she led the horse to a large flat stone beside the road
and was able, after some difficulty, to remount and start
out once more.

It was only a matter of minutes before she reached a
clearing where she could see a sugar mill; a low, dark
warehouse-looking building that she supposed housed
the plantation workers; a stable; a blacksmith shop; and
storage sheds—all gathered around a tall, two-story
white frame building like a feudal village clustered around
the foot of a castle.

She had time for only a hasty look, however, because
the rain was coming down harder now. By the time she
had dismounted and climbed the steps to the front porch
of the house, she was soaked to the skin, the skirt of her
riding habit pulling heavily at her legs.

The young Hawaiian woman who finally opened the

door to Jasmine's knocking stared at her, open-mouthed, without speaking. Jasmine wondered if it was because of her rain-drenched appearance or because visitors were so unusual at the Beale plantation.

"Is Mr. Beale at home?" she asked.

When the woman didn't answer but stood with an almost stupid look of fright on her face, Jasmine spoke more sharply. "I'm Mrs. Tucker from Palekaiko plantation. I'm here to see Mr. Beale."

The woman cast a quick, worried glance back inside the house, then murmured, "Kahu Beale not here."

Jasmine was sure the young woman was lying. Impatiently she pushed by the servant into the entrance hall. "I'll wait till he returns, then. And please have someone look after my horse."

Without waiting for a reply, she walked into a large front parlor, limping a little as she discovered that putting weight on her injured ankle was becoming more and more of an ordeal. She also discovered, as she put a hand to her head, that she had somehow lost her hat. There was a meager fire burning in the rough brick fireplace, and she held out her hands to its warmth, not sure whether the cold she was feeling was due to her wet hair and clothes or to the odd, chilly atmosphere of the house itself.

What an ugly room, she thought, staring curiously around her. The furniture was of good quality but too bulky and covered in a drab brown velvet. Mauve curtains shut out all light at the windows, and dark brown carpeting on the floor only added to the dismal air of gloom and bad taste. She hadn't heard of Micah Beale's remarrying, and she was sure that no woman had had anything to do with this dark, graceless room.

She didn't want to sit in one of the chairs with her wet skirt, so she stood, awkwardly bracing herself on one foot while trying to ignore the pain in her ankle. Suppose Micah Beale wasn't home, she thought after a few moments, and no one came to the door. She couldn't wait here indefinitely. Suddenly her whole trip began to seem foolishly impulsive. What if the man who thought he had seen Kale had been wrong, a case of mistaken identity? For all she knew, her brother might not be anywhere near Beale's plantation.

"Mrs. Tucker, what a pleasant surprise."

Micah Beale came quickly into the room, his hands outstretched. Once again Jasmine was struck by how much handsomer the plantation owner was than the minister she had met aboard the *Jeremiah*. His tanned flesh was healthier, firmer looking; even the grasp of his hands on hers, although still oddly clammy, was no longer soft, almost effeminate. He wore a coarse linen shirt open at the throat and work pants, which suited his lanky frame better than the somber black frock coat. And there was no doubt, she thought, relieved, that Mr. Beale was quite healthily alive.

Micah's gray eyes, sparkling with pleasure at seeing his guest, filled with dismay when he took a closer look. "Why, you're drenched to the skin, Mrs. Tucker."

Jasmine smiled ruefully. "The rain caught me before I reached the house, and I'm afraid that's not all. I've somehow clumsily managed to twist my ankle."

"Let me look at it," Micah insisted at once, helping her into a chair, ignoring her protests that her wet riding habit would ruin the velvet upholstery. He knelt down before her and carefully removed her boot. Although his hands were gentle, she winced when he touched the ankle.

"There're no broken bones," he said. "But the ankle's badly wrenched and beginning to swell." Without getting to his feet, he called loudly, "Moani, *hele mai*."

The servant appeared again so quickly in the doorway that Jasmine wondered if she had been lurking in the hall, waiting for the summons. Jasmine studied the girl curiously. Her creamy brown coloring and straight features, along with the full mouth and broad face, showed her *hapa-haole* ancestry. The girl would have been pretty, Jasmine decided, except for the shapeless gown she wore, which covered her lithe body so completely, and for the slight purplish coloring on one cheekbone, like a birthmark, that disfigured her face.

Micah didn't look at the young woman as he gave brusque orders. In a few moments she returned with strips of cloth soaked in cold water and a glass that contained brandy, which burned Jasmine's throat as she swallowed the liquid.

She gave Micah an amused glance, knowing how strongly the missionaries felt about not allowing any liquor in their homes.

He smiled almost boyishly as he finished wrapping the cloths around her ankle. "For medicinal purposes only, of course. And even the Bible approves of a little wine for thy stomach's sake."

He got to his feet, worried, frowning down at her. "Now, I want you to get out of those wet clothes before you catch cold. There are still some of my wife's gowns in a bedroom upstairs. You're about the same height as Mary, so they should fit. And after you've changed, we'll have a bite to eat."

"Oh, I can't stay," Jasmine said quickly. "They'll be worried about me if I don't get back to Palekaiko."

"I won't hear of it," Micah said briskly. "You can't ride with that ankle, and it's still raining. You'll spend the night here, and I'll see to getting you back to your plantation in the morning."

"Mr. and Mrs. McTavish won't know what happened to me. . . ."

"I'll send one of the stable boys with a message," Micah assured her, then, turning to the servant, who was still standing quietly, he ordered, "Take Mrs. Tucker upstairs, Moani, and help her change her clothes. Then you can put fresh linen on the bed. Mrs. Tucker will be spending the night." He smiled with awkward gallantry at Jasmine. "I'll see if the cook can't come up with something special. It isn't every day that Bonniville has guests."

He bustled away before Jasmine could protest further, and as she made her painful way up the stairs, she

decided he was certainly right about her ankle. She
supposed it would be foolish to think of trying to ride
back to Palekaiko, with the sound of the rain still beating against the shuttered windows. But as Moani showed
her into a bedroom at the front of the house, a room as
chill and gloomy as the parlor, she couldn't help feeling
a growing aversion to the Beale home.

Moani brought her several gowns and pieces of undergarments from a chest in a corner of the room. The
undergarments were yellowed, and the gowns were all
several years out of fashion, smelling of mildew as if
they had been carelessly packed away. There was only
one gown, a faded blue cotton, that looked as if it might
fit. With Moani's help, she slipped into the dress. Mrs.
Beale, she remembered from seeing the woman briefly
aboard the *Jeremiah,* had been flat-chested, so the bodice of the gown fit with uncomfortable tightness across
Jasmine's breasts. But the length and waist size was
right, she saw as she glanced into the tiny mirror on the
wall.

The servant had helped her out of her riding habit
and into the gown without speaking, although Jasmine
tried to engage the girl in conversation. "Do you live in
Nanakuli?" she asked.

"I live here," the girl replied softly.

Jasmine tried to hide her surprise. Did the girl mean
that she lived here in this house with Micah Beale?
Somehow she couldn't imagine the ex-minister taking a
native woman as a mistress. She studied the young
girl's face, the dark, fear-filled eyes. And if she were
Beale's mistress, then why did she look so terrified?
Still, it wasn't any of her business, she thought as Moani
took a hairbrush and skillfully brushed the tangles out
of Jasmine's damp hair, twisting its length into a coil
and pinning the coil at the back of her neck, then teasing the dark hair at the temples into curls that fell to
the tip of the dark, arched brows.

When she had finished, the girl smiled, pleased. "You
are very beautiful," she said shyly.

"And you are a very good lady's maid." Jasmine laughed. Reaching into the pocket of her wet riding skirt, she drew out several coins and handed them to the girl. "You must let me pay you for your trouble."

She was startled when the girl backed hastily away. "No, Kahu Beale would be *huhu* with me if I took money from you."

Jasmine frowned. "If you're so frightened of Mr. Beale, why do you stay here?"

Childish tears suddenly glittered in the girl's eyes. "I must stay," she said, her voice low, her eyes not meeting Jasmine's gaze directly. "You don't know the evil life I led before Kahu Beale found me and brought me here. Each night he comes to my room, and we kneel and pray together. He asks his *haole* god to forgive me for my wicked ways, so I will not burn forever in the fires of hell."

At the rotelike way the girl repeated the words she had obviously learned from Micah Beale, Jasmine reached out and touched the birthmark that marred the girl's lovely face. Only it wasn't a birthmark, she saw now, but a partly healed bruise.

"Did Mr. Beale do that?" she asked.

Moani flushed and ducked her head, shamefaced. "Kahu Beale says there is a devil inside of all women that makes them behave wickedly, turns them into whores tempting men into evil. And it must be so. For I remember how eagerly I once sought the caresses of my lovers. And there are nights Kahu Beale comes to my room to pray, and when his hands touch me in a certain way, my body sinfully lusts after him and ensnares him into my bed. Then Kahu Beale becomes very angry with me afterwards for shaming him before his *haole* god."

Jasmine fought back a feeling of nausea, listening to the girl's artless voice, trying to push from her mind the perverted scene the girl was describing. When she was able to speak, her voice was cold with anger. "Mr. Beale has no right to mistreat you. When I leave tomorrow, I'll take you with me to Palekaiko."

Fear contracted the muscles of the girl's face into a terrified mask. "No! I must stay. Kahu Beale is a great *kahuna* with a powerful *mana*. Last year he placed a curse upon a young woman in Nanakuli who angered his god by marrying her brother. Within the month, both the woman and her child died horrible deaths. If I leave Kahu Beale, he will place a curse upon me, too. And I will die."

"That's nonsense," Jasmine said hotly. "Mr. Beale can't hurt you with his prayers or curses." But looking into Moani's disbelieving, incredulous eyes, she knew, helplessly, that there was no way she could convince the girl. After all, it hadn't been too many years before that autocratic priests or *kahunas* had arbitrarily condemned men and women to death with their prayers and curses. If Kale and Malia both believed that Lani's death had been caused by Beale, then how could she expect an uneducated child like Moani not to believe the superstitious stories that had, no doubt, spread through the village about Beale and Lani's death after his visits to her home.

"We'll talk about this later," she said firmly to Moani. Perhaps she could persuade Mr. Beale to allow the girl to come to work at Palekaiko, although the thought of asking a favor of the man, much less having to face him across a dinner table now, turned her stomach.

The murkily lit dining room, with its dust-covered chandelier and massive table and chairs, resembled the rest of the house, but to her surprise, the food, deliciously spiced fish and rice, was very good.

When she said as much to her host, he smiled, pleased. "Li Huu was taught to cook at a plantation on Maui before I bought his contract."

"You have a Chinese cook?" Jasmine asked, startled.

"All my plantation hands are Chinese," Micah replied. "The Hawaiians are much too lazy to make good workers. And the minute you turn your back, they run away. Of course, a few of my coolies have tried to run away, too, but since they don't speak English and don't know the countryside, they're much more easily caught and returned." He smiled thinly. "And when my *luna*, Ramon, has finished dealing with those who do run away, they never try again."

Jasmine wondered if Ramon was the cruel, swarthy-faced man she had seen in the fields as she rode up to the house. She remembered the whip held loosely in the man's hand and the fresh whip cuts across the backs of the laborers. "I thought it was against the law to flog the Chinese workers," she said indignantly.

"Your soft heart does you credit, Mrs. Tucker," Micah said with a patronizing smile. "I'm sure you know, though, that there are other planters besides me who have found that applying a whip to a disobedient or slow worker is much more efficient than turning the man over to the authorities, where he will be placed in a prison on bread and water and the planter is cheated out of his labor."

"The whip isn't used at Palekaiko, and it never will be," Jasmine retorted.

"Indeed?" Micah frowned. "Then I suggest that you carry a revolver with you at all times, as I do. The coolies are pagans and worse. There is no wickedness too vile for them. They not only worship heathen idols but they gamble their wages away and drug themselves into opium stupors. Only last week on Maui, a coolie stabbed a *luna* to death. It's the height of folly to trust them."

"You told me once that you came to Hawaii to save heathen souls," Jasmine said. "I should think it would make you happy to have such a plentiful supply!"

Her sarcasm, however, was lost on her host, who nodded eagerly. "Oh, yes, it is my Christian duty to do what little I can to save their heathen souls. I make it a point to preach to them each Sunday. All the workers are required to attend my services."

Or, no doubt, be flogged if they don't attend, Jasmine thought, hoping the distaste she was feeling for her host didn't show in her face. She glanced at Moani, who was padding softly around the table in her bare feet as she served the food.

"What about Moani?" she couldn't resist asking. "She's Hawaiian, and she works for you."

A flicker of annoyance touched Micah's face as he glanced at the servant girl, his voice stiff. "Moani is another lost soul. I found her in Nanakuli after her lover had beaten her in a drunken rage and thrown her out into the street to die. I brought her here and nursed her back to health. She is still young and has shown a gratifying interest in cleansing herself of her past wickedness. I hope and pray that in time she will find salvation."

Jasmine pushed her plate away, discovering that despite the delicious food, she had suddenly lost her appetite. What a sanctimonious scoundrel the man was, she thought and began to regret fervently that she had agreed to spend the night under his roof.

"You've never told me, Mrs. Tucker. To what do I owe the pleasure of your visit today?"

The abrupt change of subject caught Jasmine by surprise. She looked up to find her host's smiling gaze fastened upon her face, but the smile didn't reach the pale gray eyes that reminded her all at once of his hands on her ankle earlier, their touch clammy and cold, oddly lifeless.

For a moment she thought of lying, but as much as she disliked and was repulsed by Beale, she knew she must at least warn him of the danger he was facing from Kale. Certainly a man like Micah Beale wasn't worth Kale's death in a hangman's noose.

"I'm looking for my stepbrother, Kale," she said. "I thought he might be here at your plantation."

"Here?" Beale shook his head as if mystified. "Why should your brother be here? I've already told you that I don't hire Hawaiian laborers."

"He wouldn't be here to work. I'm afraid he means to harm you. He holds you responsible for the death of my sister Lani."

"That's preposterous! Your sister died as a result of smallpox."

"But you did visit Lani before she died?"

Micah's voice took on a self-righteous smugness as he folded his hands neatly on the table. "I'm not denying I visited her. I told you as much that evening at your party. But only to pray for your sister's immortal soul, to try and persuade her to repent her heinous sin so that she could return to a state of grace." He gave Jasmine a quick, suspicious glance. "Surely you don't condone your sister's wicked, depraved behavior, the evil . . ."

"Lani wasn't evil!" Jasmine protested, outraged. "She was gentle and kind."

"And your brother?" Micah asked. A flush turned his neck red, spreading upward into his face in ugly red blotches as he glared at her. "Do you approve of his lascivious behavior, too? I understand he's an escaped felon now, hiding out from the law on Maui."

Jasmine felt her own face grow warm and struggled to regain her temper. It would do no good to antagonize Micah Beale, especially if she wanted to help Moani. She forced her voice to a semblance of calmness. "Of course I don't approve of what—what Kale did. But I would hate for him to hang for your murder," she added sweetly.

Micah leaned back in his chair and studied her face thoughtfully for a moment through half-lowered eyelids. "Frankly, what I find shocking is that your husband would allow you to go on a foolish, wild-goose chase like this alone."

"My husband couldn't come with me," Jasmine said, irritated again at the implied criticism of Morgan. "He had to remain in Honolulu. He sent my son and me to Palekaiko because he was concerned about the possibility of trouble in the city over the annexation treaty."

Micah nodded gravely, the angry red stain draining from his face. "Yes, it's a great concern to all of us, but with American warships in the harbor, I have no doubt that the treaty will be signed. And once the islands belong to the United States and the planters rid themselves of the unfair import duties leveled against Hawaiian sugar, it won't be long till the sugar industry dominates these islands and its government."

"And the Hawaiian people?" Jasmine asked coldly. "What of them?"

Micah seemed surprised at her question. "They will be looked after, of course, as they always have been, by white men. The kings have always been figureheads since these islands have become civilized. It's the white men who have always managed these islands; first Bingham, then Judd, and now Wyllie. It could not be any other, for the Lord has commanded the white man to subdue the earth and have dominion over it, to be monarch of all he surveys," he finished grandly.

Jasmine rose, annoyed, from her chair. She might have to spend the night under Micah Beale's roof, she thought, but she didn't have to sit here and listen to him. "Would you excuse me, Mr. Beale? My ankle's bothering me, and I find that I'm rather tired."

"Of course." He came quickly to her side and escorted her to the foot of the stairs. "A good night's rest will do wonders for you."

Jasmine noticed as she made her painful way up the stairs that this time Mr. Beale didn't direct Moani to accompany her. Did he suspect, she wondered uneasily, that Moani had told his guest more about their relationship than he preferred that she know? If so, she hoped he didn't take his anger out on the girl.

As she undressed for bed, she decided that if she wasn't able to persuade Moani to leave Bonniville with her, then she would explain the whole unhappy situation to Mr. McTavish and see if he couldn't think of some way to force Micah Beale to give the girl up.

Moani had laid out a nightgown for her on the bed. Although it was also yellowed and smelled faintly of mildew, the gown was of the finest white lawn, with beautiful, tiny, hand-stitched tucks across the bodice. Jasmine tried to imagine the young woman who had so hopefully and lovingly sewn this gown, undoubtedly for her trousseau. What sort of marriage instead had she found with Micah Beale? It couldn't have been a happy one, she thought as she slipped on the nightgown, not with a man like Beale, who seemed to regard the natural, joyous union between a man and a woman as something evil and sinful. Jasmine thought of how she felt when Morgan held her, the pleasure it gave her to give him pleasure, the closeness she felt at the end of their lovemaking, as if for a few miraculous seconds they were not two people but one.

Thinking of Morgan, though, made her wish that he were here, with his arms tightly around her, making her forget the ache in her ankle and this cold, somehow menacing, house.

When she did finally fall asleep, it was a light sleep, and she awoke instantly when she felt a hand on her shoulder shaking her, a voice whispering softly, "Mrs. Tucker, please, wake up."

She sat up in bed. The rain had stopped, and there was enough light from a watery moonlight streaming into the room through the windows for her to make out Moani's young, frightened face.

"What is it?"

The girl put a hand to her lips. "Please, no talk. Kahu Beale might hear. Come with me."

The fear in that small voice was too authentic for Jasmine to hesitate. She joined the girl at the door without stopping to change from her nightclothes, then followed Moani's slim, pale figure down the hall to a back staircase. When Moani saw that Jasmine was having difficulty walking, she slipped an arm around her waist as they crept down the stairs and stepped out into a large courtyard. The moon was hidden by the tall walls of the house behind them. It was several seconds before Jasmine's eyes adjusted to the almost complete darkness and she was able to make out the chimney of the sugar mill, thrusting whitely upward into the darkness. Closer at hand was the low, dark building she had noticed earlier, its wall forming one end of the courtyard.

The yard of the court was unpaved, still muddy from the rain, making Jasmine grimace as she realized she had forgotten to put on slippers in her haste to follow Moani. The mud made soft squishing sounds but was not too unpleasant beneath her bare feet, reminding her of when she was a child and ran around barefoot, as all Hawaiian children did.

They were halfway across the courtyard when she noticed the object in a corner of the yard: a crude wooden cross with loops of rope at either end of the horizontal bar. Jasmine had never seen a flogging post before, but she knew at once what it was, and her hand tightened convulsively on Moani's arm.

Moani turned and followed her gaze. "Ramon does the beating," she said, her voice suddenly toneless. "Kahu Beale reads from his Bible. The beating does not stop until Kahu Beale finishes his reading." She tugged at Jasmine's hand. "Come, we must not be seen."

There was a heavy board that acted like a latch across the front of the door into the laborers' quarters. Moani lifted it and let it fall silently to one side. When Jasmine stepped inside the building behind Moani, she could not breathe for a moment, the sickening stench reminding her of the hut where she had found the bodies dead from smallpox. Moani stopped to light a candle. Since there were no windows in the building, there was no danger of the light's being seen. Then she was pulling Jasmine forward again toward what looked like a bundle of old clothes flung into a corner of the room.

When Moani knelt down on the unpaved floor and lifted her candle, Jasmine saw it was a man crumpled on the floor. He had a broad, muscular, dark back and shoulders. Across the back were dozens of ugly red cuts with blood dried in the wounds.

The man, as if sensing their presence, stirred, moaning slightly as if even adjusting himself to an upright position caused untold pain on his torn and bleeding back. Jasmine saw that the man was chained to the wall, and then in the flickering candlelight she saw his face.

"Kale! My God, Kale!"

She knelt down beside him, and her brother's dark eyes narrowed, focusing against the pain and darkness as they found her face. Shock quivered through his body, his voice a horrified whisper as he asked, "Pikake! What are you doing here?"

"I brought her," Moani said. She reached out to touch lightly Kale's thick black hair, but her eyes, meeting Jasmine's over the man's head, were shimmering with fear. "I heard you and the *kahu* talking at dinner, that you had come seeking your brother. I knew then. You must get your brother away from here or Kahu Beale will kill him."

"He's already doing a damn good job of it," Kale said, groaning, with something of the old bravado in his voice. He attempted a smile with dry, cracked lips. Moani reached quickly beneath her gown and brought out a flask of water and some food left over from dinner.

"I cannot tend his wounds," she said sadly to Jasmine as Kale lifted the flask to his lips and tore into the food awkwardly with his bound hands. "Kahu Beale and Ramon would know that I had been here. I can only bring him food and water to keep up his strength."

"How long has he been here?" Jasmine asked, her mind trying to cope with the horror of the situation.

"Three days," Moani said. "And each day Ramon ties him to the post and beats him till he is senseless. Then they drag him back here. He cannot last much longer. You must help him."

"No!" The food and water had given Kale new strength. "You don't know Beale, sister. He's a madman, *pupule*. Get away from here."

"I won't leave without you," Jasmine said flatly. She was suddenly conscious of the other men in the long, narrow hut, the shelves, upon which men slept with barely one foot of space between them, built six inches above the ground. Most of the workers were deep in an exhausted slumber from working fourteen hours in the fields, but a few, she sensed, were awake, their faces impassive, their eyes unblinking as they watched the scene quietly, like wary animals.

"Can't these men help?" Jasmine asked hopefully.

Kale shook his head. "They can't even help themselves. Most of them have had a turn at the flogging post. They know what Ramon and Beale will do to them if they try to help me." He gazed frantically at Moani. "You shouldn't be here either. I've told you to stay away. You know what will happen if you're caught and that *pupule* Beale gets his hands on you."

"But why?" Jasmine asked, bewildered. "Why should Micah Beale be doing this to you?"

"You should know the answer to that, Mrs. Tucker."

Jasmine whirled, then rose unsteadily to her feet. Neither she nor Moani had heard the door opening or Micah Beale's footsteps entering the room. Behind him loomed the dark figure of his field *luna*, Ramon.

Micah smiled, almost archly, at Jasmine. "After all, you were kind enough to come and warn me, weren't you? Your brother is a prisoner here because he tried to kill me."

Chapter 28

Jasmine heard Moani give a soft moan of despair be-hind her, but she was too angry to feel anything but a black rage as she cried furiously, "I insist you release my brother at once."

"Release an attempted murderer and an escaped felon?" Micah asked, lifting a shocked eyebrow. "You know I can't do that, Mrs. Tucker."

"Then turn him over to the authorities. You have no right to hold him."

Beale stepped closer, so the candlelight played across his features. His face was split in a feral smile, a knife cut of white against the dark tan. His gray eyes held an odd, oily sheen and were so pale that they looked like hollows gouged into his face. His glance flickered unpleasantly down at Kale. "I'm the law at Bonniville. This man must be punished until he seeks repentance and begs forgiveness for his sins of attempted murder, worshipping false idols, and debauching his sister." The pale gray glance moved like a blow to Moani. "And to add to his wickedness, he has corrupted my servant, who I thought was saved."

Jasmine saw Moani stand as if frozen, her eyes wild with fear as Micah walked toward the girl. Jasmine started to step protectively in front of Moani, but Kale had staggered to his feet, his face murderous. "Stay away from the girl, Beale. I warn you I will kill if you touch her. . . ."

So intent was Kale upon Beale that he didn't notice the *luna*, who had slipped around behind him. When Jasmine saw the man's drawn revolver, she cried out a warning to Kale, thinking that the man meant to shoot him. Instead Ramon turned the gun in his hand and brought the heavy butt down, smashing into Kale's neck. Moani screamed as Kale crumpled, without a sound, to the floor.

Jasmine did not scream. She knelt quickly beside her brother, her hand on his chest, trying to find a heartbeat, her own heart beating so loudly in her ears that she wasn't sure whether it was her heart or the faint beating of Kale's that she heard.

"Strumpet! Harlot!" Micah cried shrilly as he saw the woman bend tenderly over her brother. He reached down and, clutching a mass of her hair in his hand, jerked her to her feet. "So he has corrupted you, too. Your soul is painted as black as his."

His hands slipped down to her shoulders, and he was shaking her in a violent, uncontrollable rage. Jasmine felt as if her head would snap off from her neck. But her hands were still free, and, knowing they were her only weapon, she reached up and clawed at the man's face.

He twisted away from her left hand, but the nails of her right hand dug into his cheek, drawing blood. His eyes glassy with anger, he released her, then before she could move, his hand struck out at her, catching her full in the face. She felt the shock of the pain jolting through her body, then darkness crowded into her mind and she joined her brother, in an unconscious heap, on the floor.

When she came to, she was back in the bedroom, lying on the bed. For a moment, disoriented, her eyes wandered around the room. Where was she? Why did her face ache so? Slowly she sat up in bed and swung her legs over the side. Then, as her head slowly cleared, she realized there was something wrong with her hands. She stared down at them, startled. Her wrists were bound together by a metal cuff, a length of chain reaching from the thin steel bracelets to the mahogany-railed headboard of the bed.

Memory swept back then in a terrifying rush: the foul-smelling building; Kale lying at her feet; and Micah Beale's wild rage as he screamed at her and shook her as if she were a rag doll, his face scarlet with fury.

She shuddered, remembering the glassy look in the man's eyes. Kale was right. The man was mad. Or was this all a nightmare? she thought hopefully, and she would wake up in a minute and find herself safely back at Palekaiko. But when she got to her feet, the pain in her ankle raced up her leg, and she knew that, whatever else, she was wide awake. Carefully she hobbled around the room, discovering that the length of chain was just long enough so that she could reach the washstand and mirror, and look out the windows but not touch the windows themselves. She looked hopefully into the jug beside the washstand, but it was empty of water. What time was it? she wondered absently. Judging by the pale pink sky she could see through a window, it must be just after sunrise.

The one window looked out over the front of the house, and from the other she could see a slice of the courtyard she had crossed last night with Moani. Moani! Fear knotted her stomach. What had happened to the girl? Was she a prisoner, too, somewhere in this house? She marveled at the courage it must have taken for the frightened girl to slip into the workers' dormitory at night and tend Kale, and then reveal to his sister his presence. She must have known that her punishment for disobeying Beale would be sure and swift if she were discovered. Was the girl even still alive?

No, Jasmine thought quickly, she mustn't think that, or she would lose the little courage she had left. She must believe that Beale would come to his senses and release her. Then, as she watched from the window, she saw Beale and his overseer crossing the courtyard. They both wore guns strapped to their hips, and Beale was carrying what looked like a book in his hands. They disappeared into the dormitory, and a few seconds later Beale came out. Two of the Chinese men were carrying Kale's body between them, although he was trying to walk. She could not see her brother's face, but she could imagine the grim determination there. Then Ramon came out of the building, a long, black whip snaking from his hand.

She could not see the flogging post from her window, and the house was too solidly built, so she could not hear, only imagine, the singing sound the whip made, and the crack as the lash found bare flesh and cut like a knife through skin and muscle. She was ashamed of herself for being glad she could not see Kale's proud body twist under Ramon's lash even as she sank to the floor, nausea rising in her throat. She reached the empty wash basin just in time to be violently sick, until there was nothing left in her stomach. Then she forced herself to her feet, watched stony-faced, and after a while—it seemed an eternity—she saw Kale being taken back to the building, not walking defiantly now but slumped between the two coolies.

For the rest of the day, she limped restlessly between the two windows, lying down on the bed occasionally to rest her throbbing ankle. Several times she saw Beale and his overseer come and go from the house. She noticed that Micah Beale never went out into the fields, or among his workers, alone.

No one came near her room to bring food, not even water so that she could wash herself, which at first bothered her more than the lack of food. Her feet were dirty from crossing the muddy courtyard, and her face and hands felt grimy. The pristine nightgown was ripped at one shoulder, the hemline soiled.

It was early evening before Beale, with a Bible in his hand, entered the room without knocking. She had been lying down, and she got swiftly to her feet, fighting the desire to fly at the man, to scream at him and claw at his face. She sensed that such behavior would only add fuel to the madness that she could see flickering in the pale gray eyes, the oddly stiff, hunched way he walked toward her, the fixed smile on the thin lips. It did give her pleasure to see that she had marked the man, a thin red scratch from her nails running from his mouth across his cheek.

Beale's voice as was placid as if he were commenting on the weather as he said, "I have come to pray with you for your salvation."

"I don't wish your prayers," Jasmine said coldly, averting her gaze from the man's face so that she could not see his eyes, like unclean hands, on her pale, gleaming skin revealed by the ripped nightgown. "I insist you release me at once." And then, unable to keep the anger from her voice, she said, "You must know that someone will come looking for me. They know at Palekaiko that I'm here."

"Do they?" Beale asked, the fixed smile mocking her.

The two words jabbed viciously at Jasmine. Of course, she thought, Micah Beale hadn't sent any native messenger to Palekaiko telling Mr. McTavish where she was. And she remembered, she hadn't told anyone at the plantation where she was going yesterday on her ride.

She forced herself to meet the man's gaze again. "When I don't return, they'll start looking for me. There'll be search parties up and down the coast."

Beale nodded agreeably. "No doubt. And they'll find your horse and riding habit on the beach near Nanakuli. Your immodest habit of swimming in the ocean is not unknown. It was a warm day yesterday. You stopped for a swim. The undertow at that part of the beach is treacherous."

And he saw, pleased, that the girl's face had gone pale, some of the arrogance and defiance draining from her wide, staring eyes.

"Why?" she whispered. "Why are you doing this?"

He shrugged impatiently. "I've told you. From the first moment we met, I knew I was meant to snatch you, like a burning brand, from the fire." His voice dropped unctuously as he stepped closer. "I know your sins are black, that you revel in the temptations of the flesh, flaunting your body before men, but I can help you. We can pray together that the strength will be given you to resist temptation."

When he reached out to take her arm, Jasmine jerked away, her voice taut with fury. "I'd rather go to hell than pray with you."

For a moment she thought he was going to strike her again; she could almost see him struggling to control his anger, the muscles in his face jerking. Then he nodded gravely and walked to the door. "It is early yet. True repentance takes time. I can wait."

"Mr. Beale."

He turned and she held out her bound hands to him. "At least you can remove the chain."

"I'm afraid not." He frowned. "Neither the door to this room nor the windows have locks."

"Some water, then, and food," she pleaded, hating herself for begging but unable to stop herself.

The odd, fixed smile returned to his face. "Fasting, they say, is good for the soul." Then the door closed behind him.

The next morning Jasmine watched again as Kale's body was dragged out to the flogging post, but although nausea cramped her, she had nothing left in her stomach with which to be sick.

At noontime, as she stood at the front window, she saw several men ride up to the house. Beale had evidently been watching for them. He came out of the house and went to greet and talk with the visitors. Jasmine was sure the men were part of a search party looking for her.

She pulled frantically to the end of the chain tethering her to the bed, screaming at the top of the lungs, "I'm here! I'm here!" All the while knowing that the men couldn't possibly hear her, or see more than a shadowy outline if they should happen to glance up to the shuttered second-floor window. Finally she watched, exhausted, her throat raw, as the men waved good-bye to Beale and rode away.

That evening, when Beale came by her room again, she was almost too sick with despair, too weak, to drag herself from the bed. It was pride only that forced her to her feet to face the man, a fine edge of contempt in her voice as she demanded, "How long do you plan to keep up this charade?"

Beale sighed. "You are as wickedly obdurate as your stepbrother. He, too, stubbornly refuses to confess his vile sins and save his immortal soul from damnation."

Jasmine's throat and mouth were bone dry from lack of water and fear, so when she tried to speak, her voice came out in a hoarse whisper. "You'll kill Kale. Is that what you want? You won't be able to save his soul if he's dead."

Beale frowned, as if annoyed that she had found a fallacy in his reasoning. Then, clutching his Bible, he said soberly, "It is written that there are those sinners who must die to be born again."

Does he mean to kill me, too? Jasmine wondered as she stared into the man's pale gray eyes. It was like looking through empty windowpanes into nothingness. What else can he do, eventually, when he's finished with me? He can't keep me locked in this room forever.

"You've forgotten my husband," she said desperately. "Morgan will never stop looking for me. And when he finds me, I swear he'll kill you. You know he will."

A mixture of fear and anger leaped behind the glassy panes, and she wondered if Beale was remembering the humiliation he had suffered in the garden the night Morgan had thrown him into the bushes.

His eyes burned dangerously as he stepped closer to her, his voice lifting, raging shrilly. "Men like your husband are an abomination in the sight of the Lord. Do you think I don't know of the laws of God and men broken by licentious whaling captains like Captain Tucker? Or that I haven't heard of the whores who swam naked out to his ship to fornicate with him and his men?" His face had become flushed, and his eyes shone as they fell downward from the woman's pale face to the swell of her breasts barely hidden from his sight by the lawn gown. "Even you," he muttered thickly, running his tongue over moist lips. "Do you think I've forgotten that you lay with him before you were married? Did you swim naked out to his ship like the other whores?"

Jasmine flinched as his hands tightened on her soft upper arms, tugging at her, trying to force her to kneel, his face so near she could see a thin line of spittle running from his mouth. "Confess your sins! Kneel and pray with me for forgiveness. We are all sinners in His sight."

Jasmine didn't know where she found the strength to resist him, only knowing that she could not bear the thought of those hands, those moist lips, touching her. She fought against him silently, fiercely, trying to claw at his face with her bound hands, kicking upward with her knee hard enough to have the satisfaction of hearing Beale's cry of pain as he let her go.

This time when he struck her, she sprawled backward against the bed. Although she was still conscious, some instinct for survival within her made her lie still and feign unconsciousness. She sensed that it was not an insensible victim that would answer Beale's perverted needs but a tamed, submissive creature that he could bend to his will.

She hardly dared breathe as she waited, her flesh crawling. When she heard his steps move away from the bed and the door close, she waited a few more minutes before she sat up cautiously. The room swam dizzily around her. It had grown dark outside, and as she made her way slowly to the washbasin, she was thankful that Beale, at least, had left her a candle. She studied her face in the mirror above the washbasin, the second bruise, an ugly purplish black, on her left cheek to take the place of the one that had faded until it looked like a shadow across her cheek. She couldn't hold out much longer, she thought wearily. If Morgan didn't come soon . . .

But he would come, she told herself fiercely. She knew her husband, his stubbornness, his strength, his love that would not let her go. He would move heaven and earth to find her. But suppose, she thought suddenly, painfully, he believed the story of her drowning?

A feeling of despair like an iciness crept over her, freezing her blood as she blew out the candle and returned to the bed. He will come, she whispered silently over and over again, staring wide-eyed into the darkness. It was as if only by repeating the words, by clutching them to her like a talisman, that she could hold on to her sanity when she thought of never holding her son in her arms again, never feeling Morgan's mouth on her never seeing his eyes fill with tenderness. . . .

The next day her husband did come Jasmine had waited all morning at the to be dragged once more into the time when Beale and Ramon went into the building, they came out alone. Was Kale dead, then? Jasmine wondered, an icy fear gripping her. Or was it that he was mercifully unconscious and Beale could find no pleasure in reading from his Bible over an unconscious sinner who could neither hear nor heed his words?

Late in the afternoon, she became aware of a faint burnt-sugar smell drifting into the room. She went to the front window, and she could see a sugarcane field being burned over not far from the house. The flames leaped skyward as the dark figures of men with pitchforks moved on the edge of the burning field, controlling the flames from spreading too far.

As she watched listlessly, she saw a man, alone, riding up to the house. Even from a distance she recognized the set of Morgan's shoulders, the shape of his face beneath the white-brimmed hat he wore, the easy way he rode his favorite black stallion with the white star on the horse's forehead. Unlike the other men who had come to the house, he dismounted, walking out of her eyesight with his familiar, slight sailor's gait.

Faintly she heard a knocking at the front door. She was learning to recognize the distant sounds from the household that did penetrate her room. She could imagine Beale hurrying out onto the veranda to greet Morgan, his long, grave face as he offered his condolences on the death of Morgan's wife. This time she strained at the steel around her wrists until they were rubbed raw and bleeding, but she could not get any closer to the window. Her throat was too dry for any sound, except for a faint whimper, to escape her lips. When after a few minutes she saw Morgan return to his horse, swing into the saddle, and ride away, she sank to her knees on the floor. The tears she had refused to allow herself to shed filled her eyes and slid down her cheeks as her body shook with helpless sobs.

It was growing dark when finally, her body mercifully drained of all feeling, she pulled herself to her feet and the candle. From the window, she could see that the

men were still working at burning the field, their silhou-
ettes black against the leaping scarlet flames.

When she hobbled to the dressing table, she hardly
recognized her face, swollen and tear-splotched, in the
mirror. She lifted her bound hands and slowly touched
the mirror, as if trying to recognize the reflection of the
stranger caught there. Perhaps Beale was right, she
thought, staring for a long moment at the glass, hard
and cold against her hands. Perhaps there was a devil
trapped inside of her. Surely the woman staring back at
her with the suddenly hopeful face and the wild, murderous look in her eyes was no one she knew.

When a half hour later Beale came to the room, he
saw at once that Jasmine Tucker's proud, carnal spirit
had been broken at last. The woman who sat on the
edge of the bed staring at him blankly was the woman in
his fantasy, her face tear-streaked and bruised, her
body quivering beneath his hand when he touched her
shoulder and asked hoarsely, his own body trembling
with excitement, "Are you ready now to repent your
sins and pray for forgiveness?"

She nodded without speaking, lifting her face to his,
and he saw that in spite of everything, she was still
beautiful: her eyes deep wells of shining darkness, her
flesh silken soft and tawny where the gown had ripped
away.

She held out her bound hands to him, her voice a
pleading, abject whisper. "Please, I don't want to kneel
in prayer bound like an animal."

Beale hesitated, frowning. Still, as weakened as she
was, what resistance could she make, even with her
hands unbound? Swiftly he unlocked the metal bracelet,
slipped the steel from her chafed raw wrists. "We will
fight Satan together," he murmured. "I will help you."
His hands moved up her arms, jerked her from the bed,
and she stumbled and fell on her knees before him, her
dark hair falling forward, hiding her face.

For a moment, looking down at her, he savored his
triumph like a sweetmeat on his lips, her sin driven out

of its deepest concealment, the carnal appetites within
that soft, seductive body finally crushed and destroyed.

Or were they? Suspicion flickered suddenly in the
pale gray eyes gazing down at the woman kneeling
before him. Or was she only pretending repentance,
feigning an innocence while the lustful fires still burned
within her? After all, Moani had pretended repentance,
too. He must make sure the penitence was real. His
hands trembled as he pulled Jasmine to her feet and
thrust her backward across the bed. The lawn material
of the gown tore easily in his hands. "You must not try
to deceive me," he warned hoarsely while his mouth
sought and found her breast, his hands moving roughly
over her body, over the cool, satin thighs. "I will know
if you are deceiving me, and you will be punished."

When she lay quietly, unmoving, he tore open his
trousers and half flung himself on top of her, feeling the
anger like a whip lashing at him. If she were sincere in
resisting the temptations of the flesh, she would be
fighting him off, he thought, as any decent, God-fearing
woman would do, instead of lying there with that strange
smile on her face, her legs spread out to receive him.

"Harlot! Whore!" he cried, panting. "Jezebel!"

His hand pinched at her breast, his face flushed, his
heart pounding. The pain inside of him was unbearable
now, and he knew from past experience that it would be
soothed only when he could inflict the same destructive
pain upon her, the temptress incarnate. The devil himself was laughing, taunting, ridiculing him. . . .

Then suddenly she was no longer lying quietly beneath him. Incomprehensibly, her hand had slipped beneath the pillow, and there was something sharp and
glittering, flashing in the moonlight, as it struck downward, slashing into his face.

Beale screamed in agony, flinging his hands up to his
face and rolling away from her.

Jasmine slipped unsteadily from the bed. A thin shard
of broken glass from the mirror dropped to the floor
from her nerveless hand. The next instant she was out

of the door, too panic-stricken to even notice the pain in her ankle as she ran down the hall. She had reached the stairs when her ripped gown tangled around her feet and she half stumbled, half fell, down the steps, lying for a moment, stunned, at the bottom of the staircase. Then she heard footsteps in the hall above her, and she clung to the bannister and dragged herself to her feet.

She flung herself at the front door, her hands fumbling at the carved brass doorknob. She yanked desperately at the knob before realizing that the door was locked.

She turned around and faced the staircase, sobbing softly, hopelessly, as she saw in the moonlight flooding the hall Micah Beale coming down the stairs. His face was twisted with fury, and with the blood dripping from the open wound in his cheek, he was, to Jasmine, like some monstrous figure out of a nightmare. She leaned against the door; her body, weakened by the battering of the last days, had no more strength to give her. She was caught up in the nightmare, too, her mind screaming at her to run but unable to force her body to move. He would kill her now, she thought. And somehow the thought of those hands touching her body again was more horrible than the thought of dying.

She closed her eyes to shut out the sight of Beale's crazed face. His footsteps, padding softly toward her over the parquet floor, pounded in her ears. She prayed soundlessly that the end would be swift.

Then suddenly, inexplicably, the footsteps stopped. The silence was deafening. She opened her eyes and saw, bewildered, the rage in Beale's face dissolving into abject fear. The glassy eyes turned incredulously toward the parlor door were charged with terror as if staring at death itself.

Chapter 29

Jasmine followed Beale's gaze. At first she thought it was a cruel hoax her mind was playing on her; that wanting so much to see Morgan one last time she actually imagined that her husband was standing there in the doorway, a tall, dark shadow in the pale moonlight. If she closed her eyes, she thought, confused, nothing would have changed; she would still be trapped in the web of her nightmare.

Crablike, Beale began to scramble backward awkwardly as Morgan stalked across the hall toward him, his face very still, only his eyes dangerously, murderously, alive. "Stay away from me!" Beale screamed. "I warn you. Ramon! Ramon!"

"Ramon won't be coming," Morgan snarled. His fist smashed into Beale's face, crushing the cheekbone and nose and sending the man flying backward, smashing into the wall. As Beale started to slide to the floor, Morgan picked him up, shaking him like a terrier with a rat, then raised his fist again. Somehow, with a strength borne of desperation, Beale managed to slip free and rushed for the door.

Morgan started after him, then stopped when he saw Jasmine crouched against the wall, her eyes dazed with horror. Quickly he took off his jacket and then wrapped it carefully around her. He carried her into the parlor, settling her in a chair, and, chafing her hands in his, murmured softly, "Jasmine, my love. It's over. No one is going to hurt you. Look at me, my love."

Finally, when he was beginning to wonder frantically if he would ever be able to call her back from the darkness in her mind, she blinked her eyes and sighed softly. "Morgan?"

The terrible blankness was gone, and she was burrowing in his arms, her body trembling violently, repeating his name over and over again. It was only after the hysteria, like a storm, had passed that she remembered and whispered through dry lips, "Kale . . . Moani . . . find them."

"I found Kale," Morgan assured her quickly, pulling her into his arms, cradling her in his lap. After the man he assumed was Ramon had jumped him outside the house, he had disposed of the man using the butt of the man's whip to beat him into unconsciousness. Then he had dragged the overseer into a nearby building, which turned out to be where the plantation laborers were housed. Morgan had seen filthy, crowded forecastles in his time, but even he had been shocked when he saw the conditions under which Beale's laborers were forced to live. "There was a Hawaiian girl chained not far away from your brother. She wasn't in the best of condition, but she was able to talk. She was the one who told me that Beale was holding you prisoner in the house."

"Kale's alive?"

"Barely," Morgan said grimly. He didn't see how the man had survived the brutal beatings he must have taken. It was a mercy he was unconscious. But it was Jasmine he was most concerned about at the moment, with her waxy pallor and glazed eyes. His glance searched the room as he murmured irritably, "Damn it, do you suppose Beale has any spirits in this house?"

Jasmine shook her head, whispering, "Water, please . . . not spirits. And food."

Morgan gave her a shocked glance and sprang to his feet, placing her on the sofa, then rushed from the room. In a few minutes, he returned with a calabash of water and some bread and cheese, all he could find at short notice. Then he watched, his face as black as a thundercloud, as Jasmine tore greedily into the food and would have swallowed all the water at once if he hadn't stopped her. "Slowly, my love," he said anxiously. "A little at a time."

He was relieved to see the color flowing back into her face; her voice was stronger when she leaned back and said, "I saw you leave." The horror of that moment, watching Morgan ride away, flooded her eyes before she was able to ask, "How did you know to look for me here?"

"Mrs. McTavish. She told me you had been reading the newspaper before you went for your ride, and she was sure something you read there upset you. As soon as I saw the news item about Kale's being sighted near Nanakuli, I knew. I remembered your telling me about your brother's believing that Beale was responsible for Lani's death. If Kale was at Beale's plantation, I figured you were there, too."

He had to believe it, he thought, or, having been told that his wife's riding habit and horse had been found beside the ocean, accept the fact that Jasmine was drowned. And that he could not, would not, let himself believe.

"Beale was very persuasive. He almost convinced me that I was mistaken, that he had never seen you or Kale." Morgan suddenly grinned. "But there were two things wrong with his story: one was the scratch on his face, a mark I remembered your leaving on my own face. And the second thing was that as I rode away from the house, I saw something beside the road, your feathered riding hat, mud-covered and completely unwearable now. But at least I knew that Beale had lied. You had been here. Since I didn't know what was going on, I waited till dark then circled back to the house on foot. That's when I ran into the man with the whip. The element of surprise was on my side, though, and by the time he went for his gun, it was too late," he said, smiling with relish, remembering. "He had the key in his pocket to the chains binding Kale and the girl, so I unlocked them and put him in their place, then I came up to the house. The front door was locked, but I found an open window and climbed inside. That's when I heard Beale scream, and you came tumbling down the steps with Beale after you."

A deadly anger burned deep in Morgan's eyes as he studied Jasmine's face, the black-and-blue mark on her cheekbone, the bruises on her body that he could glimpse through the torn nightgown. His voice thickened with fury. "Did Beale . . . ?"

Quickly Jasmine shook her head. "No. No, he didn't . . . hurt me that way." Her eyes were still dilated with shock, her voice trembling again. "I—I stabbed him. I broke the mirror and took a piece of the glass, and when he—when he . . ."

She could not finish. She could not tell even Morgan of those grotesque, terrible moments with Micah Beale in the bedroom upstairs. She would never be able to tell anyone ever. She felt unclean just thinking about it.

Cursing softly, Morgan pulled her back into his arms, wishing he had killed Beale when he had the chance, promising himself that he would kill the man if he ever saw him again. Then, through the open door and window, he heard an odd, high-pitched scream ululating through the night like a soul in agony.

Jasmine stiffened in his arms. "What is it?"

"Stay here," Morgan commanded sharply.

But she followed him limping to the front veranda, then sinking down upon the steps when she could go no further. She watched as Morgan, a darker shadow in the darkness around him, ran down the path to the cane fields where the flames were still being tendered by the workers. The smell of burnt sugar was all at once too sickeningly sweet in Jasmine's nostrils.

When Morgan finally returned, even before she saw the look on his face, she knew. "Was it Beale?"

Morgan nodded. "He must have been heading for the stable. He had to pass the cane field to get there."

And this time, Jasmine realized with a shudder, he had no revolver and no bodyguard with him to protect him from the coolies he had tortured and enslaved.

She swallowed hard. "He's dead?"

Morgan nodded without speaking, holding her hand tightly in his. When he had reached the cane field, Beale had been staggering down the road, his body wreathed in flames. By the time Morgan had been able to beat out the flames, it was too late. Beale was dead. As much as he could, he had examined the body, but he hadn't seen any knife wounds. Had the workers simply surrounded the terrified Beale, he wondered, threatened him with the machetes until the man had fled into the burning cane, or had they picked him up bodily and flung him into the blazing cane field?

Morgan had carried the body to the side of the road. The laborers had watched but made no move against him. Then, their faces expressionless, they had picked up their tools and gone back to work burning the cane.

Jasmine felt as if she could still hear the sound of Beale's scream trapped in the night. "How did he die?"

Morgan picked her up, started to carry her back into the house. "It was an accident," he said shortly. At least, he thought to himself, that was what he planned to tell the authorities when they questioned him.

At the front door, Jasmine balked. "I don't want to go back inside," she said.

Morgan looked at her face and nodded. "All right. We'll wait out here on the veranda. The girl, Moani, said that she was able to ride. I told her to take a horse from the stable and bring help from Nanakuli. They should be here soon." He would have gone himself, but he didn't dare leave Jasmine alone. He glanced down at her, worried. Her face was as still as if carved from marble, her body held stiffly as if her fragile bones would break if he held her too tightly. Only her eyes were still glazed with remembered horror.

"We'll be back at Palekaiko soon, my love," he said, gathering her closer in his arms even as he sensed helplessly that there was no way he could shield her from the terror clouding her mind. "You'll forget all this once we're back home."

It was weeks, though, before the memory of being bound and imprisoned in that second-floor bedroom began to fade from Jasmine's memory. Even after her ankle had healed and the bruises on her body had disappeared, she would awake at night, crying and screaming, seeing again Micah Beale's bloody face, his hands reaching out for her. Morgan was always there, his voice calming, assuring her she was safe, holding her in his arms until she would finally fall asleep again. But when he tried to do more than embrace her, she would stiffen and draw away as if even his caresses terrified her.

During the daytime, she kept her mind occupied with tending Matthew and helping to nurse her brother, whose deep wounds healed more slowly than her bruises. It was Moani, though, who stayed day and night, sleeping on a pallet beside Kale's bed, refusing to leave his side. It was clear to Jasmine that the girl was in love with her patient, and she suspected, from the way Kale's eyes followed the girl, that he was halfway in love with her, too.

"How can he forget Lani so quickly?" she complained unhappily to Morgan.

"Your brother hasn't forgotten Lani any more than you have," Morgan said gruffly. "He never will, but you have to go on living. So does your brother."

During the weeks Kale had spent at the plantation, a grudging, wary respect had grown between Morgan and his brother-in-law. Morgan had posted bail and arranged with the authorities so that Kale could stay at Palekaiko until he had recovered from his wounds and was strong enough to be turned over to the law on Maui.

"But he is innocent," Moani said fiercely to Jasmine

one afternoon when she dropped by to see how her brother was faring. "I won't let them take him to jail."

Kale was sitting up in bed. Although he winced with pain when he moved, and the doctor had said he would always bear scars on his back from his ordeal, he managed to smile teasingly at Moani.

"She is brave as a tiger for such a little one," he said proudly to Jasmine. "I would have died, chained to that wall, if it had not been for Moani. And for you, little Pikake," he said, his smile fading as he gazed soberly at his sister. "I am sorry for all the *pilikia* I've caused you. I promise you when they come to take me, I will not try to escape."

"I'm glad to hear that," Morgan said from the doorway, his voice dryly amused. "Since I'm responsible for you."

Jasmine said quickly, "Morgan's hired the very best lawyer in Honolulu, Kale. He tells us that since there were no witnesses who actually saw you attack that policeman, that your case may not even go to trial."

"If I am freed, it will change nothing," Kale said with a flash of his old arrogance, glancing warningly at his brother-in-law. "I will still fight for my people against the *haoles*. The annexation of these islands will not stop me."

"There's not going to be any annexation," Morgan said, his glance moving fleetingly to Jasmine. "The news arrived from Honolulu this morning. The old fox Wyllie outbluffed Gregg and the Committee of Thirteen, after all. He sent notes to the representatives of France and England and the United States, asking for guarantees of protection against any forced takeover of the Hawaiian kingdom. The French and British representatives agreed immediately, so Gregg had no choice but to honor Wyllie's request, too." Morgan shrugged wryly. "And with the French and British, as well as the American warships in the harbor, the filibusters knew they wouldn't stand a chance if they started any trouble."

He came over to Jasmine, smiling down at her as he

pulled her to her feet. "I think it's time you and I and Matthew returned to Honolulu."

Jasmine hesitated. "But, Kale," she protested. "I can't leave him."

Morgan cast an amused glance at Moani. "I'd say your brother is in good hands." Then frowning at his wife, he slipped an arm around her waist, adding firmly, "And there's no way I'll let you out of my sight again."

When one week later the Tucker family returned by ship to Honolulu, as they stepped onto the quay Jasmine could hear the sound of wailing, an eerie, piercing sound and the beat of *pahu* drums. From the U.S. ship of war the *St. Mary*, in the harbor, guns were suddenly fired, the explosions causing Matthew to clutch, startled, at his mother's skirt.

Jasmine swept him up into her arms and turned, frightened, to Morgan. "What is it? Is there an attack upon the city after all?"

Morgan shook his head, puzzled. "Those guns sound more like a salute of some sort. And the flag at the fort is at half mast." He stopped a passing native, an elderly man who had tears streaming down his face as he exclaimed sorrowfully, "*Auwe, Ka Moi!* Our beloved king is dead. What will happen to us now? The old ways have died with him."

The wild, rhythmic wails and beating drums followed the carriage as the Tuckers drove to their home. The dirgelike noise continued for several days and nights as the natives returned to their ancient manner of mourning, then thronged by the thousands through the palace, past the candlelit casket of Kamehameha III, flanked by towering feather *kahilis* and guarded by the *alii*.

As was the tradition at the death of kings, old men raised their voices in an anguished wailing, chanting *meles* of the dead king's goodness and valor and of his illustrious forebears.

The day after the funeral for King Kauikeaouli, Morgan and Jasmine attended Kawaiahao Church, where Prince Alexander Liholiho, not yet twenty-one, was formally inaugurated as King Kamehameha IV. Dressed in a handsome Windsor uniform, the young king spoke in Hawaiian to the huge audience crowding the church, of the new era that was about to begin. "Let us be one and we shall not fail," he said solemnly. Then speaking in English, he reminded the foreigners present of how liberally the late king had treated them. "To be kind and generous to foreigners is no new thing in the history of our race," he said proudly, and he promised to continue to welcome foreigners to the shores of Hawaii. Then, his dark eyes flashing angrily, he declared firmly, "But the foreigner who comes here seeking our confidence only to betray it, with no higher ambition than that of over-throwing our government and introducing anarchy, confusion, and bloodshed, then he is most unwelcome!"

Around her, Jasmine heard a rustle like a breeze moving through dried kukui leaves through the assembled *haoles*, and she smiled to herself, wishing that Kale could be here to hear the new king's brave words.

"There'll be no more talk of annexation," she said happily to Morgan that evening as they dressed to attend the inaugural ball. "King Alexander will not allow it."

When Morgan said nothing, she turned away from the dressing table to face him accusingly. "You don't believe these islands will remain free, do you?"

No, Morgan thought, his face sober, he didn't believe it. It might be five years or fifty, but the Hawaiian Islands were too valuable not to be eventually taken over by some stronger power. The days of the kingdom had been numbered from the first day the Hawaiians had welcomed the first foreigner to their shores. He had no desire, though, to spoil his wife's happiness in this day, and he frowned with mock annoyance at Jasmine, still in her lace dressing gown. "What I believe is that we'll be late to the palace if you don't hurry and get dressed."

"I can't make up my mind which gown to wear," she

said, frowning. "Should I wear the red silk or the yellow brocade?"

"The red silk would go better with your pearls," Morgan said casually.

Jasmine bit unhappily at her lower lip. She had forgotten all about the lost pearls. She couldn't put it off any longer, she decided. She had to tell Morgan the truth.

"You needn't worry about the broken clasp," Morgan said dryly, picking up her jewel case. Jasmine's eyes widened as he opened the box and drew out her pearl necklace, dangling it in his hand before her.

"But how . . . ?" she blurted and then exclaimed indignantly, "You knew! All along you knew and you never told me!"

"Lee Tai happens to know I like fine pearls," Morgan said. "When the necklace was pawned at his shop and not reclaimed, he brought it to me." The dark, straight brows slanted in a quizzical glance. "It seems, madam, there are a few things you've neglected to tell me, too."

"I had to pawn the pearls. I needed the money for Kale," Jasmine said and then lifted her chin firmly. "I'm sorry I broke my word to you, but you had no right to force me to promise to deny my brother."

"No right?" Morgan growled at the defiance he saw gathering in his wife's dark eyes. Then he shrugged to himself, a wry amusement touching his face. No matter how completely he possessed his wife, he suspected there would always be a part of Jasmine that would defy and elude him, that would belong to her alone. Just as he was sure that whatever country in the end possessed the Hawaiian Islands, there would always be a part of the islands that would belong, forever, only to the Hawaiian people themselves.

Jasmine, watching uneasily, breathed a sigh of relief as she saw the harsh lines in her husband's face soften. He fastened the pearls around her neck, his voice husky as he said, "All that matters is that the necklace is back where it belongs."

He turned her gently in his arms to face him, brushing her lips with a kiss. All those nights when she had awakened, crying, like a child from a nightmare, and he had held her trembling body in his arms, he had put aside his own desire, sensing her fear and uncertainty. Now, though, with her scent in his nostrils, her flesh cool and silken soft beneath his lips, he knew he could no longer ignore the sharp thrust of his desire for her.

When his hands moved to untie the sash around her waist so that her robe swung open, he saw a pulse in her throat beating wildly. Her eyes, staring up at him, were flared wide and lustrous but not with passion. He knew she was remembering, reliving the horror of another man holding her, touching her.

"Please, Morgan," she whispered, turning her face away. "Not now. Not yet."

His arms refused to let her go, his eyes blazing fiercely down at her even as he growled with rough tenderness, "Don't turn away from me, my love. I'm not Micah Beale. I'm your husband. I only wish I had the words to tell you how dear you are to me, how I would never do anything to harm you."

As he was speaking, his hand was gently caressing the rosebud tightness at the peak of her breast then moving downward to stroke lightly, intimately, the rest of her body. His fingertips were like brushstrokes, so as not to alarm her, as if this were the first time she had known a man's touch on her body.

Jasmine stood very still within his arms, her own arms pressed tightly to her side, her breath coming rapidly as she fought the nightmare of the memory of Beale's damp, cold hands at her breasts, the sour smell of his breath on her face. Then, gradually, as Morgan's lips and tongue, warm and teasing, added to the gentle persuasion of his hands, familiar, almost forgotten sensations of pleasure rippled in ever-widening circles through her body, finally driving the dark terror from her mind.

The moment Morgan felt the taut body become soft and pliant in his arms, saw the heat of desire replacing the cold panic in the dark eyes, he swept his **wife up** into his arms and carried her to the bed.

As he slipped the lacy robe the rest of the way from her body, Jasmine protested weakly, "But, Morgan, we'll be late for the inaugural ball."

"We certainly will," he agreed, grinning widely as he slipped into bed beside her and pulled her into his arms, knowing that here at least, when they made love, she would always be completely, entirely his. "In fact," he murmured as he watched his wife's eyes fill with that special look of wonder, "I wouldn't be surprised if we never got to the ball at all."

About the Author

Marcella Thum lives in St. Louis, Missouri, where she is a librarian at a military installation. Her other books for Fawcett Crest include BLAZING STAR, THE WHITE ROSE, and FERNWOOD.